Moriah's
LIGHTHOUSE
THE COLLECTION

A *Love's Journey*® ON
MANITOULIN ISLAND COLLECTION

Moriah's LIGHTHOUSE
THE COLLECTION

A *Love's Journey*® ON
MANITOULIN ISLAND COLLECTION

BY SERENA B. MILLER

LJ EMORY
PUBLISHING

To Steven

MORIAH'S LIGHTHOUSE

There is no fear in love, but perfect love casts out fear.

—1 JOHN 4:18A ESV

CHAPTER 1

May, 1998
Manitoulin Island

Moriah Robertson lay motionless in the dirt beneath the cabin floor as she stared with sick fascination at the Massasauga rattlesnake loosely coiled upon a rusty water pipe only eight inches from her nose. The snake's delicate tongue flickered, tasting the air between them. Its head bobbed, getting a fix on the heat emanating from her breath. A dry rattle warned that it was not amused by her presence.

She held her breath, shut her eyes, and willed herself to lie perfectly still. She had known of people who had survived a rattler's bite, but all things considered—she would prefer to pass.

The ticking of her watch sounded as loud as a jackhammer to her adrenaline-sensitized ears. She continued to lay deathly still in the small crawl space beneath the cabin while she counted the seconds, mentally cursing the snake, the snake's mother and, while she was at it, the slow water leak that had forced her to crawl beneath Cabin One. A few feet away, Lake Huron lapped gently at the shoreline.

It was a gorgeous day for those not being held captive beneath a cabin by a stupid snake. It was sunny and warm. In fact, it was unusually warm for this early in the year, which was probably part of the problem. Snakes didn't move around in cold weather, which was one of the reasons she rather enjoyed winter. The other reason was that she didn't have to deal with guests when there was snow on the ground.

She heard a heavy truck crunch up the gravel driveway. It stopped at the resort's lodge.

"Moriah!" her Aunt Katherine, shouted, "It's a delivery for you. I think it's that part you've been waiting for."

Apparently, the new part she had ordered for the emergency generator had finally arrived. At least that was one less thing she could cross off her to-do list—if she ever got out from under this blasted cabin.

She did not know if reptiles had ears but, just in case, she chose not to respond to her aunt's call.

"Moriah?"

Moriah stayed mute.

She heard Katherine chat briefly with the delivery man and then the heavy truck shifted into gear and drove back over the driveway and out to the main road. Moriah winced as the screen door on the main lodge slammed shut.

She was suddenly, violently, envious of her aunt who would happily spend the day laundering the resort's sheets, blankets and pillowcases inside their nice, snakeless, lodge. As usual at this time of year, she and Katherine were preparing for the guests who would begin arriving in a few days. The fishing camp they owned was their main source of income.

There was much work to do before the guests arrived. She and Katherine had divided the chores between the two of them over the years. Her aunt tended to the indoor chores, and she took care of the outside ones. At least she normally took care of the outside jobs—when she wasn't immobilized by the presence of this stupid, stupid snake!

Heat radiated through the plywood floor directly above her face. The fire she had built in the cabin's wood stove early this morning to make sure the flue worked, was probably what had drawn the rattler out of its den. She could think of no other reason a Massasauga would be above ground in Canada this early in the spring, even if it was warmer than usual.

She counted to one hundred and cracked an eyelid. The snake had apparently chosen to ignore her. It crawled along the water pipe, its black underbelly rasping slightly as it slid over the rusting metal, inches above her quivering skin. She drew a shallow breath and held it.

When it had slithered well past her face, she exhaled. Slowly. Then an unhappy thought struck. Didn't rattlesnakes travel in pairs? She slid her eyes over to her right. Nothing happening there except an empty spider web and a drift of autumn leaves against the stone foundation.

Then she looked to her left.

The few remaining nerves in her body that had not been on red alert clanged an alarm. At least five other Massasaugas lay entangled several feet from her shoulder.

She closed her eyes again and fought panic. A victim could survive one rattlesnake bite, two maybe with medical help, but no one could withstand a multiple attack. Especially not while wedged into a location where a quick exit was impossible.

Just as she thought it couldn't get any worse, a heavy reptilian body slid over her right leg, and then her left. It demanded her last shred of self-discipline not to scream and start beating her fists against the bottom of the cabin floor. A spasm twitched in the calf of her right leg. A drop of sweat began a slow, itchy descent into the hairline above her left ear. She desperately wanted to scratch the itch, but that was not an option.

Then another unhappy thought struck. What if she were lying on top of the hole from which they'd emerged?

Sweat oozed from her body, soaking her flannel shirt. Her calf muscle did a jig beneath her jeans.

She checked again. The snakes shifted as the one that had crawled across her legs joined the pile.

What on earth was she going to do? She couldn't stay here forever.

While she struggled to lay perfectly still, a long-forgotten memory floated into her mind.

When she was a child, she had seen a man at a circus seated in a screened box filled with diamondback rattlesnakes. They had buzzed and warned while they crawled all over him without biting. She had stood, mesmerized, until Katherine pulled her away.

There was one more thing she remembered about that encounter besides the memory of it giving her goose bumps. The man in the box had survived by moving extremely slowly.

Okay then. Since the snakes did not appear to be in a hurry to go elsewhere, that could be a plan. She might survive if she moved very, very slow. She dug her fingernails and heels into the dirt and began to inch her way out, butt-crawling in infinitesimal degrees toward the sunlight, expecting to feel the sting of fangs at any moment.

About an hour elapsed while she finessed her body the few feet necessary to be free of the cabin. At least she thought it was an hour. It could have been a week. Or a month. Time had lost all meaning while she was under there. The late afternoon sunlight struck her face as she emerged, unscathed, from beneath.

She was safe, but every muscle in her body was trembling, and her scalp felt like it was crawling with invisible snakes. Once she was certain she had cleared the cabin, she leaped to her feet and practically flew over the pathway toward the lodge, putting as much distance between herself and the snakes as possible. Although she knew it wasn't possible that the snakes would be pursuing her, she still glanced back over her shoulder to make absolutely certain.

At that moment, she rammed into a stranger who had apparently been standing directly in her path. He felt as solid and unmoving as a boulder while she practically climbed his body and danced on his head.

"What in blazes...?" he asked.

She clung to this marvelous human mammal, grasped both of his ears, gazed into his blue, wonderfully non-reptilian eyes and, emphasizing each word with a tug because she felt it extremely important he understand, enunciated carefully.

"I. Hate. Snakes!"

The stranger blinked, pulled her hands away from his ears, held her at arm's length and, in the type of soothing voice one might use with a wild animal or a lunatic, said, "Okay."

The stranger had red hair and freckles. She had a prejudice against men with red hair and freckles. A nine-year-old carrot top had made third grade miserable for her. Under the circumstances, however, she decided she might like to crawl inside this man's body and hide.

"There was a nest of them." She let go of him, stepped away, and wrapped her arms around her waist, giving an involuntary shiver.

"Where?" he asked.

Moriah pointed back toward Cabin One.

"You were beneath that cabin?" he asked.

She nodded vigorously. "I was trying to fix a water pipe."

Then she started shivering so violently that her teeth began to chatter. "There were snakes *everywhere!*"

"Oh, lass." His voice held the hint of Scottish burr. "No wonder you're as pale as a ghost."

At that moment the trees exchanged places with the lake and the lake moved over to where the line of cabins should be. She heard a roaring in her ears and then the ground rushed up to smack her in the face. *This is going to hurt,* was her last conscious thought.

But it didn't hurt because strong arms caught her just as everything turned black.

CHAPTER 2

Ben McCain saw the girl's green eyes roll back in her head, but he was so stunned by this raven-haired beauty running smack into him, that he barely recovered in time to catch her before she hit the ground. For a moment he simply held her beneath her arms while she dangled from his hands like a rag doll.

She wasn't all that small. In fact, when she had grabbed his ears and stared intently into his eyes, they had been nearly nose-to-nose. He was six feet tall and she was only about an inch shorter. One hundred and fifty pounds, he estimated, hefting her. It was an educated guess, based on a lifetime of working as a stonemason. He could evaluate the weight of a rock within a couple of ounces.

This girl surprised him. She looked a lot lighter than she felt. All muscle, he figured. Evidently from hard work. Her hands against his skin had been rough from callouses.

The physical strength he had built over the years came in handy as he squatted to get a better grip on her. Then he rose, cradling her against his chest. It would make sense to throw her over his shoulder in a fireman's hold, he supposed. It would certainly distribute her weight more evenly, but carrying her in his arms appealed to the romantic streak in him. It wasn't as though he often had a chance to hold a beautiful woman.

He turned in a semi-circle and pondered his next move. Behind the line of cabins hugging the shore of Lake Huron, was a large, two-story log lodge sitting atop a small rise. Perhaps someone would be there who could help.

As he hiked up the path, he felt the unfamiliar whisper of silky hair against his bare arm. Her scent rose, an odd combination of honeysuckle mixed with sweat, dirt... and the sour smell of fear.

Snakes, she had said. Suddenly he realized that this might not be a simple faint. Perhaps she had been bitten.

He began to run.

He mounted the steps to the front porch of the lodge in two bounds and kicked the screen door so hard it rattled in the frame. He decided that if someone didn't come to the door, he'd break it down. The young woman needed a doctor. He would find a phone and call an ambulance.

"Is anybody here?" he shouted.

A woman who appeared to be in her early forties rushed to open the screen. She was dressed in a flowered blouse belted over what looked to be a long, fringed, buckskin skirt. Her dark hair, sprinkled with gray, was pulled back into two long braids.

She took one look and gasped. "What happened?"

"Do you know this lass?" he asked.

"Of course." The woman's face tightened with fear. "She's my niece. Her name is Moriah. Bring her inside immediately."

As he maneuvered Moriah through the door, all he registered about the place was massive overhead beams, smoke-darkened walls and heavy wooden furniture. An old blue and white quilt, framed and protected by glass hung on the wall.

"Where do you want me to lay her down?"

The woman piled two pillows on the end of a worn, brown leather couch. "Over here."

As he carefully laid Moriah on the couch and positioned her head on a pillow, it was easy to see the family resemblance between the two women. Both had the same high cheekbones, deep-set eyes, and long, dark lashes.

"What happened to her?" the woman asked. "Where did you find her?"

"She came crawling out from under a cabin yelling 'snakes,' and then she fainted. That's all I know."

"It's too early for snakes."

"That's what I thought, but she said there was a nest of them."

"I should probably check for bites, although if she were bitten I don't think the bite alone would make her faint." The woman tugged the tail of her niece's blue flannel shirt out of her jeans and then began unbuttoning it. "Knowing Moriah's fear of snakes, even if she just saw one beneath that cabin, it might be enough to make her pass out."

Ben knew it was an emergency and all, but still... he didn't know what he was supposed to do while the aunt started to undress her. Should he leave? Stay? Turn his back? One thing he was fairly certain about was that standing there staring at them was not what the situation called for.

A blush began at the base of his neck and traveled upward toward his scalp. Sometimes he just hated being a redhead. It made it impossible to have the slightest embarrassing thought without the color of his skin announcing his discomfort to the entire world.

"Don't just stand there," the aunt said. "Pull off her boots."

Grateful to be given a job, he knelt and focused all his attention on unlacing Moriah's well-worn, steel-toed, work boots. Who *was* this girl, anyway? She had a face fit for the cover of a fashion magazine, a body that made him sweat with the effort not to notice, and the calluses of a construction worker. He carefully pulled off her boots and peeled away heavy cotton socks, revealing slender, shapely feet.

"Her skin feels cold and clammy." The woman nodded toward the other couch. "Bring me that afghan over there."

He jumped to obey and brought her the tan and blue afghan that had been lying folded. In his hurry, he tripped and nearly fell over his feet as he approached the two women.

"Goodness." The aunt snatched the afghan away from him. "You're rather a goose, aren't you?"

"Yes, ma'am," he agreed, wholeheartedly.

While he studied the ceiling, the aunt checked Moriah for puncture wounds.

"No bites, thank God," she finally said. "Keep watch over her while I go get a damp cloth from the kitchen."

Ben watched the aunt's long fringed skirt swish against her ankles as she disappeared into an adjoining room. Then he glanced down and forgot all about the aunt. Moriah, covered to her chin with the tan and blue afghan, looked like a slightly worse-for-wear Sleeping Beauty. The pallor that had worried him had left her face. Long, black eyelashes made two perfect crescents against her tanned skin. Parted lips revealed even, white teeth. Hair as shiny as raven's wings tumbled across the pillow.

A streak of dirt smeared her right cheek. He leaned over and gently brushed it away. Her skin felt like velvet.

He was awkward around women and he knew it. Always had been. Probably always would be. Being raised in an all-male household was not exactly conducive to learning how to converse easily with women. High school and college had been relatively painful, except for the academics, in which he had excelled.

Some men, if they were especially handsome, could slide by on their good looks alone—even if their main form of communication was grunts—but he was not a handsome man. Never had been, never would be. Nothing he could do about it. He was the way God created him, and that was that.

Living in the jungle for the past five years hadn't helped his social skills a whole lot, either. When this girl was properly awake, she probably wouldn't give him the time of day. That's just the way things were. Thirty-two years on this earth had given him plenty of time to get used to being overlooked by beautiful women.

Even women who weren't beautiful didn't exactly queue up to stand in line to get involved with a man who spent most of his time sitting in a hut and swatting mosquitoes, while studying the language of a remote Amazonian tribe.

Savoring this stolen moment, before she could regain consciousness, he dared to tuck a strand of her hair behind a perfectly delicate ear. He was so engrossed in studying her, that it startled him when the aunt came striding back into the room. He took a guilty step backward.

"Moriah has not fainted in a long, long time." The aunt knelt and wiped her niece's face and neck with a wet washcloth. "But when she does, it tends to go deep and last long enough to scare everybody to death."

The girl's eyes fluttered open at the touch of the wet cloth. "Katherine?"

"Yes, dear. I'm here."

"What happened? How did I get here?" She saw him standing there and blinked. "And who are you?"

"He says you found a nest of snakes." The woman refolded the washcloth and laid it again upon Moriah's forehead. "I checked for bites, but you're okay. You don't have any. This is the man who was kind enough to carry you in here a few minutes ago."

"You're the man I ran into on the path?" Moriah pulled the wet cloth away from her face. "I remember now."

"I'm Ebenezer McCain, but you can call me Ben."

"Katherine says you carried me in here?"

"Yes."

"All the way from Cabin One?"

"Actually," Katherine said, "he ran. I was in the front bedroom upstairs and heard you yelling something. The window was open. I glanced out and saw him running up the hill carrying you."

"You carried me?" Moriah's eyebrows shot up. "Up that hill? And you *ran*?"

"I was very worried."

"I'm not small."

He was certain there was something appropriate to say here, but for the life of him he did not know what it was. Instead, he simply fell back on the truth.

"You're a whole lot heavier than you look," he said. "No. Wait a minute. That didn't come out quite right."

Katherine, who had been deadly serious up to that moment, snorted with laughter.

"Thanks—I think." Moriah shifted beneath the afghan. "Can I get up now?"

Ben stared at her in uncomprehending silence for a couple of seconds. Then he understood what she was trying to say. She wanted to get dressed, and all he could do was stand there and stare.

"Sorry. I'll go wait outside..."

He hurried out the door, collapsed onto a rocking chair on the porch, and began to rock nervously. Talking to a pretty girl could sure take it out of a guy.

He stopped rocking when he heard Moriah and Katherine's voices floating through an open window.

"What did he say his name was?" Moriah asked.

"Ebenezer McCain," Katherine said. "He said to call him Ben."

"Ebenezer is a weird name. I don't think I've ever heard that one before."

"I know," Katherine said. "The only time I've ever heard it before was Ebenezer Scrooge from Charles Dicken's *Christmas Carol.*"

Seriously? They were making fun of his name? It might sound funny to them, but it had come down through several generations of his family, and he was proud of it.

"I'm supposed to have a cabin reserved here for the summer," he called in through the window.

Silence.

Moriah lowered her voice to a whisper. "I don't remember a McCain on the books."

"Try looking under Bennett," Ben prompted. "That's my employer's name. He told me his secretary made the reservations."

"The man certainly does hear well, doesn't he?" Moriah muttered.

Ben folded his arms across his chest. His first day on Manitoulin Island and things were not going at all like he had envisioned.

For the past month, he had eagerly anticipated spending the summer here. It was the largest freshwater island in the world, and he was grateful for the temporary stonemason job that would replenish the funds he needed to continue his work in South America.

A summer-long respite from the oppressive Amazon heat sounded heavenly. The luxury of having a cabin all to himself with no curious tribesmen wandering through his living quarters day and night, was attractive also.

It was only for two or three months, of course. When he finished here, he would go back to his translation work, but in the meantime, he planned to enjoy every minute of his working vacation. At the moment, however, he was tired and groggy from too much travel and too little sleep, *and* it felt like he had somehow managed to make a fool of himself to boot.

He closed his eyes in weariness. Then a frightening thought struck and propelled him to his feet. Everything he owned in the world was sitting in the middle of the path where he had dropped his luggage in his rush to catch Moriah. He leaped off the porch, ran down the hill, and came to a sliding halt when he reached the place where she had fainted.

His breathing slowed as he saw that his two duffle bags were still exactly where he had dropped them. He knelt, unzipped compartments and reassured himself that everything was intact, including every penny he owned.

He carried his belongings to the first cabin and stacked everything upon the front steps. Then he picked up a rock and strolled around to the side where he had seen a large hole in the cabin's foundation. Unlike Moriah, he had no fear of snakes, but he was curious. He threw the rock into the hole and was greeted by the eerie buzz of rattles.

CHAPTER 3

"Ben left very suddenly," Katherine said, glancing out of the window. "Do you suppose we hurt his feelings?"

"I hope not." Moriah pulled on her socks and boots. "He seemed nice enough. Did he really run up the hill while he was carrying me?"

"He did."

"I wish I could have seen that. It would also have been nice to have been awake enough to enjoy it," Moriah said. "I've never been carried by a man before."

"If you were awake, there would have been no need for him to carry you," Katherine pointed out.

You could always depend on Katherine to point out the obvious. Her aunt was the voice of reason in their house. No flights of fancy for Katherine. The woman was as steady as a rock.

"That's true," Moriah said. "He said he was going to be here all summer. Do you have any idea why?"

"From what I understand," Katherine hesitated a moment before answering. "He's been hired to work on a special project here on the island."

"What kind of a project?"

"I suppose he'll let us in on the details later if he wants to tell us."

"I liked him," Moriah tied her boot laces.

"He seemed nice enough," Katherine said. "I don't think he'll be the kind of guest who will cause us any trouble. I'll go down to the cabin and help him get settled in if he's still of a mind to stay."

"Why wouldn't he want to stay?"

"Perhaps he dislikes snakes as much as you," Katherine said. "Maybe seeing you come screaming down the path at him might have scared him off."

"I wasn't screaming," Moriah said. "I was running. In fact, I ran straight into him. The man is so strong it felt like I had hit a brick wall. Somehow I doubt that Ben McCain scares easily."

"I think you are probably right on that score. I'll go help him get properly settled in."

After Katherine left, Moriah's mind flashed back to that awful moment when she realized she had crawled into a den of snakes. She gave a little shiver. Her aversion to snakes bordered on an obsession, but she couldn't allow herself to give into it. There was too much work to do! Tourism season was starting and would soon be in full swing. Some of the cabins had been reserved, but there were plenty of drop-ins. To maximize income, she needed to have every cottage completely ready to rent at a moment's notice.

Sometimes she thought about what it might be like to be a tourist coming to Manitoulin Island instead of someone who lived there all year round.

People came to her and Katherine's resort, looked at the freshly-painted cottages, the well-trimmed grounds, the well-maintained boats and motors and had no idea how much work was involved.

Keeping the place up and running with no help but from Katherine was a little daunting at times. People could be hard on things.

Sometimes she wondered what it would be like to have the time to just hang out with friends in the summer instead of having to work all the time. Or what it would be like to dress up and go out to dinner with some nice guy— but that didn't seem likely to happen any time soon.

Single, nice guys were in short supply at the resort. Most of the men who came there were married and accompanied by their families. Or sometimes family men would come alone or with a buddy for a few days of fishing. Since the resort was her entire world, her options were limited.

Of course, if she had been bitten today, finding a nice guy would be the least of her worries. Another involuntary shudder rippled through her body. She never wanted to go through anything like that ever again. She unlocked the closet where she kept her grandfather's ancient shotgun. It was her job to get rid of the snakes, but she would do it from as far away as possible.

CHAPTER 4

"It wasn't just Moriah's imagination, was it?" Katherine said. "There really is a den of rattlesnakes under there?"

Wearing her worn leather moccasins, Katherine had startled him by approaching without making a sound.

"No. It wasn't just her imagination," Ben said. "How is your niece?"

"She's fine. Just a little shaken." From a safe distance, she peered into the dark opening. "I wonder what we should do. We can't allow guests to stay in a cabin that has a den of rattlesnakes beneath it."

He glanced up and saw Moriah striding toward them while cocking an old double-barrel shotgun. She was wearing the same jeans, work shirt, and boots that she had worn when she had passed out in front of him in the middle of the path. Her long, black hair was loose and there was fire in her eyes.

"I'll take care of them," she said. "Stand back."

Katherine and Ben stepped away.

She stopped three feet from the hole in the foundation,

dropped to her belly, aimed beneath the cabin and released the safety.

"I don't think you should do that." Katherine said.

Moriah glanced up at her. "Why not?"

"Jack rattlers are a protected species."

"I don't care." Moriah went back to sighting down the gun barrel.

"I do." Katherine said. "Killing them is illegal."

"For crying out loud, Katherine," Moriah said, irritably. "So don't *tell* anybody."

Ben listened with interest. He couldn't care less about the snakes, but he wondered if Moriah might still be a little too shaken up to have thought her plan through.

"Is there plumbing beneath that cabin?" he asked.

"Yes," Moriah said. "Why?"

"Do you really want to blow a hole in it?"

Moriah hesitated, registered what he was saying, stood back up, and un-cocked the shotgun. "You make an excellent point, McCain."

She broke open the shotgun, slipped the two shells out, and dropped them into her shirt pocket. He noticed that her hands were shaking.

"Are you okay?" he asked.

"No, but I will be," Moriah said. "I'm going to go back to the lodge and take a very long shower to get the snake stink off me. Then I'll try to pretend this afternoon never happened."

"That sounds like a good idea," Katherine said.

"You," Moriah pointed at her aunt, "are in charge of figuring out what to do about those snakes. I suggest you should get in touch with the people who think rattlesnakes should be protected. Maybe those people would like to come get them. Maybe they would like to keep them as pets."

"I'll take care of it," Katherine said.

21

Ben watched with open admiration as Moriah strode back to the lodge. "Your niece is really something, isn't she?"

Katherine looked at him, then glanced at her niece, and back at him. A worry line appeared between her eyebrows.

"I'll put you in Cabin Ten; our newest. Moriah framed it up last fall and finished the inside work just last week. You'll be our first guest to stay in it. I think you'll be very comfortable there."

"Moriah built all these cabins?" He had never met a woman carpenter.

"She built the three newest ones. My father built the others. Come along and I'll show you where you'll be staying."

Ben hefted his bags off Cabin One's porch and followed Katherine to the last cabin in the row. He was fascinated with the fact that Moriah had built it.

It was a simple design like all the others; one story, two windows in the front. A deck furnished with a small table and two chairs that faced the beach. The cabin was not large, but it was plenty big enough for a single man to live in for a summer.

"Moriah built this all by herself?" he asked.

"Yes. My niece has many skills."

Katherine unlocked the front door, walked in, and flicked a button to make the fireplace roar into action.

"You might get chilly in the night. You can use the gas logs if you want. Our older cabins have stoves that burn wood, but Moriah installed gas logs in the three newest ones. They give off an amazing amount of heat. She likes to update when she can. There's a campfire ring outside. Some of our guests enjoy sitting round it at night when the weather is warm."

Katherine waited quietly while he scanned the inside of his temporary home.

There was a combination kitchen/living area in front, while two bedrooms with a separating bathroom occupied the back. He was pleased to see that one of the front windows had a desk placed beneath it. He would have a view of the lake whenever he worked there. A navy couch and matching overstuffed chair sat against the opposite wall. A Formica and chrome table with four red vinyl chairs graced the middle of the kitchen. The walls in the combined living room/kitchen area were painted a creamy yellow. The place was pristine and perfect.

"I'm going to love it here," he said.

"Moriah will be glad you like it," Katherine asked. "By the way, how did you get here? I didn't see a car."

"I hitched a ride with a trucker from the airport in Toronto; came across the bridge at Little Current. Then I walked part of the way here until someone else gave me a lift."

"So you don't have your own transportation?"

"Not yet."

"Then you may borrow the lodge truck and get groceries tomorrow morning. If you are spending the whole summer with us, you'll need to stock up. If you need anything else, please ask."

"Thanks." He ran a hand over the smooth walls. "This is a really good paint job, too."

"Moriah did all of it." There was a smidgen of pride in Katherine's voice. "She also installed the plumbing and electricity."

"Impressive," he said.

"Yes, my niece is very competent. She has built a good life for herself." Katherine hesitated a moment before adding. "Here on the island."

CHAPTER 5

M oriah's stomach grumbled. She awoke and peered at the clock. It was four a.m. and she was hungry.

Throwing an ancient, blue, chenille robe over her flannel pajamas, she padded past her aunt's room in search of a snack. As she went down the stairs to the kitchen, she paused on the landing and glanced out the window. Ben McCain's lights were still on.

That was worrisome. There was no television in any of the cabins and no good reason for anyone to be up at this time of night unless something was wrong.

She downed a glass of milk while standing in front of the refrigerator. Then she glanced out of the window again. That light was still on. Could he be ill? Surely he would come to the lodge for help if he were.

Along with television, there were no telephones in any of the cabins either. Their guests tended to prefer it that way. This was supposed to be a basic fishing camp—a place to come and get away from it all. She and Katherine had never pretended to provide all the modern conveniences. What they had was great fishing and a dynamite view of the lake.

She knew they must be doing something right because, during the summer tourist season, they seldom had an empty cabin. Of course, it made things a whole lot cheaper for them to not have to provide entertainment and instant contact with the outside world. If anyone really needed to use the phone, there was one in the lodge.

They didn't have a computer or internet access yet. They might end up being the last hold-outs on the island, but Katherine preferred the old ways and so did she.

A package of oatmeal cookies lay on the kitchen counter. She grabbed one and took a bite, but that uncomfortable feeling that something was amiss at McCain's cabin kept niggling at her. She decided she'd better go check on him just in case.

A pair of rubber fishing boots lay against the wall where she had dropped them earlier. Now, she plunged her bare feet into their chilly depths and opened the door. Cool air struck her face.

Spring nights in Canada were chilly. Some visitors had a problem with adjusting. Maybe that was the problem at McCain's cabin. She didn't know if Katherine had taken extra blankets to Cabin Ten yet. Her aunt had been busy with the laundry when he arrived and might have gotten distracted. There was a good chance that he was cold, couldn't figure out how to turn on the gas fireplace, and didn't want to bother them at this time of night.

She considered taking him a thick comforter, and decided against it. It would look odd, knocking on a man's door in the middle of the night with a blanket over her arm. It could be easily misinterpreted as her hoping for a sleepover. It would be best to simply go check things out before she started trying to fix a problem that might not exist.

The sky was clear and a full moon illuminated the path. Her

eyes adjusted quickly as she clumped along the path beside the lake in her rubber boots. She might be afraid of snakes, but walking outside in the dark did not bother her. Manitoulin Island was a safe place. It had very little crime, and Robertson's Resort always felt like the safest place of all to her.

Small, comforting night sounds filled the air as she walked. Lake Huron lapped at the shore. The sound of the lake was a lullaby embedded so deep in her consciousness that she practically breathed according to its rhythm. A young raccoon scurried into the underbrush, leaving a lake mussel, half-eaten on the path.

"Sorry about that, little one," she said, softly. "I didn't mean to interrupt your breakfast." She tossed her half-eaten cookie toward the lake. Raccoons liked cookies. She knew this for a fact. Katherine had once accidentally left an open package of fig bars outside. It was empty the next morning and had raccoon tracks all around it.

When she arrived at Cabin Ten, light poured out from the two front windows. She quietly and carefully mounted the deck steps and glanced in, relieved to see him seated at the desk absorbed in a book instead of shivering in the corner like she had feared. Ben had apparently felt no need to pull the curtains. He had even figured out how to use the gas logs, which were burning nicely. He stopped reading, wrote for a moment, and then focused back on his book.

Relieved, she turned to go back to the lodge. She was half-annoyed with herself for even bothering to come check things out. Back at the lodge, there was a long to-do-list. Morning would come soon enough and she needed to get some sleep if she was going to...

"Did you need something?" Ben asked.

She whirled and saw him standing in the open door. With one foot in the process of descending the steps, she let out a little yelp and fell backward onto the ground, landing flat on her back.

The wind rushed out of her lungs when she hit the ground. While she fought for breath, Ben leaped off the deck and knelt beside her, lifting her into a sitting position.

"Relax, lass, and your breath will come."

The unexpected feel of his strong arms around her caused her to gasp, and her lungs filled. She began to breathe normally again.

"You'll feel better now." His voice was kind and reassuring, and she noticed the hint of a Scottish burr again. The man had a lovely deep voice. She also realized that he was continuing to hold her upright with his iron-muscled arms.

He smelled of soap and sun-dried laundry and some sort of woodsy scent she couldn't identify but liked very much. Suddenly, she wished with all her heart that she had worn something more attractive than a faded bath robe, flannel pajamas and, oh goodness, fishing boots. This was embarrassing. She pushed herself away from him and shoved herself up off the ground.

"I'm fine," she said, brushing off her bottom. "Thanks."

Ben rose and shoved his hands deep into his pockets as though he thought he had done something wrong. She saw confusion flitting across his face in the moonlight.

"It is very late," he said. "Was there something you needed?"

"I didn't need anything. I was up and saw that your light was on. I thought you might be ill or something."

His expression softened. "I should have told you that I often stay up very late. Your other guests probably turn in early, don't they?"

"Those who plan to go fishing before dawn tend to. I'm sorry I disturbed you."

"You didn't disturb me. In fact... I'm still wide awake. I slept a lot on the plane coming here. You could stay awhile if you want to."

"*Excuse* me?" Disappointment stabbed her. A handful of male guests had made the mistake of assuming she automatically came with their cabin. They had never made that mistake again, but somehow she had not expected Ben to be one of them.

"I— I mean," he stammered. "We could sit out here on the porch and talk if you want. It would be nice to have someone to talk to."

Moriah relaxed as he emphasized the word "talk". It was probably close to five a.m. now. She normally got up at six, and falling off a porch tended to wake a person up. She wouldn't be getting any more sleep today.

"I suppose I could stay for a bit."

"May I offer you some—let's see—all I have is water. I planned to get groceries tomorrow. I mean today."

"Water would be nice."

"I'll be right back," Ben said. "Wait right here. Please don't go anywhere."

He ran to fetch the water with a whole lot more eagerness than she thought the situation warranted.

She decided that she wouldn't mind getting to know Ben McCain a bit better. This was a little unusual for her. Tourist season was so intense that she seldom had the time or inclination to get to know her guests beyond a basic professional courtesy.

But there was something about Ben that intrigued her. It wasn't because of anything particularly special about his looks. His hair was sandy red, unkempt, and much longer than it should be. His hands, large, blunt-fingered and calloused, were workman's hands. His face was honest and plain, unremarkable, except for his eyes. As he'd hovered over her at the lodge, she had noticed that his eyes were an unusual shade of blue. They nearly matched the denim shirt he was wearing.

Even hunched over a book, the width of his shoulders had been impressive. Obviously, he didn't spend all his time reading books or he would not have had the strength to run up a hill carrying her. At five foot eleven and a hundred and fifty pounds, she had yet to meet a man capable of making her feel like a delicate flower, but her brief encounter with Ben McCain came close.

Ben was far from movie-star handsome... but he wasn't exactly hard on her eyes, either.

Unfortunately, with the exception of her childhood friend, Jack, she had always been a little awkward around guys. At least when it came to the possibility of dating one of them. The boys in high school shop class had respected her skill with a reciprocating saw, but they didn't exactly invite her to the prom. Of course, it didn't help that she was taller than most of them, and that she had never developed a knack for boy/girl small talk.

She caught herself wondering if Ben was married, and then shoved the thought aside. He probably wouldn't be interested in her after he got to know her. Most men seemed a little intimidated by the fact that she could take a cranky boat motor apart and put it back together again until it ran smoothly. Or that she could fix a leaky toilet all by herself.

What most of them didn't realize was that, if she didn't do the repairs, there was no one else to do them. She *had* to learn to be handy with tools. She just hoped Ben wouldn't be yet another man who would be put off at the idea of a woman who knew her way around a hammer and nail gun.

On the other hand, maybe it didn't matter what Ben thought of her. For all she knew, the man might have a wife and a dozen kids at home.

At twenty-five, she had not once been on a real date and she had no idea how to go about getting one. Being a girly-girl simply was not part of her skill set. Plus, she had no earthly idea how to flirt.

While other girls had been learning how to capture a boy's attention, she'd been fighting to keep her family's fishing resort from falling apart ever since the year she turned thirteen and her grandfather died. She could build, plumb and re-roof a cabin with the best of them, but somehow she'd never figured out the key to making a guy fall in love with her.

Nor had she met one yet that she wanted to. Until—quite possibly—now.

CHAPTER 6

B en rifled through his freezer for ice and filled two glasses. He couldn't believe his luck. An intriguing, lovely woman was sitting on his porch right now. At least he *hoped* she was still sitting on his porch. He hurried to go outside before she could change her mind.

As the screen door closed behind him, he stopped, stunned at the picture she made in the moonlight. She was absolutely gorgeous as she sat there, long pajama-clad legs propped up on the banister, a pretty blue robe draped around her. She had long, shiny, black hair and it rippled in the moonlight, reminding him of the Amazon River at midnight. She seemed utterly engrossed in the starlight filtering down on them. His heart turned over at the sight of this graceful beauty waiting for him.

Things like this didn't happen to Ben McCain. Beautiful women didn't just turn up out of nowhere in the middle of the night. Getting to spend some time with Moriah would be a nice memory to take home with him when he left.

"Wishing on a star, lass?" he asked.

"Huh?" Fishing boot clad feet came off the banister and hit

the floor with a thud. "Nope. I'm wondering how much longer that gutter will hold."

He handed her the glass of water and took the other chair, feeling a little deflated.

"It's a beautiful evening," he offered.

"Yes, it is. No bugs yet." She ran a finger around the rim of her glass. "Black flies get so thick around here sometimes they can blind a bear."

"Oh. Right."

Ben sat in silence, casting about in his mind for a new topic. Discussing black flies and leaky gutters didn't strike him as appropriate moonlight conversation but he wasn't sure what to do about it.

Moriah took a sip of water and glanced at him from the corner of her eye. "Do you have any kids?"

"Who? Me? No."

She nodded. Took another sip. "A wife?"

He had no intention of even thinking about a wife until he finished his present project. His work in the Amazon was primitive, dangerous and all-consuming. Sometimes even *he* didn't want to be there. He had no plans to drag a woman into it.

And yet, his heart swelled with the possibility that Moriah might inexplicably be interested in him.

"No," he said, happily.

"Living with anyone?"

He thought about the seventy plus tribesmen who considered his hut their own personal property and wandered through it for their private amusement any hour of the day or night.

"Not really."

Moriah glanced at him with narrowed eyes.

"What does 'not really' mean?"

His mind raced. He didn't want to get into the whole thing about his work quite yet. It was such a complicated story. Few people could understand why he had chosen to bury himself in the jungle for the past five years. He'd almost given up on trying to explain it.

"Let's just say that I have a lot of friends who make themselves at home in my house."

"Oh."

She appeared to ponder this while they both gazed out at the lake. A thin line of dawn appeared on the horizon.

"I'm going fishing," she announced.

Talking with this woman could give a man whiplash, he decided, as she drained her glass and tossed the ice over the banister. Then she said words that went straight to his heart.

"Do you want to come?"

CHAPTER 7

Moriah felt an unfamiliar flutter in her stomach as she stuck one leg into the pair of jeans that she had flung over the chair last night before bed. She already regretted having invited Ben McCain to go fishing with her. There would be chit-chat. She didn't like doing chit-chat. The chances of saying something stupid were too high. There was also the fact that she had things to do. She didn't have time to go fishing with Ben.

Except that she just wanted to.

Standing on one leg with her jeans half on, she stopped and reconsidered. Under normal circumstances she would wear yesterday's work clothes to fish in without a moment's thought and put on fresh ones after she'd finished and showered off the fish smell.

But not today.

She kicked the already-worn pants into the same corner where her giant antique library globe stood. Her bedroom wasn't fussy, but it wasn't plain either. It held only things she enjoyed using or looking at—things like old maps. Her walls were covered with a collection of framed antique maps. Her furniture was dark mahogany, built at least a hundred years ago. An authentic spy glass sat on her window sill. Katherine said that the room reminded her of a ship captain's quarters, but all Moriah knew was that she liked the way her room felt when she was inside of it.

Which wasn't often. There was way too much to do at Robertson's Resort for her to lounge around in her bedroom.

She pulled her newest jeans out of a bureau drawer. They were a little stiff, but at least they were clean. Then she threw on her best flannel shirt, slicked her hair back into a tight ponytail, ran downstairs to the extra refrigerator on the front porch where she and Katherine kept bait for sale, and then headed out to the small dock.

She was pulling two basic fishing poles and some gear from the locker when Ben came whistling through the early-morning mist. He was wearing baggy, blue jogging pants, flip flops, and a too-tight grey t-shirt that said, "Kiss me! I'm Scottish!" He carried a large backpack in one hand and a giant-sized tube of sunscreen in the other.

"That's an awful lot of sunscreen." She nodded at the yellow tube.

"I burn easily," Ben said. "I go through cases of the stuff."

"But the sun isn't even out."

"It will be." He offered the tube to her. "I'll share."

She shook her head. "I never use it."

A large pair of sunglasses sat on top of his head. He slipped them onto his nose before stepping into the boat and finding a seat.

"Again?" she said, looking around at the mist. "The sun isn't out yet."

"It will be," Ben explained. "I get really bad headaches without them."

"Whatever works." She had dealt with hypochondriacs at the

resort before and she was getting the impression Ben might be another one. Based on experience, she doubted he would last thirty minutes without asking to go back to shore. This was a grave disappointment to her. In her opinion, a man who couldn't go on an early-morning fishing trip without worrying about sunburn and headaches wasn't much of a man. Oh well.

She climbed in, settled down onto a seat and jerked the cord to start the motor.

"You sure you want to go through with this?" She jerked the cord.

"I'm sure," Ben said. "I can't wait. I live to fish."

She jerked the cord again.

Ben settled his backpack onto the floor of the boat. "Maybe you should try the choke."

"I know how to start a motor." Her teeth clenched as she gave another mighty jerk.

Nothing.

Ben reached over her shoulder and moved a lever a fraction. "Now try."

She shot him a glance, then gave one more pull. Of course, *this* time it caught and purred like a kitten. Over the years she had developed a theory that some pieces of machinery had a sense of humor and deliberately chose to embarrass the person dealing with them. This was one of those times.

"I've been repairing boat motors since I was twelve," Moriah said. "I do know how to start one."

"I'm sure you do." Ben nodded in agreement.

"I've taken this one apart and put it back together again more than once."

"I don't doubt it," he agreed. "Do you have life jackets on this boat?"

"You don't swim?"

"Not particularly well."

"There are two of them under the seat."

"Great." Ben pulled one out and tried to hand it to her.

"No thanks," she said.

"Ah." He drew his own arms through it and shrugged it on. It was a little snug. "I'm guessing that you *do* swim well?"

"Like a fish."

"What a surprise," he said.

He buckled on the yellow life jacket, then squeezed out a handful of suntan lotion and began slapping it on while she nosed the metal boat away from the dock. They motored into the mist for a few minutes then, a half-mile from shore, she cut the motor and picked up the extra fishing rod. It was an uncomplicated spinner, the kind with which she taught beginners. Ben watched with interest as she baited it.

"You ever fish before?" she asked.

"Some."

She handed him a pole with an already-baited hook at the end. "Try not to hook yourself. Or me."

Ben reached for the pole and inspected the already-baited hook. "My uncle had a saying about this sort of thing."

"About fishing? What was it?"

"My uncle always said, 'Don't ever marry a woman who won't bait her own hook.'" Ben cast in a smooth, flowing arch and began to reel. "He never told me what to do about a woman who baited her own hook *and* mine."

"Sorry." Moriah apologized. "I'm used to beginners."

"That's okay," Ben said. "It never was my favorite part of the sport, anyway."

She got her line ready, then settled back and cast it with expertise. They sat in companionable silence for several minutes as they watched the ripples from the tiny nibbles, baby fish too young to grab a proper mouthful, or mature ones wise enough not to take the entire hook.

"Can I ask you a question?" she said.

"Sure."

"Where are you from?" She inspected her hook. The nibbles had taken a toll. She rebaited and cast again.

"I was born in Scotland—no surprise there—but my father and I moved to Maine to live with my uncle when I was still a wee lad."

"Well then, that answers that."

"That answers what?"

"The bit of accent you have," she said. "It's nice."

"My accent?" He pretended to be surprised. "I have an accent? What accent? I thought I had gotten rid of it."

"Please don't get rid of it."

"If you like it, Moriah," he said, solemnly, "I will try very hard to hang onto it."

She had stopped getting any bites at all. She cast again. "You said you and your dad moved you to Maine. What about your mom?"

"My mom didn't live too long after I was born. That's one of the reasons we left Scotland."

"I'm sorry."

"So was Dad. He didn't do too well for a long time afterward. My father and uncle were far from perfect but they did the best they could to raise me." Ben reeled in his fishing line, checked the hook, and also recast. "I never went hungry and I learned to work. That's more than a lot of people can say."

"True."

"My turn to ask a question," Ben said. "Why was your aunt wearing that buckskin skirt and moccasin outfit last night?"

"You didn't like what Katherine was wearing?"

"I don't care what your aunt wears, but I've never been to Canada before. I was wondering if wearing buckskin is some sort of custom."

38

"It isn't exactly a custom. Katherine wears it because she works part time at the Amikook Centre at Wikwemikong."

"I have an extensive vocabulary," Ben looked at her with raised eyebrows. "And I speak five languages, but I have no idea what you just said."

"I don't know the meaning of the words. That's just what it's called. Katherine helps counsel and care for elderly tribal people who come to the Amikook Centre. She arranges for various activities, runs the meals on wheels program, checks on them at home if they're sick. That sort of thing. Katherine is one-eighth Ojibwe, so she dresses somewhat traditionally when she's there. It's a comfort to the older ones."

"Then that makes you...?"

"One sixteenth."

"Oh," he said. "Then that would explain your beautiful hair and lovely skin."

Moriah had no idea how to respond to that. Ben, on the other hand, was completely nonchalant about what he'd just said.

In fact, he continued the conversation as calmly as if they were discussing the weather.

"Wikwemikong? What is that?"

It took Moriah a couple of beats before she recovered her voice. It wasn't every day that a man used the words "beautiful" and "lovely" to describe her. She would have liked to savor it, but Ben had asked a question. "It's the unceded First Nations reservation over on the east side of Manitoulin Island."

"First Nations?"

"People used to call them 'Indians' but First Nations people really hate that word."

"I'll try to remember not to use it, then. What does unceded mean?"

"They never surrendered."

"Seriously? They're allowed to do that?

"Canada's native history is a little different than the States."

"Apparently so."

"Can I ask you something else now?" Moriah said.

"Sure."

"Do you have a job?"

Ben choked on a laugh. "You don't mind being blunt, do you?"

"Not usually," Moriah said. "Does that mean you don't?"

"I do have a job."

"And it is...?"

Ben shrugged. "It's complicated."

"Complicated as in 'I'm an international spy' or complicated as in 'I sell drugs to little kids'?"

"Neither!" Ben shot her a glance. "I'm a linguist. I'm translating the Bible into a remote Amazonian dialect. That's also where I've been living for the past five years."

Her heart skipped a beat at the mention of the Amazon.

"Do you like what you do?" She checked her line and added a fresh worm. Something was definitely nibbling at it out there.

"Most of the time. Why do you ask?"

"We've had morticians, electricians, airplane pilots, teachers, truckers, you name the profession and a person who makes their living at it has stayed with us—except for Bible translators. You're our first."

"Well, that's what I do."

"Why?"

"Maybe because I'm good at it?"

"I thought most people who wanted Bibles already had them."

"I wish they did. But that's not the case. There's over seven thousand languages in the world. Around nineteen hundred still do not have Bibles translated into their own language yet. I'm one of the people who are trying to whittle that number down."

"In the Amazon?"

"That's where several of the remaining languages are."

Moriah laid her fishing rod across her lap, rinsed her hands in the lake, dried them on her shirt and digested this information.

"My parents died there," she said.

"The Amazon? I'm sorry." He sounded genuinely concerned. "How did it happen?"

"Dad was a carpenter. He went there one winter to help build a medical clinic. He and my mother died in a plane crash coming home."

"Do you know where the clinic was located?"

"I've asked, but Katherine says the place didn't really have a name. I suppose it doesn't matter anymore."

"I know the country pretty well, maybe I could find out…"

"I doubt it." Moriah's stomach twisted like it often did when she thought about her parents' death. There was a blackness there that she had never understood. Her childhood memories did not go back past age six. "I'd rather not talk about it anymore."

"Okay. What do you want to talk about?"

"You don't look like a Bible translator," she said.

"No? How should a translator look?"

"You should be skinny and hunched over from studying all the time. You have way too many muscles to be a Bible translator."

"You think I have too many muscles?" Her comment surprised him. This lovely woman had noticed how he was built?

"I think that came out wrong," she said. "What I meant is, you look like you are used to working hard. That doesn't fit with sitting around translating the Bible."

"I do work hard." He recast. "Here's the deal, Moriah. Most Bible translators have to either support themselves by working a second job or they have to ask for donations from churches. My father and uncle were both stonemasons and they taught me a trade that I'm good at and that pays well. Every summer, I hire myself out for a few months and do a project or two until there's enough money for me to live on again."

"I sort of do the same thing," Moriah said. "During the winter I hire myself out to a local contractor to help with inside finish work."

"How did you learn to be so good at carpentry?"

"My grandpa was afraid that Katherine wouldn't be able to run the resort alone after he died, so he taught me how to help her take care of it. He bought me a nail apron when I was only seven. I loved following him around."

"Do you enjoy what you do?"

It wasn't a question she'd ever asked herself. Keeping the resort in good repair was pretty much a matter of survival for her and Katherine. It was simply what she did and probably always would.

She shrugged. "It pays the bills."

"The Apostle Paul supported himself by making tents. That's what my stonemasonry is. It's my tent-making job, except, unlike Paul, I haven't gotten beat up for anything yet... although I suppose it has happened to other translators."

"Oh." Her mind had wandered. The fish were not biting. Just the little nibblers. It was probably way too early in the season to go fishing—let alone take a guest, but one could always hope. "Let's go to another spot I've had good luck with in the past. It's rocky. Sometimes they're biting there."

"Could we move closer to that lighthouse?" Ben pointed. "I'd like to get a better look at it."

The mist had evaporated and the sun had burst through. The broken tower shimmered in the distance above the gentle waves of the lake. She gazed at its familiar form. As always, she silently grieved its present condition.

"Are you a lighthouse buff?"

"Not particularly, but I'd be interested in knowing more about this one. How long has it been unattended?"

"Most of the lighthouses were shut down back in the 60s, before I was born."

"Why did they do that?"

"Money," Moriah said. "A solar powered light on a pole was a whole lot cheaper than paying a light keeper and bringing food and supplies to his family."

"So it's been empty all that time?"

"I wish! Vandals came the summer I was sixteen. Outsiders. They stole the special French-made Fresnel lens in the tower. A few weeks later, they returned and broke all the windows."

"You know for sure it was outsiders?"

"Locals wouldn't do something like that."

"This is a big island." Ben said. "I read that at least twelve thousand people live here. Surely one of them could be a vandal."

"No." Moriah shook her head. She knew what she knew. "Locals wouldn't have damaged the lighthouse. The people of Manitoulin Island cherish the lights that ringed our island. The Coast Guard and government... not so much."

"Okay, so locals wouldn't have vandalized it," Ben conceded.

Moriah reeled in her line. No reason to stay here. She started the motor and began plowing through the waves in the opposite direction of the lighthouse.

"Wait a minute," he shouted over the drone of the boat. "Can't we go see it?"

"No." Moriah had no intention of becoming his tour guide to what she considered her private property. At least not right now. Maybe later, after she got to know him better. "We came to fish, not go sight-seeing."

In a few moments, she shut the motor off near a rocky outcrop toward shore. Sometimes there were good-sized perch hiding there. Ben studied the boulders deep in the clear water beneath the boat, then he dropped the pole she had given him and reached into his canvas backpack.

"I don't want to hurt your feelings, Moriah. That's a fine pole for a beginner, but I'm ready to do some serious fishing now."

CHAPTER 8

Two hours later, Moriah nosed her boat into the dock, climbed out and tied it. Ben handed her the two rods and her fishing gear. Without saying a word, she stashed the poles in the locker and rinsed her hands off under the faucet her grandfather had rigged to make it easier for guests to clean their fish.

"There's no need to be surly, lass." Ben untied his stringer from the bow of the boat and pulled it out of the water. It was heavy with bass and perch. "I can't help it if I caught more fish than you."

"I'm not being surly." Moriah dried her hands on the back of her still-stiff jeans.

He flashed a grin, and she noticed how white and even his teeth were. Ben had a great smile, even if it was a little mischievous at the moment. Her prejudice against red-heads aside, Ben was becoming more attractive to her by the minute. "You were just fishing off the wrong side of the boat, Moriah. That's all."

"There *is* no wrong side of the boat."

"Sure there is. Tomorrow morning, I'll take your side of the boat and you can take mine."

She watched the fish flip water all over his pants and shoes.

"We're not going fishing tomorrow morning."

"Okay. What *will* we be doing?"

"*We* are not doing anything tomorrow morning. I have to get this place ready for the other guests. Trust me. It's going to get really busy around here soon."

"This afternoon, then?" Ben asked. "This evening? Come on, Moriah. I've waited a long time for this vacation. Some companionship would be nice."

"Your fish can keep you company." Moriah glanced again at the large catch. She couldn't remember ever seeing someone as competent with a fly rod.

"They don't smell as good as you."

"I don't smell so good right now, either."

She felt an unfamiliar desire to—to—*flirt*. But she didn't know how.

A little confused by her feelings for this stranger, she turned and started hiking up the hill to the lodge.

"You'd better start cleaning them," she called over her shoulder.

"You'll help, right?" he shouted after her.

"Nope." She started walking backward up the hill. "My grandpa had a saying about fish, too..."

"What was it?"

"My grandpa always said, 'You catch 'em, you clean 'em.'"

With a wave she left him to his work.

As soon as she got inside the lodge, she went upstairs, stuffed her fishing clothes into the laundry basket and stepped into the shower, her mind filled to overflowing with Ebenezer McCain. He was a surprise to her in every way. Who would have thought that a man so fair-skinned he was nearly allergic to the sun, would turn out to be such an expert fisherman?

He had whipped out a featherweight, collapsible fly-casting

rod from his backpack that was so state-of-the-art she had never seen one like it. Then he had attached a tiny hand-tied fly that seemed to tickle the fancy of every fish within a hundred feet of their boat. The man was poetry in motion with a fly rod in his hand. She'd been so mesmerized by the sight that she had laid her fishing pole across her lap and simply watched.

She dried off, ran a comb through her damp hair, and began to dress. As she balanced on one foot while pulling a sock on over the other one, she looked out of the upstairs window and saw Ben cleaning fish with the same single-minded concentration she had seen as he had read and made notes the night before. His movements were quick and spare as he dropped one fillet after another into a bucket. He finished, sprayed down the concrete sink, hung the filleting knife back in its place, and looked up at the lodge. He caught sight of her watching and raised his hand in a greeting.

As he climbed the hill, she puzzled over the feeling of familiarity she felt with that particular walk, that solid build. Even his voice sounded faintly familiar. She just couldn't remember who or where she had seen someone so much like him.

"You want fresh fish for breakfast?" Ben let himself into the back door and sat the bucket in the kitchen sink just as she came downstairs into the kitchen.

"Don't you want them?"

"Of course I do, I'm starved. But I don't plan on *cooking* them. My uncle had another saying... if you catch them, and clean them, somebody else has to fry them."

"Oh." She put her hand on her hip. "Your uncle always said that, did he?"

"Always." Ben nodded solemnly. "It was on a framed embroidery sampler hanging in our kitchen."

"Your uncle embroidered?"

"Yes." Ben looked offended. "Do you have a problem with that?"

"Nope. We've had guests who did much stranger things than that."

"Okay. Maybe I exaggerated a wee bit. My uncle didn't embroider, but I *am* very hungry."

"Unfortunately, I don't cook."

"Why not?"

"Katherine does all the cooking."

Ben cocked one eyebrow, silently questioning her statement.

"My aunt and I divided up the chores a long time ago. She does the inside work and I take care of the outside. Cooking is her responsibility. I've never learned."

"Why not?"

"I just explained it."

"You explained a division of labor. You didn't explain why you're incompetent."

No one had ever said such a thing to her before. Quite the opposite.

"I'm far from incompetent and you know it."

"You said you couldn't cook."

"I suppose *you* can?"

"Of course I can, but I was hoping not to. I'm trying to have a vacation here, Moriah."

Despite the sunscreen, Ben was slightly sunburned and was starting to sound a little out of sorts. He was coming as close to whining as a grown man with a deep voice could. She had seen the same symptoms in resort children who had played hard for too long, and had gotten too hungry.

"How long has it been since you ate, Ben?"

His eyes closed as he calculated. "Except for a bag of peanuts on the plane, thirty-six hours."

Moriah was aghast. "I had no idea you were starving."

"Technically, I'm not actually starving, but I don't remember being hungrier."

"Oh, Ben! I'm so sorry!" She grabbed a skillet. "If you give me instructions, I'll attempt to fry those fish."

"In the meantime..." He grabbed a bag of potato chips lying on the counter. "Do you mind?"

"There's cheese in the refrigerator. Go ahead and snack." She turned the gas on beneath the frying pan. "This might take a while."

CHAPTER 9

Katherine walked into the kitchen just as Ben and Moriah were finishing their meal. She was wearing baggy blue capris, a white shirt, and a faded grey cardigan sweater. There were no moccasins on her feet—just regular tennis shoes. Her salt-and-pepper hair was in one long braid down her back. Apparently, she was not working at the reservation today.

He couldn't help but notice once again the striking resemblance between the two women. In spite of her everyday dress, and being old enough to be Moriah's mother, Katherine was a very attractive woman. If this was what Moriah would look like in another twenty years, her husband would be one lucky man.

"Goodness!" Katherine exclaimed. "You two have destroyed my kitchen!"

"Yes, we did," Ben said. "But I did manage to teach your niece how to fry fish."

"Moriah cooked?"

"She certainly did. Although, just between me and you..." he glanced around the kitchen, "I think she's a little messy."

Fish bones littered the table, along with an empty bag of potato chips, and two slices of leftover cheese lying on a plate.

"You had a hand in making the mess, as well," Moriah said. "You can't blame this all on me."

"And I'll have a hand in cleaning it up—but my stomach feels a whole lot better. Thanks for feeding me, Moriah."

Katherine surveyed the table. "A well-balanced diet, I see."

"I'll teach her how to cook vegetables tomorrow," Ben promised.

"I doubt that." Moriah reached for a red ball cap hanging behind the back door.

Ben noticed the insignia. "You're a Cincinnati Reds fan?"

"Not particularly." She turned the cap around in her hand to look at the front. "Oh, I see. Nope—it's just something a guest left behind in one of the boats last year. We weren't sure who and they never contacted us to ask for it back. I liked the color."

She slammed the cap on her head and pulled her pony tail through. "I've had fun this morning, Ben, but I've really got to get back to work. There are some porch steps I need to replace today. I don't want a guest to break their leg and sue us."

Ben stood and began dropping fish bones into the potato chip bag. "Thanks for taking the trouble to go fishing with me."

"No problem." She waved as she went out the door.

Katherine watched Moriah bound down the path, and then closed the door behind her.

"I just had a conversation with your employer's secretary." Katherine said. "She told me why you're here. Moriah won't like this. Have you told her yet?"

"Not yet." Ben stuffed the trash into the kitchen trashcan and started putting dishes in the sink. "To tell you the truth, until Nicolas Bennett arrives and makes a final decision about what he wants to do, I'm not entirely certain what all my job will involve."

"Whatever Nicolas decides," Katherine swept the remaining crumbs off the table into her hand and dumped them into the trash. "I'm fairly certain it will break Moriah's heart."

"What makes you say that?"

"Because," Katherine glanced up at him while clearing the table. "That's the kind of thing Nicolas does. That's who he is."

"You know him?" Ben said. "I don't understand."

"Nor do I," Katherine grabbed a damp cloth and began wiping the table's scarred wooden surface. "I never did. I have no idea what Nicolas thinks he's doing, but my main concern is Moriah. If you and Moriah develop an affection for one another it will not turn out well. Trust me on this. Please try to stay away from her."

"All she did was invite me to go fishing, Katherine."

"I know, and that is what worries me."

"Why?"

"Because Moriah hates going fishing."

"Seriously?"

"Seriously. It might be recreation to you, but to her it's work. She's taken too many beginners out over the years. I'm afraid she must already like you to invite you to go fishing."

Katherine went to the sink and began filling it with warm water. "I can't bear to see Moriah hurt. Couldn't you try to find another job somewhere else? Maybe you could talk Nicolas into hiring someone from the island to help him?"

"I gave Nicolas my word that I would at least come and check things out for him. I can't leave. Not now. Not until he shows up and we can make some decisions together."

"That's what I was afraid of." Katherine sighed, resigned. "You'll need food. I'll go get the keys to the truck. There's a Foodland in Mindemoya."

"I'm truly sorry that you're upset," he said, concerned. "But

I've only been here a day. I barely know your niece. I've done nothing wrong."

"Of course you've done nothing wrong," Katherine said. "You are a decent and good man. But I know who you are and where you came from, and I promise you, this summer is not going to turn out well. Not for any of us."

"Why do you say that you 'know who I am'?" Ben was dumbfounded. "What are you talking about, Katherine? I'm a linguist and a stonemason. That's it. There aren't any dark secrets in me. I am who I am."

"We'll discuss it later on if you stay the summer, or maybe not. I've said too much as it is." Katherine placed the truck keys in his hand. "Fill the gas tank before you return it."

CHAPTER 10

I t had been a full year since Ben had found himself behind a steering wheel and it felt good. Katherine and Moriah's fifteen-year-old white Chevy truck, however, which was emblazoned with the logo of Robertson's Resort, was shifting a little rough. He slowed down to stop at a stop sign and realized that the brakes were a little mushy too.

This made him feel a little guilty for having taken up so much of Moriah's time this morning. The girl had her hands full trying to maintain the resort with only Katherine's help. It was no wonder that the truck wasn't in the best shape.

As he drove north on Route 551, he noticed a church with white clapboards and a steeple. It was a pretty place and it reminded him of the church where he and his father had attended when he was a child. There were several cars, ladders leaning against the sides of the building, and lots of young people with brushes and paint cans. Apparently, the youth group was in the process of giving the church a little spiffing up. A man with gray hair and beard appeared to be giving instructions to the group.

Ben pulled into the parking lot. If he was going to be spending the next two or three months here, it might be a good idea to get to know someone besides Moriah and Katherine. This active-looking church group appeared to be a good place to start.

The sign out front said, "Tempest Bay Community Church." He got out of the truck and approached the group.

"Can I help you?" The man politely addressed Ben, but did not take his eyes off the youth group. Some had already scampered up the ladders and were enthusiastically slapping on white paint while the others held ladders and shouted encouragement to the ones up above.

"I'm Ben McCain," Ben said. "I'll be staying at Robertson's Resort for the summer."

"I'm Howard Barrister." The man shook Ben's hand, still watching the kids. "Preacher to this group of hooligans as well as their parents."

"Looks like you have a good crop of young ones coming up," Ben said. "Do you think they'll actually get it painted?"

"I'll be happy if none of them fall and break their neck," Howard said. "This was not my idea, but it became my job to make it happen."

Ben noticed that there was about as much paint ending up on the ground and the teenagers as was getting on the building. He sympathized with the preacher's concerns.

"Katherine and Moriah Roberts attend church here most of the time," Howard said. "Nice women. Hard workers. It's not an easy task trying to keep that resort going by themselves. In the past, I've offered to have our youth group go over and help them get ready for tourist season, but Moriah always refuses... politely, of course... but she seems to take a dim view of the idea."

"I'm not surprised." Ben said. "Hey, speaking of her needing help, the resort truck I borrowed needs some work. I think Moriah has been too busy getting ready for the other guests to arrive to tend to it. If I had some tools and a place to work on it I'd do the work myself—but I don't. Do you know of a good garage around here that you'd recommend?"

"There's Denovans down the road if you want, but my house and garage is next door here. I do most of my own mechanic work, so I have plenty of tools." He chuckled. "Working on my car gives me a nice change from trying to get my people to behave themselves."

"Thanks," Ben said. "It's been awhile since I had a chance to get my hands on a vehicle."

"How's that?" Howard took his eyes off the kids long enough to give Ben an appraising look.

"I've been living in the Amazon for a while and I don't leave often. I'm working on a Bible translation for one of the tribes."

"Oh?" Howard ignored the teenagers for a moment. "You said your name is Ben McCain?"

"Yes."

"You aren't, by any chance, Dr. Ebenezer McCain, the Bible translator who has been working with the Yahnowa?"

"Yes." Ben was a little taken aback. "I am, but how do you know about me and the Yahnowa?"

"I have a son who was attending a Bible college a couple of years ago when you were in the States. You spoke at his chapel service. He talked about it for a long time. He was so inspired he thought he wanted to become a translator too."

"Great. Did he?"

"My son?" Howard shook his head. "Nope. It turned out that learning another language took a great deal more effort than what he was willing to expend."

"It comes easier for some than others," Ben said. "It isn't work for everyone. Sometimes I wonder if even I am cut out for it."

"In what way?" Howard asked, obviously intrigued. "I imagine it isn't the translation work that's hard for you."

He liked Howard. The man seemed genuinely interested. Ben was pretty certain this church was lucky to have Howard as their preacher.

"Honestly? It's the loneliness… and getting homesick. When I first arrived, everything was new and different and I was fascinated with the work. Also, I was also buoyed up by the knowledge that I had a gift for languages and that I was doing God's work. I felt like I was in the right place at the right time doing exactly what I was meant to do."

"What happened?"

"Nothing. I'm still working at it, and I will finish the translation, but there are times when the work becomes tedious and I'm hot and itchy and the mosquitoes are driving me nuts and I would give anything just to be able to drink an ice cold Pepsi and watch a movie."

At that moment, over Howard's shoulder, Ben saw a girl in torn jeans accidentally spill part of a bucket of paint on the head of a girl with long, dark hair, who had been holding the ladder beneath her.

"Is that oil paint?" Ben said.

"Yes," Howard said. "Why?"

A scream erupted as the girl with long, dark hair realized what had happened.

"I think you have some spilled paint to deal with. I hope you have a lot of mineral spirits on hand."

Howard turned, took in the scene and sighed.

"No need to hire professional painters, the building committee said. Get the teens involved, they said. Let *them* paint the church, the committee said. It'll keep those kids out of trouble, they said."

The girl with paint dripping off her hair was dancing on the spot, yelping for someone to get her a towel, while the other girl kept apologizing down to her.

"Better see what I can do before that paint starts to dry," Howard said. "I don't think I can send her home like that. Garage is open. Go ahead and help yourself to whatever you need."

"Good luck." Ben did not envy Howard.

"It's okay," Howard said. "The one doing all the screeching is my daughter. I'll see if her mother can help me take care of it."

Ben pulled the truck around to the preacher's garage. He was getting out of it when he heard Howard talking to his daughter as they headed toward the front door. Howard was carrying a half-gallon jug of mineral spirits.

"It's okay, honey," Howard was saying to her. "Don't worry. I think you'll look good in a crew cut. Think how cool it will feel this summer without all that hair."

"Dad!" The girl wailed. "I'm not cutting my hair!"

A few minutes later, Howard came outside and asked if Ben had everything he needed.

"I'm fine, thanks," Ben said. "How's your girl?"

Howard grinned. "Her mom is taking good care of things. Pretty sure my daughter's scalp is going to be pretty raw before this is over though. Now, if you'll excuse me, I think I'd better get back over there before anything else happens."

"That would be wise," Ben said.

As he opened the hood of Moriah's truck, he was grateful for having stopped by. In addition to getting the use of the preacher's garage and tools, it looked like he had found a good church to attend this summer, and was looking forward to it.

He was also looking forward to seeing Moriah's face when he gave her the truck back, all tuned up and ready for the influx of summer guests. She would be so pleased.

CHAPTER 11

Moriah pulled a tape measure across a seasoned oak board, measured it a second time, marked it with a flat carpenter's pencil, and sawed it straight across. Along with the whine of the circular saw, her grandfather's voice rang in her ears.

Measure twice, saw once.

She drilled the oak board three times on each end, selected a nail from her leather carpenter's apron, coated it with a sliver of bar soap, then drove it through to the support board in one expert motion.

A true carpenter can sink a nail with one blow.

It bothered her that she had to resort to soaping the nails and drilling, but that had been a trick of her grandfather's, too, when he was working with well-seasoned, granite-hard oak. The sight of his skilled hands and the sound of his voice while he was working was one of her most comforting memories. He had been such an important part of her life that it sometimes seemed as though he was still with her.

Because of her grandfather's teaching, she was also competent with basic mechanical things like boat motors, but nothing felt as good to her as working with wood. Framing the three new cabins and finishing them out these past three years had meant more to her than anyone could possibly know. There was a lot of satisfaction in building something that was strong and sturdy and, as a bonus, would bring in more income.

She stood and stretched her back as she gazed out toward the lake. In the distance, she could see the battered lighthouse. Owning and repairing it had been an obsession for as long as she could remember.

The Canadian Coast Guard certainly couldn't be trusted to care for it—even though their name was presently on the deed. They did not have a good record for preserving Canada's light-houses. Several communities had lost these precious historic landmarks when the Coast Guard dynamited them out of existence in the middle of the night. No warning. Just one-hundred-fifty-year-old historical buildings blown to bits. She could quote dates and locations.

But they wouldn't do that to hers. Not Eliza's Lighthouse. Not if she had anything to do with it. Only one more season with the resort, especially with the extra cabins, and she should have enough money saved for a good-sized down payment.

She was grateful that there had been such an outcry from the Canadian people about the carnage that the Coast Guard had been forced to start selling some of the lighthouses to private individuals instead of destroying them. It was upon this that her hope was fixed. She had been besieging them with letters for the past year, offering to purchase the derelict lighthouse.

It had continued to be unseasonably warm. The sun was beating on her back. It would have been wise not to wear her black work t-shirt. Pulling a blue bandana out of her jeans hip pocket, she wiped the sweat off her face and surveyed her work.

The steps on Number Four Cabin were now sturdy and strong. No lawsuits waiting to happen there.

Cabin One needed some small repairs as well, but she was depending on Katherine to make arrangements for someone to come capture and move the snakes first. Whatever Katherine did, it needed to be soon. Only a few more days until the giant ferry boat, the Chi-Cheemaun, which meant the "big canoe", would begin bringing people across Lake Huron to the south shore of Manitoulin. Then tourist season would be off and running in earnest. She and Katherine already had most of the cabins reserved through September.

Nearly everyone came for only a week. It was rare for someone to rent for two. Someone who was renting for the entire summer, like Ben, had never happened at Robertson's resort before. The cabins were expensive. None of the rentals worth staying in on Manitoulin Island were cheap. They couldn't be. It was a matter of survival as those who made their living depended on making enough during tourist season to live on through the winter.

This was going to be a particularly interesting summer with Ben here. She really liked him. Who knew that just frying fish together could be so much fun? It had been a long time since she had laughed so hard. In fact, she couldn't remember *ever* laughing so hard.

As though conjured by her thoughts, Ben came sauntering down the path with a bag of groceries in his arms. He stopped, took a good look at the job she'd just finished, and gave a low, appreciative whistle.

"Those steps should hold for at least another century." His voice held genuine admiration.

Moriah accepted the compliment with a modest nod, but it felt good to have someone compliment her on her work. That didn't happen often. Most guests either didn't notice it or they took the care she gave to the resort for granted.

"Thanks." She felt a glow of pride as she fitted the hammer into the loop on her carpenter's apron. "But I'll be happy if they last for the next five years. People are awful hard on things."

"Oh, and speaking of being hard on things," Ben shifted his bag of groceries from one arm to the other. "Here's your truck keys back." He tossed them to her and she caught them in midair. "Katherine loaned them to me so I could go into town and get some groceries. I stopped at that church down the road where you and Katherine attend and met the preacher. Nice guy."

"We like him," Moriah said.

"Howard and I talked a bit and he offered me the loan of his garage and tools to work on your truck. I picked up some things I needed in town to help me fix the problems it was having. It should run real good now."

"Oh?" Moriah tried to sound grateful. "That was nice of Howard to loan you his tools and garage."

"I added some oil—you were low—and put on new brake pads. You were almost down to the metal."

She didn't know what to say. Truth be told, she *hated* for anyone to mess around with the truck and wished Katherine would quit loaning it out to guests. She was also embarrassed that her vehicle had been a topic of discussion between Ben and Howard. The idea of those two men discussing how she had allowed her vehicle to get into less than pristine shape was embarrassing.

"I also picked up an additive for the transmission. It seemed to help quite a lot. It was shifting a little rough when I first started out."

The tone of his voice told her that he was quite pleased with himself. She started to politely thank him for his help, but he made the mistake of saying one word too many.

"You really ought to keep on top of things like that, Moriah. I know you're busy and all, but your old truck has a lot of miles left in it if you'd take better care of it."

No one had ever criticized her mechanical ability before. There hadn't been one thing wrong with that truck. Had there? She tried to remember the last time she had changed the oil or the brake pads but she couldn't. She had been so busy lately that all her chores had begun to run together in a big blur in her mind.

Ben grinned like a small boy who had brought her a present. She knew he was waiting for her to jump for joy but his mild criticism stung.

"You've certainly been busy," Moriah said, her voice flat.

Ben stared at her, his grin turning into puzzlement. "Are you mad at me?"

"I prefer to take care of my own equipment and vehicles."

Silence.

She glanced up at him and saw that his blue eyes were fixed on her. He cocked his head to one side as though she were a puzzle he was trying to solve.

"I haven't had my hands on an engine in over a year, lass. It felt good to work on that truck. I didn't have anything else to do today and I thought I'd help you out by doing something I know how to do."

She stuffed the rumpled bandana back into her hip pocket. Ben had obviously meant well, but there was always the possibility that he didn't know what he was doing. For all she knew, in his ignorance, he could have damaged something. She really couldn't afford a major repair bill right now. Buying a new truck was out of the question—not when she was socking away every spare penny for a down payment on the lighthouse.

"I know you thought you were doing me a kindness, Ben, but from now on, please ask before you try to fix anything else."

"It's a deal," Ben said. "And from now on, you might try saying 'thank-you' when someone does something nice for you."

"I can't help it if I don't like people messing with my things."

"Seems to me like that's how you support yourself." He glanced around. "By renting out everything you own."

That, of course, was true. She rented out everything from the cabins to the boats and the motors that went with the boats. In a pinch, she had rented out the spare room in her and Katherine's lodge as well as tent space on the undeveloped acreage along the lake. She even rented herself out as a tour guide on occasions. Not to mention picking up odd jobs on construction sites around the island during off-seasons.

She made a dollar any legal way she could and there was nothing wrong with it. Her lighthouse fund was growing daily and that made it all worthwhile.

"There's nothing wrong with the way I make my living."

"No, but maybe you can understand my confusion. I thought the truck was resort property—something you lent out to guests —most of whom probably never bothered to contribute to its upkeep."

He had her there. "Actually, I'm surprised if they even bother to put gas in it."

He waited.

"Okay then," she said, reluctantly. "Thank you."

"You're welcome." Ben walked off toward his cabin.

"How much do I owe you?" she called after him.

Ben stopped, shook his head with disbelief, and kept walking.

Moriah watched his retreating back with regret. She'd done it again. Said the wrong thing. Acted the wrong way.

This is why she enjoyed working with wood and machinery. Wood didn't get its feelings hurt. She never felt like kicking herself after completing a building project. People, on the other hand... well, people were hard.

She heard the screen door on his cabin slam shut as she bent to retrieve her tools. She carefully put each one away in its place in her toolbox, then she temporarily tucked the box and circular saw under the steps she had just built, and made a decision.

Ben had tried to be kind to her this afternoon and, aside from some mild teasing, he had been nothing but nice to her ever since he'd arrived. She really did owe the man an apology. It was a relief to know that her truck was in good shape. She really was grateful, and she doubted he'd made any mistakes in the repairs. Ben just wasn't that kind of person.

She was pretty sure she knew how to make amends for her annoyance with him.

She marched down the path to his cabin, knocked on the screen door and glanced inside. He was in the kitchen area, putting some of the food into the refrigerator. At her knock, he came to the doorway, and leaned against the frame. He wasn't smiling.

"It was a gift, lass. You owe me nothing."

"I know. Thank you." She shoved her hands in her pockets. "I thought you might enjoy going with me to see my lighthouse now. I check on it every few days. You can come with me if you like."

"*Your* lighthouse?"

"Yes."

He remained exactly as he was. Arms folded, leaning against the doorframe. "Is that your idea of an apology?"

She glanced at the light fixture above his head. It needed one of those new florescent compact bulbs that she was replacing the old bulbs with.

"I guess."

He shrugged. "Okay."

CHAPTER 12

Ben marveled at the different moods of the lake. It was nearly as changeable as Moriah. Earlier, in the morning darkness, it had been as smooth as a mirror. Now, it was decidedly choppy. The late afternoon sunlight reflected off the tops of the waves which glittered like diamonds.

He pulled his sunglasses out of his shirt pocket and put them firmly on his nose. He did *not* want a headache while he was with her. It was hard enough keeping up with the woman when he had a clear head.

She looked like a woman on a mission as she steered the boat over the waves, intently focused on getting there. She had explained that going by boat was the quickest way to get to the lighthouse since the Coast Guard had allowed the dirt road leading down the middle of the short peninsula to grow into a small forest. It discouraged visitors, Moriah explained, which was okay with her.

After a few minutes, she beached the boat and, together, they pulled it far enough onto the shore that the lake couldn't reclaim it. Then Moriah climbed the gentle rise and he followed. When they reached the top, Ben found himself on a grassy plateau dotted here and there with rocks, at the edge of which stood a stone light tower soaring above an attached stone cottage.

The keeper's cottage was a story-and-a-half, and it definitely needed work, but the thing that arrested his total attention was the wicked-looking crack zigzagging up the side of the light tower. The tower was nearly eighty feet high and built out of limestone. It was beautiful, broken and dangerous.

Still, the place took his breath away. Even damaged, the tower proudly sat outlined against the blue of the sky and the lake. The cottage, with its matching stones, hugged the tower like a faithful little companion, determined to keep its friend company even if it was badly hurt.

He studied the light tower with the appreciation of a stonemason. It required time and patience to chisel stones into the shapes necessary to build such seamless walls. In spite of the damage, he could tell that a master stonemason had created the place. Such skill was rare—even back in the 1800s when the lighthouse was probably built, but thanks to his father and uncle, he possessed the ability to build as well as the old masters.

Small spring flowers were already tentatively peeking out through the grass. In spite of the damage to the place, the yard area wasn't overgrown.

"If the Coast Guard doesn't bother to keep a road open to the place," Ben asked. Who mows it?"

"I do."

"You drag a lawnmower all the way over here on a boat?"

"No. I keep one here, in the old boat shed down by the lake. That way I only have to bring a gas can with me. It's not much trouble."

"On top of everything else you have to do, you come and mow property that doesn't belong to you?" he said. "Why?"

"Because I love it here." Moriah opened her arms wide and

turned in a circle—indicating the whole small peninsula and the lighthouse. "I always have loved it here. And I'll be able to buy the place soon. Katherine and I have saved nearly enough for a good down payment."

Ben froze. "You've what?"

"Saved enough for a down payment. The Coast Guard has begun selling off some of the older lighthouses. I want to keep this one in the Robertson family if I possibly can."

"I don't understand," Ben said. "I thought you said the government owned most of the old lighthouses."

"They do." Moriah sighed. "At least on paper. But I've always believed there is such a thing as a sort of a moral ownership too. My family took care of this place for over a hundred years. They rescued people from boat wrecks, kept the light shining no matter what the weather was like, and sometimes they kept it going in spite of sickness and death. They lived their lives here."

She pointed to a patch of ground near the front of the keeper's cottage. "In a few weeks, the daffodils that my great-great grandmother, Eliza, planted will blossom here. They are the old-fashioned kind that smell so good. My grandfather always took special care of them, and I do too. One of the men she and her son helped rescue during a terrible storm, sent the bulbs to her. The man said he sent them as a living golden medal for her bravery. There's a picture of her that hangs in the great room at the lodge. Katherine put it beside that quilt she made. She's wearing a high lace collar and her hair is all done up fancy for the photographer. When you look at that photograph, it's hard to imagine her rowing out to rescue people during a storm—but she did it."

"I had no idea they ever let women be light keepers way back then," Ben said.

"There were quite a lot of them over the years. A woman named Ida Lewis was one of the most famous. Her father had a stroke soon after he moved his family to the lighthouse, so Ida and her mother kept the light going. Then her mother got sick. Ida took care of both of them, kept the light going at night, and went out and rescued by boat at least eighteen people over the years. Most of the women light keepers got their jobs under the sort of same sad circumstances that turned Ida and my great-great grandmother, Eliza, into one."

"What sad circumstance did Eliza have to deal with?"

"For Eliza, it was her husband's death. At least they thought he must have died. Liam Robertson disappeared the first winter he was employed here."

"You don't know for sure what happened to him?"

"No. It's always been a bit of a family mystery. From what we can tell, Eliza didn't know either. He just disappeared one night and never came back. It was in the wintertime, and she was snowed in with their son who was just a little boy. There were rumors that Liam went hunting for game because their food reserves were getting too low and he just never came back."

Ben could only imagine how isolated and desolate this place must have felt to a woman alone with a child. "That must have been terrible for her."

"I'm sure it was. Especially since other rumors said that he had grown tired of being cooped up with his wife and son and had abandoned them. All we know for sure is that when spring came he still hadn't shown up, and never did show up, so the government allowed her to stay on instead. Once they saw she could take care of things, they formally hired her. I suppose it was a lot easier than finding someone new and training them. She already knew how things worked. Her son, who was my great-grandfather, eventually took over when he grew up. And *his* son, my grandfather, kept the light going until the government started replacing the lighthouses with electric lights and letting the old light keepers go."

She stood, gazing at the lighthouse with so much passion and love showing in her face that it was almost painful for Ben to look at her. Especially knowing what he knew.

With this trip to see the lighthouse, things had suddenly gotten very complicated for him, and he was not a man who welcomed complications. His work was complicated enough. As she continued to tell him the history of the place, he realized how deeply rooted she was, and it made him feel sick to his stomach.

Nicolas had never told him that there was a girl building her life on dreams of restoring the lighthouse. It made everything so much worse that she was opening up and sharing her dreams with *him* of all people. If he had known the job he had been hired to do would break someone's heart, he would never have agreed to come.

"Wouldn't it take too much work to fix it up, Moriah?" he said, trying to dampen her enthusiasm a little. "Looks to me like you already have your hands full."

"I'm young. I'm strong. I'm definitely not afraid of hard work and I want to do this. I've *always* wanted to do this. It would mean the world to me if I could make this come alive again."

He could easily see all the holes in her plan, but he doubted she could. She had dreamed of this scheme for far too long to clearly see all the problems involved. Unless she and Katherine had a much larger stash of money than it seemed, trying to bring this place back to life would be impossible.

"I'd rather not run over *that* next time I mow." Moriah picked up a stone about the size of her fist and threw it toward the lake. "Sometimes it seems like the earth around here grows rocks like some sort of crop."

Ben knew that she would probably never mow the place again, but he didn't think it was his place to break it to her. But if not him, who?

Instead, of telling her what had happened, he chose to change the subject.

"How did your family end up running the resort?" he asked.

"When Grandfather saw that the Coast Guard was beginning to phase out the lighthouses—it didn't happen all at once—he bought the adjoining property and built the lodge and the first seven cabins. Tourism had just begun to hit Manitoulin Island, and land was still cheap. He hoped the cabins might provide an income once the lighthouse was decommissioned."

"And did it?"

"Yes, slowly. But the ship captains complained that the battery-operated light didn't show up as well as the old one, so Grandfather and my Dad kept the tower lit anyway on bad stormy nights even though they didn't get paid for it."

Her voice was so proud telling him this. It was obvious that her father and grandfather had achieved heroic stature in her eyes for keeping the light burning.

Katherine had been right. It had been a mistake for him to get to know Moriah because she was definitely going to despise him before the summer was over. It bothered him that apparently Katherine had known what was going to happen, but had chosen not to break the news to Moriah. Why? Did she plan on him doing it? Or had she postponed upsetting her niece while they were still in the middle of getting ready for all their guests. Perhaps she was postponing it until Nicolas's appearance forced her into it.

Moriah walked along in front of him, her long, loose hair rippling like a silken black scarf on the breeze. He could still remember the feel of her skin and the scent of her hair when he'd caught her in his arms yesterday.

Regardless of what Katherine had in mind, he knew he had to tell her. Now. This was the moment and the time. If he didn't break it to her now, she would be embarrassed by the fact that he had allowed her to go on and on about what she intended to do with the Robertson Lighthouse—especially since he knew all along what would happen.

And yet as he watched her now, glowing with enthusiasm, the words to destroy her dream stuck in his throat. She was so beautiful, so strong, and yet so vulnerable. In bringing him here, she reminded him of a little child who had offered to share her favorite toy after accidentally hurting a friend's feelings. There was something decidedly childlike about her, an innocence, in spite of the fact that she was a grown woman. It made him want to protect her, to shield her from hurt. Which made no sense at all. Truth be told, he barely knew her... and yet, in the few hours they'd spent together so far, it felt like he had somehow known her all of his life.

"We had a good year last year." Moriah confided. "So I put in a bid on the lighthouse a couple of months ago. They sent me a letter saying they would give it serious consideration. As far as I know, I'm the only one interested in it. I don't think anyone else would want to take on all the repairs. If they accept my bid, I'll have to mortgage the resort, but we'll be able to handle the payments. Especially if I keep getting winter construction work."

"What would you do with it if you had it?" Ben continued to wrestle with his conscience. Should he break it to her or not?

"I would repair the tower first. Then I'd fix the cottage and rent it out to help pay the mortgage. Lots of people would like to vacation in a lighthouse. I'd also rig up some kind of light after the tower is repaired." She turned and looked at him, her eyes so vulnerable and trusting. "It doesn't seem right not having a light in that tower. I thought maybe if I could find something that would work well, I could come over on bad nights and light it like my grandpa and Dad did. The ships don't really need lighthouses anymore—they use radar systems instead, but I'd like to do it anyway. Even with radar, there are still wrecks sometimes."

Her hopes were so naked and sweet, Ben wished the ground would open up and swallow him before he had to destroy her dream. But the ground didn't open up, and he stood mute while Moriah went on trusting him with all that was in her heart and he gathered his courage to tell her what he knew.

"If I could do that, the sailors would know that there was a real, living person here that cared about them, not just a light bulb on a pole. It might make a difference, you know?"

"It's a wonderful dream, Moriah, but I have to tell you something. I'm so sorry…"

A small, black, pontoon plane appeared in the sky, circled low over the lighthouse, flew away, and then approached again. They watched as the plane made a smooth landing near their boat.

"Who could that be?" Moriah shaded her eyes. "I've never seen anyone come here by plane before."

A head emerged from the cockpit. A fortyish man with a compact build and dark hair unfolded himself, climbed down onto the pontoons and stepped onto the beach. He was neatly dressed in navy pants and a white shirt. With dismay, Ben realized that he knew the pilot.

"I really need to talk to you, Moriah…"

"In a minute, Ben. Right now I want to find out who that is." She strode toward the plane. "If it's someone from the Coast Guard, I need to talk to them."

"Moriah, wait!" Ben hurried after her.

He caught up just as the pilot reached the top of the bluff.

"So, McCain, you're already here," the man greeted him. "Good. I'm glad. What do you think of the place?"

"I think you're a week early," Ben muttered.

"Do you two know each other?" Moriah looked from one to the other.

"This is Dr. Nicolas Bennett." Ben was furious at Nicolas for coming a week early, but there was nothing he could do about it. "He's the one who hired me to come here for the summer."

"Oh, hello," she said, pleasantly. "I'm Moriah Robertson. My aunt and I own the resort where Ben is staying."

Nicolas accepted the hand Moriah offered, held it firmly in both of his, and studied her face.

"You resemble Katherine."

"You know my aunt?"

"Since we were children." Nicolas turned to Ben. "It's getting late. I want to check out my property before it gets too dark. Since you're already here, we can get a head-start on making plans."

"*My* property?" Moriah's voice quavered. "What's he talking about, Ben?"

"I was trying to tell you..."

"Katherine didn't explain all this to you?" Dr. Bennett asked.

"Apparently not." Moriah put her hands on her hips. "Exactly what is it that Katherine didn't explain?"

"I acquired the land and buildings a short while ago. I engaged Ben to hire a crew to tear this decrepit light tower down before someone gets hurt."

"The cottage, too?"

"Yes. I doubt it's repairable," Dr. Bennett said. "I plan to start out fresh and erect a new house on the site. Now, if you'll excuse us, Moriah, I need to work out some plans with Ben."

CHAPTER 13

M oriah felt her face grow hot. She could not believe what she was hearing. How could this man, this stranger, own *her* lighthouse? It was unthinkable. It had to be a lie.

"I don't believe you."

"Excuse me?"

"I said I don't believe you."

Nicolas seemed distracted by something. He pulled a small leather-bound notebook out of his pocket and made a note with a slim silver pen. He took his time, while Moriah waited for his response. Finally, he finished writing, closed the notebook, tucked it away, and placed his pen back in his shirt pocket. "Why not?"

Moriah's dislike for the man was growing rapidly. He seemed arrogant and rude, but worst of all he seemed to be under the mistaken impression that he owned her lighthouse.

"Because I've been trying to buy this place for the past two years." She ticked off her arguments with her fingers. "I've been in frequent contact with the Coast Guard, waiting for them to decide to sell it. I've written letters, saved a down payment, applied for a mortgage. I've done everything except sign the final papers."

"Oh?" Dr. Bennett's voice was emotionless. "Well, I signed the papers and paid in cash. Apparently they didn't want to wait for your mortgage."

Tears started to well up in Moriah's eyes, but she forced them back. She did not know who this man was, or how he knew Katherine, but she was determined not to cry in front of him.

"I was getting ready to tell you, Moriah," Ben said "But Nicolas came too early. I'm so sorry."

"I need to go." Moriah spun away and strode to her boat. She had to get out of there before she broke down. How could this have happened?

As she motored across the water, she was so lost in thought that, instead of coasting in, she accidentally rammed her boat against the dock, leaving a dent in the boat's aluminum bow. Furious with herself for letting that man upset her to the point of damaging her boat, she jumped out and jerked the rope around a post so hard that she got a rope burn on the palm of hand. She needed to talk to Katherine. Maybe her aunt could make some sense out of this mess.

Katherine was hanging sheets on a line stretched between two poles placed between the lodge and the lake. She wore that shapeless gray cardigan over her clothing which, in Moriah's opinion, made her look sixty instead of forty-seven. But that was unimportant. Nothing felt like it mattered now. The one thing she had dreamed of most of her adult life had just been jerked out from beneath her feet.

"Is there something you intended to tell me?" Moriah's throat tightened at the thought of asking her aunt about such bad news. Katherine had wanted the lighthouse as much as she, and had agreed to mortgage the resort if necessary. At least she'd thought her aunt wanted it as badly as she did. "Why on earth didn't you tell me someone had already managed to purchase the lighthouse?"

"Wha...?" Katherine had clothespins in her mouth. Her hands froze in the process of straightening a wet sheet draped over the clothesline.

"I was showing the lighthouse to Ben. Then this strange man arrived and said he had bought it!"

Katherine's eyes widened as Moriah's words tumbled out. She waited for her aunt to explode with indignation and mirror her own outrage, but instead, Katherine merely paled, removed the clothespins from her mouth, and finished pinning the sheet. Her hands were shaking so badly she could barely complete the easy task.

"I didn't expect him to come so soon." Katherine's voice was low and tense. She lifted the empty laundry basket and held it tightly against her side. "He's here a week earlier than his assistant said. How did he get here? I didn't hear a car."

"Pontoon plane." Moriah stared at her aunt, confused. "Why does it matter how he got here? Are you telling me you actually know this man? This Nicolas? And you never bothered to mention him to me?"

"I hoped to never have to tell you about him."

"Even though you knew he was coming?"

"I hoped he would change his mind," Katherine said. "Nicolas does things like that... change his mind at the last minute."

If Moriah thought she was confused before, she was completely at a loss now. Why was Katherine acting so weird? She had never seen her aunt so flustered and upset.

"I have to leave." Katherine clasped the empty clothes basket and whirled in a circle as though unsure of where to go. "I need more time. I need to get out of here. I can't bear to face him yet."

"What is *wrong* with you?" Moriah asked.

"I just need to leave, Moriah. Right now."

The sound of a plane motor coasting through the water made them both turn toward the lake. As it nosed in beside the dented boat, Ben jumped out and tethered it to the dock.

Nicolas Bennett pulled himself out of the plane, carrying what appeared to be a black leather overnight bag with him.

"Look at that," Moriah pointed out. "Carrying an overnight bag. How presumptuous. Do you suppose he actually expects to stay here?"

Katherine stood as still as death as Nicolas approached her.

"Katherine?" Nicolas's voice sounded tentative and hopeful. The impatience he had shown with Moriah was gone and in its place was a man filled with what seemed to be a sort of awe.

Katherine didn't respond, or even move. Moriah had never seen her aunt look so upset.

"It's been such a long time." Nicolas dropped the black satchel and held out his arms as though reaching for a hug.

Katherine took an involuntary step back.

When the hug didn't materialize, he picked his satchel back up and said, "You look well, Katherine."

Moriah was stunned to see tears glide down her aunt's cheeks. Katherine was the most stoic person she had ever known. Not once had she ever seen her aunt cry. Never.

Not until this moment. What had this man *done* to her?

Katherine pressed her knuckles to her lips as she backed away. Then she dropped the laundry basket and fled toward the lodge's parking lot. As the three of them watched, she climbed into her ancient brown Ford Taurus and sped away, leaving behind a cloud of dust.

Moriah realized her mouth was hanging open and shut it.

She'd never seen Katherine run away from anything. Her aunt was upbeat when money was short—which was nearly always—and had patched up more accident-prone tourists than Moriah could count. She faced everything straight on without flinching. The Katherine who Moriah thought she knew would have given Nicolas a piece of her mind and then shooed him off if she felt he needed to be shooed off.

Nicolas shook his head, as though in sorrow, hefted his satchel and wearily trudged back to his plane while Ben stayed behind with Moriah.

"Do you have a clue what that was all about?" Ben asked.

"None." Moriah's world had just shifted on its axis. "Do you?"

They watched as the plane roared to life and taxied far out into the lake before taking off. "Where do you think your friend is going?"

"I have no idea. I'm not even entirely sure I want him as a friend—not after the way Katherine acted."

The pontoon plane had barely disappeared when a second cloud of dust rose from the end of the driveway and grew denser as a van neared the lodge. It was filled with what appeared to be a very large family. When she saw who it was, her heart sank. They had such terrible timing.

"It's the Kinkers from Michigan." Moriah told Ben, exasperated at their sudden, unannounced appearance. "That's just what we need right now."

"Moriah," a large blonde woman trilled, waving through the open window of the front seat. "We're back!"

Moriah glanced at Ben and shrugged. "Excuse me, but I've got to go to work now."

Happy shouts filtered out to them as four small towheaded boys piled out of the van carrying fishing rods, beach balls and luggage. The assorted debris of a family who had traveled many hours tumbled out onto the ground, completely unnoticed by anyone in the van.

"The boys were so excited about coming we just couldn't hold them back any longer, so Farley closed down the shop and we came a little bit early. I knew it wouldn't matter. We've stayed here so often I feel like we're as close as family. Can we have our usual cabin?"

Ben and Moriah watched Camellia Kinker struggle to get out of the van. She was a thin, tall, blonde, and appeared to be at least nine months pregnant. Moriah sighed. This could get complicated.

She made a quick calculation. Although she usually put the Kinker family in Cabin One, the cabin closest to the lodge, the rattlesnake problem hadn't been addressed yet. From sad experience, she knew that the Kinker boys were too curious and undisciplined to be put in such close proximity to a den of rattlesnakes, although she felt a twinge of pity for the rattlesnakes.

"I think we'll put you in Cabin Nine, Camellia. It's one of the new ones."

"Don't you charge extra for the new ones?" Farley Kinker was a tiny man whose head barely reached his wife's shoulder. Moriah often felt, looking at him, that the exuberant and often clueless Camellia and their four rowdy children had somehow drained all the life out of him. There seemed to be nothing left to him except a constant hum of worry about expenses.

"Not for loyal customers like you," Moriah said.

"You'll put that in writing?"

"I'll put it in writing, Farley."

Having the Kinkers arrive first thing in the spring was actually a good thing, she supposed. It always helped her appreciate the guests who came later.

"I don't care where we stay." Camellia kneaded the small of her back. "Just get me to a bathroom."

CHAPTER 14

After Moriah had deposited the Kinker family in Cabin Nine, she gathered all the trash that had fallen out of their van and threw it in the garbage. She took some pleasure in her decision to put them in the cabin next to Ben. It would serve him right to have this chaotic, noisy family next door. She knew it wasn't fair to be aggravated with him, but he should have told her this morning why he had come here. Instead, he allowed her to be blindsided by Nicolas's sudden announcement.

Before returning to the lodge for the evening, she carefully blocked off the hole beneath Cabin One with cinder blocks. Last summer, the Kinker boys had spent the biggest part of a week beneath Cabin One's porch, accompanied by any food they could sneak out of the lodge's kitchen when she and Katherine weren't looking. She shuddered, thinking of the possibility of one of them crawling beneath the cabin before something could be done about those snakes.

By the time she finished getting the hole blocked and the Kinkers settled, the sun was setting and she was exhausted. The day had started at four in the morning when she felt compelled to go check on Ben. It had been filled with a rollercoaster of emotions, including the devastating news about the lighthouse and Katherine's strange behavior when Nicolas came to call.

The worse thing was that, as full as the day had been, the only productive thing she had accomplished was rebuilding those cabin steps. Everything else involved getting acquainted with Ben, going fishing with Ben, fixing breakfast with Ben, taking Ben to the lighthouse...

The lighthouse. The Kinkers had been a momentary distraction but now the realization that it was lost to her came flooding back into her heart. Without the exciting goal of bringing the lighthouse back to life, the future looked like nothing more than years of summers with her and Katherine going about their routines, waiting for the tourists to show up, and years of winters hiring out for indoor carpentry work.

She knew she should be grateful for her life—and she was—but the lighthouse had given her something truly wonderful to look forward to. Some people saved up for their vacations all year long. That seemed to put an extra bit of excitement into their lives, but she already *lived* where other people came to vacation. She wished she had a dollar for every time some guest told her how lucky she was to live on Manitoulin Island.

What exactly was it that Nicolas said he was planning? If she remembered right—and she was dealing with shock at the time her mind was whirling—it sounded like he planned to tear everything down and build some sort of a vacation house on top of the original foundation... or something like that.

She went to the back side of the lodge porch, the side that faced the lake, and sat down in her favorite porch chair—a split hickory rocker that felt as comfortable as an old sneaker. The view of the sunset was magnificent from this vantage point and nearly always soothed whatever troubles she had.

Tonight, however, the setting sun merely illuminated the

view of the lighthouse she had cherished since childhood. She was angry, but she wasn't even sure who to be the angriest at. The mortgage company in being so slow to approve her application? The Coast Guard for selling the lighthouse out from under her? Nicolas for scooping it up from right under her nose.

Or should she be angry at herself for allowing herself to believe that her love for the place gave her some sort of special claim. She should have pushed harder for that mortgage. Paid closer attention. Instead, she'd concentrated on scraping together enough money all while daydreaming about how wonderful it was going to be to own it.

Funny. She had never dreamed someone from the outside would come in and steal it away from her. The lighthouse had always felt like it belonged to her—a broken down guardian that would someday come alive again. Making enough money to secure it legally had been the focus of her life ever since she was old enough to understand what that ownership needed.

As the sun sank beneath the lake and darkness settled in, she bit her lip in an effort to hold back the tears, but the sharp pain didn't help. If Nicolas had truly purchased the lighthouse—and she had no reason to doubt that he had—there was nothing she could do about it. No legal recourse.

With no one around to hear, she finally gave in to grief over the death of her dream.

Ben was investigating the boat dock to see if he had left his sunglasses there. They were his best pair and he had misplaced them. Then he heard Moriah's quiet sobs and forgot all about his sunglasses and pretty much everything else on his mind.

The lodge was completely dark. She hadn't even turned on

any lights. Katherine's car wasn't in the parking lot, so Moriah must be all alone... and crying.

He wanted to go and try to comfort her, but intruding on her privacy might upset her even more than she already was. After all, they didn't really know each other all that well yet. He didn't know whether to intrude or not. Still, he suspected that it took a lot to make Moriah cry. Listening to her sobs was breaking his heart. He wished he could do something that would help.

He tried to ignore the sound as he headed back to his cabin, but it just wasn't in his nature to walk away from someone in pain. He turned around and headed back toward her even though his head continued to debate with his heart the wisdom of approaching.

Personally, he could not care less about the lighthouse. In his eyes it was, after all, just a pile of rocks. There was nothing sacred or eternal about it. He had the expertise to tear it down and build another just like it if he wanted to. In fact, with enough time he had the talent and skill to make an even better one. Tearing down the lighthouse was nothing more than a job to him... except for the fact that he would be tearing Moriah apart with each heavy stone he took from it. Even though he'd only known her a day, he already cared about her. He didn't want to cause her any unhappiness.

He approached quietly then, when he got to the porch, he stood for a moment and watched. She didn't seem to know he was there. Her legs were drawn up against her chest, her arms wrapped around them, and she sat with her forehead pressed against her knees. Her whole body shook as she wept.

He quietly walked over to her, knelt down in front of her and put his hands on the arms of her rocker.

"Moriah?" he said, softly. "Is there any way I can help?"

Startled, she jerked upright, her legs flew out, and she kicked him square in the chest.

Surprised and in pain, Ben suddenly found himself sitting on the porch floor, legs splayed.

"Ben!" Moriah exclaimed. "What are you doing here? You scared me to death."

He rubbed his chest where she had kicked him with her steel-toed work boots. Hanging around Moriah was most definitely not for sissies.

"I heard you crying. I wanted to see if there was anything I could do?"

"Oh." She wiped her eyes with the back of her hands. "Okay."

He pulled a handkerchief from his back pocket and offered it. "It's clean," he said. "I think."

"Thanks." She accepted the handkerchief and blew her nose. "I'd rather be alone right now, Ben. If you don't mind."

"You don't have to talk to me." He dragged a chair over and sat down beside her anyway. "I just came to keep you company."

"I don't need any company."

"Maybe *you* don't, but I certainly do," he said. "It's been a rough day."

"You've got the Kinkers next door. You could go keep them company. Go talk to them."

"I think they're pretty busy talking to each other at the moment. That family makes more noise than any group of people I've ever been around. Even the littlest one goes around screeching, apparently just for the fun of it. Or maybe so he can get noticed. The other three just argue with each other most of the time. Farley yells at them from time to time but they pretty much ignore him."

"Do I need to put you in a different cabin?" She gave a soft laugh, then hiccoughed from having cried so hard. "Are they too loud for you?"

"No. They aren't too loud. I'm used to noise. The jungle is never quiet. In fact, I'd place the noise that the Kinker boys make somewhere between a tree full of frightened monkeys and a puma's growl. I have learned to sleep through both of those. But, if they bring out some drums and start banging on them, I might have a little difficulty. Drums are really hard to sleep through. Trust me on that."

"You're serious?" Moriah sniffed and blew her nose again.

He was pleased to see that, not only had she stopped crying, she seemed to be somewhat interested in what he was saying, so it seemed to be a good idea to keep talking.

"Well, truthfully, I still have a little difficulty sleeping through a puma's growl. My hut isn't all that substantial. Where I live sometimes feels... a little unsafe."

"Are there snakes there?"

He nodded. "Big ones."

"And yet you still plan to go back?"

"I have to."

"Why?"

"It's in my DNA."

"What do you mean?"

"I made a promise." He shrugged. "And I keep my promises. It's kind of a thing with McCain men. At least it was with my dad and my uncle. They didn't make promises quickly—they always gave it some thought first—but once they made a promise, they kept it."

There was a long silence as Moriah digested this.

"So, how did Nicolas and you get together? How did he even know how to find you out there where you were living?"

"That's easy. He's a doctor. He came to help the people I'm working with. We met there and got to know each other. It had nothing to do with who or what I am."

She released a shuddering breath, the kind that comes after a hard cry. Ben heard it and knew that the storm was over—at least for now.

"Nicolas doesn't seem to be the type to do charitable work," she said.

"That's what I thought, but he told me that, now he's retired, he's looking for something to do with his time. Some way to give back. I got the impression he doesn't quite know what to do with himself. At first I thought he might be one of those people who just thinks working in the jungle with a remote tribe is romantic."

"Is it?" She turned in her chair to look at him, fully engaged.

"Is it what?"

"Romantic. Do you enjoy living in such an exotic place?"

"At first it felt romantic and exotic. Plus there was the extra joy in feeling like I was doing what I was meant to do. In the beginning everything was new and different. It was all an adventure. But not so much after the first hundred mosquito bites. That and the heat can kill off the romance of the place pretty quick."

"You didn't take mosquito repellent?"

"Of course I did. Quarts of the stuff. But those insects get so hungry the repellent doesn't always work as well as the labels claim. Plus, did I mention it's hot? Pretty easy to sweat the repellent off."

Ben hoped he'd managed to distract her away from the subject of Nicolas with his tales of mosquito woe, but he hadn't.

"What made Nicolas go after my lighthouse? Do you have any idea what brought him here?"

"He said he had lived there when he was small."

"That's very odd," Moriah said. "He appears to be about Katherine's age. If he stayed here, he would have known my father and aunt, but I've never heard her mention him. She never said anything about another child living here with them. My grandfather never mentioned it, either."

"I don't know anything except the little I just told you. He stayed with me a couple of weeks. I don't have the most comfortable living conditions, but he never complained. While we worked together, he mentioned that he was considering buying a lighthouse on an island in Canada, but he said it was in really bad shape. When he discovered that I supported myself as a stonemason, he showed me a picture and asked if I had the skill to disassemble the stones and incorporate them into a new dwelling. I said I might, but I needed to inspect it on site first. The next thing I knew, a few weeks after he left, he sent word that he had bought it and that he had made arrangements for me to come here for the summer."

"Why did he choose to show up to work with your tribe?"

"His mother was responsible for having a small medical clinic there. He wanted to see it. He didn't know I was a stonemason until he got there. I think that might have triggered his desire to tear down the lighthouse and do something else with it."

"So, I remembered exactly what he said after all." Moriah rose from her seat and began to pace. "He's planning to tear everything down and just build a house there."

"Not entirely. There are some beautiful stones in that tower that can be salvaged." Ben hoped he could calm her down. "He's already had an architect draw up some basic plans. He's hoping to incorporate those old stones into the new place. I've seen the plans and they're nice. If you weren't so emotionally attached, I think you could see the wisdom of what he is doing. At least he's going to do something good with the old stones. He's not planning to allow them to be trucked off, or tossed into the lake."

She sat back down in the chair and began to rock rapidly. "You don't understand, Ben. You didn't grow up seeing that lighthouse from your window every morning of your life. It always made me feel... safe. Even back then I longed to see a light in it each night."

"Look, Moriah." Ben placed a steady hand on the rocker's arm to slow her down. She was rocking so violently, he was afraid she would rock herself right off the porch. "If it means that much to you, I won't do it. I'll ask Nicolas to find someone else to do the job. That will slow things down considerably because, trust me, he won't find someone to replace me easily. Good stonemasons don't grow on trees."

"You would do that for me?" She stopped rocking and looked straight at him. As he looked into her eyes, it hurt him to see the weariness and pain there. "What about your DNA and all that talk about keeping promises?"

"I made a promise to the Yahnowa people and to God. I promised that I would bring them a copy of the New Testament in their own language. Barring death, I will keep that promise. I never promised Nicolas that I'd take on this job. All I promised him was to look at it and give him an estimate. I can always find another job. It's no big deal to me to refuse this one—especially if it's going to break your heart."

"You were going to give him an estimate?" Moriah sighed. "I can only imagine what it would be."

"The place is dangerous, Moriah. You do know that, right?"

"You're talking about that big crack in the tower?"

"It's hard to miss."

"I know. It keeps widening every winter. I've been so worried. I wasn't sure what to do about it. Stonework isn't one of my skills. I'd hoped to hire someone—but didn't know for sure who to choose. I don't think any of the stonemasons I know would want to tackle it."

"Anyone with any sense would blow it up and start over," he agreed.

Her eyes blazed at him. "Don't say that!"

"Sorry," he said. "I was thinking out loud again. I need to stop doing that."

"Can I ask you something?" Moriah said.

"Of course."

"Let's suppose I *did* own it and I hired someone like you to fix it."

"Okay."

"How much would it cost to restore it? Give me a ballpark figure."

"But you don't own it," he pointed out. "And I don't think Nicolas is going to give it up."

"Humor me," Moriah said. "I'm just curious."

"I can't say exactly. I know what my time is worth, but I'd also need heavy equipment and a work crew."

"I know that," Moriah dismissed it with a wave of her hand. "But what would have to be involved to bring it back to its original condition?"

"The lighthouse would have to be completely dismantled, the stones numbered, a new foundation poured and then rebuilt, stone by stone. The damaged stones would have to be replaced. My best guess is that it would probably cost way more than you could ever save up no matter how many extra jobs you took on each winter. Depending on how much labor costs on this island, a million dollars would be a very low estimate."

There was a quick intake of breath as Moriah took this in. Then she turned and stared out at the lake in the direction of the darkened lighthouse. He could easily imagine her as a young girl, orphaned by a plane wreck, drawing comfort from it. Possibly even then dreaming of bringing it back to life.

"So you are telling me," Moriah's voice dropped. "That even if I already owned it, I could never afford to repair the place properly."

"Probably not. Not unless you and Katherine have a small fortune tucked away somewhere."

"We don't."

"Do you own the resort outright?"

"Yes."

"And yet it still doesn't seem like you're making a good living off of running it. Since you were going to have to mortgage the place to buy the lighthouse, my guess is that there is a very good chance you might have lost the resort. Things always cost more than you expect—especially when you're restoring and building."

"I don't know what we would do if we didn't have the resort."

"Look, lass," he said. "Nicolas isn't such a bad person, he was very kind to the Yahnowa people he helped, but he is sad. His wife died awhile back and they never had any children. He strikes me as someone who doesn't know what to do with himself. He says some of the happiest moments of his life were spent out on that peninsula. I've seen the plans he had drawn up. The new structure he wants built with the stones won't be an eyesore. I can promise you that. Once you get used to all the changes, you might not even be aware that he's there."

"Oh, I'll know he's there," Moriah said. "And Katherine will know, too. I have no idea what happened between those two, but whatever it was, I think it's pretty obvious that it wasn't good."

CHAPTER 15

Moriah had a restless sleep, and awoke to an early spring drizzle. The morning was so overcast it hardly seemed worthwhile to get out of bed. The gloom that filled her bedroom matched her mood.

The wooden floor felt damp and chill after she slid out from under her blankets. She shivered, dug into her dresser, and pulled on some heavy woolen socks.

In spite of what Ben had told her the night before, the sick knowledge that she had lost the chance to save the lighthouse her family had tended for generations clouded everything.

She ran her fingers through her tangled hair. Then she walked over to the most precious thing in her room—the giant, waist high globe of the world that sat in a wooden stand taking up one whole corner. She had bought it two years ago from one of the antique shops in town. It had been a great extravagance, but she had seen it, been mesmerized by it, and bought it within minutes of entering the store. Next to the tools her grandfather had left to her, it was her most prized possession.

Katherine had appreciated the globe's beauty as well but,

when she suggested keeping it in the main room of the lodge, Moriah had balked. She wanted it where she could study it all she wanted to, with no one to see or think it odd.

Sometimes, she played a private game with it when she was feeling down. Like now. She closed her eyes, gave the globe a spin and put a finger lightly upon it, feeling it glide beneath her touch as it spun. When it stopped, she peeked beneath her finger. Greece. That would be a nice place to go. It was probably warm and dry in Greece. Maybe she would go to Greece someday.

Thinking about going someplace besides Manitoulin Island was a fantasy in which she often indulged. Some people were afraid of heights. Some were afraid of speaking in public. Some had a great fear of being alone. Her problem—much, much, greater than her very reasonable fear of snakes—was her inability to leave the island.

She had fought it, prayed about it, tried to read up on ways to overcome it, but it was what it was. The thought of leaving the island made her knees weak and her heart palpitate and she hated herself for it.

This weakness, this inability to leave the sanctuary of Manitoulin Island, was her greatest shame and her deepest secret. Only Katherine knew.

It was at the root of why she had bought the globe. She kept thinking that maybe imagining herself in all those faraway places might someday help give her the courage to leave the island. At least thinking so kept the hope alive that she could overcome her weakness someday.

She glanced in the mirror and did a double take. Her eyes were swollen from her meltdown last night. Greece forgotten, she headed for the door. She had much work to do before more guests arrived.

Coffee would help. Some very strong coffee. Maybe an

aspirin or two. Then a long, hot shower. Then what she needed was a heart-to-heart with Katherine—if she could find her.

Her aunt had not come in last night. That was not particularly unusual. Katherine had many friends on the island. Some of them were elderly with no relatives to help care for them. If there was sickness, Katherine would sometimes stay with them for several days, spending the night and helping the best she could. She seemed to have quite a knack for knowing what to do when someone was ill.

Moriah hoped it was a medical reason that kept her aunt away last night, but Katherine's behavior around Nicolas yesterday had been so odd that it undermined her faith in her ability to understand her aunt at all.

She shuffled down the staircase still in her flannel pajamas and heavy socks, momentarily forgetting the fact that the Kinkers had arrived the night before. The minute her feet hit the bottom step on the stairs, she heard four little voices arguing.

"It's my turn."

"No, it's *my* turn!"

"I had it first."

"Nuh-uh, I'm telling Mom.""

Silently, she backed up the stairs, one step at a time. Since it was raining, Camellia and Farley had apparently sent the children over to play in the lodge's great room where there was a collection of board games as well as a small library of paperbacks that had been left behind by guests. Rainy days often found half a dozen tourists reading or playing games and visiting together by the fireplace.

But usually not at six-thirty in the morning.

Her heart sank at the thought of having to deal with the Kinker boys today. No matter what project she got into, they would be underfoot and into everything. As parents, the Kinkers were... interesting. They did not believe in discipline of any

94

form. Therefore, the boys were only slightly better behaved than monkeys. She was definitely not in the mood to deal with them right now.

A stair tread creaked beneath her and she froze. If the boys heard that she was up, they would be on her like a pack of wolves.

Then she heard the door to the lodge open.

"Hello? Anybody home?" It was Ben.

A quartet of young voices greeted him.

"Hey, mister, you wanna play checkers?"

"Well, I, umm…"

"No!" One of the boys shouted. "Not checkers! I want to play Clue!"

"Clue and checkers are for dummies," the oldest yelled. "I want to play chess."

"Well," Ben said reluctantly. "I guess I could probably play one board game."

Moriah heard him close the front door of the lodge behind him and begin discussing game choices with the boys. Grateful for the reprieve, she quickly retraced her steps to her room, grabbed her blue robe and ducked into the bathroom. Her priorities had changed. A shower first… while Ben babysat the Kinker boys. Then maybe, after she had dressed, she would go check on that coffee. Ben could probably use some as well as herself.

CHAPTER 16

Forty minutes later, hair dry, dressed in a fresh work outfit of jeans, gray t-shirt, work boots and a black and red plaid flannel shirt, Moriah came downstairs feeling ready to face the day. The scene she found in her great room surprised her. No board games were spread about. Instead, four little boys of varying ages were grouped around Ben as he sat in the middle of the dark leather couch.

The two littlest were on either side of him, cuddled up against the big man. The two biggest perched on a footstool nearby. All were big eyed and engrossed, while he told a story that seemed to involve an inordinate amount of growling.

He was wearing faded jeans and a dark, rust-colored sweatshirt that went well with his red hair. The sleeves were pushed up. His hair was still so wet that she could see the furrows his comb had made as he slicked it straight back. It was too long, and curled behind his neck. His blue eyes danced with good humor as he entertained the children.

As though knowing she was watching him, he glanced up.

Their eyes met, and he smiled a greeting that was so filled with warmth that she felt it all the way to her toes.

No man had ever affected her that way before.

Befuddled by her reaction to him, she turned to go into the kitchen and accidentally walked straight into the closed door.

"Ouch!"

"You all right?" Ben asked, concerned.

"Yes." She rubbed her nose. "I need coffee."

"Obviously."

He chuckled and returned to his story.

While she hunted for coffee filters, she found herself rubbing her hip from the fall she had taken off his porch yesterday morning. It occurred to her that she might have a few more bruises and bumps before the summer was over if she didn't hurry up and get used to having Ben around.

Katherine nearly always had the coffee started by six a.m. but Moriah could not find the filters anywhere. Apparently, Katherine had chosen to put them in an odd place.

After giving up on coffee filters, Moriah swallowed the two aspirin she had been promising herself, and wandered back into the great room nursing a glass of orange juice.

Ben had finished his story and the boys were begging him for another.

"Don't you think it's time for breakfast?" His voice held a hint of desperation.

The boys looked at Moriah with hope in their eyes.

"Nothing cooking here," she said. "But your mom and dad might be awake by now. Go see if they can fix you something."

The boys shot out of the lodge.

Moriah and Ben glanced at each other as the sound of a slammed door reverberated through the air.

"You think they're hungry?" Ben asked.

"It's been my experience that the Kinker boys are *always* hungry." Moriah sat down beside him. "Don't worry, Camellia manages to feed them, even if she doesn't believe in disciplining them. Thanks for keeping them occupied while I pulled myself together."

Ben gave a great stretch, and happened to leave his arm on the couch above her. "Are you feeling better this morning?"

"Some. You did get through to me last night about the financial realities of the restoration project, but I'm still not at all happy about what Nicolas has planned."

"I couldn't sleep for a long time last night," Ben said, "And I got to thinking about something. I came over this morning to discuss some things with you."

"You mean you didn't just come over to babysit the children?" She pretended to be shocked.

"As fascinating as the Kinker boys are, no, I did not come to babysit. I've been thinking about the job."

"What about the job?"

"If I do decide to work for Nicolas—and I'm not saying that I'm going to—I'll need a crew. You happen to know the skilled labor on this island and could steer me toward the people we could depend on to do a good job. I could also really use your carpentry expertise when we start to build. That's an area I'm weak in."

The idea had no appeal to her. In fact quite the opposite. She was hurt that Ben would suggest such a thing to her.

"This resort will be filling up with people soon." She shook her head. "It's almost more than Katherine and I can handle under normal circumstances. I'm just not interested."

"Maybe you and your aunt could hire some help?" he suggested. "One thing I know is that Nicolas is planning to pay really well."

"How can he?" Moriah said. "You said he's retired, but if he and Katherine were children together, he's still twenty years or so off of normal retirement age. He couldn't have accumulated that kind of money just being a doctor could he?"

"I got the impression that his wife was the one who had the serious money," Ben said. "I'm guessing he inherited."

"I wish I knew where Katherine is." She glanced around. "She didn't come home last night."

"Should we be worried?"

"I don't think so. At least not yet. I think it might have been her day to work at the Amikook Centre. I'll call her workplace when it opens up. If she's not there, then I'll panic."

The sound of a plane landing in the lake filtered into the lodge.

"Well my goodness. Nicolas's here. How lovely," Moriah said, dryly. "What are you going to tell him?"

"I'm going to give him my professional opinion." Ben shoved his fingers back through his hair. "I just haven't decided exactly what that will be yet. I've not yet been able to inspect the place as thoroughly as I need to. I've only had been able to take a glance at it so far."

Most of their guests had fallen into the habit of simply walking into the lodge during daylight hours, but Nicolas knocked. When she opened the door, he stood stiffly on the porch wearing black dress pants, black wingtip shoes, and a gray silk shirt. She wondered briefly if he had also dressed in business attire while working with Ben with the Yahnowa.

"May I come in?" he asked.

Moriah held the door open. "Of course."

"Ben." Nicolas nodded an acknowledgment as he stepped inside.

"Nicolas," Ben acknowledged.

Silence filled the room.

Moriah pulled her red ball cap off a peg on the wall. "If you'll excuse me, I have work to do."

"Please don't go," Nicolas said.

Moriah stopped and waited.

"I owe you an apology," he said. "I wasn't entirely truthful yesterday. I did know someone else was trying to close on the property. I deliberately undermined the bid. What I did *not* know until I arrived here yesterday was that I had taken the lighthouse away from Katherine's niece."

"Katherine knew about this?"

"I'm not sure. Katherine and I have not spoken for many years. I didn't want our first conversation to be over the phone. I had my secretary call to make arrangements for Ben. I think she might have mentioned the fact of the purchase to Katherine, but I'm not sure." Nicolas glanced around the room, "By the way, where is she?"

"I haven't the foggiest."

"I'd like to speak with her."

"I think it was pretty obvious yesterday that she didn't want to talk with you. Looked to me like that's why she left—to get away from you. She still hasn't come home." Moriah shoved the cap on her head and pulled her ponytail through the back. "How do you and Katherine know each other, anyway? If you spent part of your childhood growing up with her, why hasn't she ever mentioned you before?"

"I'd rather not talk about any of that right now," Nicolas said. "Not until I've had a chance to speak to Katherine."

"Whatever." Moriah turned on her heel, annoyed with all the secrecy.

"Moriah," Ben said. "Please wait a minute. Nicolas and I planned to go back to the lighthouse today. I would appreciate it if you would go with us. Will you?"

"I have work to do." She rifled through a drawer and came out with her favorite pair of work gloves.

"Please, Moriah. You know that place better than either of us. There might be questions you could answer that we need to know."

She hesitated

"I tentatively offered Moriah a job this morning," Ben explained to Nicolas. "You'll need a good carpenter to accomplish what you are planning and she's first-rate."

Nicolas stared at her. "I don't believe I've ever known a female carpenter before."

There might not have been an intended insult behind his words, but the surprise in his voice made her feel like some sort of oddity. Why was it surprising that a woman could create things with wood and nails?

"She's worked with several contractors on the island," Ben interjected before she could respond. "I've seen her work. In fact, I'm living in one of the cabins she built. She's good."

"When you were small," Nicolas said. "I could never have imagined that you would become a carpenter and builder."

"You knew me when I was a child?"

"You were a beautiful little girl," Nicolas said. "And everyone loved you. Including me. Please accompany us out to the lighthouse today. I would consider it a great favor."

Moriah weighed her options. She really did have an awful lot to do. For one thing, she'd hoped to patch the roof on Cabin Four. Mentally, she calculated the odds of keeping the Kinker boys off the ladder. Zero to none. The drizzle had stopped, and the sun was out, but rain was still in the forecast. It wouldn't be wise to be on the roof if another downfall started. She could probably put the job off for a day.

Besides, if her beloved lighthouse was to be torn down, it didn't seem right to abandon it. Like a dying loved one, she felt that she needed to be there, no matter how painful the process might be.

"I'll go," she said. "And I'll take the boat. You two can ride with me if you want. Seems like a plane is a bit unwieldy for such a short trip."

CHAPTER 17

As Moriah pulled away from the dock, Ben glanced back at
the pontoon boat.

"Is the cockpit locked?" Ben asked Nicolas.

"Yes, why?"

"Oh, nothing." Ben mentally wiped his brow in relief. He had
just had a vivid mental image of the four little Kinker boys flying
off into the sunset.

The view, as they skimmed across the lake, reminded Ben of
a Dresden plate he had once seen, all blue and white. Blue lake,
blue sky and white clouds. In the distance stood the white limestone light tower. The only thing that spoiled the beauty of the
day was Moriah's total silence as she piloted the boat. He could
only imagine all the things going through her mind.

She beached the craft and jumped out into the water before
he could move. Ben felt silly sitting there while she hauled the
boat onto the beach. Nicolas calmly stepped out onto the dry
sand as though he were used to other people taking care of him.

"I would have done that," Ben whispered to Moriah as they
approached the bluff.

"Why should you when I am used to it?"

Ben shook his head in exasperation as they climbed the rise. He wasn't particularly knowledgeable in the social rules between men and women, but he was fairly certain Moriah wasn't playing by them. If he ended up taking the job and staying the summer, he wondered if there was a library on the island with a book he could read that would give him a clue as to how to go about dealing with her. He was good with books. But being raised in an all-male household had left him fairly clueless about women.

He was also good with stone. Very good. As they approached the lighthouse, he forgot the emotional tempest surrounding him and surveyed the structure with a critical eye.

A portion of the roof on the cottage sagged. Slate tiles were missing from the roof, blown away and scattered nearby. All the windows had been smashed out of both structures. The front door of the light keeper's cottage hung from one hinge. A large, square room connected the cottage to the tower, and an entire corner of it was missing.

"How did all this damage happen?" He gestured toward the gaping wound in the side of the single room connecting the light keeper's cottage to the tower.

"This was where they kept the steam-powered foghorn," Moriah said. "Some local boys tried to start it a few years ago just for the fun of it. They didn't know what they were doing and were nearly killed by the explosion. They ended up in the hospital. That's what caused the crack in the tower, plus most of the other damage. I started to try to fix what I could, but a government official who was inspecting it told me to stop. He said they did not want civilians in here. He said they would do what repairs were necessary."

"Let me guess," Ben said. "They never did."

"No," Moriah said. "They didn't. The official didn't say anything about staying away from the outside of the place, so I just tried to keep it mowed enough that the trees and weeds didn't take it over. I knew if I ever managed to buy it, I'd have my hands full with the inside repairs. I didn't want to have to take a bulldozer to the grounds to get to it."

"Well," Nicolas said. "Since the government has relinquished title to it, I believe we have the right to inspect it. Let's go see how bad it is inside."

Moriah entered through the ragged opening and Ben followed, hoping nothing would fall on his head. Nicolas trailed behind.

Except for the damage to the roof nearest the foghorn room, the cottage seemed fairly intact. Moriah led him through it, explaining the various rooms and what they had been used for.

"This kitchen was built large," she explained, "so the early keepers could use it to preserve the food they had to grow in order to survive. Otherwise they were forced to depend entirely on a ship they called a light tender. Its primary purpose was to bring them supplies in the early years. The problem was, the light tender couldn't always get through the ice in the early spring for those keepers who chose to winter in the lighthouses. That first winter Eliza and her son nearly starved because the boat couldn't get through and it was too far for them to walk out without risking freezing to death before they could get help."

"How did they survive?" Ben asked.

"My grandfather told me that some of the villagers got so worried they hired a man with a dog sled to take her some food that they donated. Even though she had always been a city girl, the next summer she taught herself how to grow a huge garden —which she preserved for the following winter just in case such a thing ever happened again."

"Desperation can give a person the determination to do things they never thought they could do before," Ben said.

"Exactly," Moriah said. "That was the winter her husband

disappeared. She never knew for sure what became of him. Since she had nowhere else to go, she asked the government for the job as light keeper and they gave it to her. She tended the light for many years."

"Alone?" Ben asked.

"Not entirely. She had a young son who learned to help her. He stayed on and cared for the light when she no longer could do so. I think there might have been an assistant at one time, but I'm not sure."

"There was an assistant," Nicolas said. "The man with the dog sled who came helped out in the summer months and made a living with his dog sled in the winter. I think he and Eliza might have married at one time. I'm not sure."

Moriah looked at him, questioningly. "How would you know that?"

"I spent a great deal of time here. I paid attention to the stories. I'm probably as familiar with the lore of your lighthouse, Moriah, as you."

Moriah's expression softened, slightly. Ben was grateful to see the change. Perhaps the knowledge that Nicolas wasn't a complete outsider would help alleviate some of her disappointment.

The living room was about half as large as the kitchen. A potbellied stove stood in the center. Its chimney pipe had dislodged from the wall and a pile of soot lay on the floor. Old, pink and green flowered wallpaper hung in strips.

"Was this their only means of heat?" Ben had never been inside of a lighthouse before.

"There is a fireplace in the keeper's office, but there are none in the sleeping rooms upstairs. Katherine said they were frigid in winter. That quilt of Eliza's we keep on the wall in the lodge is the only one that survived. Katherine said she made others, but most of them were worn out from helping keep her family warm for many winters here."

The office was directly off the living room. A fireplace dominated one wall and a huge, scarred, built-in oak desk dominated another. A few uninvited visitors had gouged their initials and dates into the wood.

"This desk is the only furniture left," Moriah said. "It was built into the wall and was too large to fit through the door. Everything else got auctioned off by the Coast Guard when they shut the place down."

"It's a shame," Ben said. "Someone put a lot of time and skill into that desk."

"I was a studious child." Nicolas ran his hand over the surface. "I worked way harder than I needed to. I often did homework here. I remember your grandfather building up the fire in the fireplace in here for me so I wouldn't get chilled. If I had a lot of homework to do, it wouldn't be long before your grandmother would come in with some hot chocolate for me. They were always so kind..." Nicolas's voice drifted off. Then he seemed to gather himself. "Oh well. The past is past. Let's go upstairs now."

Moriah shot a questioning glance at Ben. The sadness and longing in Nicolas's voice was a revelation to both of them.

"How do we get upstairs?" Ben asked.

"The staircase is over here." Moriah disappeared into a small door.

They followed her up a narrow, spiral staircase, emerging moments later into what appeared to be an empty attic that had been divided into two large compartments. The walls were covered with a thick, brownish wallpaper. The partition still consisted of raw, un-milled lumber.

"The theory was, one side for the girls, one side for the boys. That took care of any size family," Moriah explained. "Sometimes the light keepers would need to rescue people from shipwrecks and they would stay here too, men in one room, women in the other, until it was possible to get them home. The light keeper and his wife slept in the bedroom on the main floor."

Nicolas wandered over to a low beam and carefully ran his hand over it as though searching for something.

"Are you looking for something?" Moriah asked.

"I carved my name into this beam when I was a boy. It's still there." He smiled and shrugged. "Childhood memories. Nothing important."

"Okay," she said. "I have to ask. Why were you staying here?"

"My mother and your grandmother were great friends," he said. "They grew up together on the island."

Ben faded out of the conversation. Moriah and Nicolas could figure out family connections without him. His only interest was in the structure and whether or not it was reparable. He glanced out of the window at the light tower. "Is there a way into the tower from the house?"

"Yes," Moriah said. "Through the foghorn room."

"Will you show me?"

"Of course."

Together, the three went back down the stairs to the outside and inspected the large crack in the tower.

"It keeps getting bigger each winter," Moriah said. "Water gets into it and freezes and the rocks pry farther and farther apart."

Ben backed several steps away and gazed up. "Why is there a portion of the top missing?"

"Fire," Moriah answered. "Someone started a fire in it after the Fresnel lens was stolen. I've never understood why someone would want to destroy something so beautiful."

"Some people build. Some destroy. Some do nothing at all." Nicolas said. "I prefer those who build. I've had my architect draw up some preliminary sketches of the house I plan to put here. I have enough sentiment for this place that I'd like to incorporate as many of the stones as possible."

Ben saw Moriah's face grow pinched at the mention of tearing down the lighthouse again.

"It can be fixed," Ben said.

"What do you mean?" Nicolas frowned. "I didn't think that was an option."

"We could salvage the stones and build something else with them, but frankly, Nicolas, it seems a shame."

"What are you suggesting?"

"The cottage isn't in too bad a shape. Mainly it's just water damage. Besides needing to install double insulated windows, most of the rest is cosmetic. I could rebuild the foghorn room and finish out the attic. Repairing the light tower will be a challenge, and expensive, but it can be done. If you wanted to, you could probably make the money back that you spend on repairs by charging admission for people to go to the top of the tower. Put some telescopes up there. Tourists are always looking for some place different to go see."

Nicolas turned to Moriah. "What were your plans for this place?"

"I wanted to restore it, of course." Moriah said. "Rent it out. Maybe live in it someday."

"No," Nicolas dismissed her plans with a shake of his head. "I mean, what had you thought to do in the way of restoring it? Were you going to take it back to the authentic lighthouse in which Eliza lived? Replace the foghorn? Live with oil lamps?"

"No," Moriah said. "I had planned to turn the foghorn room into a large study/bath combination. With dormers, the attic could be made into two large, conventional bedrooms. I would leave the ground floor bedroom, living room, office and kitchen alone except for updating everything. It would have to be gutted, wired and plumbed. Electricity would need to be brought in."

"And the tower?"

"Ah. That I would want to take back to the original design.

Repair it, of course. I wish it was possible to still buy an original Fresnel lens, but it isn't. They are much too rare. Most are either in museums or private collections. Instead, I had planned to check into getting some sort of large spotlight for stormy weather. I'd hoped to install a good quality telescope for clear nights. Manitoulin Island has almost no light pollution, so it's an ideal spot for amateur astronomers."

"Could it be finished by autumn?"

Ben's gaze flew to Moriah's face. She was stunned. It took her a couple seconds to find her voice.

"Excuse me?" she said. "What exactly are you saying?"

"All I need is a place to retreat to from time to time," Nicolas explained. "I do not have many friends so I do not need a lot of space in which to entertain. If both of you think it can be restored and repaired without anyone getting hurt or killed in the process, that's good enough for me." He turned away, as though dismissing them both, and studied the view, deep in thought, his hands behind his back.

Ben saw Moriah's continued wide-eyed look of surprise and he wanted to make certain he was hearing what he thought he was hearing.

"Are you serious, Nicolas?" Ben asked. "Instead of tearing everything down and rebuilding, you want me to restore this place based on Moriah's ideas?"

"Yes." Nicolas was engrossed in the horizon and didn't turn around. "Moriah, you will take your work orders from McCain. I'll share the oversight of the repairs until I can see if you are competent enough to be entrusted with the work. Inform Katherine that I'll require the use of one of your cabins whenever I fly in. I shall require one for the entire summer. Tell her she doesn't have to talk to me unless she wishes to do so."

Ben saw her eyes cloud over and knew there was trouble

brewing behind them. He knew why. Nicolas sounded like a general giving commands to an underling.

"I appreciate the fact that you won't be tearing down the lighthouse, Nicolas." She removed her cap, pulled her ponytail holder off with one fluid motion and let her hair swing free. "And we do have space for one more summer-long visitor. But I have a resort to run. It takes all my time. I'm afraid you'll need to find someone else to do the job for you. I have my own business to run. As for Katherine... whether or not she talks to you is her business. I don't intend to be giving her messages from you."

She headed back to the boat, her stride as athletic and sure as a gymnast. She was so beautiful and strong. Ben's throat went dry just watching her, but he wanted to wring Nicolas's neck. You didn't talk like that to a girl like Moriah.

"Was it something I said?" Nicolas said, surprised. "After all the drama yesterday when I arrived, I thought she would be delirious with my decision. I thought I was being kind."

Ben dragged his attention away from Moriah. "Did you have servants or something when you were growing up, Nicolas?"

"No. Why?"

"You sure do sound like it sometimes when you talk to people."

"I don't understand."

"Moriah would love to be part of bringing that lighthouse back to life, regardless of who owns it. But she's a skilled craftsman. A person of value. My advice to you is to never talk down to her again."

"Don't be ridiculous," Nicolas said. "Good paying jobs aren't all that plentiful on the island. She'll come around. In the meantime, hire whomever you wish."

"No," Ben said. "I'll hire the workers Moriah recommends to me. I don't know the people on this island. She does."

CHAPTER 18

The three of them rode back to the pier in silence. Each deep in their own thoughts. After Moriah docked the boat, Nicolas asked to borrow it to go back to the lighthouse. She wasn't happy about lending it to him, but he said he needed to search for a special pen that had dropped out of his pocket while they were exploring the place.

Depend on Nicolas to have a pen that was so special he needed to go retrieve it. Moriah had never had a pen she gave a second thought to.

"I wish you hadn't done that," Ben grumbled as he and Moriah entered the lodge.

"Done what?"

"Turned Nicolas down." He dogged her footsteps as she went into the kitchen.

"I told him the truth," she said. "I do have a lot to do."

"You're cutting off your nose to spite your face. You know that?" Ben said. "You know you're itching to be part of bringing that lighthouse back to life but you're too proud to work for him."

"You're right. I don't like Nicolas and I don't want to work for him."

"You don't have to like someone to work for them. If I had to like everyone I worked for I'd be broke and homeless."

"As opposed to what?" she shot back. "Living in the middle of nowhere in a hut?"

"That's unfair, Moriah," he said. "I could have a house if I wanted to. I could have a very nice house. There is a difference."

"I apologize, Ben," Moriah said. "I respect what you do and I appreciate what you just did back there when you convinced Nicolas the lighthouse could be repaired. Unless Nicolas changes his mind, you've spared me the heartache of watching it destroyed. But why is it such a big deal to you for me to be part of this project? After all, it's Nicolas's lighthouse. Not mine. I already *have* a job and I'm way behind in it."

"Look, Moriah. I'm a stone worker and a translator. I build things. I translate things. Stone upon stone. Word upon word. That's what I do. That's who I am. *You* take boards and nails and make something strong and good with them. I thought working together would be nice. I thought we could make something together that we could both be proud of. But evidently I was wrong. Go ahead and do whatever you want."

"That's been my plan all along." She grabbed a pile of folded towels lying on the kitchen counter, and headed toward the door.

Ben stepped in front of her. "I'm not finished with this discussion. Where are you going?"

"I'm going to take these towels to Cabin One for your boss."

"You can't be serious. You're putting him in the cabin with the rattlesnakes?"

"I'm sure he'll be fine."

"You're kidding, right?"

"Yes. The idea's tempting, but no, I'm not going to put him in

Cabin One. He'll stay in Cabin Eight, on the other side of the Kinkers. Perhaps he and the boys will bond. At the very least, they should provide him with hours and hours of entertainment."

In spite of his irritation with her, the idea of the emotionally remote Dr. Bennett staying next door to the Kinker children, made Ben laugh.

"I have to admit," he said. "That would be interesting."

"I get my kicks where I can," Moriah said. "Why in the world that man ever decided to become a doctor is beyond me. I thought people who wanted to be M.D.s needed to actually *like* people and want to help them. He seems so… cold."

"Sometimes it is the people who feel things the deepest who have the hardest time expressing themselves. I saw great kindness in Nicolas when he came to my village. There's more to him than you give him credit for."

The front door to the lodge slammed.

"Help!" a child's voice yelled. "Somebody help!"

"What's wrong?" Moriah ran into the great room with Ben directly behind her.

"My mommy's sick!" The oldest Kinker boy grabbed the sleeve of her flannel shirt and tugged, "Come quick."

She whirled, shoved the clean towels into Ben's hands and ran with Ben following close at her heels.

Farley Kinker emerged from his cabin the moment they clattered onto the porch. His sparse hair was standing on end.

"Camellia's gone into labor, but something's wrong." Farley wrung his hands as he talked. "She's never had trouble having babies. But this time there's something different happening. She's having terrible pains."

"How long has this been going on?" Moriah asked.

"She didn't feel so good this morning," he said. "That's the reason we sent the boys to the lodge. She thought maybe we'd have a new baby by the time they came back."

"Why didn't you take her to the hospital?" Ben asked.

"It's an hour away. Besides," Farley glanced at Moriah, "you know how I feel about hospitals."

"How does he feel about hospitals?" Ben asked Moriah, his arms still stacked with linens.

"Farley doesn't like them, or doctors. They cost too much."

"I vote we drive Camellia to the hospital," Ben said. "Right now. How about it, Farley?"

"She'll be fine." Farley set his jaw and shook his head. "This one is just a little harder than the others, that's all."

"I wish Katherine was home," Moriah fretted. "She would know what to do. She always knows what to do."

"Where is she?" Farley asked.

"I don't know, but I'm hoping she's at work by now. I'll make some phone calls."

Ben and Farley stared at each other for a long minute, while the child who had come for Moriah danced a nervous jig between them. Ben knew next to nothing about childbirth. The closest he had come to it was hearing moans from a neighboring hut and then watching as a tribal woman stepped out with an infant in her arms.

At that moment, a high-pitched scream came from inside the cabin and three scared little boys ran outside. Farley blanched. Ben felt a little light-headed.

"About that hospital thing…" Ben began.

"Mommy says for you to come back inside *right now!*" the littlest boy commanded.

Farley gave Ben one wild-eyed look and then shuffled into the cabin like a man going to his execution.

"Hey, mister. You want to play checkers?" the oldest boy's

voice quavered, trying to be brave. "Or maybe tell us another story?"

He looked down and saw that all four children were grouped closely around him. Two were leaning against his legs and gazing at the open door from which loud moans now emerged. The youngest vigorously sucked his thumb and stared up at Ben with wide blue eyes.

Ben didn't know how long this birth process was going to take, but he figured the best use of his time would be entertaining these four little boys until it was over. One thing he could not do was overrule a man about what was best for his wife. With all his heart he hoped Moriah could reach Katherine. Or someone else who knew what they were doing.

"Is there a Monopoly game at the lodge?" he asked.

"Yes!" four little voices chorused.

"Then go get it." He might not have any experience in birthing babies but he did know that Monopoly would take a whopping long time to play. The least he could do was keep the children out of Farley and Camellia's way until whatever it was that would happen, happened.

In moments, the boys came running back with two of them fighting to carry the board game at the same time. It was an old set and the cardboard box was coming apart. Pieces and cards dribbled out of it as they ran.

"Whoa. You're losing things," Ben called.

"I told you so, dummy!" one of them said, smacking one of his brothers.

"You!" Ben used his deepest voice and pointed. "The one who just hit his brother. Go back to the lodge and pick up everything the two of you dropped."

Don't have to," the child said, in a sort of sing song. "Can't make me."

"That's right," Ben's voice was calm. "You don't have to and I can't make you. On the other hand, you can't make me play a game with you, either."

"Go on, do what he says," the younger brother said.

Grudgingly, the boy sauntered back up the path, picking up game pieces and sticking them into his pockets while giving Ben dark glances over his shoulder.

A loud moan pierced the air and Ben winced. He wished he could do something for the poor woman, but keeping the boys out of her and Farley's hair was the best he knew to do for now. That and pray—which he was fervently doing.

While he and the three other boys waited for the fourth one to finish retrieving game pieces, he also heard the sound of a car practically flying over the gravel driveway. With a rush of relief, he saw it was Katherine. Moriah came running out of the lodge. They spoke for a moment and Moriah gestured toward the cabins. Katherine reached into the backseat of her car and emerged with a large, blue tote bag.

"Now what, mister?" the oldest boy said, his task completed. "Where do you want us to play?"

"Inside my cabin," Ben said, distracted by Katherine's arrival. "Go set the game up on the kitchen table. I'll come in a moment."

The children skipped happily into the cabin they had formerly been forbidden to enter.

"Can you help her?" he asked, as Katherine and Moriah strode past him, women on a mission to the Farley's cabin.

"I have no idea," Katherine's said. "I'm not a midwife, but I do have some basic knowledge. My main objective is to override Farley and get an ambulance here whether he wants one or not."

"Thanks." Moriah took the clean towels out of his arms. "We might need these."

Ben watched with admiration as the two women mounted the porch steps. In his opinion, something like that took real courage. He wondered how many other crises they'd dealt with over the years with various guests.

"How are we doing, Camellia?" Katherine called out cheerfully as they entered the Kinker's cabin. "I hear we're going to have a baby today."

CHAPTER 19

M oriah had seen her aunt in action many times before. As
a teenager, she had often accompanied her to the island
homes where she ministered to various people who needed her.
Even though Katherine was not a nurse, she seemed to know
more about dealing with various health issues than anyone
Moriah had ever known.

Some of the people on the island spoke about Katherine with
awe. They said she had magic in her fingers and that she could
draw pain away by her very presence. Moriah knew better. In
the wintertime, in the evenings when there was little to do,
Katherine read anything to do with medicine she could get her
hands on. It was like a hobby with her.

"Brew Farley some tea," Katherine said to Moriah as they
entered the bedroom together. "He looks like he could use some."

Camellia lay on the bed red-faced, panting and straining.
Farley cowered beside her, his face pasty white.

"I don't like tea," Farley protested.

"Put plenty of sugar in it," Katherine instructed. "You've had a
shock Mr. Kinker. Hot tea and sugar will help you get past it."

Moriah knew that Katherine didn't really care how Farley fared. Telling Moriah to fix him tea was her way of telling Moriah to get him out of the way. There was nothing that annoyed Katherine more than having someone hovering nearby in her way who couldn't be of any help. She especially didn't like having someone around who seemed likely to come down with the vapors—especially when it was a man.

One look at Farley, and Katherine wanted him out of the way.

"Come into the kitchen, Mr. Kinker." Moriah ushered the pale, shaking little man from the bedroom.

"I just don't understand it." He hung his head and stared at the floor while Moriah filled a kettle with water. "Camellia's never had any trouble before. All four boys came quickly. At home."

Moriah listened with half an ear as she searched the cabinets for a tea bag and a container of sugar.

More moans came from the bedroom as she and Farley waited for the water to came to a boil.

"Where did Camellia put the tea and sugar, Mr. Kinker? I remember she loved tea and always brought some with her."

"What?" He lifted his head.

"Tea? Sugar?"

"I think the boys ate all the sugar last night. I don't know where she put the stuff."

Heavy, guttural panting came from within the bedroom, followed by a thin, high-pitched squeal. Mr. Kinker's eyes grew large and the area around his mouth turned a sickly shade of green.

Moriah made a quick decision. "Go to the lodge, Mr. Kinker. There's tea and sugar in the canisters on the counter. Make some, drink it slowly, and then bring some back for your wife. She'll need it after the baby comes."

"Are you sure I should leave?"

"I'm sure."

The man nearly fell over his feet in his haste to leave the cabin.

After he left, Moriah glanced into the bedroom. Camellia's hair had come undone from its perpetual bun. It was now wet with sweat and stringing down her face and back. Her face was puffy

"Push harder, Camellia!" Katherine said, sharply.

Moriah's head jerked back in surprise. Her aunt never used that tone of voice.

"How's it going?" Moriah asked.

"Camellia's doing great," Katherine said, with strained cheerfulness.

From the sound of her aunt's voice, Moriah knew she was lying—for Camellia's sake.

"What can I do to help?"

Katherine motioned for Moriah to bend down where she could whisper into her ear.

"Go call an ambulance," Katherine whispered hoarsely. "We have to get her to a hospital."

"Don't move me!" Camilla had overheard. "It hurts!"

"Could I be of some help?" A clipped, male voice rang out from behind Moriah.

"Oh Nicolas! Thank God!" Katherine said. "It's a shoulder dystocia I think. A bad one."

Moriah moved out of the way while Nicolas pulled up the sleeves of his dress shirt and rushed into the small adjacent bathroom. Moriah stood back and heard water running.

"My antibiotic soap is on the sink, Nicolas."

"I've got it, Kathy."

Kathy? In spite of the crisis, Moriah was surprised. Katherine had never allowed anyone to call her that.

"Dr. Bennett will be in here in a moment, Camellia," Katherine said, soothingly. "He knows a great deal about difficult births. You're going to be fine, honey."

Camellia strained again, the awful keening sound filled the room.

"Help him get the gloves on, Moriah," Katherine barked. "There's a box in my basket. Camellia, push!"

Moriah glanced down as Camellia strained and the baby's head emerged. Then, strangely, it disappeared. Something wasn't right.

"Did you try the Woods Maneuver?" Nicolas accepted the gloves Moriah slipped on him and took Katherine's place at the foot of the bed. "Weren't you taught that in medical school?"

"I tried it twice but it wasn't successful," Katherine said.

The baby's head emerged once more and Nicolas slid his hand in beside it. Moriah heard Camellia scream and suddenly she could not bear to be in the same room a moment longer.

Moriah raced out of the door and to the lodge, where she placed a call for an ambulance. There were only two on the island and sometimes it took a while for one of them to get there. She hoped they would arrive in time.

Having never given birth or assisted at one, Moriah knew she was no expert in childbirth, but she did know that a shoulder dystocia was not good news. One of her friends had suffered through that kind of birth. It meant that the baby's shoulders were simply too big to crowd through the birth canal. It was rare but, without expert intervention, it could sometimes be fatal.

After running back to the Kinker's cabin, she heard Camellia continuing to cry out from behind the closed door, and Katherine and Nicolas's voices trying to encourage her.

There was nothing more she could do except wait, hope Nicolas knew what he was doing, and pray.

She sat down on the couch and bowed her head. Preacher

Howard said it didn't work this way—that God didn't want to be brought out only for special occasions, but she couldn't help herself. It had always felt to her like God had enough to deal with, so she tended to try not to bother him except in emergencies. This situation definitely qualified as an emergency. The baby's life hinged on the next few seconds.

There are few sounds harder to bear than a mother's screams during a difficult birth...

...and few sounds are sweeter than a newborn baby's first cry.

Moriah's communication with God was interrupted by the wail of a gloriously indignant—but very much alive—newborn. Tears of relief stung her eyes.

In a few seconds, Katherine strode out with the infant wrapped in a clean towel and laid it in Moriah's arms.

"We have a little girl, Moriah. Hold her while Nicolas and I take care of Camellia."

"He called you Kathy," Moriah said. "He said you were in medical school."

"We'll talk later," Katherine said, and left the room.

The baby fussed and waved her tiny fists in the air. Coming into the world had been quite an ordeal. She needed a bath, a snack and her mommy.

"Soon, baby girl, soon," Moriah crooned. She stood up and paced the floor, bouncing the newborn gently in her arms. As she passed a window, she saw Farley strolling down the path with two teacups in his hand.

"I've decided I like tea now." Farley entered the cabin with both teacups in his hands.

"I don't think Camellia wants any quite yet," Moriah said. "Maybe in a few minutes."

He sat the extra cup on an end table. "I'm feeling a lot better. The trick is putting enough sugar in it. Oh," he eyed the baby, "it's here. Good. Maybe things can get back to normal again."

Then he calmly sat down and sipped his tea.

"Camellia had a really close call," Moriah said, annoyed with Farley's complacency. "If Dr. Bennett hadn't come when he did, you could have lost her."

"A doctor?" Farley seemed disturbed. "Where did a doctor come from?"

"That's not the point. You almost lost the baby and maybe Camellia. Dr. Bennett came along just in time to save their lives. You should be grateful."

"Camellia never had any problem having kids before," he muttered, taking another slurp of tea.

Katherine emerged from the bedroom, checked on the baby and saw Farley sitting on the couch.

"Dr. Bennett is finishing up," she told him. "Camellia needed quite a few stitches, but your baby is fine."

"And just how much is all this going to cost me?"

"I don't know." Exasperation laced Katherine's voice. "Why don't you come in and ask the doctor yourself."

"I think I'll just do that." Farley sat his teacup on a side table, got to his feet, hoisted his pants, and followed Katherine toward the bedroom where Dr. Bennett was administering stitches.

Moriah seriously enjoyed hearing the loud thud Farley made as he passed out cold before he even got through the bedroom door. Evidently he had encountered a sight that was a bit upsetting.

Katherine calmly stepped over him and went back to assisting Nicolas.

Moriah sat back down on the couch, cradling the newborn. She touched the baby's tiny button nose with her finger.

"Welcome to the big wide world, little girl." She smiled as the baby yawned, blinked and stretched.

Moriah leaned back against the couch, the baby tucked carefully into the crook of her arm, and replayed the past few minutes in her mind. She knew her aunt had a better than average knowledge of medical things, but she'd never once mentioned medical school. Why had Nicolas said that?

"How's it going?" Ben entered the cabin, bringing a rush of fresh air in with him. "I heard the yelling stop. I'm hoping that's a good sign?"

He saw Farley stretched out on the floor. "Oh."

Then he glimpsed the tiny bundle in Moriah's arms. "No wonder the yelling stopped. Is everyone okay in here?"

"Yes." Moriah sighed with relief. "Everyone's okay—except for Farley. He decided to check out for a while. Where are the boys?"

"Taking the Monopoly game back to the lodge. The game didn't turn out so well. Half of the pieces were missing. I promised to play Scrabble with them instead."

"I don't think we have Scrabble."

"You don't. I noticed that this morning." Ben grinned. "How long do you think it will take for the boys to figure it out?"

"Probably not long enough." Moriah pulled a corner of the towel away from the baby's tiny face. "Check this out."

Ben ignored Farley and sat down beside her to admire the baby.

"Boy or girl?"

"A little girl. She might be a football player someday. Her shoulders were almost too big to make it through the birth canal. Apparently, Dr. Bennett came just in the nick of time. I've never seen Katherine so scared. She didn't know what to do and that's unusual."

"Farley's a lucky man." Ben touched the infant's damp wisp of brown hair. "I'd love to have one of these someday."

"What? A little girl?"

"Girl or boy. It wouldn't matter. I'd just like to have a family of my own. I've lost both my dad and my uncle. It would be pretty wonderful to have a houseful of my very own kids someday."

Moriah looked into his eyes. He was dead serious.

"You're lonely," she said.

"Sometimes."

"But you've got a whole tribe depending on you back in the Amazon."

"I do. They treat me with respect. Sometimes I suspect they may even feel some love toward me, but they got along without me for a very long time and will continue to do so after I'm gone. They also have very tight-knit family groups and I'm not part of any of them."

There was a rustle near Ben's feet. They both looked down. Farley opened his eyes, saw them staring at him, and suddenly sat up. "What happened?" he said, rubbing his forehead.

"Your wife gave birth," Moriah said, calmly. "And you passed out."

"Congratulations, Farley," Ben said. "You have a beautiful, healthy little girl."

"A girl?" Farley let out a disgusted sigh as though he were greatly put-upon. "That means we'll have to buy girl clothes instead of using the boys' hand-me-downs."

"Perhaps instead of counting the cost, you should count your blessings," Ben said, softly. "Your wife and child are alive, mate. You should rejoice."

"I can't help it." Farley's voice was laced with self-pity. "I told Camellia not to get herself pregnant again, but she wouldn't listen."

Moriah was suddenly sorry she was holding the baby. It had been such a close call for Camellia. She had suffered much to bring this child into the world, and Farley was so ungrateful. She wished she could smack him.

She didn't have to. Ben was done dealing with the man. Apparently, Farley had managed to get on his last nerve. Ben stood up, reached down, grabbed a handful of Farley's shirt and lifted him easily with one hand until they were nose-to-nose and Farley's feet were no longer touching the ground.

"I said," Ben's voice was quiet but deadly. "Your baby girl is alive and so is your wife. Without Katherine and Dr. Bennett's help, you could be planning a funeral right now. Do you know how much funeral's cost, Farley?" He gave him a shake, still holding him in mid-air. "Do you? Let me tell you. A funeral costs a whole lot more than a few sweet little girl clothes."

Without warning, he dropped Farley, whose knees gave out from under him and he crashed back onto the floor.

Moriah's mouth hung open. She closed it and swallowed. Farley was not a big man, but he still had to weigh at least a hundred and forty pounds. Ben had held him up in the air like he weighed no more than a small sack of potatoes. If she didn't have the baby in her arms, she would have applauded.

Until this moment, she had no idea that her new friend had an angry bone in his body but, under the right circumstances, Ben was quite a force. Who knew?

"Daddy?" Four little boys tumbled into the room as Farley picked himself up off the floor for the second time.

"Way to go," Moriah whispered in Ben's ear as he sat back down beside her. He didn't acknowledge her comment. His breathing was rapid, and his jaw and fists were clenched. As angry as Ben appeared, she was impressed that the only thing he had done to Farley was give him a shake and a good talking to.

Farley tucked his wrinkled shirt into baggy pants, and regained a sliver of dignity as he pointed the boys toward Moriah. "Children, we have a new baby."

The boys rushed to Moriah's side to admire their latest sibling.

"Can we play with him?" the oldest one asked.

"Her," Moriah corrected. "You have a sister. And no, you can't play with her yet. She's still brand new."

They nodded soberly, accepting Moriah's judgement. Brand new things were rare in the Kinker household and not to be taken lightly.

Katherine stepped out of the bedroom, took one look at the children and quickly closed the door behind her.

"Your wife is stable, thanks to Dr. Bennett's skill. The baby is fine, as far as I can see. But they both need to go to the hospital for an evaluation. Camellia and your new daughter have been through quite an ordeal."

"But…"

"Farley," Ben warned. "Don't go there."

The bedroom door opened again and Nicolas strode past all of them. The children's eyes went wide as he ripped off bloody latex gloves, stepped on the pedal that opened the metal trashcan in the kitchen area, dropped them in, and let the lid drop with a bang.

"Excuse me, but Camellia wants to see her baby." Katherine lifted the infant from Moriah's arms and disappeared into the bedroom.

"Moriah," Dr. Bennett said, "Please go to the lodge and call an ambulance." He pulled a cell phone out of his pocket and waggled it with disgust. "Apparently there's no service here yet."

"I already did," Moriah said. "They should be here soon."

"Wait," Farley said, sidling away from Ben as though he feared being dangled in the air again. "Is it absolutely necessary to have an ambulance come?"

"Yes," Nicolas said, flatly. "Katherine and I will go with

Camellia and the baby in the ambulance. I don't know how skilled the EMT team is on the island and I don't want to take any chances with her. Ben? You bring Moriah. The two of you can take Katherine home later. I'll stay at the hospital overnight just in case. Considering Mr. Kinker's propensity for fainting at inopportune times, it might be best if he stayed here with his children."

Moriah felt her chest tighten at Nicolas's instructions and her palms grew sweaty. The nearest fully equipped hospital was in Espanola. Across the bridge. On the mainland.

Not on Manitoulin Island.

"I'd rather not." Moriah said. "Farley can go. I'll stay here with the boys."

"You aren't still giving into that old problem are you, Moriah?" Nicolas sounded exasperated as he rolled down his shirt sleeves and buttoned the cuffs. "I expected you to outgrow that issue years ago."

"Nicolas." Katherine had just come back into the room. She placed a hand against his shoulder. "That's enough."

"What are you talking about?" Ben was puzzled.

"Moriah won't leave her safe place," Nicolas explained. "I doubt she's been off Manitoulin Island since she was five. Do I have that right, Moriah?"

"I can't see it's any of your business," Moriah said. She had stopped disliking Nicolas for a few moments while he saved the baby's life. Now her aversion came flooding back.

"How little you know." Nicolas's voice was edged with bitterness. "It was once very much my business."

The sound of a siren drifted into the cabin.

"Ben, you can drive Katherine's car," Nicolas hurriedly gave out assignments. "Farley, you can drive your own. Moriah... I guess you can stay here with the children."

A few minutes later, Moriah and the children watched the

small caravan leave the resort. The ambulance was in front. Ben and Farley followed behind.

She felt humiliated as Ben drove past. It felt as though she were one of the children, watching the grownup drive away.

What was *wrong* with her? Why did she have to be this way?

The self-hatred she felt as she turned to deal with the Kinker boys was bitter and intense.

"What are you going to play with us?" the oldest boy demanded. "We couldn't find the Scrabble."

The last thing Moriah felt like doing right now was play with the Kinker boys.

"I have something in my room you might like to see," she said.

"You mean we get to go upstairs?"

They had never been allowed upstairs before.

"You'll have to be very good." She heard the ambulance turn on its siren as they pulled onto the main road. "But yes. You'll get to go upstairs."

"What is it you're going to show us?"

"The world." She hoped that spinning the huge globe and watching the countries slide slowly past would keep the boys entertained for a few minutes—perhaps long enough for her to compose herself and gather the strength to face spending the rest of the day with them. "I'm going to show you the world."

CHAPTER 20

"Could you explain what Nicolas was talking about back at the resort—that thing about Moriah not leaving the island?" Ben shifted his body as he sat on the hard plastic hospital chair. He was finding it impossible to achieve a comfortable position.

The acrid smell of burnt coffee drifted across the room from an untended coffee pot, which made Ben's stomach churn. He wished he had remembered to bring his sunglasses. The headache he had acquired on the drive to the hospital was a killer.

Katherine sighed and dropped the magazine she had been staring at onto her lap. She had been clutching a tissue that she now began to nervously tear into small pieces.

"I guess you should know. To make a very long story short. Moriah was so traumatized by the death of both of her parents, she did not speak for two solid years," Katherine said. "She also refused to leave the island."

"Were you able to get her any kind of help?"

"I tried. At least I got her what little help there was that was available on the island back then. Moriah was so frightened by the loss of her parents, I tried to reassure her by telling her that, even though her parents were gone, she was safe. I told her that Manitoulin Island was the safest place in the world. I knew better, of course. There's nothing special about our island. Bad things can happen on Manitoulin Island just like anywhere else. But she was a child. I thought if I created a little bit of magic for her, it might help. Instead, I think I managed to make everything worse."

"She was only five when her parents died?"

Katherine nodded. "She had been talking in full sentences by the time she was three. Moriah was such an outgoing, happy little girl until we lost my brother and sister-in-law. I took her to our family doctor—we only had two here on the island at the time—and he said that, with enough reassurance and stability in her life, she would eventually outgrow the silence and fear."

"He was wrong?"

"Unfortunately, yes. A year later, when she still hadn't spoken, I heard there was a psychologist who had established a practice in Espanola. I tried to take her, but every time I started to drive over the bridge she would start screaming and couldn't seem to stop."

"That poor little girl." Ben's heart broke at the thought of Moriah being in such distress.

"She was never a spoiled child so I knew her terror was real. I always weakened and turned the car around. Maybe if I had hardened my heart and ignored her pain and gotten her to a real professional, she wouldn't have this problem now. I have so many regrets."

"But she must have begun to talk again sometime."

"Yes, eventually. The doctor was right about that, but she's never been able to make herself leave the island."

It was hard for Ben to accept the idea that such fear could

reside in someone so competent, so outwardly stable, so physically strong.

"But Moriah is no longer a child."

"No, and she's built herself a good life on this island. Everyone respects and likes her. But she's dreadfully ashamed of this weakness. She refuses to speak to anyone about it. Not even to me anymore. It was cruel for Nicolas to bring it out into the open like that."

Ben was still trying to wrap his mind around the enormity of the problem. "She won't leave the island? For anything?"

"It's not a matter of *won't* leave the island, she *can't*," Katherine said. "There's a big difference. Every time she's attempted it—and as an adult she's attempted it many times— her body goes into a full-fledged panic attack that is so severe it has all the symptoms of a heart attack. I've watched her try so hard, but her body rebels each time."

Ben's temples ached badly from the drive and now this information was pounding in his brain as well.

"I've read a lot about it over the years," Katherine said. "I think that what Moriah is dealing with is a form of agoraphobia."

"That's when people can't leave their houses, right?" Ben said. "Moriah doesn't seem to have any problem doing that."

"She doesn't, thank goodness. But sometimes agoraphobia will present itself as the inability to leave a certain geographical location."

"Like the island," he said.

"Exactly. And sometimes other phobias get mixed in with it. Like a fear of bridges. That's a fairly common one for agoraphobics. Even footbridges can become an issue. The experts believe that this sort of thing is rooted in early childhood trauma."

"Seems like psychiatrists tend to believe that everything goes back to early childhood trauma, don't they?"

"Seems like it," Katherine said. "I haven't read anything about well-meaning aunts causing it—but I think I had a big part in making her the way she is."

"Sounds like you did the best you could," Ben said. "I'm sure Moriah was lucky to have you to care for her."

"I suppose so, but I think my father did her the most good. He was so patient, and he taught her many useful things."

"She's the most competent woman I've ever met," Ben said.

So, the woman who was taking over too many of his waking thoughts was incapable of leaving the island. It was hard to imagine, but he had no reason to think Katherine would make it up.

"You need to realize that if you do stay the summer to work on Nicolas's lighthouse project, when it is finished, if you go back to your other work, Moriah will stay here. Unless God grants us a miracle, she will always remain here."

As he digested the reality of all of this, Ben's head throbbed so badly he wished he could wrench it off his neck.

"How did her parents die again?" he asked dully.

Katherine hesitated and then avoided his eyes by staring down at the torn tissue which now lay scattered like snowflakes across her lap. "A plane crash."

CHAPTER 21

I t was the sort of island day for which vacationers traveled hundreds and sometimes thousands of miles each summer. The lake made tiny kissing sounds as it gently lapped at the beach. The air was fresh and cool. Loons spoke to each other in their wild, reedy calls—a call echoed by Native American flute music playing on the CD player she'd placed inside the light-house. A sunrise was just peeping over the horizon. A pink sky, but so many different shades of pink reflected in the lake. Such a lovely view.

It would be even lovelier from the top of the light tower. The thought of climbing those steps yet again, in spite of the damage, was tempting.

The music floated out through the open window while she sat on the top step outside the light keeper's cottage. From here, she could see the resort clearly. No one was stirring yet.

That was a good thing. She didn't want to have to deal with anybody yet. Or—in the mood she was in right now—have to deal with anyone ever. She wished she could just live out here and have everyone leave her alone.

She could still feel the sting of Nicolas's harsh words as they sliced through her joy in the baby girl's birth. It had been humiliating.

There were so many different ways to be handicapped. So many different ways to be crippled. For some people, the disability was visible. It was hard to hide a wheelchair or crutches or a hospital bed. For some people, like her, the handicap was very carefully hidden away, but there it remained—a fear so paralyzing that no amount of rational thinking could dissolve it.

The problem with trying to keep her greatest shame hidden, was the energy it took to protect it. A secret such as she carried was a heavy load.

It was so much better to simply build and repair things instead of trying to deal with people. Nails that she pounded into wood stayed exactly where she put them. People did not. Nails didn't judge you. People did.

The morning sun, as it rose now on Lake Huron, distracted her with its soundless pageantry. The rays were turning from pink to gold, burnished with bright oranges and reds, magnified and reflected in the surface of the lake. The red was a little worrisome, there might be rain before the day was over, but still, it was an extravagant display that she never tired of watching. Being here, watching the sunrise from the steps of the cottage, had long ago become her greatest antidote to pain.

Her grandfather had taught her this.

"There's healing here," he said, the day after the doctors announced that he only had a few months left. "I've felt it ever since I was small. After I'm gone, if you start to feel sad, come here to this spot and remember what I said. And while you're at it, take time to remember how very much I love you."

She had been just shy of her thirteenth birthday, and life had felt very dark and unfair the day he broke the news to her.

"I don't think I can stand it, Grandpa," she'd said. "I can't bear to lose you."

"But it's only this old wrinkled body that's going away. It hasn't worked good for a long time. Kinda glad it's almost time to get me a new one," he chuckled. "When I see God, I'll ask him to make me good-looking this time."

"Don't talk like that, Grandpa," she said.

"Why not? It's just the way life is. My body will be gone, but my love for you will never go away. Just like my love for your grandmother and your parents have never gone away. Love is the only thing that matters, Moriah. Great love never goes away. It is eternal."

While R. Carlos Nakai's wilderness-sounding Canyon Trilogy flute music played softly inside the cottage, she began to feel her spirits lift, as the emotional cleansing she always felt here began to work its magic.

If her grandfather had lived, would she have gotten over her fear of leaving the island? If her parents had not been taken from her when she was so little, would she have grown up normal? How could losing one's parents create so much trauma that she would still be suffering the effects of it?

As she sat on the steps, remembering her grandfather's words about love, her mind drifted to Ben. He had occupied her thoughts an awful lot these past three days. The moment between them yesterday morning when they had admired the newborn baby together had been special. She had never been so attracted to a man before in her life, not like this. She felt as though she were being drawn to his very essence, to his soul and spirit.

Last night when he had confronted Farley for not valuing his good fortune in having a healthy baby and wife, she had seen another side to him. Ben was amiable, but he wasn't a pushover. Goodness! That moment alone, when he lifted Farley off the ground and gave him a good talking to was almost enough to make her fall in love with him.

The image of Ben with those four boys grouped around him yesterday morning as he told them stories was something she would remember for the rest of her life as well. He would make an excellent father someday, not to mention being a great husband to some lucky woman.

She was already three years older than her mother and father had been when they got married. Of course, they had grown up knowing each other. Ben and she had known each other for such a short time, but there had been a look in Ben's eyes each time they'd been together that made her think he was as interested in her as she was in him.

Then Nicolas had to go and make his big announcement about her weakness last night. Her cowardice. Her paralyzing fear. He had torn away the careful façade she had built over the years—the pretense that nothing was wrong with her. The truth of the matter was, there was a great deal wrong with her and now Ben knew about it.

He had been noticeably absent last night when he came home from the hospital.

He had gone straight to his cabin after they had all gotten back from the hospital. Katherine said it was because he had a headache, but Moriah suspected it was because he didn't want to be around her anymore. What man would? What man would want a woman who was so emotionally crippled that she could not bring herself to leave an island?

Silly. She reprimanded herself for taking up valuable time pondering Ben. It was ridiculous to even think about maybe falling in love with him. Ben was just a guest and would be leaving when the lighthouse project was finished. He would be going back to a place she would never see.

There were so many places she would never see.

It was a little chilly this morning and sitting on this stone step wasn't making her any warmer. She should go back to the resort and start in on a project—the lavatory in Cabin Six had a crack in it and needed to be replaced. Three kitchen tiles were coming loose in Cabin Three and needed to be re-glued. One of the poles where Katherine hung the sheets out to dry was leaning and needed to be reset.

There was plenty to do, but Nicolas had taken the heart right out of her last night.

"Want some company?" Ben, wearing jeans and a safari-like tan shirt, climbed up the porch steps, took off his sunglasses, dropped his scuffed leather backpack on the small porch and settled down close beside her.

"Where did you come from?" she asked. "I don't see a boat."

"I walked. Or at least I attempted to. After fighting my way through that tangle of trees and briars to get here, I can certainly understand why you prefer to take the boat." He pulled his backpack toward him and started undoing buckles.

"I figured you would want to sleep in after the big trip to the hospital."

"Nope." Ben pulled a grease-stained paper sack and a thermos out of the backpack. "Farley was clearing out the cabin and packing up the kids."

"Where was he taking them?"

"Camellia has a sister who lives up near Sudbury. The sister is a nurse and wants the family to come and recuperate at her house. Last night, Nicolas told Farley it would be okay to take Camellia and the baby there tomorrow. He says that if Camellia is doing well enough he thinks she can leave by then. The hospital agrees. The sister is coming to take the boys with her today. Farley will stay with Camellia until the hospital releases her."

"All of them? That poor sister!"

"I don't know. She came to the hospital last night and seemed capable of dealing with all seven of them, even Farley." He pulled something wrapped in a napkin out of the sack. "Fried egg sandwich. I thought you might be hungry."

"Thanks." Moriah took the sandwich with gratitude. She'd been too upset earlier this morning to eat, but now that Ben was here with her, and not treating her like a freak after learning about her problem, her appetite had come back.

"She's a stronger woman than I am if they are going to stay with her very long." Moriah took a big bite of the sandwich.

Ben poured a paper cup of cocoa and handed it to her. "I'm impressed you could get out of bed this morning after babysitting the Kinker boys most of yesterday."

"I didn't babysit them."

"Then who did?" Ben handed her a paper napkin before getting down to business with his own sandwich.

"I didn't babysit them, I hired them. You can get a lot of work out of those boys for a dollar."

With a fried egg sandwich in one hand, cocoa in the other, and Ben close beside her, Moriah watched the ever-changing lake and was surprised by realizing that she was feeling happy.

They ate in a silence broken only by the lapping of the lake and the raucous calls of dozens of seagulls wheeling above them.

"They want a handout," Moriah said. "But don't give it to them."

"You don't want me to feed them?" Ben tentatively held a morsel of food in the air. "That seems a little harsh."

"Better not." She pulled his hand down. "They'll call in all their relatives and overrun the place before you know it. They get annoyed with you when you run out of food. Seagulls are very rude."

He obligingly stuffed the rest of his sandwich into his mouth and then brushed off his hands and showed them, empty, to the seagulls. The birds, disappointed in not getting an easy meal, wheeled and squawked their disapproval above them, then went in search of a more promising food source.

"You know?" Ben said, after he'd swallowed the sandwich, stretched out his legs and leaned back on his elbows. "I always wanted to watch a sunrise with a beautiful woman. I didn't expect to have to fight my way through a half-mile of wilderness to get to her, but it was worth a few scratches and gouges to get here. Now, go ahead and tell me what you got the boys to do. I'm all ears."

There it was again. Ben had called her "beautiful". It always took her breath away when he used that word. It took her a moment to regain her bearings.

"Well," she had to think. "For starters, the two older ones got to rake our entire beach to prepare it for swimmers. I had the two younger ones go through all the games in the lodge's great room and make sure all the pieces were in the right boxes. For another dollar apiece, they vacuumed and dusted the entire lodge."

"Did they do a good job?"

"No—but I didn't tell them that. They were trying, and they really liked getting an entire dollar for each job accomplished."

"I should have thought of that. It would have been a whole lot easier than trying to play Monopoly with them while Camellia was trying to have her baby."

"How was Camellia and the baby last night?"

"When I left, everyone seemed to be doing well enough. They named the little girl 'Rosie' by the way."

'What about Katherine and Nicolas?"

"What about them?"

"How did they act?"

"You mean together? Katherine and Nicolas were a little self-conscious around each other at the hospital. Quiet. Professional.

141

Nicolas kept looking like he wanted to say something, but never quite got the nerve. Katherine seemed determined to ignore him. It was all business between them. I thought the ice was broken once they had worked together to save little Rosie, but once Katherine had thanked Nicolas for his help, she grew cold toward him again, like she acted that first day when they met."

"I'm not wild about the man, of course," Moriah said. "I think I've made that pretty clear, but I've never seen Katherine act like this before. I wish I knew what was going on."

"Apparently they wish you didn't, or Katherine would have mentioned something about Nicolas a long time ago. She didn't say a word to me about him in the car coming home."

"Not a word?"

"Not about him. We talked a bit about the upcoming tourist season, but she was pretty much into her own thoughts. Should I have pried?"

"No," she said. "That would have been a mistake. I think it would be best to allow Katherine privacy for now."

It felt so good having him beside her. He was sitting close enough that she could smell the faint woodsy scent that usually clung to him. It wasn't overpowering, and she liked it very much.

"What's the name of that aftershave you wear?" she asked. "It's nice."

"I don't use aftershave."

"You must use something."

"What does it smell like?"

"I don't know. It's woodsy with some kind of spice."

"Oh," he said. "That's just my shaving soap. It has sandalwood in it. Taylor of Old Bond Street. It's what my dad and uncle always used, so I ended up using it too."

"The scent seems familiar to me, but I don't know why."

"Beats me. It would be unusual for you to come across it. Most men don't use a shaving brush and soap anymore, but I like it. When I was a little boy, it fascinated me to see my dad lather up. He'd hand the shaving brush to me to dab some on my face—and then, after he'd finished shaving and rinsed the razor off, he'd take the blade out and let me pretend to shave the soap off. It's a nice memory."

"So you use the same shaving soap that your dad did? That's sweet."

"No, it's practical. One of those bars lasts forever. With what I do, it makes a whole lot more sense than toting around a bunch of aerosol shaving foam cans." He laid his arm carelessly around her shoulder. "What are you doing out here today? Saying goodbye? Or avoiding me?"

"Why would I avoid you?"

"Possibly because of the look you gave Nicolas last night when he made an issue about you not being able to leave the island. He embarrassed you. I'm sorry he did that. Katherine explained it to me—about what happened after your parents died. I wish you hadn't had to experience that."

He kept his arm draped loosely around her shoulders. It was not a romantic gesture. It was simply the comforting touch of a friend. The warmth of his body felt exactly right against hers. It was only now that she realized how badly she'd wanted him to come and be with her this morning. How badly she'd needed him to let her know he was not repelled by her weakness, her cowardice, this weird form of agoraphobia that she struggled with.

She was too vulnerable when he was around. She was already starting to care too much about what he thought about her.

CHAPTER 22

S he had been so engrossed in her thoughts about Ben that at first she didn't notice the sky growing dark. When she saw that rainclouds were gathering, she thought of the old mariner's rhyme:

Red sky in morning, sailors take warning.

That rhyme had been drilled into her every time her grandfather stood at the resort window and looked out into a reddish early morning sunrise. Sometimes, if there was a reddish sky in the evening, he would quote:

Red sky at night, sailor's delight.

Then, they would talk about what all they would accomplish the next day because they knew the weather would be fine. The sunrise this morning had been especially spectacular, primarily because of all the reddish hues in it, but the sky had been so clear and blue she thought maybe the old rhyme was going to be wrong this time. Apparently it wasn't.

Even with storm clouds gathering overhead, she felt reluctant to leave the stalwart comfort of Ben sitting beside her here. Problem was, that sky wasn't going to hold off for long.

"Are you going to give me a ride in that boat, lass, or make me walk back through all that overgrowth?" Ben's voice broke into her thoughts.

It was the sky that decided her next actions as small droplets of rain began to hit them.

"Let's get inside." She jumped up. "The roof on the old office is still intact. At least enough, I think, to keep us out of the rain. It wouldn't be wise to head out onto the lake right now. Too much danger of lightning. You don't want to be sitting in a metal boat when lightning starts to strike."

"No, I don't." Ben quickly gathered up the napkins and sack, crumpled them and stuffed the wad of paper into his pants pocket. Then he grabbed the empty thermos. "That's an adventure I would rather avoid."

At the clap of thunder, they scrambled into the cottage and Moriah led him through the ruined, empty rooms to the old, lighthouse office. Unlike the rest of the dwelling, the one window in the office room had been left whole and only a tiny rivulet of water ran down the stone wall. The only thing in the room except themselves was the fireplace and hearth, and a large wooden desk built into a corner.

Ben and Moriah stood in the middle of the room and listened to the thunder volley off the stones of the cottage.

"That's pretty intense," Ben said.

"It gets that way out here." Moriah grabbed hold of Ben's arm as a sudden flash of lightning struck close by. She quickly released it and apologized. "Sorry."

"You didn't hurt me, lass," Ben chuckled. "That strike about made me jump out of my skin too. Did you, by any chance, happen to check what the weather was going to be today? Any tornadoes predicted? Hurricanes? Earthquakes?"

"It never occurred to me. I felt the need to be here, so I came."

"I think we might be stuck here for a while," he said. "I hope you don't mind, because I certainly don't."

"Is standing around in a damp, cold, lighthouse while it pours buckets of rain outside your idea of a good time?"

"No, but it's a lot better than sitting outside of a damp, cold, lighthouse while it pours buckets down your neck. Besides, I have you for company. That's always a bonus."

"I'll show you a family secret if you won't tell."

"Your family has secrets?" Ben said. "I would never have guessed."

Moriah punched him lightly on the shoulder. "Don't judge."

Then she turned around and wriggled a small stone out of the face of the fireplace directly behind her.

Ben folded his arms as he watched her. "This should be interesting."

"It will be." Moriah reached inside of the hole created by the removal of the stone and brought out an old iron key.

Ben watched with interest. "Does the key open a pirate's chest? Is there a treasure map? Perhaps a hidden staircase in here?"

"Sorry." She polished the key on her jeans. "No treasure map. No pirate's chest. No hidden staircase."

"What then?"

"The key opens a compartment in the bottom of that desk in the corner. The desk was built into the wall and was too cumbersome to move out when the lighthouse was shut down. In the end, Grandpa simply locked it up and put the key back where he always kept it—behind the loose stone. Of course, he showed me where it was."

"I'm surprised someone didn't take a crowbar to it to get into it."

"I don't think anyone else knew the compartment was there. My great-great grandfather, Liam Robertson, built the desk.

From what I understand, he had been a ship's carpenter once. Apparently, a good one. He lined the compartment with cedar and my family kept things in there they thought valuable."

Moriah knelt in front of the desk and fit the key into an invisible lock that was hidden well beneath the desk. There was a small click as she turned the key.

"I've never seen a desk designed like that." Ben ran his hand over the scarred surface.

"Grandpa said you could tell that the man who built it had spent time on a ship because of the sturdy way it is designed. Underneath all the dirt, it is made out of seasoned red oak and is as hard as a rock."

A door swung open beneath the desk and Ben caught a faint whiff of cedar. Moriah reached deep inside and pulled out a thick sleeping bag, a folded blanket and a pillow. She arranged it all in front of the fireplace and sat down cross-legged on it.

"I'll share." She patted the seat beside her.

Ben happily settled in next to her. He looked at the fireplace where a stack of logs and kindling lay.

"I wish we had some matches."

"Do you want a fire?" she asked.

"It would be nice. Especially if it continues to rain."

"You underestimate me, McCain." Moriah rose and dug into the deep recesses of the desk again, producing a clean mayonnaise jar filled with small boxes of safety matches. She held out her hand. "Give me that sack you stuffed in your pocket right before we came inside, please."

Using the grease-stained paper wrappers from their meal beneath the dry kindling and logs already stacked in the fireplace, Moriah created a blaze in minutes.

"You were the one who stacked those logs here?" Ben said.

"You never know when you'll need a good fire," Moriah said. "Sometimes in the summer our guests start getting on my last nerve and I come out here for a while. I always keep a few supplies here so I'll be able to have a getaway."

Everything felt better and more cheerful as they sat near the fire watching it blaze against the storm. Eventually, the fire grew so hot that they moved farther away from the hearth, propping themselves against the opposite wall with the sleeping bag beneath. They watched the fire burn, sometimes popping and cracking almost in unison with the lightning. The rain thrummed steadily on the slate roof.

"How long have you been keeping things like this out here, Moriah?"

"From the day Aunt Katherine allowed me to come out here by myself."

"You were..."

"Thirteen and miserable. That was the year my grandpa died. It didn't happen all of a sudden. Katherine and I took care of him for several months. Sometimes watching him go downhill would get to be too much and I'd have to escape out here until I could pull myself together. Then I'd go back and help."

"Who cared for the resort then? You?"

"Not entirely. I was still a kid." She yawned. "We hired a man."

"Sleepy?"

"A little. I had a hard time getting to sleep last night."

The wind audibly changed directions and rain pelted against the window. Thunder hovered and grumbled directly above them.

Ben scooted to the far end of the sleeping bag, took the pillow and laid it down beside him.

"Lie down."

"What?"

"Lie down and sleep. I'll watch over you and your lighthouse while you take a nap."

"You sure?"

"I'm sure."

Moriah didn't fight it. The crackling of the fireplace and the roll of thunder had created a sort of lullaby to her. She laid her head on the pillow and pulled the blanket over her shoulders. The rain sounded like it had settled in to stay. There was no way they could leave until it stopped.

But when she closed her eyes, she found that she couldn't drift off after all. She was too aware of Ben's nearness.

"Tell me about where you live."

He began to gently stroke her hair. She didn't mind.

"What do you want to know?"

"Everything. Every detail. I want to know what the people wear, what the trees look like, what they eat. What it sounds like and smells like. Everything."

"I don't know if I can tell you everything." There was a smile in his voice. "Even if it rains a really long time."

"Then tell me something. Apparently I'll never see anything except Manitoulin Island. I'd like to hear details about some faraway place—especially the one where you live."

"Well, okay, then." He paused. "It is more beautiful than you can imagine, Moriah, and more dangerous than most people ever realize."

Listening to Ben's voice while she lay gazing into the fire felt delicious. Even though they were caught in a tumbledown cottage with torrents of rain sluicing all around them... she didn't remember ever feeling so warm and safe.

"How is it dangerous?" She pushed the blanket down to her waist. It was beginning to grow warm in the small office.

"In so many ways. For instance, have you ever heard the old saying that both fish and guests start to stink in three days?"

"Aunt Katherine has said that a few times about certain guests."

"I bet she has." Ben chuckled. "Sometimes it's true even with primitive tribes. If they are at peace at the time, they're happy to see a foreigner the first day you arrive. You are new and interesting. The second day, you're still fairly welcome. By the third day the novelty has worn off and they've grown tired of entertaining you. Especially if they are responsible for feeding you. Most of the tribes live a subsistence lifestyle at best and even a handful of outsiders can quickly deplete their food stores. If a traveler doesn't take the hint and move on, he or she can find themselves in mortal danger."

"Still? In this day and age?"

"Still," Ben said. "I have felt threatened more than once when I've traveled outside my tribe's geographical area, even when I didn't overstay."

"Why does the Yahnowa allow you to live with them?"

"I bring my own provisions, of course. They don't have to feed me. But primarily they allow me to stay because of the great work a young medical missionary did. She's the one who first began to live among the Yahnowa. They loved her. It opened up opportunities for others to minister to them, including me."

"And Nicolas. It's hard to imagine him in that situation."

"Nicolas may not be easy to talk to, and I agree that he can be a little arrogant—but he's trying to do some good things. I got the impression he had received a rather large inheritance from his wife and, along with his own savings, he's looking for positive ways to use it."

Moriah didn't want to hear any more about Nicolas. She wanted to hear about Ben. His life. His work. "So you're completely alone there?"

"I'm never alone. There's always and forever, God, who has become especially real to me these past five years. Plus there are the Yahnowa people, whom I love and respect. Then, there's Abraham Smith, a retired minister, and his wife, Violet. They are an older couple that settled there about eight years ago. They use their retirement income to support themselves. He tries to teach the Yahnowa and she was a nurse most of her life. She does what she can with some basic medical supplies."

"I wish I could see it someday."

Ben's hand, which had been stroking her hair, stilled. "I wish you could, too."

He began describing the flowers and trees, animals and people in his village. His voice soothed her, a lullaby of words, and she drifted off.

When he saw that she was sound asleep, Ben stopped talking. He had not gotten much sleep either. All he could think about was the revelation he had received from Nicolas and Katherine. There was a good chance, a very good chance, that Moriah would never be strong enough emotionally to leave the island. Falling in love with her could get a bit awkward.

Who was he kidding? Falling in love with Moriah would be devastating. Life would be much simpler if he wasn't so fascinated with her.

The position in which he was sitting began to feel uncomfortable. He stood and walked over to the small window and looked outside. It was too dark to see anything, until a bolt of lightning streaked through the air and for one quick moment lit up an image of the lake lashing against the shore.

How many people had stood here in this spot, looking out at the wild fury he was witnessing? How many times had the various light keepers had to leave the solid sanctuary of the stone lighthouse to man a rescue boat when a ship went down. Had Eliza, Moriah's ancestor, ever done such a thing in those early years when she cared for the lighthouse?

He could see Moriah risking her life in a rowboat to save

others. He was fairly certain she wouldn't hesitate or consider her own peril. To think that this strong, young woman couldn't manage to leave her island refuge was ridiculous—except for the fact that it was true.

He turned from the window and watched the firelight play over her face. He was grateful that she was getting some rest. The past couple of days had been hard on her. Sleep might make it easier for her to deal with things.

There was a sketchpad in his backpack. He had brought it to make rough drawings of the various changes Moriah had considered making to the place. Before he began the work, he wanted to make sure Nicolas approved her ideas. For instance, she'd mentioned turning the foghorn room into a combination study and bath. That would need to be drawn out and discussed. It was the main reason he'd come out here this morning.

Now, sitting across from her, watching the shadows and light from the fire dancing over her face and body, he was caught up in the desire to draw her—just as she was—hair all tangled from the boat ride across the lake, eyes closed. Completely unaware that he was studying her.

Ben had never considered himself an artist, but he had developed an ability with pen and pencil over the years that came in handy when he was trying to envision a project, or capture an idea of a client. This was easier for him to do than most because, from the time he was a child, he had entertained himself by drawing whenever there was a lull in school, or whenever he was alone and needing to entertain himself.

Now, he wished he'd actually taken real art classes so he could capture this image of Moriah exactly as she was right now.

Oh well. It was just for him. It didn't have to be perfect. He didn't even need to ever show it to anyone. He placed another log on the fire and punched up the glowing embers so he would have more light. Then, as the rain continued to beat against the roof, he settled back against the wall with his sketchpad on his knees and began to sketch.

Moriah and her best friend, Karyona, lay together in the sleeping hammock, their little girl arms and legs entwined. Light from the fire that Karyona's parents kept in the middle of the hut danced on the ceiling. Moriah was having a great deal of trouble getting to sleep. It was hard to even close her eyes when she was so excited.

Today was her fifth birthday and, since she was such a big girl now, Mommy had allowed her to sleep over in Karyona's hut. It was the first time, ever, that she'd slept apart from Mommy and Daddy. Being here by herself felt a little strange, but she was determined to make it through the night without asking to go back to them. She was a big girl now, and needed to be brave. Besides, this was something she had been begging to do for weeks.

"Do you think there's any reason not to let her?" Mommy had asked Daddy.

"Not that I can see," Daddy said. "We are close by. If she gets frightened it will only take Akawe a moment to bring her to us."

Akawe was Karyona's daddy, and Napognuma was her mommy. Their hut was directly across from the clinic Mommy and Daddy were helping Doctor Janet build. They were Christians and Napognuma helped Mommy sometimes. There was much to learn about living in the Amazon forest, and Napognuma knew everything there was to know. Mommy loved learning about all the plants and animals. She said it was all so different from Manitoulin Island.

"If you get scared, have Akawe bring you back," Mommy said, smiling and giving her a hug as she left her at Karyona's hut. "Sometimes little girls change their minds on their first sleepover and need to come home. If that happens, it's all right, no one will mind."

Moriah played with some of Karyona's hair as she lay there curling it around and around her finger, listening to the even breathing of all of Karyona's family. They all lived together in one room. Her big brother, Rashawe, slept there, too. Rashawe was old. Already fifteen and a very good hunter.

Moriah wished her mommy and daddy and Doctor Janet and Petras could all sleep in the same room like Karyona's family. She had suggested it at dinner, but her mommy shushed her and said that big people needed to sleep in separate rooms. Moriah didn't see why. It was nice having everyone all together.

Moriah wriggled her toes with pleasure. She loved living here with the Yahnowa people in the winter. She especially liked getting to play all day outside with the other children instead of being cooped up in the lodge back home.

She had a pet monkey here, too!

Last winter the fluffy snow at home was taller than her head and she had to stay inside the lodge all day every day for weeks and weeks. She hated not getting to go outside.

But this winter was different. Daddy had packed his best carpentry tools. Then they came in a big airplane to the jungle to help build another room on Doctor Janet's clinic.

Doctor Janet was pretty but Moriah didn't think she was as pretty as Mommy. Mommy had big blue eyes and curly black hair and very light skin. Daddy teased Mommy and called her a paleface because he was part Ojibwa and had shiny black straight hair and skin that was brown and never burned. Just like Moriah's. Mommy always teased her and said that she was terribly jealous of Moriah's beautiful skin and good looks that she had inherited from her daddy.

She liked taking after her daddy. It made her feel special when they were together and people looked at them and laughed.

"Spitting image," they would say.

She had no idea what spitting had to do with looking like her daddy, but she liked how proud he acted when people said that.

The Yahnowa called her "Little Green Eyes" because her eyes were *the only thing that set her apart from the other black-haired, brown-skinned children in the village. She liked having a special name.*

It was fun here. She was able to blend in with the other children so well that her mother allowed her to dress like them, which meant wearing very little. Her daddy had frowned, but her mother had said, "Oh goodness, Jake, she's only five—let her be. She'll grow up soon enough. Let her be a wild child for these few weeks."

That's how she liked to think of herself as she played with the other village children. She was a wild child.

She took the strand of Karyona's hair between her fingers and twisted it together with a strand of her own. They were both puddles of black in the moonlight. All around Moriah were the sounds of Karyona's family sleeping. She wondered why Mommy said big people had to have separate rooms.

She was just dozing off when she heard a sharp crack outside of the window and a quick shuffling sound. Wild animals sometimes snuffled around the village at night but this sounded different. She lifted her head, straining to hear.

The muffled sounds moved away. Then a light flickered against the wall of the hut through the cracks between the bamboo poles of the wall. Moriah heard a shout, then another one and then a scream. The scream sounded exactly like Mommy the day she'd found a snake under her bed.

Moriah struggled to sit upright in the hammock. Had Mommy found another snake? In the middle of the night? Daddy would kill it like he'd killed the last one and would tease Mommy about her reaction to it in the morning.

Then shouts filtered through the bamboo wall and made her feel really, really scared. Maybe there were a lot of snakes over at the clinic. She thought she heard her father yelling now.

Silently, she slipped out of Karyona's hammock and padded to the door. Moriah opened it just enough to see out. She knew she wasn't supposed to go outside after night, and she wouldn't, but she didn't think she would get in trouble by just looking.

What she saw through the slit in the door had nothing to do with snakes and everything to do with men lifting machetes up and down while Daddy and Petras tried to protect Mommy and Janet. But Daddy and Petras didn't have machetes, they just had hands and their hands and faces were bloody. The bad men kept bringing the machete down over and over and Mommy was crawling and Daddy was trying to go to her and...

She couldn't see her mommy and daddy anymore. Petras had backed against the door that Moriah had been looking through. He was grunting and fighting the bad men with his big fists. She wanted Petras to fight hard. Petras was big. Bigger and stronger than Daddy. Maybe he could win against the bad men. Moriah knew they were bad men now, bad Yahnowa men with painted faces.

Hot urine ran down her leg, soaking into the dirt floor.

"Petras!" she screamed, but a hand went over her mouth and shut off the scream. She felt herself lifted away from the door and carried to the far side of the hut to the platform where Karyona's mommy and daddy slept. She tried to get away, but Akawe held her tightly, with his hand firmly over her mouth.

Tears came then, tears of anger and fear. They dribbled over Akawe's hand and ran down onto Moriah's neck while he kept her immobilized and silent. Napognuma had pulled Karyona out of her hammock and now held her in her arms, rocking back and forth, staring at the closed door. Fifteen-year-old Rashawe, already a warrior, crouched in front of the door, a spear in his hand.

"Chief Moawa," Karyona's daddy whispered to Napognuma as Moriah struggled and kicked to get away. "He must not find out that we shelter the white child."

"No!" Moriah screamed, desperately fighting the hands that restrained her, kicking at the blanket tangled around her feet. "Mommy!"

"Shush, Moriah, sweetheart, you're just having a bad dream."

Disoriented, Moriah sat up and gazed around wildly. The room felt alien to her. There was a wood floor instead of packed dirt. Stone walls instead of bamboo. She didn't know where she was. She wasn't entirely certain *who* she was.

"Petras?" she said to the big, solid, red-haired man beside her.

"That was my father's name, honey. I'm Ben."

She realized that she was drenched in sweat. "Where am I?"

"You're in the lighthouse cottage. There's been a thunderstorm, and you've been having the worst nightmare I've ever seen. I couldn't wake you for the longest time."

Moriah drew Ben's hands into her own and examined them. "You have Petras's hands." She touched a strand of his hair that had fallen over his forehead. "You have Petras's hair."

"Why are you talking about Petras?" Ben said. "Who is he to you?"

"He was fighting." Moriah's brain was still fuzzy from the nightmare. She fought to come fully awake but the nightmare was still so fresh upon her that she felt as though she were still partially in it. "He was fighting for his life... and my mother's... and Doctor Janet's... and I think... at the very last... he was fighting for me. I know it had to be a nightmare, but it felt real. So very real."

One last volley of thunder hit, along with a streak of lightning that lit up the room and Moriah began to tremble.

Ben gathered her up in his arms and held her against him. Rocking her. Comforting her.

"Do you know what my father's name was, Moriah?" Ben asked, softly. "Have I ever mentioned it to you?"

"No," she answered against his chest. "You've talked about your dad, but you never said his name."

"My father's name was Petras," Ben said, tears choking his voice. "And I know absolutely that he would have fought for you."

MORIAH'S FORTRESS

He only is my rock and my salvation, my fortress;
I shall not be shaken.

— PSALM 62:6 ESV

CHAPTER 1

May 1998
Manitoulin Island, Ontario

Through the dirty window of the old light keeper's office, Moriah watched the wind and rain whip Lake Huron into a frenzy of white topped waves.

The lake had so many moods. There were times when it rested, still and smooth as glass. Other times it was cheerful, lapping at the sandy beach of Tempest Bay as though inviting everyone to come play. In winter it could be treacherous, enticing people out onto ice that was not always as sturdy as it appeared. And some winters it chose to become almost magical by creating glistening ice caves out of the freezing wave action it threw against the shore.

This afternoon, it seemed to be lashing out in hurt and confusion, which perfectly matched her own inner struggle.

"I need to get out of here," she told Ben. "I need to talk to Katherine."

"We'll go soon," Ben said. "It would be suicide to try crossing right now in that metal fishing boat of yours."

"I know." She sighed in frustration.

It was unusual for her to want to leave the ruins of the old lighthouse. For as long as she could remember, it had been her private sanctuary—a fortress against all the things that could go wrong in life.

The day her grandfather died, it was here that she fled, curling up on an old sleeping bag and crying herself sick, while the walls of the light house cradled her. It was within these walls to which she often ran in the summer when the guests at the fishing resort where she worked got on her last nerve. It was here that she had come to recuperate from all the angst and worries she'd experienced during high school.

But the storm combined with the violent nightmare she'd just experienced, made the place feel ominous and threatening today instead of a fortress against life's problems.

She had no idea why her mind had decided to serve up such a nightmare. Ben and she had simply been discussing and making notes on the upcoming restoration of the ruined light-house—a pleasant task—when the storm came up and they took shelter inside the keeper's cottage. To while away the time, she'd asked him to tell her about his translation work with the Yahnowa tribe. Unfortunately, she had been exhausted, and had fallen into a half-sleep while he was still talking.

His descriptions of the Yahnowa people and the jungle had somehow brought on such a terrifying nightmare that she was still trembling from the shock of it. In it, she had been a small child in the Yahnowa village, peering through the slats of a neighboring hut while her mother and father were slashed to death by murderous, painted, half-naked Yahnowa men. She'd even dreamed that a man by the name of Petras had stood outside the hut fighting for her life. Petras was Ben's father's name—a fact she didn't remember having ever known.

The whole thing was such a disturbing image it had shaken her to the core, but she knew it could not be based on any sort of real-life experience. Her mother and father had died in a plane crash on their way to do mission work. She had been raised by her grandfather and aunt from the age of five. Except for being orphaned at such an early age, she had lived a very ordinary life.

Her hope was that her aunt might be able to help her figure out why she'd experienced such a mixed up, crazy nightmare. Katherine often knew things that she did not.

Ben was nearly as confused as Moriah. Nicolas had never mentioned the fact that Moriah might be the daughter of the missionaries who had been killed in the same massacre that had taken his father. The name of Robertson was a fairly common one. It had never occurred to him that Moriah's parents could have been those people. Especially since Katherine had told him that Moriah's parents had been killed in a plane crash.

And yet…the Yahnowa people still spoke fondly of a little girl who had once lived among them, a child they called Little Green eyes.

Moriah's eyes were strikingly green.

With her screams from the nightmare still ringing in his ears, he decided to not upset her further by mentioning his suspicion to her. If there was any possible way that she *was* the child who had survived the massacre, it was not his place to tell her.

A lightning bolt hit nearby so close that they both jumped. Even though the structure they were in was made of stone, Ben knew they were not safe. His greatest concern was the roof. He hoped it held, but he'd noticed that it was starting to rot in many

165

places. He did not like their chances if the heavy, soggy, roof fell on them.

"It might be best for us to get away from the window," he said. "And it probably wouldn't be a bad idea to stay out of the middle of the room. I know this roof is weak."

Moriah glanced up. "You're right."

She went back to the spot where they had been sitting and dropped down onto the floor. She leaned her back against the stone wall and drew her knees up to her chest, still trembling slightly.

"Are you okay?" Ben sat down beside her.

"I will be," she said. "But I'm having trouble wrapping my mind around what just happened. That nightmare was so real! I can still smell the smoke of the little cooking fire inside the hut."

"Must have been scary."

"It was."

They sat in silence for a while. Then Moriah asked the question he had hoped she wouldn't until he'd had a chance to speak privately with Katherine.

"How did your father die, Ben?"

There it was.

Ben was an awful liar, so as usual, he simply fell back on the truth.

"My father was killed by the Yahnowa, as was Nicolas's mother."

He winced when he heard her sudden intake of breath.

"I'm feeling very confused right now," Moriah said.

"I was just a kid when Dad went there," Ben explained. "My dad met Nicolas's mother, Dr. Janet Bennett, on a trip. He was so impressed and intrigued by her and her work he went to go help in whatever way he could. I stayed with my uncle while he was gone."

"So, you and Nicolas both had parents who were killed by the Yahnowa? When did you find out about each other?"

"We knew of each other from the beginning of my dad and his mother's relationship, but I never met him until last fall. That's when he closed his medical practice and came to see if any of the clinic his mother built in the Amazon still existed."

"Does it?"

"No. At least not much of it. The clinic was abandoned for a long time after Dr. Janet died. Finally, some veteran missionaries, Abraham and Violet Smith, braved going in. The jungle had completely taken over the few structures when I got there. It never was all that much of a place to begin with."

"What about the tribal people?" Moriah asked. "Have they ever talked with you about what happened that night?"

"Not much, and there's no good reason to bring it up. We know what happened. The older ones who still live in the village are embarrassed by what happened. They weren't part of the killings, anyway."

Moriah began to braid a strand of her hair. He'd noticed this before. It seemed to be a reflex comforting action—something to keep her hands busy when she was under stress or thinking hard.

"Do you suppose that was the village where my parents were headed when their plane crashed?" Moriah said. "My grandfather and Katherine never talked much about where my parents were going. I got the feeling it made them sad to talk about it, so I seldom brought it up, but I probably overheard some things over the years. Do you suppose when you started talking about the Yahnowa my brain did something weird with the information and triggered a nightmare?"

Ben dodged the question. "I'm no expert on nightmares."

He noticed a lessening of the wind and rain as the lightning moved further away. Moriah heard it, too.

"The storm is starting to calm down," Moriah said. "Maybe we can leave soon."

"Maybe."

He watched as she rubbed a hand over the cracked linoleum floor. There had once been a floral pattern to it, but most of it had worn off.

"My great-great-grandmother, Eliza Robertson, nearly starved here her first winter. I often wonder what it might have been like to live here back then. "

Ben was grateful for the change of subject. "How much do you know about her?"

"Not a lot. There aren't any written records I've been able to find. Even the old log book was taken away by the government when the lighthouse was decommissioned. I know her husband, Liam, disappeared and was never found. The spring thaw was late. The lighthouse tender—that's what they call a ship that is specially made to bring supplies to the lighthouses—wasn't able to get through. She had one child with her when it happened, a little boy."

"Did they ever find her husband?"

"No. Once the ship was finally able to break through the ice and get to them, the authorities came and searched. They never found a trace."

A rogue gust of wind blew down the chimney and scattered smoke and embers from the fireplace.

"As first dates go," Ben rubbed the smoke out of his eyes, "I'd say this one has not gone particularly well."

"I was not aware this was a date."

Ben ignored her comment. "Let's see; we've had tears, screams, and nightmares from when you fell asleep. I got scratched up from all the brambles and pine trees I encountered trying to walk that old road here. We're damp from the rain. My backside is killing me from sitting on the floor. I'm hungry. We both smell like smoke. That rain-soaked roof might collapse at any moment. Did I happen to mention I made the acquaintance of a black bear on the way here?"

"You did?" Moriah said.

"I only caught a glimpse of him or her from a distance, but I was impressed." He stretched out his legs. "You sure know how to show a guy a good time, Moriah."

She leaned her head back against the wall beside him. "And to think, I wasn't even trying."

CHAPTER 2

The rain finally stopped completely. Ben stepped outside for a moment and was treated to the glorious sight of the sun breaking through the clouds over the water.

"It's over," Ben said. "I think we can make it home now."

"Good," she said.

The rainfall had been heavy. When they reached the beached boat, they had to bail out the water before they could climb in. To his surprise, Moriah didn't take over control of the motor. Instead, she chose to sit at the front of the boat.

"You trust me to drive?" he asked, surprised.

"The way I'm feeling right now," she said. "I trust you a whole lot more than I trust myself."

A few minutes later, Ben guided the little fishing boat through waves still choppy from the storm. It felt good to get away from the dark and damp lighthouse. It was one thing to be there when the sun was shining and things were cheerful. It was another thing entirely when it was raining and dreary. Especially when his companion was screaming in terror.

Like Moriah, he couldn't help but wonder how depressing

and lonely it must have been for the light keepers and their families when it grew dark out there on the tip of the peninsula, especially when provisions were low and the nearest neighbor was miles away. Those old lighthouse keepers did not have an easy life, no matter how much people tended to romanticize the profession.

Spray from the waves flew into his face. He kept his chin down, trying to avoid as much of it as he could. Moriah faced the front of the boat with face uplifted, as though the spray felt good on her skin. Perhaps, she hoped it would wash away the lingering horror of that terrible dream.

For Moriah's sake, he was trying to act calm about the whole thing, but he had been stunned listening to her describe not only what could have been her mother and father's murder, but his own father's death, as well. He had never known the details of that night. There had been no non-Yahnowa witnesses, except the one child. Now, he would forever bear the image of his father fighting to protect that little girl. It was so typical of his dad.

He could see his father so clearly in his mind. The man had been heavily muscled, even in middle-age. He could just imagine him fighting with those strong, stonemason fists. It was exactly the kind of thing his dad would do. Petras had once been nearly as good of a fighter as he had been a stonemason.

Petras. It meant rock. The name so aptly described the man.

When they reached the small dock, he climbed out and tied off the rope while Moriah stayed huddled in the boat so deep in thought that she didn't seem to notice where she was.

"We're back," he said. "We will soon be warm and dry up at the lodge."

Moriah was young, strong, and healthy. Normally, she bounded out of the boat like it was nothing. Now, she climbed out as stiffly as an old woman. He grabbed her hand and helped steady her.

"A hot bath. Some cocoa. Warm, dry clothes." He steered her toward the lodge. "You'll be as good as new, lass."

He hoped he was right about that. He had never been a lover of secrets, and he had a suspicion there had been way too many of them in the Robertson family.

CHAPTER 3

"Was it worth it, Kathy?" Nicolas said. "I've always wanted to know."

Katherine's way of dealing with worry and stress was to cook. It had been her release and comfort most of her life. Moriah sometimes joked the amount of food on the table was a good barometer of Katherine's worry level.

At the moment, there was a large pot of chili simmering on the stove, hot cornbread sitting on the counter, a fruit salad in the fridge, and several dozen oatmeal cookies cooling on a white dishcloth spread on the table.

But Katherine was not hungry.

She had been fighting the urge to cook obsessively ever since Nicolas purchased the abandoned lighthouse and moved into one of the vacant cabins at the fishing resort she and Moriah owned.

Actually, she felt a little sick to her stomach, truth be told. Probably because ever since Nicolas had settled into that vacant cabin, he seemed determined to force a conversation between them.

A conversation she absolutely did not want to have.

It had taken a long time for a scab to form over the wound in her heart. It had taken an even longer time for the wound to heal enough that she didn't think about Nicolas every moment of every day. She was terrified if she spent any more time with him the old wound would begin to bleed again. If that happened, she didn't know if it would ever stop.

When would Moriah and Ben get back, anyway? She did not want to be alone with this man.

"Please answer me, Kathy," Nicolas said. "Was it worth it?"

Maybe she should bake a cake. She had all the ingredients. She pulled flour out of the cabinet, found the baking powder…

"Kathy, stop that," Nicolas demanded. "Look at me."

She didn't want to look at him. He looked too good. His dress shirt was opened at the collar and was slightly rumpled. The sleeves were rolled up. His black pants fit him as though they were tailor-made for his body, and knowing Nicolas, they probably were. A lock of dark hair fell over one eye. It gave him a boyish look.

The love of her life, twenty years older, fit and strong and still able to make her heart skip a beat.

She knew she had not aged well. With him gone from her life, there had been no reason to care or fuss about her looks. She didn't so much as own a tube of lipstick anymore. The leather skirt and calico blouse she was wearing was probably the nicest outfit she owned, and it was ancient. She hadn't been to a beauty shop for years.

She had heard his wife was gorgeous and seriously rich.

Would he never leave this lodge?

Suddenly, she heard the sound of a boat motor roaring across the lake.

"Maybe that's Moriah." She headed toward the great room.

From the window, she could see that it was, indeed, Moriah,

and Ben was with her. That was even better. She would feed them all and the conversation would be general. And *then* Nicolas would leave. Or she would leave. There was no way she could have the talk he seemed determined to force on her without breaking down. She was on the verge of tears now. And there was no way she was going to cry in front of the man who had abandoned her when she had needed him most.

"You can't avoid me indefinitely, Kathy," Nicolas said. "I'm going to be here all summer. We *are* going to talk."

"Talking won't fix anything, Nicolas."

With an effort, she broke her attention away long enough to greet Moriah and Ben as they came through the door.

"Where have you been?" Katherine asked, her voice more stressed than she intended. "I've been worried."

"We got trapped by the storm out at the lighthouse," Ben said.

"You both look upset." Moriah glanced at Katherine and then at Nicolas. "What's going on?"

Nicolas was silent. He laid his forearm across the thick, wooden mantel and gazed down at the dying fire.

"We were just having a discussion," Katherine said. "It was nothing important."

Nicolas barked out a short laugh as though disagreeing with Katherine's description of the situation.

"There is something weird between you two. There has been from the moment Nicolas arrived. I want to know what it is."

"Leave it alone, Moriah," Katherine said. "Please. It's none of your business."

"I disagree, Kathy." Nicolas turned away from the mantel. "It's very much her business. I think she should know."

"Know what?" Moriah said.

"It's time to tell her," Nicolas said. "She should know what you sacrificed. If you don't, I will. She's not a child anymore."

There was a knock on the door. Ben went to open it.

A family of four were standing outside—a mom, dad, pre-teen son and daughter. All were dressed in white Bermuda shorts, flowered shirts, and flip flops. All were wearing sunglasses. All looked as though they had been taken by surprise with the chilly weather.

"We're the Wrights from Florida," the man said. "We have a reservation."

"Please," Katherine said, grateful for the interruption. "Come inside."

She went to the desk where she took care of the paperwork with the man, while the wife and two teenagers huddled around the fireplace. Nicolas drew away from them and began examining the bookcase although Katherine knew he wasn't particularly interested in any of the dog-eared paperbacks guests had left behind over the years.

The Wrights were interesting. What had they have been thinking when they dressed for this trip? How could they have missed the fact Canada was much further north and colder than Florida?

"How was your trip?" she asked, pleasantly, while Moriah grabbed fresh towels, sheets, and pillowcases and hurriedly ducked out the door to prepare their cabin. Nothing got in the way of taking care of guests. Sickness, worries, emotional storms —the business had to go on.

"Much longer than we expected," Mr. Wright said. "The ferry wasn't running, so we had to go the long way around, up through Michigan."

"I'm sorry to hear that," she said. "But I'm happy you made it here safe and sound."

Her tone was cheerful while she evaluated these new guests. They hadn't realized the ferry wouldn't be running yet? They had not had enough sense to try to make a reservation for the Chi-cheemaun? These people were definitely novices.

She saw Ben throw a couple more logs on the fire to help the Wright family warm up.

"Thanks, Ben."

"No problem," he said. "While you sort everything out here, I'm going to my cabin to change into some dry clothes. I'll be back in a few minutes."

"The weather is a little chilly here at night," Katherine told the family. "There are usually some sweatshirts and sweaters in the lost-and-found box in the corner. You are welcome to help yourself."

Almost before the words were out of her mouth, the mother was rummaging through the box, tossing sweaters and woolen scarfs to her children. By the time the mother was finished, the whole family looked a little strange in an odd assortment of clothing, but they had stopped shivering.

"I'll show you to your cabin, now," Katherine said.

She was grateful for an excuse to leave the lodge. It would prevent her from spending another minute alone with the man who had broken her heart.

CHAPTER 4

M oriah had changed into dry clothes and was sitting on the end of one of the couches. A bowl of chili sat untouched beside her on the side table.

"The Wrights are set for the night," she said. "We are not expecting any other guests until tomorrow. Now, would you mind telling me what's going on between you two?"

Ben had already consumed two bowls of chili and was giving serious consideration to having a third. He nursed a cup of coffee while he listened.

"Honestly," Katherine said. "It's really not important. Would anyone like more chili?"

"Kathy and I grew up together," Nicolas interrupted with a quick glance at Katherine. "My father left my mother when I was only three. She fought her way through medical school with no help except from your family. My mother and your grandmother were close friends. Both had grown up here on the island."

"Why didn't you tell me about him, Katherine?" Moriah asked. "All these years and you never mentioned knowing Nicolas? Why?"

"Probably because the subject was too painful," Nicolas said. "Am I right, Kathy?"

Katherine bit her lip and nodded.

"My mother dreamed of becoming a medical missionary," Nicolas continued. "I was six when she left me permanently with her friends, the Robertsons, while she went to establish a medical clinic in the jungles of Brazil."

"She did visit, though," Katherine said.

"Yes, but even when she came here, she went to the reservation every day to help out."

"True," Katherine said. "Nicolas and I would follow her around. She really was quite gifted."

"Brilliant woman, my mom." Nicolas's voice held a tinge of bitterness. "Great doctor. Absentee mother."

Katherine looked around, brightly. "Does anyone want cocoa? Or cookies? I baked cookies."

Ben thought he did...

"Please, Katherine," Moriah said, "I don't want cocoa or cookies. I just want answers."

...and decided he didn't.

Katherine sighed. "I wanted to be a doctor, too, just like her. She always made it seem so noble. I studied hard. I applied for scholarships. Your dad, my big brother, helped. Nicolas and I were in our first year of medical school when we called off our engagement."

"Engagement?" Moriah gaped at them, and Ben choked on his coffee. "You and Nicolas? You have to be kidding! You actually considered marrying someone like Nicolas?"

"He's sitting right here, lass," Ben reminded her. "He can hear you."

"I'm sorry, Nicolas," Moriah said. "But seriously, you and Katherine? It's pretty hard to imagine. She's so kind and caring, and you..."

"And I bought the lighthouse out from under you," Nicolas added. "I committed the unpardonable sin. You've made that abundantly clear."

"Nicolas can come off as being a little cold, sometimes," Katherine said, defensively, "but that isn't who he is. I always knew him as the sweet, shy little boy who cried at night for his mama."

Nicolas made a surprised sound. "You knew about that?"

"I heard you crying, Nicolas," she said. "We all did, but there was nothing any of us could do."

"So why did you break off your engagement?" Moriah began to braid a small lock of her hair nervously.

A long look passed between Katherine and Nicolas. It was a look that went deep. Ben felt like he had just seen a lifetime pass between them.

"Oh, nothing, really," Katherine passed it off. "The timing just wasn't quite right."

"That's the understatement of the century," Nicolas said. "Tell her the truth, Kathy."

"What good will it do?"

Ben felt his stomach tighten, as though anticipating a punch to the gut. Whatever Katherine's next words were, he was fairly certain they were going to hurt Moriah, and from what little he knew, she had been hurt enough.

"Did I have something to do with it?" Moriah said. "Was I the reason you broke off your engagement?"

"After your parents died, the only family you had left was your grandfather and me. Dad was too old to raise you by himself, and he had lost a son, a daughter-in-law, and a beloved wife in the space of two years. I needed to stay and take care of you. I couldn't leave."

A sick dread built inside of Ben as he watched and listened. This story was not going to turn out well.

"Nicolas didn't understand how I could drop out of medical school to care for you. I was a good student, and I worked hard, but he was scary smart. By the time your parents died, he had focused his sights on becoming a top surgeon. He wanted it more than anything else in the world, and he was capable of achieving it."

Katherine looked down at her hands, which were clutched together in her lap.

"So?" Moriah prompted.

"In the end," Katherine's voice was low, "he wanted it more than he wanted me."

Nicolas gazed at Katherine but said nothing. Instead, he slowly shook his head as though refuting everything she had just said.

"Nicolas is a surgeon?" Moriah asked.

"No," Nicolas said, "I'm not a surgeon. My mother was an obstetrician. After her death, I specialized in high risk pregnancies. I suppose I thought it would bring me closer to her, somehow."

"That's why you were able to save Camellia's baby."

"Camellia's birth was easy, compared to some of the situations I've had to deal with, but yes, that's why I was able to help her."

"So, let me see if I understand what you're saying," Moriah said. "You, Katherine, thought you could not leave the island because of me. You quit medical school because I went into a meltdown every time you tried to take me across the bridge, and you didn't feel like you could dump me on my grandfather. And Nicolas, you couldn't face being tied down forever on Manitoulin Island. Is that correct? Am I reading this right? I managed to ruin both of your lives?"

"You couldn't help any of it," Katherine said. "You were a child. I was only twenty-two, myself. Too young to know how to help you. Not wise enough to deal with your problems in a healthy way. All I knew to do was to keep reassuring you that you were safe here with me, but my reassurances apparently only made the situation worse. Besides, if Nicolas had loved me enough, he would have found a way to work something out. He married within the year." Katherine glanced at Nicolas as she continued. "I heard his wife was very beautiful and quite wealthy."

"Correction," Nicolas said. "If you had loved *me* enough, *you* would have found a way. And for the record, I soon discovered that my 'beautiful' wife was incapable of loving anyone besides herself. I made a terrible mistake, but I was already bound to her by the time I found out."

"Then why did you stay with her?"

"I am not my father. I had made a vow to her, and I kept it."

Nicolas and Katherine were so intent on one another they had apparently forgotten Ben and Moriah were in the room.

"You were the one I loved, Kathy. Always. From the time we were children. You were the only one. My marriage was created in a selfish fit of temper and I have suffered a lifetime for it."

"You did throw a lot of tantrums when we were small," Katherine smiled, remembering. "They were memorable, but they never accomplished much."

"I grew up, Kathy. My wife died fourteen months ago. I cared for her until the end." He waited for the impact of these words to sink in. "I've done a lot of good with my life. I've done the best I knew how. But now, all I really want to do is come home. That's the only reason I bought the lighthouse, Kathy. I'm so tired. I just want to come home."

Katherine, who was seated in one of the leather chairs, hesitated a moment, then she reached out her arms to him. Nicolas rushed over, knelt in front of her and they embraced. Nicolas held onto to Katherine like a drowning man, as she stroked his hair and crooned soothing words.

"This is our cue to leave," Ben whispered to Moriah.

"I know," Moriah said, "but I still need to ask Katherine about my nightmare."

"Later," Ben said. "Those two deserve some time alone."

"I'll see you in the morning, then." Moriah reluctantly went upstairs, and Ben let himself out while Nicolas and Katherine simply clung to one another.

CHAPTER 5

Ben, a good night's sleep under his belt, filled with hot oatmeal and good-will toward men, walked toward the lodge in the early morning sunshine. He could hardly wait to see what new things might transpire today. Being around Katherine, Moriah, and Nicolas was nearly as good as having television, except it was real people dealing with real problems. He genuinely wanted only the best for all of them.

When he arrived at the lodge, Katherine was bustling around the kitchen and she was humming. That was new. She was dressed in her buckskin outfit again, so he supposed she was going to work today. Nicolas was standing over a skillet of scrambled eggs with a spatula in his hand. He was wearing khaki pants with a plaid shirt. His shirt was not tucked in. For Nicolas, this was casual in the extreme.

Moriah came in about the same time as Ben. She was ready for work, dressed in a brown flannel shirt and jeans, her hair pulled back into a tight braid. He searched her face. She didn't look like she had slept well.

"There's fresh juice in the fridge if you want some," Katherine said. "We'll have breakfast ready in a jiffy. Are you eating with us, Ben?"

Ben could smell bacon in the oven. Suddenly, hot oatmeal didn't seem like nearly enough breakfast to get him through the morning.

"Sure!"

"By the way," Katherine said, "I called Sam Black Hawk early yesterday morning. He specializes in snakes. Sam promised to come take a look at our little problem under Cabin One."

"Does he think he can help?" Moriah asked.

"He said not to worry; he can take care of it."

"Great. I was beginning to think I'd have to burn down the cabin and start all over."

"I don't think he has anything that drastic planned."

"Will it be expensive?"

"Probably not. Your grandfather was a good friend to Sam, and I helped his mother get through some difficult times. He seemed happy for a chance to help us."

"That's a relief."

The radio was playing soft, classical music as Katherine pulled the pan of crisp bacon from the oven and plated it. Nicolas dished out the eggs; Ben made himself useful by pouring out the juice. Moriah buttered the toast, then brought out the plates and silverware. Katherine made fresh coffee. The morning sun poured through the windows.

Everything was lovely as Katherine asked Ben to say grace. He did, with thankfulness pouring from his heart. As they ate, he felt blessed to be sitting with these people in this room at this moment. Life was good until Moriah spoke.

"Why did you lie to me, Katherine?"

Ben sighed inwardly. Things had been going so well.

"My love for Nicolas was a painful memory." Katherine said. "I had no desire to relive it by sharing it."

"I'm not talking about Nicolas."

Katherine looked puzzled.

Moriah carefully laid her knife and fork on her plate. "Tell me about my mom and dad's death."

Katherine hesitated. "Your parents died in a plane crash on their way to do mission work. You know that."

"Why was I not with them?" Moriah asked. "You told me last night that you were in medical school. My grandmother was already gone. Even though my grandfather was always kind to me, I doubt my parents would have left a five-year-old alone with him for an extended period of time. Why was I not in the plane with them?"

Ben watched Katherine struggle for an answer. Moriah's logic had blindsided her. She had no ready explanation.

"You were the one person in the world I trusted completely," Moriah said, when Katherine didn't answer. "Why did you feel the need to lie to me about how my parents died?"

"She was afraid you would stop talking again." Nicolas intervened. "She couldn't bear to see you re-traumatized and was afraid that's what would happen if you knew."

"If I knew what?" Moriah crossed her arms. "What exactly were you afraid that I would find out?"

"She's a grown woman now, Kathy," Nicolas said. "She deserves to know the truth."

"I was there, wasn't I?" Moriah said. "I actually saw my parents being murdered."

It took a moment for Katherine to answer, but when she did, her voice was low and steady. "You were a child. I did what I thought was best for you."

"I've been an adult for a long time."

"You seemed to remember nothing," Katherine said. "Considering the horror of what you had been through, I thought that was a good thing. I was grateful. The last thing I wanted was to bring any of it back to mind. Even your doctor thought it best not to bring it all back up. I believe his words were something along the lines of letting sleeping dogs lie."

"I think those sleeping dogs have awakened," Ben said. "Tell them what happened yesterday at the lighthouse, Moriah."

She described the nightmare in all its horrific detail.

When she was finished, no one said anything or wanted breakfast anymore, not even Ben. When no one made any comment, Moriah got up and walked out of the room. Nicolas quietly cleared the table. Ben went to the porch and watched Moriah walk away along the water's edge. It did not seem wise to him to follow her, but he could keep an eye on her from this vantage point. Katherine came to stand beside him, also watching. Every now and then, they would see her stop, stare at the lake and then start walking again.

"The bodies were too mutilated and decayed to bring home," Katherine said. "Who tells a child something like that? I certainly couldn't. I bought a headstone to put in the church cemetery with the names of Jacob and Mary Ann Robertson on it. I wanted to create a place where Moriah could lay flowers on her parent's grave, but nothing is there except the headstone. I did what I thought was best. Maybe I was wrong."

Katherine shook her head with regret, then walked back inside the lodge.

For the first time since arriving on the island, Ben almost wished he was back with the Yahnowa. He hated to see such suffering. Especially when there was nothing he could do about it.

After a while, he saw Moriah turn back toward the lodge. Her steps were steady. There was a determination to her pace. Apparently, she had come to some sort of a conclusion during her solitary walk.

He went inside the lodge where Nicolas and Katherine were washing dishes. "She's coming back."

"Thanks for warning us," Nicolas said.

The three of them were seated in the great room when she entered. All three were steeled to answer whatever she asked. They heard her mount the wooden porch steps. Then the door swung open. She stood there with her feet braced. Hands clenched. Cheeks flushed. Her hair had come loose from its braid. She had obviously prepared herself to face whatever they told her.

"So, what happened?" she said. "I'm not five anymore and I need to know."

CHAPTER 6

The more they talked, the more Moriah realized somewhere in the back of her mind, much of this information had been stored. Apparently, her mind had been either unwilling or unable to examine it until now.

"My mother," Nicolas explained, "managed accidentally to do something that set one of the tribal headmen off. I've not been able to find out what it was, nor has Ben. We're still not sure exactly what happened. Most of the Yahnowa were grateful she was there. But one particular man, Chief Moawa, who was from a neighboring Yahnowa tribe, was not happy with her. He gathered several of the younger men and got them stirred up about the outsiders. Unfortunately, in addition to my mother, the 'outsiders' happened to be Ben's father and your parents. They were innocents, just trying to help make a better life for these people."

"And I was there."

"You were there," Katherine said. "Apparently, you saw it all. The only thing that saved your life was you were spending the night with a little friend in the hut across from the clinic. That family hid you and got you out of the village before Chief

Moawa figured out where you were. They put themselves in great danger to do so. What little we know about what happened, we found out from the Catholic priest to whom the family took you. They didn't know what else to do. He brought you to Detroit and that's where Dad and I got you. I've never been so happy to see someone in my life."

"So, you remember everything now?" Nicolas said.

"I don't know. I think I witnessed my father and Petras trying to protect Dr. Janet and Mom. And at the very end, I'm fairly certain Petras was fighting to protect me."

"Please don't be angry at me," Katherine said. "Your doctor said it would be best if the memories came back on their own. He said if we told you about it before you were ready, it might reopen wounds you couldn't deal with. You were so little and you were so traumatized."

"But why did you make up the story about the plane crash?"

"Once you began to speak again, you started asking where your parents were. I had to tell you something, but how could I tell a fragile five year old her parents had been murdered? Maybe it was wrong. I don't know. I'm sorry you're hurt. But I was trying to do the best I could for you."

"You've had a lot of years to tell me the truth."

"When would you have been ready to hear your parents had been hacked to death by the very tribe they were trying to help? Did I really need to put that image in your mind?" Katherine pressed her hand against her heart. "I didn't even want that image to remain within my *own* memory! I didn't know what to do, nor did your grandfather. We decided to try to give you the most normal childhood we could. I'm sorry if that wasn't enough."

"I don't know if you did the right thing, either, Katherine. I really don't, but I understand why you did it," Moriah said. "I also appreciate how good you have been to me, and the sacrifices you've made down through the years. What I don't understand is why you, Ben, chose to work and live where your father was killed. How could you do that?"

"I have a gift for languages, Moriah. They come easily for me. When I started considering where I might best use my gift, the first place that came to mind was the Yahnowa tribe. It was a way to continue my dad's work. I didn't want his death to be in vain."

"And Nicolas, you have recently gone back there also. Why?"

"The main culprit," Nicolas explained, "was Chief Moawa. He gave the young men who followed him jungle intoxicants. Afterward, there was no more clinic, and they were sorry. But by then, it was too late. I tried to ignore that place for a long time, but in the end, I had to go back. When I saw what Ben was doing, I decided to help. Once we get the lighthouse finished, I'll concentrate on seeing what I can do to fulfill my mother's dream."

"I see." Moriah voice was bone tired.

"I know all this is a shock," Katherine said. "Would you like to go lie down for a bit?"

"I would very much like to crawl into bed, pull the covers over my head, and stay there until my life makes sense again. But…" She glanced at the wall clock and stood up wearily. "Dale Trowbridge will be here any minute with that big load of gravel I ordered for the driveway. I need to get things ready to start spreading it."

"I can take care of that," Ben said. "Nicolas can help me."

Nicolas seemed a little surprised to be included in a project that required manual labor, but he agreed as well. "Yes, I'll help, too."

Ben was happy he'd offered when he saw the look of relief on Moriah's face. That job would take her, working alone, the rest of the day or longer. Helping was the least they could do.

"Thanks," she said. "I appreciate it. The rakes and shovels are in the tool shed. Nicolas, grab some work gloves or you'll get blisters. Katherine, you'll need to write a check when Dale gets here."

The gravel came, the check was written, and Ben and Nicolas spent several hours helping rake two truckloads of gravel smoothly over the driveway. The sun was setting when they finished. Moriah took off her hat, leaned on her rake, and surveyed the work they had done.

"It looks good. Having you two help made a huge difference."

"*Now* you can go to bed and pull the covers over your head," Ben said. He wasn't joking. Moriah was so tired she appeared to be standing only by sheer will-power. There were dark circles beneath her eyes that had not been there the day he met her. Struggling with the realities of her past was taking a toll.

"I believe I will do just that." She walked away, carrying her rake with her.

"By the way." She stopped and turned to face them. "If you two still want me to help pull the lighthouse project together, I'll do it."

"Great! What changed your mind?" Ben asked.

"If both of you can be forgiving enough to go back to the people who killed your parents, I guess I should do the same."

"You are thinking of going to the Amazon?" Nicolas asked.

"Of course not," Moriah said. "Didn't you say that you will start concentrating on fulfilling your mother's dream after we get the lighthouse project finished?"

"I did."

"I can help you get it done faster. Ben's right. I do know all the contractors and skilled labor on the island. I know who we can trust to show up for work and do a good job. I can save you a lot of headaches."

"That's a relief," Nicolas said. "Thank you!"

"You're welcome. Frankly, I think both of you need to have your heads examined going back there. I never want to see that place again as long as I live. But I can help move your schedule up. Consider it my contribution."

Moriah hefted her rake and left without another word.

"She's probably right." Ben smiled. "We probably do need to have our heads examined."

"All I can think about is Katherine, right now, anyway." Nicolas shrugged. "Wouldn't it be something if we got back together after all these years?"

"It would," Ben said. "I think I'm going to head back to my cabin now. I have no plans to go to bed and pull the covers over my head, but I do have some work to do."

He saw that he was talking to Nicolas's back. The man had already headed back to the lodge. He thought Nicolas acted as though he was afraid Katherine would disappear if he didn't keep her in eyesight at all times.

When Ben got back to his cabin, he pulled his sketch pad out of his backpack and looked long and hard at the rough drawing he'd made of Moriah while she had been asleep out at the lighthouse. That was before the nightmare, when things were still relatively simple. The drawing had turned out pretty well. He tore it off the tablet and stuck it into the corner of the frame of an old picture. It gave him pleasure to see it there.

Then he sat down at his desk and began to sketch again. This time, it was the light tower and cottage. He was getting a good understanding of how to recreate both into something everyone could be proud of when the job was finished.

Now that all the secrets had been brought out into the open and forgiven, he thought life was going to be much easier for everyone.

Moriah showered off the gravel dust and sweat from leveling the driveway, wrapped her hair in a towel, donned her robe, and went to her bedroom. There, she softly closed the door and locked it. There was no need for a lock, and she seldom used it. Katherine would never walk in without knocking. They always respected one another's privacy. Nor was she concerned about guests wandering in. The great room downstairs in the lodge where they greeted and checked in guests was, by necessity, a public place, but a sign at the bottom of the steps let everyone know the upstairs was private living quarters. So far, no one had ever been rude enough to ignore the fact.

There was no reason at all for her to lock her door tonight, except it made her feel a little better. She needed to shut out the world tonight. The day had been overwhelming in every way.

She tossed the damp towel on the foot of her bed, combed out her wet hair, exchanged her robe for flannel pajamas, and then fell face forward on her bed. If any of her guests had an issue in the middle of the night, Katherine would have to take care of it. Moriah was done.

Then she opened one eye and noticed her giant globe sitting in the corner. She crawled off the bed, gave the globe a spin, closed her eyes, and let her finger glide over the surface until the globe stopped spinning. Then she opened her eyes and peeked beneath her finger. Trinidad. That would be a nice place to visit. It would always be warm in Trinidad.

For a moment, she gave into a fantasy of stepping onto an airplane, flying to Trinidad, and exploring the island. What wonders would she discover there if she ever got to go?

Unless something changed drastically within her, that was something she would never know.

CHAPTER 7

"Why did they let it grow up?" Ben shoved his fingers through his hair as he stared at the wall of new-growth forest and brambles that stood between him and Robertson's lighthouse.

His hair was getting so long it was starting to bother him. Maybe he should talk Moriah into cutting it. Then it hit him that Moriah cutting it would also involve Moriah running her fingers through his hair. The thought made his knees go weak, so maybe that wasn't such a good idea. He needed to find a barber, preferably a male barber.

He reminded himself it would not be wise to get romantically involved with Moriah. As much as he admired her, now that he knew everything, falling in love with her would be a disaster. He had important work to do in Brazil, and she would be a hindrance. The girl needed a nice, normal Manitoulin Islander man in her future, not him.

"It was never more than packed dirt, anyway." Standing a few paces in front of him, Moriah jammed her hands into her back pockets and planted her boots firmly apart as she surveyed the dense woods. A dark blue baseball cap printed with the words "Robertson's Resort" was pulled low. Her plain, white tank top showed off the firm muscle in her upper arms and back.

To Ben, her stance was entrancing. She was especially cute when in full work-mode.

Forget it, McCain, he warned himself again. He forced his attention away from Moriah and back to the subject at hand.

She seemed completely unaware of his attention. "After the Fresnel lens was stolen, the Coast Guard deliberately let the road grow over to discourage sightseers and vandals."

"That's the third time you've mentioned a Fresnel lens. What's so special about it?"

"It was revolutionary. In the early 1800's, when most of the light towers were built, the lights on the Great Lakes were nothing more than oil-burning lamps with reflectors behind them. It required as many as ten lamps to make a light bright enough to warn a ship. Then, a Frenchman by the name of Fresnel experimented with creating layers of specially cut glass surrounding and reflecting one lamp. A Fresnel lens is lovely. It looks sort of like a huge, multifaceted diamond with a light glowing inside. I've seen miniature replicas sold as jewelry in lighthouse catalogs. Ours was called a second order light, which was one of the largest on the lakes. It was nearly as tall as a man."

"And it's not possible to buy one anymore?"

"Not to my knowledge. I don't know where you could ever get one, unless you could talk a museum out of one of them, which is not likely. There are lighthouse history buffs who keep lists of every Fresnel lighthouse lens known. Even the one we had wasn't new when it arrived, back in the 1800's."

"How did your people end up with a used lens?"

"It started out inside a light tower on the shores of southern Georgia. The light keeper grew so afraid the Union army would destroy or take it that he secretly dismantled and buried each lens in the sand. The story goes that he was so destitute after the war, he secretly sold it and blamed it's disappearance on the Union troops."

"When did it disappear from the Robertson lighthouse?"

"Soon after my grandfather's death. The Coast Guard had already installed their automated light pole, but the road was still passable then. The lighthouse became a favorite place for late-night beach parties, and since we didn't own it, there was nothing Katherine nor I could do. The lens disappeared soon after. It was either destroyed, or someone got a lot of money for it. There's an extremely strong market for original lighthouse memorabilia."

"Did you know your grandfather well?"

"He helped Katherine raise me as long as he was able. I learned quite a few things about tools and carpentry trotting around behind him, getting underfoot. Eventually, I became competent enough to be a bit of help to him. I was thirteen when he died."

Moriah pulled off the baseball cap and let her hair swing free, ruffling it with her fingers.

"It's warm this morning." She twisted her hair into a loose knot and tucked it beneath her cap again. It was such an innocent, womanly gesture that it made Ben swallow hard.

Even though he had only known her a few days, he wished with all his heart it was within his power to give her the lighthouse for her own. He also wished he could give her the Fresnel lens and, while he was at it, the sun, the moon, and the stars. But he was just a stonemason, not a magician. The best he could do was put the tower back together. Maybe seeing it in good repair would be gift enough.

He cleared his throat. "Well, we can't start until we get a road in. Are you sure you're okay helping me with this project?"

"I am," she said. "Even if I don't own it, I couldn't bear to see someone else mess it up. There might be some on the island who are better carpenters, but no one cares about it more than me. It would probably drive me nuts not to be involved in bringing it back to life."

Ben felt a combination of relief and excitement tinged with worry. To have Moriah around all summer as they worked on a project together—well, he wasn't sure life could get much better than that. But, he reminded himself yet again, he couldn't afford to get too attached to the girl.

"The road is impassable," he said. "I barely made it through that one time I walked to the lighthouse to see you. We'll have to make it into a road again before we can do anything else. Do you know of a good heavy equipment operator?"

"Let's go see my buddy, Jack." Moriah turned toward him and smiled. "He can use the work, and you'll like him."

"I don't have to like him. All I need to know—is he any good?"

"Jack is so good, he can just about do brain surgery with a backhoe." Moriah tossed him the keys to her truck. "You drive."

CHAPTER 8

After driving a couple of miles, Moriah directed him to pull into the driveway of a small, white frame house. Beside it stood two bulldozers, one slightly larger and newer than the other, as well as a backhoe and a large flatbed trailer. In front of the garage was a red Ford pickup.

Her buddy, Jack, might be a great heavy equipment operator, but apparently he didn't know how to operate a lawnmower. Knee high weeds and grass decorated the front yard.

"Your friend's not much into yard maintenance, is he?" Ben followed Moriah up the front steps.

"He's pretty busy," she admitted, "but it isn't usually this bad. Jack's proud of his home. He worked hard to buy it. He and Alicia have probably just been a little overwhelmed with their new baby."

Moriah knocked, but no one answered the door.

"That's odd. His truck's here." She knocked again. "He's usually wherever that truck is."

When no one came to the door, she tried the doorknob. It opened easily. Moriah poked her head in and gasped. Ben looked over her shoulder. The living room had been completely trashed. The couch had been overturned, pictures hung askew on the walls, and curtains puddled on the floor. The place looked like a tornado had hit it, except there had been no tornado.

"Jack?" she called.

No answer.

"Jack? It's Moriah. Are you home?"

"Maybe we should call the police," Ben suggested.

Moriah ignored him. "Jack?" She tiptoed down a hallway, peeking into each room. Ben stopped and stared at the kitchen as he followed her. Every cabinet hung open; every piece of china lay smashed on the floor. Someone with a violent temper had definitely been at work here. Feelings of *deja vu* swept over him. This scene was sickeningly familiar to him.

"Ben!" Moriah called from the back of the house. "Come here. Quick. Something is wrong with Jack!"

Ben made his way toward her voice. He passed a room to the left of the hallway and glanced in. Unlike the rest of the house, peace and order reigned within. It was a nursery, pink, pristine and perfect. At least, in there, nothing had been disturbed.

At the end of the hall, in the master bedroom, stench and filth greeted him.

A man, whom Ben presumed to be the marvelous backhoe operator, Jack, lay clothed in pajama bottoms on a disheveled bed. Dirty clothes and decaying food were scattered about.

Moriah stood in the middle of the disarray, looking bewildered and vulnerable.

"Jack?" She bent over and shook the inert figure on the bed. "Where's Alicia and little Betsy?"

The man mumbled something into the pillow along the lines of wanting to be left alone.

"Please, Jack. Tell me what's wrong." She shook his shoulder again. "Are you sick?"

Ben leaned against the doorframe, crossed his arms, and took in the situation. It wasn't hard to read. What surprised him was that Moriah didn't seem to understand what was going on.

"Does your friend like to drink, by any chance?" Ben asked.

"A little," Moriah said, "but he stopped when he fell in love with Alicia. She wouldn't marry him unless he did."

"I think he might have started again."

"Is that what's wrong with him?" She glanced up at Ben from Jack's bedside. "He's not sick? He's just drunk?"

"Yep. You need to leave, Moriah," he said. "Let me take care of this."

"But, what if he needs…"

"Out!" He wanted Moriah gone from this stinking room. "Now. Please."

With one last glance of concern for Jack, Moriah obeyed.

"Get up," Ben growled at the semi-conscious figure, once he heard Moriah moving around in the kitchen.

"Leave me alone."

"Get *up!*" Ben fisted his hand in Jack's dirty blonde hair. The desire to shake some sense into the man was overwhelming. This was Moriah's good friend?

Jack opened one red-rimmed eye, squinted, and peered at him. "Who are you?"

"I *was* the man who was going to give you a good job for the summer. I don't think that's going to happen now."

Jack let loose a string of curses, then awkwardly swung his legs over the side of the bed and pulled himself up into a sitting position.

"Was that Moriah in here?"

"Yes."

Another string of expletives split the air. "I didn't want her to see me like this." He leaned over and cradled his head in his hands.

"Where are your wife and baby?"

"I didn't touch them if that's what you're thinking."

"Did you do all this damage while they were still here?"

"No. After they left. Quit asking me questions; my head hurts."

Ben breathed a sigh of relief. He hoped Jack was telling the truth.

"How long have they been gone?"

"What day is it?" Jack scrubbed his hands over his face, as though trying to wake himself up.

"Saturday."

"Alicia took Betsy to her mother's two weeks ago."

"Good for her," Ben said.

"I'm not a drunk." Jack glared at Ben.

"Could've fooled me."

"She shouldn't have left." Jack shook his head. "I need her with me to stay sober."

"Your wife showed good sense. She got herself and your baby to a safe place. Now, get up before Moriah comes in to check on you again. I hear her out there, right now, trying to clean up the mess you made."

"I was mad." Jack stumbled to his feet, knocking over the bedside lamp in the process.

"Mad is a choice." Ben righted the lamp and shoved his shoulder under the swaying man. "So is being stupid."

CHAPTER 9

Moriah heard the shower turn on. She peeked around the kitchen door as Ben came out of the bathroom and marched down the hallway. He emerged a moment later, grim-faced, steering a wobbly Jack from the bedroom into the bathroom.

She decided to trust Ben with her friend and returned to the task of retrieving broken crockery off the floor and dropping the pieces into a trash can she had found in the adjoining laundry room. Alicia would be so upset if she came home and found her kitchen like this.

A thump and a groan came from the bathroom then a yelp. She didn't know exactly what was going on in there, but she heard steel in Ben's voice as it penetrated into the kitchen.

"I don't *care* if you don't want to take a shower," Ben said. "You stink, man. I'm not letting you near Moriah until you clean up."

She decided she didn't envy Jack one bit. He was the larger man of the two, but Ben was built like a rock. If Jack was putting up a fight about taking a shower, she would bet on Ben winning.

The last shard of pottery had been gathered when the bathroom door banged open and Jack staggered out. He was dressed in clean clothes, and his hair was combed. Ben steadied him from behind.

Ben's longish red hair had curled in the steam of the bathroom, giving him a wild look. His jaw was set. His shirt was drenched. His eyes blazed, but his voice was under control. He spoke to her with a calm that belied those smoldering eyes.

"I think some black coffee might be a good idea, Moriah, if you don't mind."

"All the coffee cups are broken," she said. "Maybe we could go down to the lodge and get some?"

Ben propped Jack against the wall with one hand, reached into his own pocket, and handed her the keys. "Good idea. You drive."

CHAPTER 10

The cab of the truck was too small for three grown people to sit comfortably. Moriah's shoulder was wedged tightly against the side of her door as she drove. No one spoke, not even when they arrived at the resort.

Ben pulled Jack out of the truck and guided him up the steps into the lodge, while Moriah followed. Fortunately, Katherine was already in the kitchen preparing lunch. A coffee maker gurgled merrily on the counter. The cozy scene was reassuring to Moriah after the chaos of Jack's house. Nicolas was sitting at the kitchen table working a cross-word puzzle. Katherine was humming a little song and smiling as she worked at the counter.

"Jack needs some black coffee, Katherine, if you don't mind." Ben sat the blonde man down at the kitchen table beside Nicolas and pulled out a chair for himself.

Katherine turned away from her lunch preparations and took in the situation.

"The coffee isn't quite finished yet. Have you eaten today, Jack?"

"No, ma'am," Jack mumbled.

"I have chicken salad sandwiches and vegetable soup."

"Thank you, ma'am."

Katherine looked at Ben and Moriah. "What about the two of you?"

"I'm not hungry." After working on Jack's nasty kitchen, Moriah thought it might be a while before she felt hungry again.

"I'd like some, if there's enough," Ben said.

"I made plenty." Katherine turned back to the stove and stirred a pot. "Nicolas and I were making plans while I chopped vegetables, and I'm afraid I accidentally made enough soup to feed a small army."

"Plans?" Moriah reached to take two bright yellow soup bowls out of the cupboard.

"Your aunt and I are getting married!" Nicolas announced.

Moriah froze. "*Excuse* me?"

"It's true." Katherine said. "Please be happy for me."

One of the soup bowls slipped from Moriah's grasp and crashed to the floor. She stared at it, focusing on the yellow pieces. More broken crockery to deal with.

"You're joking." Moriah's voice quavered in spite of her attempt to steady it. "Right?"

"Kathy and I have always loved each other," Nicolas said.

The fact he had announced their plans instead of allowing Katherine to do so, annoyed Moriah almost as much as the announcement itself. Besides, her nerves were already on edge.

"You think the fact you played together as kids gives you the right to come in here and marry my aunt?" Moriah said. "You dumped her. Remember? Just because you didn't want to be burdened with me."

"No, Moriah. We're not joking." Katherine gazed at her steadily, as though waiting for her reaction to run its course. "I've never been surer of anything in my life."

Moriah knew she needed to be careful about what came out

of her mouth next. Very deliberately, she sat the remaining bowl on the counter. "When?"

"Soon," Nicolas answered, "sometime this summer, as soon as you and your aunt get through the worst of tourist season and can have some time to prepare for a wedding. You'll be Kathy's maid of honor, of course."

Now, he was telling her who would be Katherine's maid of honor? That was her aunt's place, not his. This man would take over their lives entirely if Katherine married him. In fact, it looked like he already was.

Moriah was so exasperated she spoke without thinking. "Have you lost your mind, Katherine?"

Katherine's expression of happiness melted, and Moriah watched her aunt's face freeze into her professional expression of calm—effectively shutting her out.

"As a matter of fact," Katherine lifted her chin as though daring her niece to argue with her, "I've not lost my mind. I feel like I've finally found it. I've thought of Nicolas every day for years. There's no need for us to lose any more of our lives. We might not even wait until the end of summer. We might just go to the courthouse tomorrow. So, don't worry about being my maid of honor. I'm too old for a formal wedding, anyway."

"But you said..." Nicolas objected.

"That was just daydreaming, Nicolas. A church wedding would look silly for an old maid like me."

"Excuse me," Ben interrupted. "Is that coffee ready, yet?"

Moriah glanced at Jack, who seemed ready to slide beneath the table. She quickly selected the largest mug she could find and filled it to the brim. The coffee hadn't finished flowing through the coffee maker and several dribbles sizzled on the burner. She didn't care. Her hand shook as she poured.

Her aunt, her rock, was getting married to a man who got on Moriah's nerves with every word he spoke. Every time she thought Nicolas was becoming likable—for instance, when he helped her and Ben with the driveway—he'd say something that would set her teeth on edge again. Just thinking about the ramifications of him coming into their lives so intimately made her stomach feel queasy.

Things had been so much simpler before he showed up.

She handed the cup to Ben, willing him to take Jack and leave the kitchen so she could have it out with Katherine and Nicolas. As she bent to give him the cup, he whispered in her ear. "Be careful, Moriah. You've already said too much."

She jerked upright. Be careful indeed. It wasn't *his* aunt getting married to this man. "Can we go someplace a little more private and talk, Katherine?"

"Maybe later, dear. Nicolas and I have more to discuss." Katherine ladled soup into a bowl and placed it in front of Jack. "By the way, now that Nicolas has retired from his obstetrics practice, he says he thinks he would enjoy having a hand in running the resort. You'll be working on the lighthouse anyway, and I could use the help."

Moriah looked at Katherine and saw her aunt's heart in her eyes. *Please,* Katherine's eyes pleaded. *Please don't ruin this for me.*

The room was silent as though everyone, including Jack, were waiting for Moriah to release them from some sort of evil spell. Nicolas didn't even look at her. He just toyed with the edge of his napkin, probably waiting for another outburst.

Twenty years her aunt had pined for him? Twenty years with no other man in her life?

There really was no accounting for taste.

Moriah loved her aunt. She realized there was only one decision she could make if she was to keep their relationship intact.

"Congratulations, Katherine." She put her arms around her aunt. "You deserve all the happiness in the world. I'll be honored to be your maid of honor, and I'm happy Nicolas will be helping you with the resort this summer."

Still hugging her aunt, she narrowed her eyes and gave Nicolas a meaningful look over her aunt's shoulder. She hoped the message was clear to him. Don't even think about hurting this woman again, or you'll have me to deal with.

CHAPTER 11

B en found Moriah later, on the roof of Cabin Four, pounding nails into shingles with much more force than necessary.

"I drove Jack home," he called up to her.

She sunk a nail.

"We cleaned the rest of the trash out of the house."

She sunk another one.

"Can you hear what I'm saying?"

"Make yourself useful, Ben. Bring me up some more nails."

Ben found a box of unopened nails lying near the house's foundation. He grabbed them and mounted the ladder.

"Did you hear anything I said?" He poked his head over the edge of the roof.

"I heard." She furiously pounded two more nails into the gray shingles then tossed the used-up empty box to the ground and motioned for him to come the rest of the way up.

Ben crept across the roof to sit beside her.

"Nice place." He laid the fresh box of nails on the roof near her feet, hoping she wouldn't accidentally brain him with the hammer. "You come here often?"

Moriah slid him an angry glance, grabbed some nails, held them between her lips, and started nailing again.

Ben wasn't entirely certain he was safe up here with her so angry, so he scooted away and prepared to descend.

"Please don't go," Moriah mumbled around a mouthful of nails.

Ben contemplated the risk, then he scooted close and tried to comfort her by patting her on the back.

"You'll get used to him being around," he said. "Nicolas might even be useful. Maybe you won't have to work so hard if he's helping at the resort."

"Seriously?" Moriah spit the nails into her hand. "Can you picture Nicolas crawling underneath one of the cabins to fix the plumbing? Or unplugging a toilet? Or doing anything useful?"

"He certainly knows how to deliver a baby and rake gravel," Ben said. "You have to give him that. And he makes your aunt happy."

It really wasn't all that bad, he thought, sitting on top of a roof in Canada in the spring sunshine with a beautiful woman. She smelled faintly of sun and strawberry shampoo. Things could be worse. He could be Jack, for instance.

Speaking of which, he had good news that might cheer her up.

"I told Jack he could ride with us to church next week."

She pulled away to stare at him.

"Jack agreed to go to church?"

"Yes."

"I'm surprised. Jack's a great guy, but he hates church."

"Yes, he made that clear, but he's not a great guy, Moriah. He's an angry drunk. How long has he been like this?"

"I don't know. He used to drink when he was younger, but

when he fell in love with Alicia, that all changed. I wonder what set him off?"

"Apparently, he hasn't had a lot of work lately. He broke his promise to her, had some beer with some friends. She found out and got upset, and then he got upset. Then she left, and instead of going after her, he made the brilliant decision to binge."

"How on earth did you talk him into going to church?"

"I kind of made it a prerequisite of getting the job. Plus, I told him if he wants to work for us for the summer, I'll need proof he's going to AA every week."

"You blackmailed him into staying sober by offering a job." She laughed. "That's not fair."

"Of course, it isn't. But whatever works." Ben was silent for a moment, thinking and remembering. "Did he ever hit Alicia or the baby?"

"Not to my knowledge. Jack's more likely to take it out on things."

"What do you mean?"

"I saw him put his fist through a windshield once."

"Whose windshield?"

"His own."

"Good for him!" Ben said.

"Seriously?"

"I think Jack might be a lot like my Dad used to be," Ben said, "except Dad sometimes hit people instead of things."

Moriah caught her breath at this revelation. "Your dad hit you?"

"Sometimes." His eyes were on the horizon, remembering. "Sometimes he hit me a lot."

She turned her face toward his as the meaning of his words sunk in. "I'm sorry, Ben. I always figured you must have had a great father."

"I did. He *was* a great father eventually. But we had a pretty rough patch there for a while."

"What happened?"

"I told you about Mom dying when I was little?" He took a deep breath. "Dad didn't deal well with losing her. He couldn't get used to having me around instead of her. I think he must have started drinking, at first, to anesthetize his grief. Nicest person in the world when he was sober, but oh man, was he ever a mean drunk!"

"You're telling me the Petras I remember trying to protect me during the massacre was a mean drunk?"

"He was for at least part of my childhood. If Dad hadn't followed me into an empty church when I was trying to hide from him one Saturday night, I'd probably be ten times worse off now than Jack ever thought of being."

"But he stopped hurting you?"

"Finally. He got sober, realized what he was doing, and got help. He didn't have a choice." Ben chuckled. "The preacher threatened to whip him if he didn't."

"The *preacher* threatened him?"

"Paul Bascomb. He had a very short fuse when it came to dads who hurt their kids."

The memory washed over him, and it was as though he were there again—shivering, terrified, a little boy trying to make himself into a very small ball.

"Tell me."

Moriah's voice was so gentle; he wondered if this was the same woman who had been taking her anger out on nails a few moments earlier.

"There was an old church near our house that always kept its doors unlocked," he said. "Sometimes I would go there to hide. That's what I was doing when the new preacher found me. He saw me hiding beneath a pew, saw how terrified I was, and barely had time to process it all before Dad hit the door and came roaring in. I knew I was in for the beating of my life because, not only was Dad a mad drunk, he hated preachers and churches."

"What happened?"

"The most amazing thing. The preacher put his body between me and my dad and told him that he'd better not lay a hand on me."

"And your father listened to him?"

"Of course not. Dad loved a good fight, especially when he was drunk. He figured a preacher would be an easy knockout."

"Was he?"

"Nope." Ben grinned. "Dad had big hands, and he was very strong. I think he could have cold-cocked an elephant with those fists. He went after Brother Bascomb like an enraged bull, and even though I was just a little boy, I knew at that moment the preacher was going to die and I felt sorry for him."

"What happened?"

"Dad charged the preacher, and a second later, my dad was lying flat on his back, looking up at the ceiling."

"You're kidding!"

"Nope." Ben laughed. "Brother Bascomb had taught self-defense in the military before he became a preacher. Dad hardly knew what hit him."

"Then what?"

"After several more attempts to win the fight and several more times finding himself on his back, Dad got the message. He'd finally met a man he couldn't whip. The first, actually. Strangely enough, the respect he gained for the preacher that evening made him agree to get help. The preacher took me home to his family for a while, until Dad sobered up and made good on his promise."

"Why didn't the preacher just call Children's Aid?"

"You'd have to have known the man. It wasn't his way. He did things himself. And it worked. Dad started going to Alcoholics Anonymous, while meeting with Bascomb every week. One Sunday—I'll never forget this—I was sitting beside the preacher's wife, chewing on a stick of Juicy Fruit gum she had given me, and suddenly, here came my Dad, lumbering down the aisle. Only this time, he wasn't angry; he was sobbing. I'd never even seen him cry before. He changed his life that Sunday morning, gave it over to God, and never looked back."

"Never?"

"Nope. Not that I ever knew, and I probably would have known."

"So, there's hope for Jack?"

"There's hope for anyone."

"So how did he end up working at a clinic in the jungle?"

"He saw an article in National Geographic about a place called Machu-Pichu. That's a city famous for its ancient rock dwellings on a mountain in South America. As a stone mason, he became fascinated with the place. He wanted to study the techniques they used in ancient times. Finally, he went on a trip just to see it for himself. Kind of a reward, he said, to commemorate five years of sobriety."

"I've never heard of the place."

"A lot of people go there every year. I've been, too. I think you have to be a stonemason to truly appreciate it. Anyway, while he was there, he met a woman. She was a doctor, a missionary taking a little vacation from a clinic in the Amazon. When he called and told me about her, I was happy he had met someone. She sounded nice. My uncle had moved to the U.S., and I was living with him while Dad was away. I daydreamed that, maybe someday, Dad would bring home a mom for me."

"Did they get married?"

"No. I gathered from the letters he sent he had hopes they

would, but she thought they needed more time together before taking such a big step. When he discovered there were others on their way to help build an addition to her small clinic, he volunteered to help. It was a win-win situation, he said. More time with her, and a way to pay God back for some of his bad years. After he got sober, my dad spent his few remaining years trying to make up for all the damage he had caused."

"And now you're translating the Bible for the exact same tribe that killed your dad."

"Yes."

"I still have a hard time wrapping my mind around that. I admire what you are doing, but I don't think I have it in me to forgive to that extent."

"Let me try to explain how it feels to me." Ben pointed out toward the lake. "Do you see your lighthouse standing out there?"

"You mean Nicolas's lighthouse?" There was a hint of sarcasm in her voice.

"Right."

"Of course, I see it. I've seen it every day of my life."

"How many ships do you suppose it saved during the years it was in service?"

"Hundreds," Moriah said, "maybe thousands."

"How many lives?"

"I don't know. I'm sure there were records kept of the wrecks and the people dredged out of the water, but it would be impossible to know all the ships and people who simply sailed safely on by. Why?"

"My life as a young boy was a nightmare, Moriah. Then everything changed. A light came on in the darkness of our house, much like the light your family kept going in that light tower for so many years. God's message changed my father completely and kept us from crashing into the rocks and sinking.

It turned him from being a tortured animal that lashed out at everyone to being a man with joy and purpose. He became the father I'd dreamed of, a man who was kind to me all the time. Suddenly, I felt safe with him. More than safe. I felt *protected*. Something like that has a profound impact on a kid."

"I can understand why."

"There was one night, soon after he turned his life around, he borrowed a hymn book from the church. He sat by my bed with it and sang all the words to Amazing Grace. He had a good, deep voice. I was eight years old, and it became his nightly lullaby to me. He told me the words were talking about someone like him."

Ben stretched his hands out in front of him and flexed them.

"My father had big hands. Mine are a lot like them. I watched him take down men twice his size in bar brawls. I was so afraid of those hands. And then, suddenly, through the grace of God, those hands combed my hair and washed my face, tucked me in, and held hymnbooks so that he could sing to me at night. I was twelve when he went to South America. My uncle, with whom I lived, was a lot older than my father, and his house was gloomy, but I went to school every day the proudest kid in that school. I told everyone my dad was a missionary, and they believed me because he sent me things from Brazil that my teacher displayed on a special shelf."

"But he never came back."

"He never came back. I cried for a while after he died and begged my uncle to let me go to him. I couldn't believe he was actually gone. When I was older, I still wanted to go to him, but in a different way. I studied hard, got a degree in linguistics, and found the tribe he was working with when he died. I figured, if God's word could turn a man like him into the man he became, it could change the hearts of the people who had killed him."

"Does Nicolas know all this?"

"No. Funny thing, if Dad and his mom had lived, we probably

would have become stepbrothers. That's created a small bond between us, but I've not talked to him about my dad."

"Why not?"

"Partly because it's none of his business, partly because Nicolas is not the easiest man to talk to. I think that's one of the reasons he loves your aunt so much. They created a relationship when they were children that I don't think he's ever experienced with anyone else. He struck me as a very lonely, cold man the first time I met him. Since being here with Katherine, he's already different, happier."

"If they get married, I bet I'm going to have to live under the same roof with that man." There was sadness in Moriah's voice.

"You could come to the Yahnowa village with me, instead," he teased. "You could build me a new hut. I really need a new hut."

"What you need to do is help me finish this roof, so I'll be free to start work on the lighthouse."

"True. I'll help you. Then I need to start pulling a sermon together."

"A sermon?" Moriah asked. "Why?"

"While you were up here nailing shingles like you were killing snakes, your minister came around and asked me to speak for church next week."

"That should be interesting."

"I know." Ben said. "I can hardly wait to find out what I'm going to say."

CHAPTER 12

It had been several weeks since Moriah had been to church. It wasn't a matter of faith; it was a matter of having a business to run that took every spare minute preparing for and surviving tourist season. She was a lot better about showing up in the winter. This morning with Ben speaking, however, going to church took on a whole new significance.

She stood in front of her closet and pondered the fact that she owned nothing pretty to wear. It wasn't really that she was against nice clothes; it was just that her church had a very relaxed dress code—one that, fortunately for her, included jeans, t-shirts, and flannel shirts.

Most of the time, she didn't care all that much how she was dressed. Since she was constantly working at some sort of project, jeans, t-shirts, and flannels seemed good enough most of the time. But today, she had a yearning to wear a dress, a pretty one, something really nice that Ben would like.

Except she didn't have a pretty dress. All she had were a couple of okay ones that didn't fit all that well.

Without much hope, she reached into the back recesses of her closet and scooted all the clothes to the front.

A lone pantsuit appeared. It had been left abandoned in a closet in one of the cabins last fall. It was her size, so instead of putting it in their Lost and Found box, she'd had hung it here, ready to mail it off the minute anyone called to claim it, but thinking she might need it someday if no one contacted her about it. It had eventually gotten shoved to the back. She had forgotten all about it.

Pulling it out, she admired the rich fabric. It was a thin, creamy wool, perfect for a Sunday morning in spring. Why someone brought it along to a fishing camp, she had no idea. People did the strangest things, but she was grateful.

Then she slipped it on. The slacks fit well. The short jacket nipped in a little too much at the waist, but it would do. She carefully laid the jacket and slacks on her bed.

Rarely did she do anything with her straight hair, except wash and trim it with her aunt's sewing scissors. But this morning, she pulled it on top of her head, securing it with a ponytail holder.

There was a curling iron in her room she had experimented with a couple times and then abandoned as a waste of time. This morning, she heated it and attempted to create a cascade of tendrils like she had seen in a magazine. If her new hairstyle didn't turn out well, she figured she could always put it back in a braid.

She had never felt the need for much makeup, but she did have some lipstick she used on rare occasions. Carefully, she applied it on her lips, then rubbed just a little on both cheeks.

She put on her black dress flats, buttoned the jacket, and hurried down the hall to the bathroom, where there was a full-length mirror.

The image that greeted her was nothing like what she had

hoped for. The black shoes looked awful with the pantsuit, the jacket was definitely too tight, and her hair simply wasn't going to work. It was too straight to stay in curls. She had been kidding herself even to try.

She trudged back to her bedroom, kicked off the black flats, and ripped the fastener from her hair. She unbuttoned the jacket and sat, dejected, on the side of the bed, contemplating her short fingernails and calloused hands. There was nothing she could do about them now.

This was what she got for telling herself she had too much work to do to care about her appearance. She couldn't even look nice when she really wanted to!

Ben would be here to pick her up for church in a half-hour, so she had to do something fast. She attacked her hair again and brushed it out straight. Maybe she would try something different. She pulled it into a low ponytail, and with great concentration and many bobby pins, she managed to fashion it into a semblance of a chignon.

There was an apricot-colored tank top she sometimes wore beneath her flannel shirts, so she put it on, then slipped the jacket over it, leaving it open. She checked the mirror in the bathroom again. Not too bad. She used a hand mirror to check the chignon. Actually, not bad at all. Kind of classy, actually.

Feeling a little better about things, she tried to figure out what to do about shoes. If only she had some that were a little fancier and a lighter color.

She thought back to the Lost and Found box. It was kept in the corner of the great room downstairs. She vaguely remembered a pair of light-colored low-heeled sandals being stored there.

Running down the stairs in her bare feet, she dug through the box, creating a pile of discarded games, books, clothes, shoes, bathing suits, goggles, sunglasses and... a pair of strappy, cream-colored sandals with a low heel. They were beautiful. And only a half-size too big.

"Please, God," she breathed and tried them on. She took a couple hesitant steps in her borrowed shoes and heard a low, heartfelt whistle.

"You look beautiful," Ben said.

Moriah whirled around and stifled a gasp. Ben was dressed for church, and Ben dressed up for church was something worth seeing.

He wore a white shirt, open at the throat, a dark charcoal tweed jacket, and light gray dress pants. There was something else different about him. She blinked.

"When did you get a haircut?"

"Yesterday evening. I found a barber in town. I was starting to scare myself when I looked in a mirror. I thought the people at church would prefer their speaker not to look like a wild man."

Moriah swallowed. "It's a nice haircut."

It was a great haircut. She could hardly believe the transformation.

"Are you ready, Moriah?" Katherine called from the top of the stairs. She was wearing a khaki shirtdress and was intent on fastening her watch. When she got it fastened, she looked up, stopped, and stared.

"What?" Moriah asked, defensively.

"I don't remember seeing you so dressed up for church before. Isn't that the outfit you found in Cabin Three's closet last summer?"

Moriah had always loved her aunt. She had always respected her aunt. But right now, at this moment, she wanted to strangle her aunt. Did Katherine *have* to tell Ben she had dressed in a guest's leftovers?

Ben turned to Moriah with a beatific smile. "You dressed up

just for me?"

"No." Moriah raised her chin and shot a rebellious, hot glance at her aunt. "I just like to look nice once in a while."

Ben's smile faded a shade, but he made an effort to be gallant. "Looks like I'll be escorting the two most beautiful women on the island to church this morning."

"Correction. You'll be escorting one of the most beautiful women on the island to church this morning." Nicolas breezed through the door. He wore a black suit with a red-and-black striped tie and looked, to Moriah, like a lawyer ready to try a case, instead of a retired doctor or any man she had ever seen enter the door of their laid-back church. Nicolas was definitely going to stand out against the rumpled, casual clothing of the tourists and islanders who would be attending this morning.

"Kathy, my dear." Nicolas held out his arm as her aunt joined them. "Shall we go?"

"I'm sorry," Katherine whispered as she passed Moriah. "I should have thought before I said anything."

Moriah didn't have a chance to reply. As soon as Katherine put her hand inside the crook of Nicolas's arm, he led her out to the shiny, black Mercedes he had driven back from Toronto. Moriah watched as he opened the passenger side, tucked "Kathy" in, and closed the door after her.

Katherine didn't even look back as he whisked her away. It was the first time in twenty years Moriah and her aunt had not gone to church together.

"I noticed your aunt is not wearing buckskin today," Ben observed.

"Do you think Nicolas will change her too much?"

"For a while, maybe," Ben answered. "I don't think anyone can change someone else all that much, unless they want to be changed, especially someone your aunt's age."

"Katherine's only in her forties."

"Nicolas is robbing the cradle."

"That's not funny."

"Actually, it is." Ben stuck out his elbow in a parody of Nicolas. "Moriah, my dear, shall we go? It would appear that Nicolas and Katherine have forgotten us."

Moriah suppressed a giggle as Ben ushered her, with exaggerated self-importance, out to the resort truck. He opened the passenger door, removed a white handkerchief from his pocket with a flourish, laid it on the seat for her to sit on, and then closed the door

"Let Katherine have her day in the sun, Moriah," he said as he threw the truck into reverse. "Nothing you can say is going to make her stop caring about Nicolas, so you may as well try to enjoy her happiness."

CHAPTER 13

When Ben pulled up in front of Jack's door, Moriah could barely believe her eyes. Jack was waiting for them, sitting on the steps of his house. He had on clean jeans and a pressed blue dress shirt. His wet, blonde hair still held the tracks of a comb.

Moriah scooted over, carefully dragging the handkerchief along beneath her. She hadn't thought, when she had donned the light-colored pantsuit, how dirty her truck might be. The last thing she wanted was to parade up the aisle in front of Ben with dirt stains on her backside. She eyed Jack's jeans enviously. Denim was so much less trouble.

Jack filled so much of the cab, she was forced to move close to Ben, which wasn't exactly a hardship. She enjoyed the intimacy of being pressed shoulder to shoulder with him. Briefly, she wondered if it were possible to become addicted to a scent. Ben always smelled of soap and sunshine, she analyzed, but there was that touch of spice there, too, something that made her think of jungles and exotic places.

"I appreciate you coming with us." Ben pulled back out onto the road.

"I had to think about it." Jack gazed out the side window, his head turned away from Moriah. "I only have to go to church twice to get the job, right?"

"That was the deal," Ben said, "plus, AA once a week all summer."

"I suppose going to church twice won't kill me."

"Hasn't killed me yet," Ben said.

They lapsed into silence the short distance to the church.

Moriah felt extremely self-conscious strolling in with the two men. Katherine was sitting with Nicolas in an entirely different place than usual. Since the church was already filling up, Moriah had to proceed almost to the front with Ben and Jack before they found a pew with enough room to accommodate the three of them.

She sat down and scooted over, while Ben ushered Jack in beside her and then chose the aisle seat. She didn't know if he was trying to make it easier to get up and go to the pulpit, or if he was trying to make certain that Jack didn't bolt.

"Ebenezer!" Howard Barrister, their preacher, had worked his way down the aisle greeting people. Now, he materialized beside them and pumped Ben's hand. "How's that truck running?"

"Fine. Thanks again for the use of your garage and tools."

"Hello, Moriah." The preacher nodded at her. "I couldn't believe it when Dr. Ebenezer McCain arrived at my doorstep. I've been following his work for several years. Fascinating. You and Katherine must be thrilled to have such a celebrity as a guest. And Jack Thompson, you are certainly a sight for sore eyes. Hope you enjoy the services."

As the preacher worked his way through the congregation greeting people, Moriah leaned forward and looked across Jack at Ben.

"Doctor?" she asked. "What's he talking about?"

Ben had the grace to look uncomfortable. "Just a Ph.D. in Linguistics. It's no big deal."

"You have a Ph.D. in Linguistics? Why didn't you tell me?"

Ben shrugged. "It never came up."

"Anything else you haven't told me?"

"I also have a Ph.D. in Biblical studies." Ben shrugged. "Sorry. School came easy for me, and I like to learn."

Services began with a prayer, and Moriah bowed her head, thoughts still whirling, trying to assimilate everything she had learned recently. First of all, with the exception of Jack, she seemed to be completely surrounded by people much more educated than her. Ben held a PhD, Nicolas was an M.D., and even Katherine had gone to medical school. All Moriah possessed in the way of formal education was a high school diploma and a certificate in carpentry from the local vocational school.

The prayer ended. She stared down at her hands, rubbing at her callouses, then she hid her hands beneath her thighs.

Jack glanced over and saw her hiding her hands—something he had chided her about since way back in high school. He pulled one work-worn hand out from under her thigh, held it in his, and gently smoothed out her fingers. Then he put her hand back onto her lap, patted it, and whispered, "Don't let it shake you—you're worth ten of him."

She straightened her shoulders, and folded her hands on her lap. Jack was right. She might not be worth ten of anyone, but she had come by those calluses honestly. No one could ever say she didn't work hard.

"We have a special guest with us this morning," Howard announced. "Dr. Ebenezer McCain is presently working on a translation for a tribe in the Amazon jungle. He'll be visiting our island for the summer. Would you care to say a few words to us now, Dr. McCain?"

Ben glanced apologetically at Moriah and then slowly got to his feet. There was a rustle in the church as the congregation settled, expectant and eager to hear someone new.

"The Yahnowa are historically a warrior tribe," Ben began.

With sinking heart, Moriah watched Ben turn into someone she didn't know.

His fine, deep voice rang with assurance. She saw people leaning forward as though to catch every word.

"In the recent past, Yahnowa manhood has been determined by kills. The worst thing a man could be called, the vilest cut he could be given, was to be called a 'no man killer'. Killing was their mark of masculinity, their recreation, their social status, and their life. We don't know how many tribes have become extinct throughout the ages solely because of intertribal warfare. This has begun to change, thanks, in part, to missionary efforts. Violet and Abraham Smith, a retired couple in their seventies, have worked with our tribe for many years. They were there when I arrived and have been instrumental in bringing about what peace exists in that area. The Yahnowa tribes are relieved by these changes. Like us, they prefer to live their lives and raise their children in peace."

Moriah found herself mesmerized, along with the rest of the congregation, by Ben's description of the living conditions of the people with whom he worked. One part of her listened, while another watched the man. Gone was the hesitancy she sometimes heard in his voice. Gone was the awkwardness he had often exhibited around her.

"But there are other concerns for these people of the rain forest. The greatest challenges today are the rapid deforestation by lumbering companies, the slash and burn farming practices, illegal gold miners, and the devastation brought by western disease—to which many of the more isolated tribes have no immunity."

"My personal efforts are a two-pronged approach. I am translating the New Testament into their language because I am convinced that the true applications of the teachings of Jesus can affect everything from marital relationships to intertribal friendships for the better. As I've become fluent in the Yahnowa language, I'm teaching the people, not only how to read and write their own spoken language, but how to communicate in the other languages with which they are surrounded, primarily Portuguese, Spanish, and English."

As he expressed his passion for the Yahnowa, he turned into a gifted speaker. It was obvious he loved the people with whom he worked.

"These Amazonian tribes survive by hunting, gathering, and gardening. The women tend gardens, where they grow as many as sixty crops. They also collect nuts, shellfish, and insect larvae. Wild honey is highly prized and the Yahnowa harvest fifteen different kinds. Men, women, and children all love to fish. Nutritionally, many of them have a better diet than we do. Although people think of them as primitive, much of their culture is enviable. For instance, no hunter ever eats the meat he has killed. Instead, he shares it among his friends and family. If he eats meat at all, it will be that which has been given to him from the kill of another hunter."

It was fascinating, but Moriah felt her heart drop with each sentence. Even though she had only known Ben for a short while, she had begun to daydream that he might choose to stay on the island after the lighthouse was finished. The jungles of Brazil had seemed far away, mystical, invisible, and therefore nonexistent. They seemed as unreal as the place names on the giant globe she kept in her room.

Ben leaned forward in his borrowed pulpit. "They have a

huge botanical knowledge and use about five hundred different plants for food, medicine, and for building shelters. All of this is threatened by the factors I mentioned earlier. It is my belief that one way my skills can help them survive is to equip as many leaders of the Yahnowa as possible with the ability to communicate with government officials. My hope is to help them have a voice."

She had been so focused on the drama of the recent events in her own life she hadn't even begun to grasp the reality of his. This was not a man who would be content to live on this island, just as Nicolas had not been willing to give up his own freedom twenty years ago.

Her mind drifted back to the day on the roof when Ben had invited her to come to Brazil with him. They both knew he was joking, but she also knew he liked her. There was a spark between them she had never experienced before with any man. She also knew someone Ben's age needed a wife and was probably looking for one, but now, listening to him speak of his life's work, Moriah knew it couldn't be her. Unless...

Maybe she would try again. Maybe something within her had changed. Maybe knowing the truth about what she had been through as a child and understanding the reason behind the trauma would help her heal.

Unfortunately, crossing the bridge to the mainland was only part of the problem. She might manage to cross it, but could she ever get to the point she could also continue on to an airport, board a plane, fly to another country, live in such an alien environment?

No. She couldn't. The very thought of such a challenge made her chest hurt. Just the thought of it was enough to make her feel the beginnings of a panic attack. It was impossible. She could never do it.

Deliberately, like a surgeon incising a tumor, she cut away the fledgling thought of ever traveling with this remarkable man.

Ben finished his talk about his work with the Yahnowa and then sat down.

"Thank you, Dr. McCain," the preacher said. "That was very enlightening. Now, church, I think we need to pass the basket for a contribution to help him with his work…"

"Excuse me." Ben stood up. "That's very kind of you but no. The Yahnowa are not impoverished. They don't need western money. They have created what they need from the forest for hundreds of years."

"But you must need help with your own expenses," Howard said.

"Not really. I make more than enough to support myself." Ben sat down then stood up again. "I appreciate the thought, though, and thank you for the opportunity to speak."

"Will wonders never cease," Jack whispered to Moriah. "I like this guy, even if he did nearly drown me in my own shower."

"I think it's time to go," Ben said, jolting her out of her reverie after the church had sung a final hymn. She glanced around and saw people gathering their things and getting ready to go. A buzz of conversation filled the air.

Moriah dreaded working her way through the crowd today. Usually, she enjoyed talking to her friends, most of whom she had known since childhood. This morning, however, she didn't think she could carry on a lucid conversation with anyone. Ben was much more important than she'd ever dreamed. He was so far out of her league she could hardly believe he had been spending time with her. Already, he'd been taken over by a cluster of women from the church. Three of them were unmarried. Moriah averted her eyes.

Ben didn't belong to her, and he never would. It was time to toss that little daydream right out the window.

A lovely brunette made her way toward them, balancing a baby on her hip. Moriah snapped out of her emotional fog the minute she saw who it was.

"Hi," Alicia handed Jack the little girl. "Betsy has missed you."

Jack caught his daughter in his arms and nuzzled her neck. "I've missed her, too. And you." His voice caught.

Jack and Alicia had been in love with one another since high school. Moriah knew this as a fact. She had been there and watched. To think these two were having marital troubles was beyond sad.

"I'm surprised to see you here." Alicia fingered the lacy hem of her daughter's dress. "You never came when I asked."

Moriah waited for Jack to explain. When he didn't say anything, she felt compelled to step in. "We have this job for Jack over at the lighthouse and…"

Jack shot her a warning glance, and she stopped in mid-sentence.

"I'm sorry, Alicia," Jack said. "I should have come a long time ago, when you first asked me." He touched the brim of the tiny sunbonnet his daughter was wearing and rubbed a knuckle over her pink little cheek. "Can you trust me enough to start over?"

Moriah beamed at the couple.

"You'll stop drinking?" Alicia asked.

"I already have."

"Not a drop?"

"Not a drop, at least not since last week."

"You'll come to church with me?"

"It's not as bad as I expected."

"It's been really hard living with my mom, Jack." Alicia sighed with relief. "She's so bossy. I want my own husband and my own house and my own kitchen and my own stuff."

"About your stuff…" Moriah began. She was silenced, once again, by a look from Jack.

"Let's go home, Alicia." He turned to Moriah, dismissing her. "I'll see you Monday morning. Ben tells me we have a road to clear."

Moriah watched the tiny pink sunbonnet peeking over Jack's shoulder as the couple walked away. She couldn't help but smile when she heard Jack say, "About your kitchen, Alicia..."

"Are you ready to go?" Ben touched her arm.

"I guess so." Moriah was surprised he had extricated himself from the gaggle of women so quickly.

"Do you think we could go out the back way?" He eyed the crowd between them and the front door. "I don't want to turn down any more lunch invitations."

"You don't have to turn them down."

"Yes, I do."

"Why?"

"Because I want to have lunch with you." He steered her past the pulpit and out the back door. "Someone told me there's a really good restaurant in Little Current."

"We could go back to the lodge. Katherine usually puts a pot roast in the oven on Sunday mornings."

"You're looking forward to having lunch with Nicolas?"

"Good point. Lunch in Little Current sounds lovely. Nicolas and 'Kathy' would rather be alone, anyway."

"They do have wedding plans to make."

Moriah grimaced. "Don't remind me."

CHAPTER 14

B en had never felt prouder than he did standing beside
Moriah as they waited in line at the old Anchor Inn Hotel
in Little Current. The delicious aromas wafting in from the
kitchen made him happy he was hungry. He couldn't wait to try
whatever the special was today.

He loved the way Moriah had done her hair. Two wisps had
escaped their pins on the drive here, and he was entranced as he
stood behind her. The wisps danced upon her neck, moved
about by a stray current of air.

This was the closest thing they'd had to a true date, and he
was thrilled she had accepted. He was also happy Jack had gone
home with Alicia, so he didn't have to share Moriah with anyone
today. All in all, it had been a great day, so far.

He wondered if he might keep her out all afternoon—maybe
a trip to the other side of the island, a walk along the far beach. It
would be nice to stroll along the beach with her.

He had noticed the way she had looked at him while he was
in the pulpit. He might be an amateur with women, but he would

bet his new fishing rod that those green eyes gazing up at him were interested in more than just the information he was giving the people about the Yahnowa.

It was amazing that a woman like her would be interested in him, but he was pretty sure the signs were there. And, the best part of it all was that he had an entire summer to explore a relationship with her. He had high hopes she would be able to beat her problem about leaving the island. She was such a strong person. Certainly, she would be able to overcome such a little thing as driving over a bridge, especially now that she knew the reasons behind her phobia.

Ben was flooded with a sense of well-being as they waited for their table.

A young man with a bad complexion, a tattoo on each arm, and two small rings piercing his left eyebrow, stepped up to wait upon them. The piercings he sported didn't faze Ben. He had seen more impressive ones with the Yahnowa. He briefly pictured the boy decorated in paint and carrying a spear, and he chuckled. In spite of this boy's dangerous appearance, he would starve to death in the jungle if he didn't get eaten alive first.

"How many?" the young waiter asked, fingering his eyebrow ring as though to reassure himself it was still there.

Ben had seen the same gesture with Yahnowa, when the piercings were new and they had much on their mind. People were surprisingly the same, he had discovered, no matter where they lived. "Two." He drew out the word, savoring the taste of it on his tongue.

Two was such a nice number, he thought, as they followed the waiter to a small table beside a window overlooking the channel separating Manitoulin Island from the mainland.

Two was so much nicer than the number one. Not as nice as the number three, if the third was a little daughter or son. He felt a stab of envy thinking about Jack ambling out of church with that doll-baby of a little girl in his arms.

There were seasons in a man's life, Ben mused, as the waiter laid the menus on their table. Right now, he was in the season of wanting a family. For the past few years, even before meeting Moriah, he had yearned for a wife and child but had prepared himself to wait until the translation work was finished. Now, he wasn't at all sure he was willing to wait that long.

The waiter surprised Ben by gallantly drawing out Moriah's seat. Ben frowned. He had wanted to do that, and he doubted this particular waiter was always so solicitous. It was Moriah. She was beautiful, and her beauty wasn't lost on the waiter.

After they had been seated, she studiously scanned her menu while he studied her. Moriah's creamy, light-brown skin was flawless. Not one single freckle marred it, unlike him. The only way he could ever match Moriah's color was if all his freckles ran together.

Her hair, pulled back like it was, showed off the delicacy of her features. He flashed back to that moment, the first day, when he had brushed the dirt from her face while she was unconscious. She had the velvetiest skin he had ever touched.

Her lashes made delicate black fans on her cheeks as she gazed down, her fingers splayed, balancing the large menu. He loved her hands. They were so skilled, so competent. In the short time he had known her, he had seen them do everything from bait a hook to shingle a roof to cradle protectively a minutes-old baby. He would trust his life to those hands.

Moriah's eyes flicked toward the window, then she resolutely studied the menu again.

She glanced out the window again, realized he was watching, quickly closed the menu and laid it down.

"You ready?" The waiter materialized beside them with a stubby, yellow pencil poised over the order pad.

"I'll have the butter chicken," Moriah said. "What will you be having... Dr. McCain."

He gave his order. Another specialty. Pork chops with blueberry sauce. The waiter disappeared.

"I told you," he said. "School came easy for me, especially languages. Having a couple doctorates isn't that big of a deal."

"I think it is a very big deal. My guess is that you worked harder than you let on. It couldn't have been easy." She folded her napkin into tiny pleats, still darting quick glances out the window.

"Of course, I worked. I had nothing else to do but work. My uncle died while I was still in undergraduate school. I had no family. All I had was a trade that paid a good wage and a goal."

"I'm proud of you for what you've accomplished." She smoothed her napkin onto her lap and stared out the window again, preoccupied with something outside. Ben wondered what it was she found so fascinating. There was nothing out there, except water and the bridge that connected the island to the mainland.

"Building a cabin from scratch and keeping a resort going is a pretty big deal, too," he said. "You've done that. You're an amazing woman, Moriah."

Once again, she simply stared out the window. Then suddenly, when he began to think she hadn't heard him, she faced him. "Do you see that bridge out there?"

He looked at the massive black iron structure. It looked like it had been built a hundred years ago, when sheer weight and mass equaled strength.

"I came across it when I arrived," Ben said. "Of course, I see it. Is that the one that has given you so much trouble?"

"I really can't cross it. A few months ago, I tried. Again."

"And?"

"Each time I try, my heart pounds so hard it feels like it's going to explode out of my body. My chest hurts. I can actually hear my heart beating inside my head. My body goes hot then cold. My legs and arms go numb. I can't get enough oxygen. It feels like—it feels like I'm dying."

"I'm sorry, Moriah." And he was sorry, but he simply could not imagine not being able to leave the island. Surely, there was some way for her to leave. If he were the one with the problem, he knew he would figure something out. "What about the ferry?"

"There is a long gangplank you have to cross to get on and off the Chi-Cheemaun. That's even worse because it's much narrower, and it sways and clanks. I've tried. It was really a lot of fun freezing on that gangplank in front of everyone. People behind me were waiting for me to move. Two men had to help carry me off because I was hyperventilating. No thanks. I won't be going through that again in this lifetime."

"Couldn't you just take your little fishing boat across?"

"Lake Huron is too dangerous to cross in a small boat, but I've taken it across here, at Little Current, beside the bridge. Do you know what's on the other side of the Little Current Bridge? Goat Island. Do you know what's on Goat Island? Not much. Do you know what's on the other side of Goat Island? Another bridge. And another island. And another bridge until eventually you arrive on the mainland, where, presumably, there will be more bridges. I don't do bridges, Ben. And the world outside Manitoulin Island is full of them. If we're going to be friends, it's only fair that you understand something—I really can't leave this island."

"I wish I could think of some way to help you."

"I wish I could think of some way to help me, too," Moriah said.

"Want to go try to drive across the bridge again?" Ben said. "Maybe it would be different with me cheering you on."

"It's not a baseball game. Having a cheerleader isn't my problem."

"Will you at least try?" Ben asked. "Maybe after we eat?"

"Okay." She sighed. "I'll try. But don't expect a miracle. I've tried so many times."

CHAPTER 15

K atherine and Nicolas were not at the lodge when Moriah
and Ben came home. She was grateful for that. Her
attempt to cross the bridge had been disastrous. The minute they
got home, Ben went straight to his cabin with a headache. She
ran upstairs to her room, relieved not to have to deal with
anyone after what had just happened.

She took off her pretty pantsuit, angrily kicked it into a
corner, and then flopped onto her bed. She would never wear
that silly outfit again. It would forever remind her of the
moment she had resolved to give up any hopes of a future with
Ben or anyone else who might want to live someplace other than
Manitoulin Island.

The chignon bothered her. The hairpins pricked her scalp.
She sat up again, plucked the hairpins from her chignon, and
shook her hair out. How foolish she had been to try to look
pretty this morning!

From now on, she would be the handyman and caretaker of
Robertson's Resort. That's all. It was a good life. It was her life. It
was the best life she could expect.

There was something wrong with her, and she didn't know how to fix it. The best thing she could do was cope the best way possible, just like she'd done her whole life.

Her attempt to cross the bridge after lunch with Ben had been ill-timed. By the time they drove to the bridge, it was almost two o'clock. That wouldn't have mattered for any other bridge in the world, except for the one at Little Current.

It was a swing bridge connecting the island with the mainland. It was old and built low. Many boats could not sail beneath it. So, every hour on the hour, during daylight, the bridge would swing a full fifteen degrees. Then it would stay like that for fifteen minutes so boats could pass through.

She and Ben got there just as the bridge began its slow movement out over the water. It didn't stop until it was completely parallel with the island.

They were the first in line to cross when it came back into position to accommodate the highway again, so she was treated to a front row seat of watching the heavy bridge move.

She had been geared up to try very hard not to disappoint Ben. The poor man was trying to help. But the longer she waited and watched, the worse her anxiety grew. Within the first five minutes of watching boats pass in front of them, she went into a full-fledged panic attack, which involved her begging him to get her away from there. It was difficult for him because there was a long line of cars backed up behind them. He had to maneuver the truck around while cars honked, and she went into a complete meltdown, crying and fighting for breath.

So very attractive. He'd probably make sure to avoid her for the rest of the summer.

Why did she have to be this way? When she knew absolutely there was no danger, why did her body keep reacting like someone was waiting to kill her if she set foot off Manitoulin Island?

As she lay there, another bit of memory floated to the surface for the first time...

"Quiet, little one," Karyona's daddy said. His hand was still held firmly over her mouth. "Quiet like a little mouse."

Moriah was glad Akawe was holding her because she knew Mommy and Daddy trusted him. She was scared, but she trusted Akawe, too. Karyona's big brother, Rashawe, crouched as still and as deadly as a young panther in front of the door.

The screams stopped, and the five of them listened. Moriah knew Akawe wouldn't let her go to her mommy now. Even in her child's heart, she knew it was too late.

They sat like that for hours or, at least, it seemed like hours. As morning dawned, the villagers ventured out to see what was left of the clinic and the people, but Moriah was not allowed to go outside. Instead, the village elders crept to Akawe's hut, staring at Moriah as though she was a rare and unwelcome animal.

Moriah understood enough of the words they used to know the young warriors from Chief Moawa's tribe had killed all the white people at the clinic. Every last one of them were gone, except for her. Now, the village elders were discussing what to do with her.

Napognuma pulled Moriah away from Akawe, onto her lap, and nervously braided her hair while the elders discussed what to do. Karyona leaned against her mother's side and tightly grasped Moriah's hand.

"Little Green Eyes cannot stay," an elder said. "Chief Moawa hates the Jesus worshippers, and his tribe is more powerful than ours. He has many warriors, and we have few. He'll come for her when he hears a white child survived. There is danger for us if we keep her."

"This is true," Akawe said. "I have thought about this through the night. I think she should be taken to the convent school many mountains from here. The people there will know what to do with her."

"It is a very long way," the same elder pointed out, "and there are many dangers."

"I will have Rashawe." Akawe glanced proudly at his son, who stood silently, respectfully, near the doorway. "We will go together."

The elders nodded in agreement. "This is a good plan. Go swiftly. Before Chief Moawa remembers and returns to search for her."

When the village elders left, Napognuma bound Moriah tightly to Akawe's shoulders with strips of cloth. Then she handed him his spear and a parcel of boiled manioc.

"May our God go with you, my husband, and with you, little one." She kissed Moriah on the forehead as Akawe opened the door.

With Rashawe close behind him, Akawe started on a mile-eating trot through the forest that surrounded the village. Moriah glanced back at the charred clinic from which her parent's bodies had mercifully been removed. Her last memory of the village was seeing Karyona clinging to her mother's legs while they both waved good-bye.

The pain of remembering was too great. Moriah purposely shut it down. Was this the way things were going to be from this point on? Random, miserable, memories floating to the top, unbidden?

"Why do I have to be like this?" Moriah gritted her teeth against the emotional pain, the humiliations, the anger, all the disappointments. She jumped up from the bed and strode over to the giant globe and gave it a vicious spin. "Why can't I just be normal!"

CHAPTER 16

E arly the following day, Ben heard Jack coming long before he saw him. He heard the chug and rhythmic metallic thump of the bulldozer as it made its way down the road.

"Why didn't you use a trailer?" Ben shouted, when Jack rolled into the lodge's parking lot.

"It's got a flat. Figured it would be easier just to drive ol' Boss Hog on down here. It's not that far." Jack set the dozer's motor to a huffing idle, climbed out onto its metal tracks, then leaped down to the ground.

"You're ready to start?" Jack asked.

"Absolutely," Ben said. "Looks like you are, too. Doing okay?"

Jack smiled, white teeth lighting up a tanned face. "I'm still sober, if that's what you meant."

"That's what I meant. How are Alicia and the baby?"

"She's buying new dishes today," Jack admitted. "I spent a big part of last night doing the final clean up. We're going to be okay. We have to be. I won't lose my wife and baby girl again. Once was enough."

Ben appraised the handsome giant. Today, by the grace of God, Jack was sober. Now to keep him that way. He would pray, of course, but he knew work was especially valuable when a man had private demons to fight. Many times, he'd seen good pay attached to honest labor go a long way toward getting a person back on track.

"You can tell where the old road bed is, right?" Ben shaded his eyes with both hands as he scanned the line of new growth trees. The sun was bright through the early morning mist.

"I've lived here my whole life, Ben. I know exactly where the road bed is."

"Do I need to get a chainsaw crew in there first?"

"Nope. Boss Hog and me can move everything out of the way, no problem." Jack patted the huge dozer affectionately. "In two days, you'll be driving over a road so smooth you'll think you're driving on silk."

"As long as we can get through." Ben wasn't impressed with Jack's boasting. In fact, he considered it a bad sign. Men who truly did good work didn't have to brag about it; they let the work speak for itself.

Jack mounted his dozer, pulled it out of idle, and then roared off toward the mouth of the old roadbed, which lay at a right angle to the resort's private driveway.

The two properties were so linked it was probably just as well Nicolas and Katherine were going to get married. Otherwise, there could be some major property disputes.

As Jack began to cut a swath through the scrubby pines, Ben went in search of Moriah to make sure she'd made it through the night okay. He was upset with himself for trying to talk her into crossing the bridge yesterday. How arrogant he had been, as though being with him would provide some sort of magic elixir that would make it possible. Watching her experience a full-scale panic attack had been disturbing, but it had also convinced him her pain was real. As silly as her phobia had seemed to him at first, Moriah wasn't playing games. Her fear of leaving her island went deep.

CHAPTER 17

He found Moriah and Katherine standing on the path in front of Cabin One. They were watching a pair of new running shoes attached to skinny, denim-clad legs, which were sticking out from a hole in the foundation.

"The snake man from the reservation is here." Moriah said, staring intently at the running shoes. "He just now crawled in after them. The only tools he has with him are a pair of gloves and a gunny sack. He's my new hero."

"Shhh," Katherine said.

A high-pitched quivery singsong wafted out from beneath the cabin.

"That must be a native snake-charming song he's using." Moriah's voice was filled with awe.

As Ben listened to the chant, he thought it sounded strangely like "Achy Breaky Heart." At least it did to him, but he was no judge of First Nation snake songs.

The shoes slowly emerged, then the legs and body of a tall, slender man. He wore a red cowboy shirt tucked into faded blue jeans. His hair was white and hung in two long, thin braids. Deep wrinkles creased his cheeks, and intelligent, brown eyes looked out from deeply recessed sockets. His running shoes were at odds with the rest of him. They were obviously new and expensive-looking

"It was a small den. There were only eight," the snake man said, holding a squirming burlap bag in his leather-gloved hands.

"Eight?" Moriah moved several feet away from the writhing sack. "There were *eight?*"

"Sam Black Hawk." The old man drew off one glove with his teeth and reached out to shake Ben's hand.

"Ebenezer McCain." Ben was surprised by the strength of the man's grip. "Thanks for taking care of the snake problem."

"These? These snakes are not a 'problem.' They are beautiful specimens. In fact, two of the females are gravid."

"Gravid?" Moriah hugged herself, nervously rubbing her arms with her hands.

"Filled with young."

"You mean we almost had baby snakes?" Moriah edged a couple more feet away from the sack.

"In a few weeks, yes. There could have been as many as forty young beneath your cabin. Of course, they would not have all stayed there. They have to hunt to live, and there are not enough mice under one cabin to support such a large community of reptiles."

"Thank goodness you came!" Moriah danced in place as though in a hurry to leave. "I'll go get the checkbook. How much do we owe you?"

"Are you all right, Sam?" Katherine looked closely at the old Ojibwa. "They didn't strike at you, did they?"

"Today is the exact right temperature for capturing Massasaugas. Cool enough to make them slow and sluggish, not cold enough for them to go back underground. The pregnant ones, they cannot move so fast, anyway. Do you want to see?"

"No. No. That's okay," Moriah protested.

"But they are beautiful." Black Hawk slipped his leather glove back on and opened the mouth of the sack. His hand darted in and came out grasping a writhing snake just behind the head. "Here, hold this." He handed the bag to Ben. "Do not hold it against your body, though," he warned, "or lay it on the ground."

Ben held the sack carefully at arm's length. He wasn't particularly afraid of snakes—it would be impossible to make a living as a stonemason and be too fearful of the creatures that so frequently lay beneath the stones. But he wasn't particularly fond of them, either.

"You have a terror of rattlers?" The old man focused on Moriah.

"I *hate* snakes!" Moriah admitted. "I don't know why God ever made them in the first place."

"I do not pretend to know the mind of God," the old man said, "but I know this—he made them with great care. Come closer, daughter. I will hold this little mother-snake carefully so she cannot bite. Let me show you this miracle God made."

Ben's arm was already getting tired holding the bag straight out from his body. Who would have guessed a few rattlers would be so heavy? Gingerly, he switched arms as Moriah carefully approached the old man.

"That is good. You are a brave woman to fight your fear," Sam said, "and a wise one to keep your wits about you and to crawl so slowly away when you were under the cabin. A rattler will not strike at body heat that moves slowly. It is used to prey that runs away quickly. Moving slowly confuses it."

As though mesmerized, Moriah crept a few inches closer to Black Hawk as he held the snake's head firmly in his gloved hand, supporting the rest of it with the other. Over two feet of snake stretched between the man's gloved hands.

"You should touch this little snake now," Black Hawk said.

"Touch it while you're completely safe, and let your fear leave you."

"I don't think I can." Moriah's hands were jammed deep into her pockets.

"Some people think snakes are slimy, but they are wrong. The skins are smooth and dry. It will feel like satin beneath your fingertips, and you will carry that feeling with you the rest of your life. It will help take away some of the fear."

Ben watched as Moriah visibly struggled with herself. She was trembling as she slowly stretched out her hand—then jerked it back as though from a burning coal. She took a deep breath, reached out a second and third time, quickly yanking her hand back before touching the snake.

"You can do this, daughter," the old man said. Once again, he began to sing softly the wild, high-pitched song that had drifted earlier from beneath the cabin.

Whether or not it affected the snake, Ben would never know, but it seemed to give Moriah heart. She reached out a steady hand this time and touched the snake without jerking back. She stroked it. Once. Twice.

"Look at her face, daughter; see the little black mask she wears across her eyes? She is trying to fool you into thinking she is a robber, a bandit. She thinks she is fearsome, wearing this mask. But she is only a little mother-to-be, who is hungry and wishing this old man would let her loose, so she could go running into the grass to find a nice fat mouse to fill her belly."

"She does feel like satin." Moriah smiled hesitantly up at Black Hawk.

"Would you like to hold her? I can show you how, so she cannot bite."

Moriah jammed her hands deep into her pockets and took two steps backward. "Nope. I think that's all I'll do today."

"You have done well. Now that you have seen a Massasauga

up close, you will never have to be afraid of any other snake you see on Manitoulin."

"Why not?"

"Because the Massasauga is the only one on our island with venom. All the others are harmless. You may play with them if you want."

"I don't think I'll be playing with snakes any time in the near future," Moriah said, her hands now twined behind her back.

"That is just as well, because they are shy animals who prefer to be left alone."

"What will you do with these?" Katherine asked.

"They are very territorial, so I must take them far away to keep them from returning. I will take them by boat over to Lonely Island. There are so many Massasaugas on that island eight more will not make a difference."

He deftly thrust the snake into the sack Ben held, then quickly closed and twisted the neck.

"Would you mind carrying this to my truck, my son?" Black Hawk asked. "It is a long way for an old man to walk with a heavy sack."

"Of course, I'll be happy to help."

"What do I owe you?" Moriah asked. "I want to pay."

"For *your* family? Nothing. You have done much for us already. It is good to give something back."

"Thank you," Katherine said, "more than you can ever know."

Ben watched Moriah and Katherine chatting together as they walked back to the lodge. Moriah didn't seem to be too traumatized by her meltdown yesterday, and he was relieved.

He turned back to Black Hawk, who'd pulled a handkerchief out of his pocket and was tying it around his left arm.

"Give me that bag before you drop it and hurt them," Black Hawk commanded. His voice had changed, grown stronger, lost some of the old man quaver. Ben handed him the bag, which

Black Hawk grabbed easily with his right hand. He then lifted the back of his hand to his mouth for a moment, sucked, spit, and headed toward his truck, which was parked in back of the cabins.

"I thought it was too heavy for you to carry so far," Ben protested, following him.

"Don't be ridiculous. I could hike to the other side of the island and back with it. I run marathons, McCain. The only reason I wanted to drag you into this was because I wanted a chance to talk with you alone about Moriah."

"You run marathons?" Ben was amazed.

"I placed first in Canada's over-seventy senior's division this year," Black Hawk said. "But that's not what I wanted to..."

"That's the reason for the new running shoes!"

"What did you expect? Beaded moccasins? Yeah. I have to buy a new pair every five hundred miles. It's kind of like getting new tires; the old ones wear out."

"Have you always run?"

"No. I started in my sixties. At first, it was an excuse to get away from the grandchildren and great-grandchildren. They all live close to us, and sometimes, they about drive me nuts." He preened a little. "Also, my wife likes for me to be buff."

Ben's mind was reeling from the sudden change in the man's personality. "What about all that mumbo jumbo back there, the chant, the 'courage, daughter' stuff."

"You liked my chant?" Black Hawk chuckled. "The Ojibwe do have a snake dance that is supposed to be healing. It mimics the shedding of skin and all that stuff. It's very impressive, but if we have a chant for pulling snakes out from underneath a cabin, I never heard of it. I just make 'em up so people think I've got something mystical going on. It seems to keep everyone calm."

"It doesn't have any effect on the snake?"

"Of course not," Black Hawk said. "Snakes aren't Billy Ray

Cyrus fans. At least, Massasaugas aren't. I'm not sure about the others."

"So that *was* 'Achy Breaky Heart' you were singing!"

"Don't tell Moriah. She needed confidence; the song helped. Don't argue with success, McCain."

"All that was a show for Moriah?"

"Of course, it was. She went through a terrible ordeal beneath that cabin. I wanted to help her get over it if I could."

"Are you really a snake expert," Ben said, suspiciously, "or are you pretending about that as well."

"Certified herpetologist. I have a B.A. in Zoology." Black Hawk grabbed a piece of twine from the back of his truck and tied the bag closed. "Class of '57.' I milk Massasaugas for venom and sell it to laboratories so they can make antivenin—which, by the way, I could use some of right now."

"What do you mean?"

Sam Black Hawk stripped off his leather gloves and sucked at the back of his hand again. He spit then audibly sighed at Ben's ignorance as he leaned against the tailgate of the truck. "Rattlesnakes have a limited amount of venom—so they control the amount they put in their victim—using just the tiniest amount to paralyze a mouse, for instance, until they can digest him. The reason they hold back is because, if they use up all the venom at once, they'll have to go hungry for a few weeks until their bodies replace it."

"What does that have to do with you needing antivenin?"

"Moriah was in mortal danger under that cabin. Rattlesnakes never have as much venom as when they've just come out of hibernation. It's all built up. Had she tried to get out of there quickly, making it possible for them to track her body heat, they would have struck at such a large target with all the venom at their disposal. She would have died. Painfully." He reached into his pants pocket. "Here," he said, tossing his truck keys to Ben. "You drive."

"You didn't answer the question."

Black Hawk cinched the handkerchief more snugly around his arm. "One of those Massasaugas managed to give me a little 'kiss' while I was beneath the cabin. I think it might be a good idea if we headed for the hospital."

The old man's face was beginning to turn gray as Ben spun gravel all the way out of the parking lot.

Black Hawk glanced at Ben before closing his eyes. "Don't you dare tell Moriah about this."

CHAPTER 18

Ben waited at the hospital until Black Hawk's hand had been put in ice, the wound had been cleansed, bandaged, and a shot of antivenin administered. The bite was light, they said. No venom had reached his heart.

"I just hate it when that happens," Black Hawk complained as Ben helped him climb back into the truck.

"Getting bit?"

"Yeah, I really hate snakes."

Ben stood on the brakes. "But you're a herpetologist!"

"I know." Black Hawk sighed. "Ain't it a mess?"

As Ben began driving again, Black Hawk explained, "Being a First Nations male, who is terrified of snakes, is embarrassing. I first studied snakes to get over the fear, and by the time I'd gotten over the fear, I was too fascinated by them to leave them alone."

"But you just said you hated them."

"I never said it had to make sense." He adjusted the bandage on his hand. "I was pretty good back there with Moriah, though, wasn't I?"

"You were great."

"I hear you and she are going to be restoring the lighthouse."

"News gets around fast. How did you find out?"

"Would you believe drums?"

"I don't think so."

"How about smoke signals."

"Nope."

"Would you believe Katherine called me on my phone and told me?"

"Yes. That I would believe."

"Is it true? Are you going to restore it?"

"Looks like it. Jack began putting in the road today, so we can start getting supplies to it."

"This will probably come as a surprise to you, but Moriah's grandfather was my second cousin, as well as my blood brother."

"I don't think anything you could say right now would surprise me, Black Hawk. But that blood brother stuff, do you guys still do that?"

"With the possibility of AIDS and Hepatitis C and STD's? Are you kidding? No way. But back when we were kids and the world felt pure, it still seemed like a good idea. It was hard on me when he died. I miss my old friend badly some days."

"I can imagine." Ben slowed down as he crossed the bridge onto Manitoulin. "By the way, where am I taking you?"

"Back to Katherine's lodge. I'll drop you off. I feel fine now. I can drive myself home from there."

"Are you sure?"

"Yes, I'm sure. I'm the snakebite expert, remember? Besides I have to take those snakes over to Lonely Island. We still got eight rattlers in the back of this truck."

"Why don't you take them home and milk them or whatever you do."

"I've already got more than enough. These islands are crawling with Massasaugas."

"Then why are they on the endangered species list?"

"I don't know. Makes the government feel important, I guess." Black Hawk fingered the bandage on his hand again. "McCain?"

"Yes."

"Are you going to restore the lighthouse completely?"

"As close as possible."

"Even the tower?"

"Especially the tower. Moriah wants to put a big telescope there and a beacon."

"I thought maybe she was thinking about putting the light back in."

"Someone stole the lens a long time ago."

"I know. I remember. But if she had a true Fresnel lens, do you think she would put it back in?"

"She says it's not possible to buy a new one, and the old ones are either in museums or private collections."

"Hypothetically speaking," Black Hawk said, "do you suppose the Coast Guard would press charges if the lens accidentally turned up?"

"I have no idea. Hypothetically speaking, could the lens possibly still be in good shape?"

"The lens could hypothetically be in excellent shape."

Black Hawk pulled the bandage off his hand and stuck it in his pocket as Ben pulled into the resort parking lot.

"Darn thing was bothering me," Black Hawk said.

"I noticed." Ben climbed out of the truck, leaving the keys dangling in the ignition. "When the tower is finished, I'll give you a call."

"No need." Black Hawk scooted behind the wheel. "I'll already know."

CHAPTER 19

One week later, Moriah surveyed the fresh road to the lighthouse and nodded in appreciation. She was proud of Jack. He might have a few personal issues, but he was a world class heavy equipment operator. He'd done a great job, just like she had expected. Things with that little family of his was getting back on track as well. So far so good.

"Not bad," Ben said. "Are you ready to start?

The earthy scent of freshly turned dirt and uprooted tree roots filled the air. The road was as straight and level as a gun barrel, with the lighthouse centered at the end.

"I am. This week will be a little frantic, but I think we've finally got things under control. Nicolas has been following Katherine around like a puppy, helping wherever he can. I actually saw him mopping the kitchen floor this morning. Plus, I hired Alicia part-time to take care of helping with reservations and greeting people as they show up. She can do that and still take care of little Betsy."

"Is it always so busy the first week of tourist season?"

"Yes, and it pretty much stays that way. Once the Chi-

Cheemaun starts bringing in tourists, it always gets a little crazy. We'll usually get a few like the Wrights and Camilla's family, who drive in from the north over the Little Current bridge so they can get here early, but it's when the ferry starts running that the season truly begins."

"Do you enjoy doing this for a living, Moriah?" he asked.

"I never really thought about it. It's all I've ever known. Seems like I've spent most of my life either preparing for or recuperating from the day the ferry starts bringing the usual crush of summer travelers up from Tobermory on Bruce Peninsula, to South Baymouth here on the island. A large part of our population earns the bulk of our yearly income in the space of these next three months."

"It sounds intense."

"It is."

She doubted Ben had any idea how intense it could get. Guests would begin arriving at all hours of the day and night, bringing with them pleas for extra linens, dishes, and folding cots. Concerns about plugged toilets, mice, and cranky cook stoves were a daily chorus to which Moriah automatically responded. She had grown up with it. She dispensed advice on everything from the best fishing spots to an occasional on-the-spot family intervention when frayed tempers flared.

Except, this year, she would be doing it while attempting to restore her lighthouse.

Nicolas's lighthouse, she corrected herself.

Although, now that Katherine was back in his life, Nicolas seemed content to give Moriah and Ben complete freedom with the restoration. Unless Moriah was mistaken, he seemed to have lost all interest in the place. Perhaps that was because he had a new goal—moving into the lodge with Katherine.

That would be rather awkward for her, but Katherine was

half-owner of the resort. If she wanted to marry Nicolas and let him move in with her, then that's the way it would be.

"What do you think, Moriah? Can we do it?" Ben nodded toward the derelict lighthouse.

She looked at him, studying his sturdy build, his determined eyes, his capable hands. There was something about Ben that increased her confidence and strength and made the horrific jungle flashbacks she continued to have almost bearable.

"I think, together, we can do just about anything we set our minds to, McCain."

CHAPTER 20

"We'll dismantle it, stone by stone." Ben peered through the camera he had brought with him as he circled the light tower, snapping pictures from all sides. "The stones will have to be taken down, one at a time, numbered, and re-laid after the new foundation is poured. I'll use that inner wall in the old office to mount these photos, so we can reference them easily."

"We need to start assembling a crew," Moriah said.

"Besides Jack, who do you know?"

"I've had a mental list of my dream team for restoring the lighthouse for about two years now."

"Get them. Just make sure I've got a couple of your most dependable people with me on that tower. Will Jack be one of the guys you hire for that, or does he take on work besides heavy equipment?

"Jack's pretty good at everything. I think he'll jump at the chance for more steady employment this summer."

"I'll need some real muscle beside me when we begin to

dismantle the tower." Ben shot a picture of the outside of the cottage. "I think Jack would have the strength."

"I'm sure he would."

"I know it's none of my business," he moved over a few paces and clicked a picture of the broken foghorn room, "but did you and he ever have a thing?"

"A thing?"

"Like back before Alicia."

"Me and Jack?"

"Yes, you and Jack. The man resembles a Greek god when he's cleaned up and sober," Ben said. "And you've always been friends. I figured maybe..."

"A thing?"

"You know, in a romantic way."

Moriah was surprised. "We grew up together, Ben. No, he's always just been a friend."

Ben studiously kept his eyes on the viewfinder of the camera. "I'm glad."

Moriah's heart melted. Apparently, Ben was still interested in her, in spite of her limitations. After that meltdown at the bridge, she was surprised he hadn't run screaming back to Brazil. She hoped this summer went well. If he really learned to like the island, maybe he would consider living here on the island and make trips back to the Amazon, instead of the other way around.

"I don't want anything to happen to you or to Jack," she said. "Is taking down that tower going to be as dangerous as I think it will be?"

"Yes." Ben didn't hesitate. "It will be."

In spite of the lurch in her stomach at his words, she appreciated the fact that he was not candy-coating the danger. It showed her that he was truly seeing her as an equal in this job.

"Then we'll need plenty of freestanding scaffolding on the

outside of it," she said. "Metal, not wood. I might need to have it special-built. Do you plan to work exclusively from the outside?"

"I don't think anyone should be within that tower during the dismantling. After the new foundation has cured and we begin to rebuild, it will be safe to work inside. I'm figuring I'll concentrate on the tower if you are comfortable being in charge of the cottage and foghorn room. Does that work for you?"

"Let me see." Moriah took stock. "I'll need new timbers for the roof, new insulated windows, new slate tiles. I'll keep the antique locks and hinges. They'll need to be scrubbed and oiled. The moisture from the lake eventually ruins anything metallic..."

"Hold on." Ben pulled a small notebook from his pocket. "Let me make a list."

"The walls need to be scraped clean of about a hundred years of peeling wallpaper. Those wooden floors in the kitchen, where all the rain has come in, will have to be replaced. The rotten linoleum has to go. Maybe, I can find some that matches it. I liked that floral pattern, and it would lend an air of authenticity. I'll check into wallpaper patterns from the 1800's, as well. I'll need to install bathrooms, in addition to plumbing the kitchen. Everything will have to be wired, not to mention putting in some form of central heat. Of course, I'll keep the potbellied coal stove and fireplace for authenticity."

"You sure you're up for all that?" Ben asked.

She squared her shoulders and lifted her chin. "Piece of cake, McCain."

Ben draped an arm around her shoulders.

"The girl of my dreams," he said with utter sincerity.

The big problem was figuring out what to do about it.

CHAPTER 21

During the next few weeks, the tip end of the small peninsula, where the lighthouse stood, took on the appearance of a tiny, bustling village.

By the time Moriah managed to get her team assembled and the work had begun, nearly everyone on the island had heard the news of the restoration.

A good number of the older Manitoulin residents seemed intent on watching. It seemed to be high entertainment for the elderly. Many came day after day, bringing folding chairs with them. Now that the road was open, it was easy access as long as the weather held. Quite a few packed a lunch.

These ancient owners of stories and memories chatted about storms and rescues, while craning to see everything. Some spoke with nostalgia about the picnic parties her grandparents had held there so long ago.

Each story felt like a gift to Moriah, a treasure she stored in her heart. She was inspired by the fact that her family's dedication had meant something, not only to the ships where lives and cargos had been saved, but to the community, as well.

"You swing a hammer just like your daddy, Missy," an older gentleman said as he watched her replacing a rotten windowsill. He was dressed in a well-cut dark suit and leaned on a gold-headed ebony stick

She was distracted by her work. The board she was nailing was a smidgen short. She had measured carefully, but mistakes happened when a carpenter got tired. Reluctantly, she pried up the board and threw it on the scrap pile. It was time to call it quits for the day.

"Let's pack it in, men!" she called, gathering her tools. "Time to go home." Only then did she realize she had been rude to the old man. "I'm sorry, sir. What did you say?"

"I said you swing a hammer just like your daddy." He smiled. "You're the spitting image of him."

It felt good to hear that phrase again after all these years. "You think so?"

"It's a fact." The old man took a step closer. "I remember coming here one day when you were just a tyke, not much more than three or four years old. Your daddy was doing some repairs, and you were toddling around behind him, wearing a little bitty tool apron. I went home and told my wife all about the little carpenter's daughter. Cutest thing I ever saw."

Moriah noted the kindness in the gentleman's eyes and was grateful for the gift of memory he was giving her.

"I remember very little about my father, and I don't remember the tool apron at all. Are you sure?"

He nodded. "He said your mother had made it. Your daddy was a wonderful carpenter and a good man. It was obvious how much he loved you."

Moriah's throat swelled with emotion at the man's words. "Thank you. I appreciate you taking the time to tell me that."

"You're welcome." He glanced over at the partially deconstructed light tower with its necklace of metal scaffolding. "It's an important thing you're doing here. I'm certain your father and grandfather would be proud of you."

Moriah smiled. "You think?"

He nodded. "We all are. Everyone one on the island is proud of what you're doing here. A piece of our heritage was nearly gone, but you and Jack and that stone mason fellow are bringing it back to life. Thank you."

Moriah watched as the old man limped back to where a driver and car were waiting. He waved briefly before the driver backed away.

"Do you know who that was?" Jack asked

"I have no idea."

"Isaac Jones. He used to be a ship captain back when your grandfather manned the lighthouse. I was talking to him earlier."

"Did he tell you anything else?"

"A bit." Jack grinned. "Just the small fact that your grandfather saved his life and several of his crew."

"Oh wow. I wish I'd known."

"Don't worry about it. He told you what he came to say; that you're doing something important here." Jack gazed about them at the sturdy crew of workers packing up their tools. "I have a feeling we all are."

CHAPTER 22

Even with the lighthouse requiring all of her and Ben's attention and with tourist season heavy upon them, Nicolas and Katherine managed to find time to plan an August wedding. Fancy invitations went out in the mail, and catalogs of wedding finery piled up around Katherine's favorite chair.

Nicolas surprised everyone by rolling up his sleeves and doing an excellent job, not with the lighthouse, which he rarely visited, but with the running of the resort. He donned his khaki shorts, a t-shirt emblazoned with the words "Robertson's Resort," and seemed utterly content. Moriah even came upon him once as he hung freshly laundered sheets on the line. To her astonishment, the man was whistling.

In the evenings, when Moriah came back to the lodge, she noticed her aunt was softening into a younger-looking, much happier version of herself. Katherine's expression was no longer that of stoic acceptance. Instead, she smiled more often, her eyes lit up at the smallest things, and Moriah had heard her humming as she cooked. Moriah knew that Nicolas was the cause of that new happiness, and she was grateful.

In spite of the upset Moriah had experienced earlier, her days now fell into a seamless rhythm and routine as she, Ben, and the crew worked together. Stone upon stone, bracings and chisels and rock dust, roof trusses and fresh new flooring, it was exhilarating to see her dream coming together.

Moriah loved the feeling of straining her muscles to the maximum each day alongside the company of the workmen, eating a quick sandwich with her back braced against the shady side of the cottage, then swigging down the icy water from the newly restored well and outdoor hand pump. Ben often came to sit beside her in the shade of the cottage for a few minutes to figure out some small challenge that might have arisen. She appreciated the fact that he respected and valued her opinions. Then, they would swing back into the task at hand, renewed.

It was the happiest she had ever been in her life.

Each day, some satisfying portion of the restoration was accomplished. Each evening after supper, Moriah stood in a hot shower, soaking her sore muscles. Then, she would put on clean clothes and meet Ben, who always waited for her on the back-porch swing. They'd spend at least an hour each night in the privacy of the swing, talking about their day, planning the next. It was the best part of the day.

Later, Moriah would crawl into bed, exhausted. Each morning, she awoke looking forward to the day with eager anticipation. Much of that eagerness was in looking forward to seeing how much they would accomplish that day, but some of it was knowing she would get to see Ben again.

Neither of them spoke about what would happen when the summer ended. They were careful with each other, holding back, determined to continue to maintain their friendship, knowing that saying too much too soon could destroy it.

No matter how early she rose, however, Ben was always in the lodge's great room a bit earlier, working on his translation.

He insisted he was so used to working in a village with a dozen children underfoot that he felt lonely working in his cabin.

Neither Nicolas nor Katherine brought up all that had been said the day of her nightmare out at the lighthouse, the day of the thunderstorm. Everyone skirted around the issue, avoiding it, all four of them almost too busy to breathe. They had no time to delve into the issue, so they left it alone. They all seemed content to wait for her to bring it up if she wanted to, and she chose not to.

After the restoration of the lighthouse was accomplished, after the last guest had left, after she had buttoned up the cottages and prepared them for winter, then she and Katherine would have months to sort things out. Winter often felt never-ending this far north. There would be plenty of time then to talk.

For now, she was grateful they left the subject alone. Now that she understood the reasons Katherine had fabricated a different reality for her all these years, she craved time to sort things out in her mind, especially since bits of memories kept trickling into her conscious, triggered by simple, everyday things.

One day at the work site, while wiping her forehead with the blue-patterned work handkerchief she kept in her pocket, she abruptly had an image of her mother in the jungle, tying her hair up off her neck with one exactly like it.

A child's wooden toy left on the path in front of the cabins suddenly dredged up a picture of Petras whittling out clumsy little tigers and monkeys for her and the other children in the village.

But images of the massacre kept creeping in, too. Her child's impressionable mind had apparently taken a photographic snap-shot of those moments and then tucked that snapshot away until she was old enough to look at it. She could now recall, with accuracy, even the clothes her parents had been wearing.

She dealt with this hodge-podge of rediscovered mental pictures the best she could. Sometimes, while she worked, she fit pieces together in her mind, making new discoveries every day. Many things made sense to her now.

For the first time, she understood why she had always struggled with a low-grade sadness, so different from the other children growing up on the island. For the first time, she realized that, along with the four lives that had been taken during the massacre, four other innocent lives had been nearly destroyed. The trauma wasn't hers alone. Ben, Katherine, and Nicolas had suffered, also.

Ben had pieced together a life by devoting himself to the very tribe where his father had met his death. But even Ben was not entirely whole. He still mourned the father he had come to love so much.

Katherine had sacrificed marrying the man she loved and her dream of becoming a doctor in order to care for a damaged niece. Moriah now realized just how seldom she had ever seen her aunt smile. She suspected that competent, wise Katherine had been as sad as Moriah, until Nicolas, with all his faults, stepped in.

And Nicolas. Ah, Nicolas. A gifted medical student when his mother died, he had given up his dream of becoming a surgeon by incomprehensibly taking on his mother's profession of obstetrics, a specialty Moriah felt certain he was emotionally ill-suited for. She found herself wondering, sometimes, if his hasty and poorly chosen marriage might have been the worst fate of them all.

Then, there was herself. Moriah wished she could go back in time, take the silent little girl she had once been, and hold her in her arms. Her heart swelled with pity for that little girl, pity for all of them, crippled, yet in their own way, valiant. They had all tried so hard to put the pieces back together and make lives for themselves.

As Moriah's hands sawed and hammered, her mind imagined their separate lives integrated into a jigsaw puzzle, scattered onto the floor by Chief Moawa's violent hand. Then, she imagined God patiently picking up the pieces, one by one, placing them all together—here, right now, on this island, fitting their lives together so they could finally heal.

She realized, now, part of her initial attraction to Ben was based on what had happened in that jungle village. Petras was her friend when she was a little girl. He made toys for her. Along with the other adults, he had watched out for her. She felt safe with Petras.

There had been something familiar about Ben from the moment she saw him striding up the hill after their fishing trip. And she was right. Those familiar broad shoulders, that unruly red hair, those stonemason hands had once, long ago, deliberately stood between her and death.

Just like she had felt safe with his father when she was a child, she felt safe with Ben now. She tried very hard not to think about the vacuum he would leave in her heart the day he left.

CHAPTER 23

B en found Moriah walking back and forth on the beach in front of the lighthouse.

"Something wrong?" he asked.

"Not really," Moriah said. "I'm just trying to gear myself up to tackle a carpentry job I don't want to do."

"What carpentry job?"

"Removing that built-in desk that's in the lighthouse keeper's office."

"The one you kept your sleeping bag and matches in?"

"That's the one."

"Why do you have to take it out?"

"The wall behind it is damaged. There's been a slow leak for years. I can't just patch around it. The desk will have to be removed and the wall repaired and painted. If I can keep from destroying it in the process I'll take the desk to a guy I know in Kagawong who will strip and refinish it. After that, I hope to re-install it."

"Sounds like a good plan." Ben skipped a rock across the

water's surface. The lake had chosen to be as smooth as silk today. "So, what's the problem?"

"That wood is more than one hundred fifty years old. To take it out might damage it."

"Can you just crawl in and unscrew whatever is holding it to the wall?"

"Afraid not." She kicked a pebble into the water. "Screws were invented back then, but they weren't readily available. This desk is anchored with large, hand-wrought nails."

"You're saying you'll have to use a crowbar."

"I'll have to use a crowbar," Moriah said, "which could possibly split the wood and ruin the desk my great-great-grandfather made. I love that desk. If I destroy it, I'll never be able to live with myself."

Ben took her by the shoulders and gently turned her around to face him. "I know it has a lot of sentimental value to you, but it's just a desk. It doesn't feel anything. It's not alive. It doesn't have a soul. Liam Robertson made a nice desk. It was useful. People enjoyed it for decades. People will probably use it for decades more, but if you accidentally turn it into firewood, in the larger scheme of things, it really doesn't matter. Life gets so much simpler when you don't love things that can't love you back, lass."

"You're right." Moriah took a deep breath, let it out, and made herself relax. She stood looking at the lake for a moment longer and then smiled.

"Time to go get a crowbar. We'll see how this turns out."

An hour later, Ben was high up on some scaffolding. He glanced down and saw Moriah, Jack, and one of the other workers wrestling the oddly-shaped desk into her pickup. It appeared that it was still intact. Then Moriah and Jack climbed into the truck and sped off, presumably to take the desk to the refinisher. For Moriah's sake, he hoped it turned out well.

CHAPTER 24

M oriah pulled her hair into a casual braid, donned her usual work boots, jeans, and t-shirt, and entered the lodge dining room with a light heart. They had made it into June with no mishaps, and the changes to the lighthouse tower were hard to miss. The top third of it had disappeared.

Ben expected to be finished taking down the tower by the end of June. The first part of July, they would pour a new concrete foundation. After the forms had been taken away and the concrete had cured, Lord willing, they would begin to lay the first course of stone.

Things were moving right along, and she was thrilled.

Even though she'd gotten up earlier than usual, Ben was already in the kitchen, a coffee cup at his elbow, his worn Bible and notebook in front of him.

It was interesting to her how much Ben had changed without really changing. The first time she'd laid eyes on him, she'd not thought he was particularly handsome. She had never liked red hair or freckles on a man. Now, when she came into the room, it struck her that he was one of the most gorgeous men she'd ever met. She had never realized how much getting to know another person's heart changed the way their outside appearance was perceived.

"Don't you ever get tired of the translating work you do?" She pulled out a chair and seated herself across the table from him.

"Actually, no." He thrust both arms up and stretched. "It's my cross-word puzzle, my chess game, my…"

Moriah held up a hand. "I get the picture. You enjoy your work."

"I enjoy my life, Moriah, especially now that you're in it. It's all play when your heart is joyful."

"Not if you're not a morning person, it isn't." Nicolas wandered into the dining room and plopped down beside of Ben. "I thought retirement would mean sleeping in."

"Didn't you sleep well?" Moriah went over to the kitchen counter, where the coffee pot gurgled, and poured a cup.

"No. I most emphatically did not."

Moriah held the pot out. "You want some?"

"Of course, I want some," Nicolas grouched. "Do you have an IV? If so, I shall inject the liquid directly into my veins."

Moriah sat a cup of steaming liquid in front of him. "What happened?"

"Your aunt came to my cabin in the middle of the night and asked me to go with her to help birth another baby on the reservation. Apparently, the word is out that an obstetrician is available at Kathy's beck and call. This is my third this month." He raised his voice so Katherine could hear him in the kitchen. "Why do these people insist on having so many babies during tourist season?"

"Long autumn nights, dear," Katherine called.

"Was the mother having a problem?" Moriah asked.

"No. She just had no way to get to the hospital. Probably not enough money, either. Everything went fine. In fact, after everything was over, while Kathy tended to the mother, I got to hold the baby."

"There's nothing sweeter than a newborn," Moriah said.

"I did enjoy it," Nicolas admitted. "I never got to hold them much when I was in private practice. The nurses always whisked the babies away to the pediatrician to be checked out." He traced a line down the white tablecloth with his finger, absorbed in his own thoughts. Then he glanced up and smiled. "Kathy promised to make biscuits as a reward for helping her last night."

"You're getting homemade biscuits for breakfast this morning?" Ben's voice was hopeful. "All I ate down at my cabin was cold cereal. I'm already hungry again." He raised his voice, "Hey, Katherine, wake me up next time you get a call for Nicolas. I bet I could figure out how to catch a baby. Let Nicolas sleep. I love babies, especially if homemade biscuits are involved."

Sometimes, Ben reminded Moriah of a big, cheerful, dog who regularly showed up at the lodge, hoping for a meal. Katherine rarely disappointed.

"And sausage gravy," Nicolas said.

"Wow." Ben sighed.

"I hear that," Katherine called. "And I've made enough for everyone, but it'll be a couple more minutes."

Nicolas peered at Ben's open Bible. "I forgot my glasses. How far have you gotten?"

"I'm starting into First Peter this morning. "

"You're making good progress, then."

"Yes, but I'm dreading Revelation. That's going to be a tough book to put into the Yahnowa language. I don't think they have a term for Great Dragon in Yahnowa."

"You might try using the term for Great Anaconda," Nicolas said. "They must have a word for that."

"They definitely have a word for that," Ben said.

Nicolas stifled a yawn. "I need a refill, I need my glasses...and

I need a good-morning hug from Kathy." He wandered off into the kitchen.

Moriah grimaced.

"What?" Ben asked. "What's that face about? Don't you want your aunt getting a hug?"

"I just wish they weren't so...you know...so..."

"In love?"

"Well, so open about it."

"Think about it, Moriah. Neither of them dreamed they'd ever be together again, and now, they are. It's okay with me if they want to act like teenagers. Besides," he teased, "I think you're jealous. You want a good-morning hug, too." Ben pushed his chair back.

"I don't need hugs. I just..."

"Of course, you do." Ben stood, leaned across the table and gave her a bear hug that lifted her completely off her chair. Then he dropped her back into it.

"There, feel better?"

Moriah shook her head in mock dismay. "You are way, way too happy in the morning, Ben. "

"I'm living on a wonderful island, in a great cabin, spending time with a beautiful woman. What's not to like?"

Ben had called her beautiful again.

"In fact," Ben said. "I'm often surprised any of the men out at the work site can get any work done with you around."

"Yeah, right." Moriah made a face.

She knew Ben wasn't serious. In eighth grade she had shot up almost to her full height, towering over the other kids until some of them caught up in later grades. She had once overheard a boy call her "that big horsey girl" to some other kids. They had all laughed. It had hurt, of course. That was how she had thought of herself ever since, as a big horse of a girl.

Ben apparently saw her through different eyes, and she was

happy about that, but she hadn't yet figured out how to grace-fully react to Ben's compliments.

He closed his Bible, put his pens and papers in their case, and tucked everything beneath his arm.

"I need to gather a few things before we go to work." He headed out the door. "I'll be back in a few minutes."

As he left, she pictured the first day she had met him, how awkward he had been around her. That awkwardness hadn't lasted long. He was, at heart, a confident, intelligent, and talented man. He was a man who deserved to love and be loved by someone special. Someone who could go with him to the Amazon.

CHAPTER 25

M oriah saw Chief Moawa's vicious, painted face behind every bush, behind every tree, behind every boulder. She was terrified and could not stop sobbing.

"Be quiet," Akawe demanded in a rough whisper. "If you want to live, stop crying!" She bit the inside of her mouth until it bled, swallowed her sobs, trembled with the effort to keep silent.

In spite of her valiant attempt to be quiet as Akawe and Rashawe maneuvered across a wet, creaking, rope bridge that spanned a deep gorge, a sudden cry escaped her lips. Akawe, startled, lost his balance. For an eternity, he fought, suspended over the gorge. Then, Rashawe thrust his spear toward him. Akawe caught it and regained his balance. Moriah, frozen with fear, immobilized and helpless, believed with all her heart that all three would plunge to their deaths if she ever again made the slightest sound.

With Katherine and Nicolas in the kitchen and Ben down at his cabin for a few minutes, Moriah poured herself a second cup of coffee and wandered over to the fireplace. She felt a little chilled, even though it was the dead of summer. The coldness, she knew, came entirely from within and the memories she now had to deal with almost on a daily basis.

Part of her wanted to shove them back inside the mental Pandora's Box from which they'd emerged, but she knew she had to have the courage to face them if she was ever going to be whole. She sat down on one of the sofas, pulled an afghan around her shoulders, and closed her eyes.

The lift of the plane was frightening as it spirited her away. She felt small and helpless flying through the air with a stranger, a missionary priest from the convent school. He had been assigned to a new parish in Michigan and was packing for his trip when Akawe brought her to the school. Since the priest was already leaving, it was faster for Grandpa and Katherine to meet him at the airport in Detroit than for them to try to come to her. They were already on their way to Michigan, he told her.

The priest, a kind man, kept trying to cheer her up with little games and stories, but the knowledge that her mother and father were gone knotted her stomach into a giant, painful fist. She even shook her head at the snack the stewardess offered.

Her aunt and grandfather were waiting for her at the Detroit airport when she disembarked, and she clung to them, wordless, afraid to let go, afraid they'd disappear. They thanked the priest for accompanying her, and when her grandfather lifted her up in his arms, his face was wet with tears.

Katherine tried to comfort her as they drove home. "See Moriah? We're crossing the bridge back into Canada. We're getting closer and closer to home."

She buried her head in her aunt's lap as Grandpa drove and she chewed the ear off a stuffed bunny Katherine had brought along. She tried to ignore a roaring in her head that sounded like a giant waterfall as they crossed the long, rumbling bridge into Canada.

They traveled for hours into the heart of Ontario. Then, they waited in line to pull up onto a huge gangplank and into the bowels of the giant Chi-Cheemaun ferry. She heard the great clank of the motor and fought like a wild animal when Katherine tried to make her leave the car.

Katherine told her the other children ran about the ferry playing tag. Other children tossed bread crusts to seagulls circling the open deck. Other children begged nickels and dimes off their parents and ran to buy candy at the concession stand. It was fun on the ferry, Katherine said.

But Moriah refused. She wanted to stay in the car.

Staying in the car was not allowed by the ferry officials. They said it was dangerous. She fought like a tiger to stay. In the end, Katherine had to overpower her and carry her up the steep stairs of the ferry and into a large, open room. Moriah spent the rest of the two hour ferry ride in a fetal position ripping the other ear off the bunny with her baby teeth, while her aunt sat next to her, stroking her hair and crying.

After the ferry docked and they were allowed to get back into the car and drive off the ferry onto dry land, Katherine lifted Moriah to look out the window.

"We're on Manitoulin Island now, sweetie." She smoothed Moriah's hair away from her eyes. "You're safe here. Grandpa and I won't let anything bad happen to you. You won't ever have to go away to that bad place again. You're back on Manitoulin Island with us. You are in the safest place in the world."

Moriah jumped up from the sofa and pasted a smile on her face when Ben returned for breakfast. Nicolas and Katherine were carrying four plates heaped with food to the table.

"Katherine," Ben ogled the biscuits and gravy, "Will you

marry me? We can have biscuits and gravy every morning? It will be a good life."

Nicolas sputtered and nearly dropped the plates. Moriah seated herself at the table, ignoring Ben's banter. She wasn't hungry. Not now. Not after reliving her trip from the jungle back to Manitoulin.

Katherine calmly sat the two plates she carried onto the table in front of Ben and Moriah. "Just say grace, Ben, and quit annoying Nicolas."

"Father, please keep us and our workers safe on the job today. Thank you for this food as well as for the gift of Katherine, who prepared it, and thank you for the fact that Moriah adores me. Amen." He slanted a glance in Moriah's direction.

"Just eat, Ben," she said. In spite of the melancholy she had felt moments before, she felt a little better. Ben's good nature had revived her, as usual.

"So, what are your plans today?" Nicolas shook out his napkin and centered it on his lap.

"Still working on bringing down the tower. It's tedious work. Plus, I suspect that the only thing holding some of it up was the metal stair structure inside." Ben poured a glass of juice from a pitcher sitting on the table. "We're having to disengage the inner staircase from the stones before we can bring them down. It isn't easy, but it can be done if we're careful."

"Will you be able to salvage the staircase?" Nicolas asked.

"I think so."

"I have an idea for the lighthouse, I would like to mention." Katherine said. Everyone stopped eating to stare. Katherine was the only one of them who'd not yet expressed an opinion about the restoration, even though she was the only one who had actually lived in the place. If she had an idea, they wanted to hear it.

"I think the appearance of the entire structure would benefit by laying a stone wall around it, cottage included." Katherine's voice was slightly apologetic. "I know it would be a lot of work, but my mother saw a picture of a lighthouse once that had a low stone wall surrounding it. A flower garden had been planted within, and my mother always wanted to do the same. She and Dad had to move out before they could get around to it."

Everyone was silent, contemplating the image.

Nicolas made a decision. "I'll pay extra."

"What do you think?" Moriah asked Ben.

"She's right. I should have thought of it earlier. It's exactly what the place needs. A dry stone wall, one without mortar, would be best. It could shift with the extremes of temperature that you get on this island. There is much loose stone lying around, and it would be a good way to use some of it."

"Could you teach me?" Moriah said. "I'd like to learn how to build a stone wall."

"Of course," Ben said, "I'll give you a lesson today if you want."

CHAPTER 26

"Okay," Moriah said as soon as they'd given assignments to the other workers. "How do I start?"

"You start by gathering lots of stones," Ben said.

"Then what?"

"Then you get lots and lots more stones."

"Okay already. I heard you. Then what?"

"Then you get more stones."

Moriah put her hands on her hips, tilted her head to one side, and lifted an eyebrow. "Stop it."

"I'm serious. A job this big is going to require days of rock gathering. Before I can teach you a thing, we have to gather a big pile of stones."

With a sigh, Moriah pulled on a pair of gloves and bent to lift a large stone lying at her feet.

As she lifted it, something moved beneath, and she jumped back so quickly, she stumbled and fell backwards. A snake slithered out of a small crevice beneath the rock and wound its way quickly down the hill toward the lake.

"Are you okay?" Ben helped her up.

"It wasn't poisonous." She nervously rubbed her hands up and down her arms. "If it isn't a Massasauga, and it's on Manitoulin, it's not poisonous. That's what Black Hawk said."

"Very good. Does that mean you aren't afraid of them anymore?"

"Not quite as much as I was."

"Good girl." He patted her on top of her head.

She batted his hand away. "Aren't you afraid of them?"

"No, I'm not. I avoid them, but I can't allow myself to fear them, or I'd never be able to build. Snakes enjoy hiding around stone, so they kind of come with the job. The only thing worse than snakes is a wasp or hornet nest. Now *those* are fun to stick your hand into."

"That's happened to you?"

"Oh yeah. More than once." Ben grimaced.

"I don't know what a stonemason gets paid, Ben, but whatever it is, it isn't enough."

"And I think that is something you need to tell Nicolas," he said, solemnly. "Now, about these rocks you'll be helping me gather…"

He hefted the one she had dropped. "Building a wall is a whole lot like working a jigsaw puzzle, except it's a lot better than a puzzle because, when you finish, you will have created something that can stand for generations."

He squatted, picked up another rock from the dozens dotting the immediate area, and then experimentally fitted them against the one she had selected.

"Every stone is different. They all have their own unique personalities. That's what makes rock walls so much more interesting and pleasing to the eye than standardized concrete blocks. The eye naturally enjoys variety."

He selected another stone and placed it beside the others. "There are always a few stones that don't seem to fit anywhere.

You keep trying to fit them in, and you keep trying, but they don't work. Then, all at once, you'll find a hole that seems like it was made for that odd-shaped rock you were ready to toss."

He placed a fourth stone. "A rock wall always reminds me of a church. There's always someone who doesn't seem to fit. Then, one day, that person finds the right niche, the right ministry, and the church community is stronger for them being there."

Moriah knelt beside him, watching his hands, listening intently.

"When the hard winters and the hot summers come, the wall can expand and contract and remain intact longer for the very reason that each stone is different from the others. It's a nice thing to remember when you fall into thinking the world would be a better place if everyone was exactly the same as you."

He placed another stone beside the others. "Bet you didn't expect a sermon *and* a lesson on building walls."

"Is that the kind of stuff you think about when you build?" Moriah asked.

"Sometimes. Laying a dry stone wall takes patience and persistence. It gives a person plenty of time to think."

Ben stood and stretched his back. "Now, you try your hand at this while I gather more stones."

CHAPTER 27

Moriah worked on the stone wall all day with Ben's encouragement and supervision. If it began to veer a bit to one side or another, he always found just the right rock to make up the difference.

"You're doing great," Ben said. "This isn't easy to learn. Most people give up, but you're doing it. I'm proud of you."

She was discovering that her back had muscles she'd never known existed, and all of them ached, but Ben was so pleased with the job she was doing, she was determined to keep going.

Instead of working on the tower, he left Jack in charge and spent the day gathering stones from all around the peninsula. She was amazed to find there were so many different colors, shapes, and sizes. She had never really noticed the variety before.

Occasionally, he had to place a large one, a rock bigger than she could lift, in the wall to work the smaller ones around. It gave the wall strength and character, he said, and then he pointed out that it was like when God made people with greater gifts to help hold the church together.

Moriah had never given any thought to her place in her

church—her part in holding up the "wall." As she fitted the rocks together, she realized that, in her obsession to make and save enough money to purchase the lighthouse, she had allowed herself to become a rather small pebble at her church.

Ben was right. Building a stone wall gave a person plenty of time to think. Maybe too much.

Petras was carrying rocks from the river near their village, preparing to build a room onto the clinic. She was not allowed to go to the river, but he was a grownup man, so he could go wherever he wanted. Seeing him go back and forth from the river to the clinic, carrying dripping rocks, was fascinating. She crept closer and closer. Before long, she had followed Petras almost the whole way.

"You are a curious little lass, aren't you," he said. "I'd better get you back to your mother." He dropped the rock he had pulled from the river onto the path and picked her up. He placed her on his shoulders and walked back toward the village.

She had never ridden on Petras' shoulders before. He was bigger than Daddy, and she liked being up so high. She did not like it when he stopped in the middle of the path and stood completely still.

"Go!" she urged.

Petras told her to shush and pointed up the path several yards.

At first, she didn't see it, and then she did. A giant snake was slithering across the path. It was very big, and it took a long time for it to cross. Petras waited and waited, standing very still, even long after it had disappeared.

"What was that?" she asked.

"It was an Anaconda," Petras said.

"What's an Anaconda?"

"A very large snake." He started walking again.

"Does it bite?"

"No," he said. "It swallows things whole."

"Does it eat little girls?"

"Sometimes," he said, "especially little girls who disobey their mother and go to the river when they have been told not to."

He gave her back to her mother with a warning about the big snake. Her mother did not have to chastise her. Moriah was too frightened ever to go to the river again. She didn't want to get swallowed by a big snake.

At the end of the day, with Ben's occasional help, she had completed a course of stone wall ten feet long and three feet high. In spite of having worn work gloves, her fingers were bruised and scraped in several places. She stood back and admired her work with as much pride as she had taken in the first cabin she had ever built.

"It usually takes a lot longer than this to teach someone how to lay stone," Ben said. "You're quick."

"It doesn't seem like I got all that far."

"It's not how far you get in one day; it's how well you build, how strong. A wall like that will stand a hundred years and beyond with only minor repairs from time to time. You did well."

"Thanks." She drew off her gloves and stuffed them into her back pocket. "Let's go see how much the guys have gotten done inside the cottage today. Are we on track for the light tower?"

"Two more weeks and I should be able to start rebuilding your precious light tower." Ben tugged her braid. "You are as bad as a kid at Christmas."

CHAPTER 28

"You've added, what? Another five feet?" Ben said, when he came at lunchtime to check on her. "Good job!"

She stood up, wiped her face with her forearm, and took a step back to admire what she had done. "Feels like it should be a mile, as hard as it has been."

"But you're enjoying it."

"I am."

"Katherine will be very pleased."

"She should be." Moriah stretched her back. "Every bone in my body aches. I think I'm going to have as much muscle as you by the time I get this wall finished."

"That's okay," Ben said. "I'll still love you."

Moriah's stomach flipped over. Had he actually meant to say that he loved her? Or was it just a phrase he had used, something he'd tossed out without thinking?

Ben seemed not to realize the impact his words had on her. He was already talking about something else. She missed everything, except the last two words.

"…more stones." He looked at her expectantly, waiting for her reply.

"Excuse me?" she said.

"I said you've almost run out of stones. Your pile is nearly gone." He pointed down to the lake, where a tumble-down stone boat house squatted at the edge. "I was asking if you thought it would be a good idea to bring those rocks up here and incorporate them into the wall. The boat house isn't really usable anymore."

"Sure," she said. "I'll get right on it."

"No need," he said. "You keep working here. I'll take the truck down and select the best ones. It won't take long. I'll get Jack to help me."

"Sounds great, thanks."

Moriah was so intent on what she was doing that she didn't pay any attention to what was going on at the old boat house. In fact, she had rarely ever paid any attention to it. At one time, it had been used to house a small life boat in case the keeper needed to go rescue people from a ship wreck. After the lighthouse was decommissioned, the life boat got stolen, and vines took over the small stone structure. Taking it apart would remove an eyesore.

She felt a touch on her shoulder and turned around. It was Jack, and he had a strange look on his face.

"Moriah, I think you need to come with me." His voice was gentle.

"What's wrong?"

"Ben…"

"Ben!" She whirled around to look at the old boat house. "Has he been hurt?"

"No. He's fine. He just said you need to come down there."

"Why?"

"He's found something in the boat house we think you need to see."

Moriah ran down the hill to where Ben was. It looked like he and Jack had already moved the old boards that had once been part of a low roof. Quite a lot of stone from it had been moved to the truck. She saw that Ben was kneeling on the ground inside the boat house looking at something on the ground.

"What's wrong?" she said, when she reached him.

He stood up, and she noticed that he had a dry paint brush in his hand. She could think of no reason he would need a paint brush down here.

"I'm sorry, but I think you need to see this, Moriah."

She looked at the place where he had been kneeling. Suddenly, she saw why he was holding the brush. She gasped and threw her hand over her mouth.

He bent over and flicked a bit more dirt away from a human skeleton.

"What on earth!" she said. "Who?"

"I have no idea," Ben said. "But I'm pretty sure they've been here a very long time."

CHAPTER 29

"How did you find this?" Moriah asked.

"When we got the vines cleared away a bit, I saw there were some large, flat stones that formed the floor. I thought they might be useful to make a bit of a patio outside the back door of the cottage, but when I pulled them up, there were ashes beneath."

"Ashes?"

"We thought that was odd, but we went ahead and moved all the floor stones, anyway. While we were scuffling around, carrying them out of here, we noticed that there were bones beneath the ashes. It's a very shallow grave. That's when Jack got me a clean paint brush and I started brushing the dirt and ash away from it."

"How are things going?" Katherine called.

Nicolas was walking behind her, carrying a large basket. "We brought a picnic. Katherine thought it might be nice to come out, see how things are progressing, and relax a bit...what are you three looking at?"

"The question isn't what we're looking at, it is *who* we are looking at," Ben said. "Apparently, someone buried a body here."

"Seriously?" Nicolas handed the basket to Katherine. "Let me take a look."

Ben, Jack, and Moriah stood aside so the doctor could see what they had discovered.

Nicolas crouched beside the skeleton and brushed away more dirt, revealing that the person had been buried in a heavy, ragged, woolen coat. The pants, which were thinner, had rotted away, revealing long underwear laced with holes. He also wore disintegrating leather boots.

Nicolas stood up. "Male, about 6 feet tall. Looks like maybe size twelve shoes."

Bending over, he brushed away more dirt from what would have been the face. As the dirt fell away from the skull, it was possible to see the teeth. A glint of gold captured their attention.

"Is that a gold tooth?" Katherine asked.

Nicolas flicked away more loose dirt. "It certainly is."

"Liam Robertson had a gold tooth," Katherine said.

"Your great-grandfather?" Nicolas asked. "The one who went missing?"

"Yes. My grandfather told me that *his* father, Zachary Robertson, had once mentioned that his father, Liam, had a gold tooth. It was rare to have one in these parts back then. He got it somewhere overseas while serving in the Navy."

"The state of the skeleton and clothing could be from that far back," Nicolas said.

"That's what I thought," Ben said.

"Look at this." Nicolas picked up the skull and turned it so everyone could see a large, ragged, hole in the back of it. "I know I'm an obstetrician with no forensic training, but if this is Liam Robertson, I think there's a strong chance that he didn't just disappear into the woods. This looks like blunt head trauma."

"I'm going to go call the police," Moriah said. "Even if the body is over a hundred years old. I don't know what else to do."

"I believe I've just lost my appetite for ham sandwiches," Katherine said. "I'll go with you."

"Why the ashes, I wonder," Ben said, after Moriah and Katherine left to go back to the lodge to make a phone call.

"You've never spent a winter this far north, have you?" Nicolas said.

"No, I haven't."

"Then you don't know that a death in the middle of winter causes all sorts of complications, even today," Nicolas said. "Back then, many families had to keep their deceased frozen in a shed until spring, when the ground warmed up enough to dig a proper grave. Sometimes, if for some reason they were truly desperate to bury a body, they would create a huge bonfire and keep it going to help things along by thawing out the ground beneath. In the middle of the winter, when Liam was supposed to have disappeared, it would have taken a large bonfire to make it possible to dig even a shallow grave. Instead of six feet, this one is what, maybe a foot deep? It was probably all they could manage during a hard winter. Even today, the undertaker has to keep the body of the deceased in cold storage until the ground thaws enough to dig a grave."

"But do you really think it might have been murder?" Ben said.

"I don't have enough training in that area to know for sure," Nicolas said. "But if it was an accident, like a bad fall, then who buried him? Only his wife and son were with him. Who else would be around to do that in the middle of winter? And why would Eliza Robertson tell the authorities that her husband had disappeared if she already knew he had died from some sort of accident?"

"Do you suppose someone else might have killed and buried him without her knowing?"

"I don't think she could have missed seeing a giant bonfire." Nicolas said.

"So, you think Eliza might have killed her husband, buried the body, and pretended that he disappeared?" Jack asked.

"If this is Liam, it's possible." Nicolas said. "The story I remember Kathy's father telling me was that Liam and Eliza had been cooped up all winter, alone with their child. The nearest thing to civilization was something like eleven miles away. Cabin fever can do strange things to human minds. People under those kinds of circumstances have been killed for not much more than looking at someone the wrong way."

It took the Manitoulin policeman about twenty minutes to get there. Word spread fast, and the crew soon put down their tools and came to see what was going on. Some of the older people, who loved to watch the progress on the lighthouse, also came to take a look.

"Murder or not, there's not a whole lot we can do about it now," the young policeman said.

"I have a friend who teaches forensics in Toronto," Nicolas said. "Can you help make arrangements to have what's left of the body taken to him?"

"We can do that." The officer nodded, pleased to have a direction. Murder was rare on Manitoulin, but he knew the protocol just in case. He hadn't been sure what to do in a case like this and was happy to follow Nicolas's suggestion.

CHAPTER 30

T he stones from the boathouse were removed, the flat ones incorporated into a back patio that he built with them. The other boathouse stones were used in the wall Moriah had just finished with a good bit of help from Ben. There was nothing left to indicate there had ever been a boathouse or a shallow grave, which was just as well.

"You're finished with the wall?" Nicolas walked over from the lodge, while she and Ben were admiring their handiwork. "Kathy's going to love this."

"I hope so," Moriah said.

"I came over to tell you that I got a call back from my friend in Toronto, the forensic expert," Nicolas said. "I thought you might want to hear his report."

"Definitely," Moriah said.

"His findings match the time period when Liam Robertson would have lived. We didn't search his clothing, but my friend did. An inside pocket held a cheap pocket watch with Liam's name engraved on the back. I don't think there is any doubt that the skeleton was of your great, great grandfather, Moriah."

"So, could your expert tell for sure how he died?"

"It looks like I was right in my original assumption. It was the head injury as far as he could tell. No one comes to my mind as a suspect except Eliza."

"How very strange to think that Eliza might have done something like that," Moriah said. "She's always been a heroine of mine, taking over the duties of a light keeper after her husband disappeared. Raising her son out here alone."

"Sometimes even decent women are driven to do bad things," Nicolas said. "If she killed him, apparently, she lived a virtuous life from that moment on. There was never any suspicion about her when I was growing up here. It would be interesting to know what drove her to it, assuming she did."

"About all we have are assumptions," Moriah said. "I wish there was a way to know for sure. I wish we had the logbook."

"I doubt the logbook would say anything along the lines of, 'Oh, and by the way, I killed my husband today,'" Ben said.

"True," Moriah said. "Well, regardless of what happened, I want to give him a proper burial when we get his remains back."

"I agree," Nicolas said. "He was your blood kin, one of the first light keepers on this island, and he deserves to have a dignified burial."

CHAPTER 31

It was a beautiful evening in July as Moriah built a fire on the sandy beach. They and their crew had accomplished a staggering amount of work. Of course, there was still much more to do.

The temperature was balmy. A small breeze blew in gently off the lake, just enough to make the bit of warmth from a bonfire feel welcome. A full moon cast light on the water. Most guests stayed from Sunday afternoon to Saturday morning, so the Friday night bonfire on the beach had become a tradition to wrap up the week.

There was usually a general camaraderie that developed between guests over the space of a vacation week at the resort. Friday night, before they went home, tended to become a time of reflection, soaking up the last moments of unhurried vacation, enjoying the wild sound of a loon, once more, as it wafted over the lake from their secret places. There were lazy discussions about large fish either caught or lost. Some of the guests brought folding lawn chairs. Some preferred to relax on blankets on the beach. It was Moriah's favorite time of the week.

This had been an especially good week for her. Everything had worked properly in the cabins, all the toilets' flushed, everyone got along, and no one fell overboard during their fishing excursions. Nicolas had become quite the inn keeper as he helped Katherine. Baby Betsy had charmed guests as Alicia lent a hand each day. The baby had taken her first steps only yesterday. Having Alicia and Nicolas there meant Katherine could get in a few days at her part-time job at Wikwemikong.

In other words, it was working.

She took mental stock of all they had accomplished. The slate roof on the cottage had been removed and new trusses set up. Then, a new roof was installed using as many of the old slates as possible. Once that was in place, the work on the inside had begun. The basics of plumbing and furnace installation took up some of the time. A sewage system was put in, insulated windows installed. The limestone of the cottage was power-washed of decades of grime. The inside was still unfinished, but from the outside, the cottage shone.

In the midst of all this organized chaos, they buried Liam Robertson's remains in the small family cemetery that had been filling up with Robertson relatives for over a century. With Ben officiating, they laid one of the area's first light keepers to rest in the ground with a proper service. Ben created a headstone out of one of the hand-hewn pieces of broken limestone they were replacing on the light tower.

"It's beautiful," Moriah said, when she saw the image he'd carved. "Thank you."

It was an image of their light house with waves crashing about it, above Liam Robertson's name, date of birth, and approximate date of death.

"I don't get to indulge often," he said. "But I do enjoy a bit of fancy work every now and then."

Except for a few scrapes, bruises, and a couple strained back and shoulder muscles, none of their crew had suffered any harm. No rain was expected for several days, so the foundation had been poured today. They would let the concrete cure over the weekend; come Monday, the process of rebuilding the tower would begin. The weather was supposed to be fine for several days so the timing was working out perfectly.

She could hardly wait to see it rise, strong and new. Ben was right. She was as excited as a kid at Christmas.

As the resort guests began to gather, Moriah sat back in the shadows, contentedly watching and savoring their enjoyment.

There was a lot to complain about in running a place like this, but there were many blessings, too. Tonight, it felt as though the blessings far outweighed the complaints.

It pleased her that one of the guests had brought his guitar to the Friday night gathering. He and his wife made their living as musicians, and they were very good. The wife had brought her violin with her. They tuned up, and soon, a sweet folk melody began to fill the soft summer air.

Work finished for the day, Nicolas and Katherine sat with their backs against a log, holding hands, relaxing with their guests. Moriah watched the firelight flicker over her aunt's face and saw true joy there. They had set their wedding day for the end of August. It would be very simple. There was little time to do anything too elaborate, but Katherine would have her church wedding, and Moriah would be the maid of honor. She had never seen her aunt so happy. She closed her eyes and allowed the music and the feeling of contentment to flow over her.

She opened them again, when she caught the scent of Ben's shaving soap, and felt his body settling down next to hers on the sand.

"Nice fire," he said. "What a lovely night!"

She nodded. "All of it. The wind, the lake, the sand, the music, the full moon. It's pretty close to perfect."

They were such good friends, so comfortable with each another. Aside from Ben's teasing compliments, they had managed to make it through much of the summer without embarrassing themselves by openly acknowledging the attraction they felt toward one another.

But right at this moment, with the music and the moonlight and the soft breeze from the lake, plus the intimacy of sitting somewhat apart from the rest of the group, with Ben's shoulder just touching hers, she couldn't help wishing they could be more than friends.

Apparently, Ben felt the same way. With no warning, he pushed her hair back behind her ear, leaned in, and kissed it.

"Ben!" She was shocked and delighted. "Someone will see!"

"I doubt anyone would be surprised."

"But, Ben…"

"I know what you're going to say. We have issues. I agree. I can't stay, and you can't go. But, I've wanted to do that for such a long time."

Her skin still tingled from the touch of his lips. "Since when?"

"Since I saw you lying on the couch after I carried you to the lodge. Katherine was in the kitchen getting a wet cloth for your forehead, and you were still unconscious. I took the liberty of brushing your hair back out of your eyes and tucking it behind your ear. It struck me then that you had the velvetiest skin, the silkiest hair, and the longest lashes I had ever seen. I had never met anyone I thought more perfect."

"I'm far from perfect," she said. "You know that."

"I think the eye of the beholder gets to decide that."

His gaze upon her was so intense that she had to look away. Two more seconds of looking into his blue eyes, and she would fling herself at him and beg him to marry her.

She couldn't let that happen, even though her heart was breaking from the effort of holding back. Unless she could overcome her cursed weakness about leaving this island, she was going to lose him. She turned her head, so he wouldn't see the tears that were beginning to fill her eyes.

"I stepped over a boundary that I shouldn't have," he said. "I apologize, lass. It was the music and the night. Let's just enjoy this beautiful evening together, without trying to figure anything out."

CHAPTER 32

As the light tower grew and the keeper's cottage neared completion, the preparations for the wedding escalated.

Then, suddenly, the wedding day arrived, and everyone was scurrying around, either helping or getting in the way. Moriah had given the crew the day off in celebration and a chance to come to the wedding if they wanted.

The phone was ringing as Ben entered the lodge, but no one answered. He heard the shower running upstairs, probably Moriah getting an early start on preparing for her big day as Katherine's maid of honor.

The tourist season was finally winding down as families went home to get children ready for school, but several of the remaining guests were pitching in to help with the wedding. Today, all of Katherine and Nicolas's plans and preparations would come together.

Since no one seemed interested in the fact that the phone was ringing, he answered it.

"Robertson's Resort. Can I help you?"

"Ben?" The voice sounded far away.

"Yes."

"It's me. Abraham."

Ben's heart lurched. Abraham and his wife, Violet, were the two elderly missionaries helping him with the Yahnowa tribe. If Abraham was calling, something was terribly wrong. It was a hard, two-day trek from their village to the nearest telephone.

"What's wrong, brother?" Ben gripped the phone tightly against his ear.

"It's Violet. She's sick."

"How sick?"

"She doesn't want me to tell you about it."

"Why?"

"She's modest."

"I know she's modest, but what's wrong?" Ben's chest was pounding. He had hated to leave those two alone. Abraham was a hale seventy-year-old, but Violet was frail. She compensated by possessing a lion's heart and an enormous love for the Yahnowa people, but still...

"She thinks she might have bowel cancer, Ben."

"How long has she suspected?"

"Since before you left."

"And she didn't tell anyone?"

"She hoped the problem would go away. Even I didn't know."

"Where is she now?"

"Back at the village. She feels too bad to trek out. I'm arranging for a helicopter, but she's worried about leaving our people. She thinks there will be trouble if one of us isn't there."

"Why?"

"There's been some revenge killings by two tribes near us in the south. There's been talk. She's afraid it will spread to the Yahnowa. You know how that kind of thing can spill over."

"Yes. I know." Ben pondered the situation. Amazon tribes frequently made the feud between the Hatfield's and McCoy's look like a tea party. Entire tribes had been wiped out before the arrival of the missionaries and after.

"I'm sorry to ask this, Ben, but we need you to come back as soon as possible. Aren't you nearly done there?"

Ben made some quick calculations. He had intended to finish mortaring the top run of stone on the tower by noon, just in time to get ready to be Nicolas's best man.

The shower shut off above him, and he stared at the ceiling. He hated the idea of breaking the news of an early, unexpected departure to Moriah

"Ben?" Abraham's voice was uncharacteristically querulous. "Ebenezer? Are you there?"

He had no choice. He had an obligation greater his desire to spend more time with Moriah.

"I'll leave tomorrow morning," Ben said.

"You need to plan to stay awhile, Ben," Abraham said. "Even if Violet doesn't have cancer, I don't think we'll be coming back. I've been having a few dizzy spells, myself. I'm afraid we're done. We'll try to find someone to come take our place, but it might take some time."

"I understand. I'll take care of things." Ben's mind began to calculate logistics.

One day. He only had one day left with Moriah, and it was already filled with a wedding.

"Thank you," Abraham said. "I knew you would come."

"Give Violet my love. Tell her I'm praying for her."

Ben hung up. He grabbed the phone book, dialed, and scheduled his flight. Leaving Manitoulin Island...and Moriah...was going to be the hardest thing he had ever done, but he no longer had a choice.

CHAPTER 33

Ben mortared the last stone into place and completed his portion of the light house. There was still the lantern room to build on top of the tower, with metal bracings and new oak beams. It would take Moriah awhile longer without him, but she had a good crew; she could do it.

Working from old photographs that Katherine had unearthed, Moriah planned to duplicate that lantern room exactly with the exception of the Fresnel lens. His task had only been to make the tower strong again—and that he had done.

Moriah had worked wonders on the keeper's cottage. It still needed a bit more attention, but it was looking good. Katherine had come to the work site with the bed of the resort truck filled with nursery annuals. She had planted flowers all along the stone wall. It was already looking spectacular.

He had gone to see Sam Black Hawk, hoping for information about the Fresnel lens, but he didn't tell Moriah he believed it might have survived the vandalism. There was no reason to get her hopes up, unless it was actually in his possession. The visit had been a disappointment. Black Hawk pretended to have no knowledge of the lens and denied he had ever mentioned it.

Ben and Moriah had already planned the celebration party for the completion of the lighthouse. They intended to invite everyone from the community. He had planned to rig some sort of illumination in the tower, creating a grand finale—the light glimmering on the lake again after so many years of darkness.

Now, he was going to miss it.

But that wasn't all he was going to miss. He had been holding off until the tower was completed to propose to Moriah. Even though they had not yet expressed it, he knew she was in love with him, and he loved her. He had visualized the moment for weeks, intending to ask her to marry him while they were standing high atop this massive work that they had both poured their hearts into. To him, it was symbolical, a sign that, with God's help, they could conquer anything—even her inability to leave the island. Somehow, someway, he knew they could find a way to be together without breaking his promise to the Yahnowa and to God.

He struggled with himself. To ask her now would mean to abandon her tomorrow morning. To *not* ask her now, to leave with nothing but a hug might mean losing her altogether.

Ben wiped his hands on a rag and climbed down the scaffolding. Tomorrow, his crew would begin attaching the original iron spiral staircase to the inside of the light tower. The staircase would wind its way up the eighty feet of limestone he had just finished setting.

He wished he could be there to see it all come together.

Moriah would be able to finish the rest of the work without him. He was certain of that. His only concern was leaving her with an all-male crew to supervise. Jack would watch out for her, he reassured himself. No one would dare try anything with that blonde giant about.

Ben smiled at the image. Jack was big enough to put the fear of God into any man who might be bold enough to lay a finger on Moriah. Of course, Moriah was fully capable of braining a man with a shovel if he tried anything with her, as well. It was one of her many charms.

He dropped off the bottom rung, put his tools away, and climbed into the truck. Nicolas and Katherine's wedding would take place in two hours. It was the only reason Moriah wasn't here beside him. Because of the wedding, she had made an unprecedented appointment at Brenda's Barbering and Hairdressing. He couldn't wait to see her in the maid-of-honor finery that Katherine had bought for her in the mall at Espanola.

If he asked her to marry him, would she follow him later to Brazil? Could she?

He knew she had made a couple trips alone to the bridge this summer that she hadn't told him about. Nicolas had seen her one night pacing the ground in front of it. He said she had stood for the longest time, staring at the bridge. Finally, she had turned around and came back home without crossing. Sam mentioned that he had heard from others who had seen her haunting the bridge as well.

Ben was certain she was trying to overcome this problem all by herself, and he wasn't happy about it. In fact, it hurt a little. He would go with her. He would hold her hand while she crossed, or carry her over on his back if she wanted.

He had hoped her fear would go away, once her memory had returned, but she avoided the subject each time he tried to bring it up. He had done the only thing he knew—prayed until he hoped God would become so tired of his entreaties that He would answer Ben's prayer just to shut him up. He didn't have the knowledge or the skill to make Moriah well. God did.

He glanced at the rearview mirror. The tower stood tall and straight behind him. Stone upon stone. Word upon word. That's what he knew how to do. The inner workings of Moriah's mind remained a mystery to him.

Covered in mortar and rock dust, he entered his cabin and emerged forty-five minutes later in a black tuxedo, white shirt, and an emerald vest and tie.

The whole wedding had become a much bigger deal than Ben had expected. Even though she'd kept the decorations relatively simply, Katherine had expanded her plans to a wedding with what seemed to be half the island in attendance. The church would be filled to capacity this afternoon.

When he arrived at the lodge, caterers from the mainland were putting the finishing touches on a feast. He hoped there might be some spare bite of food lying about as he wandered into the dining room.

"Hello, Ben. "

He gulped. One glance at Moriah, and he forgot all about being hungry. She looked incredible. Her hair was pulled up into a cascade of glistening black curls, tendrils spiraling down around her face. Her eyes and mouth had just the right amount of makeup. Her dress was an off-the-shoulder emerald green that exactly matched her eyes.

She smiled at his reaction, the whiteness of her teeth enhanced by her tawny skin and the deep shade of burgundy on her lips. Luscious lips. He had never thought of anyone's lips as luscious, but it was exactly the right adjective for Moriah's.

Was this truly the same woman who had worked beside him all summer?

She had lost a little weight—not that she had needed to, of course—but her dress showed off a perfect waist and shoulders. It draped about her, flaring slightly at the bottom. She made a little gesture and held it out.

"I feel like a trussed-up turkey, Ben."

"You look like an angel. No, that isn't right. You look like an

Irish fairy princess. That's better." He was nearly stuttering in his appreciation. There simply weren't words to describe his Moriah. "You look like a mermaid. You're..."

"Stunning," Nicolas supplied the word Ben had been searching for, "as is her aunt."

Katherine practically floated down the staircase. She had opted for an ankle-length ivory gown of lace with a high collar. The dress reminded Ben of a much earlier time. He was no expert on women's dresses, but he had heard this kind of style referred to as Victorian. Her hair hung loose, a dark cloud of soft curls with tiny, white flowers tucked here and there. He had never seen Katherine without her hair scrapped back into tight braids. For the first time, he could see a glimpse of the girl with whom Nicolas had once fallen in love.

Brenda-the-hairdresser must be really, really good, Ben decided, or maybe, it wasn't entirely the beautician's magic; maybe it was love that was giving Katherine that glow. He could only imagine what it must have cost Nicolas to give her up when they were young. With all his heart, he silently congratulated them on the new life they were starting together.

"Is the groom supposed to see the bride before the wedding?" he asked. "I thought I heard somewhere that's bad luck."

"I don't believe in luck," Nicolas said, "and there's no good place at the church for our girls to change into their finery. So, Ben, are you ready to help me escort them?"

Ben's reply was heartfelt. "Anytime, anywhere."

CHAPTER 34

M oriah held her bouquet in her lap and sat very still, trying not to disturb her hairdo, as she sat in the backseat of Nicolas's black Mercedes. She had decided, while her head was being lathered over a bowl, that if she was smart enough to build a cabin, repair a lighthouse, and build a stone wall, she was probably smart enough to figure out this girlie stuff, and she wanted to. It was worth the time and cost to see that look of awe on Ben's face. And it was much nicer than chopping her own hair off every six months with Katherine's sewing scissors.

While traveling to the church, she surreptitiously admired her fingernails. Long, lovely nails, and they were all hers. She had paid good money for them. Her fingers had never looked so graceful.

Ben glanced down, focused on her hands, and she eagerly anticipated his reaction. Nothing there to be ashamed of today. No ragged cuticles, no broken nails, just a smooth, unbroken, satiny burgundy nail polish.

"What in the world?" Ben peered at her hands. "What did you do?"

"I had my nails done."

"Why? They were fine before."

"Oh, Ben. I didn't want to look like a man today."

"Lass," Ben's voice was strained, "with that body and that face, you couldn't look like a man if you tried."

Moriah smiled. Yes, the trouble she and the women at the beauty shop had gone to was worth it.

"You're hands look pretty, sweetheart." He took one of her hands in his and studied her fingernails. "But then, they always do to me."

He lifted her hand to his lips, gazing at her with those deep blue eyes of his, and kissed it.

It took her breath away.

He had also taken her breath away when she first glimpsed him as he strolled into the lodge wearing that tux. His latest haircut had grown out, curling slightly over the stiff, white collar. His blue eyes were startling against the tan he had gradually obtained in spite of the sunscreen.

He did not release her hand but continued to hold it as they drove to the church.

She was grateful they had another month ahead of them while they completed the project. There was unspoken hope in her heart that he would decide to stay. There were good signs. He never complained about being on the island, and he was making a lot of friends among the people at church and the crew. She knew he admired and cared about her.

She would never ask him to stay here to be with her, but if he decided on his own to live permanently on the island, instead of going back to live in the Amazon, she would not fight him about it.

If they were to be together, he would have to stay.

She had secretly tried to leave the island this summer. Over and over. In the middle of the night, while everyone else was asleep and she knew the swing bridge wouldn't be moving to accommodate ships.

She had tried driving across it; she had tried walking across it. Nothing had worked. She told no one, not even Ben. This was her fight, her struggle. The failure she felt each time her fear defeated her was not something she wished to share with anyone.

Her attempts had felt like death each time. The dizziness, the chest pain, the shaking, and the dry mouth. The same feelings that had terrified her as a child washed over her each time she tried.

Except now, she had the desperation of her love for Ben and the horrific flashbacks to her childhood in the Amazon to add to her private bag of misery.

Ben was worth it, she told herself each time she arose in the middle of the night to drive to Little Current to attack the bridge again.

Ben was worth everything.

CHAPTER 35

The church was filled with friends, while Katherine and Nicolas made their vows to each other. Nicolas had a surprisingly hard time getting through the service without crying. Katherine was serene and happy.

Ben and Moriah gazed into one another's eyes, while standing beside the bride and groom as vows were said. Moriah fantasized about repeating the same words to Ben someday.

The wedding was beautiful, and the reception came off without a hitch. Then, after the reception, Nicolas and Katherine drove away in a flurry of good wishes. Katherine blew the crowd a kiss as they turned onto the highway. There was a collective sigh from the crowd as the newlyweds disappeared from sight, bound for a well-deserved honeymoon.

The caterers made quick work of cleaning up the debris. The guests went home, and the few tourists who were still staying at the resort, drifted back to their cabins. Moriah found herself alone in the lodge with Ben, both still dressed in their wedding finery.

"It was a nice wedding," Moriah said. "I didn't expect Nicolas to be so emotional."

"I had a pretty big lump in my throat, as well." Ben captured one of her hands and drew her down onto the couch beside him. "All I could think about was how much I wished it was us saying our vows."

She hesitated a moment and then said, "I was thinking the same thing."

There. It was said. The feelings they had for each other were out in the open. Now what?

Moriah's heart beat so hard she wondered if he could hear it. "But I still can't leave the island."

She waited for him to tell her that if she truly couldn't leave the island, he would stay. Instead, his brow furrowed, and he looked pained and worried.

"Are you sure, Moriah? A lot of things have happened since the summer began. You are a stronger person now than you were."

"I've tried to cross the bridge several times since you came, Ben, but I can't. I just can't do it. I'm so sorry, Ben."

"I love you. I can't imagine ever wanting to spend the rest of my life with anyone else, Moriah—but I can't stay. I have to go back."

They looked into one another's eyes, both searching desperately for a way to solve the problem. Both miserable as they contemplated the very real possibility that they had no idea how to solve this problem.

"There's a small airport here on Manitoulin," Ben said. "Maybe you could fly out."

"I tried that once."

"And?"

"I threw up and begged the pilot to let me out."

"That kind of thing happens to a lot of people their first time in the air, Moriah, especially in a small plane."

"He hadn't started the motor, Ben. "

"Oh." He scratched his chin. "You were a child, sweetheart. It would be different now."

"It was last month. I thought my chest would explode. It's not the method, Ben. It's the island. I'm hard-wired to think it's the only place I can be safe."

"What about some kind of therapy?"

"There are no psychologists or psychiatrist here. Even if there were, I saw a show on TV about panic disorder or whatever it is that I have. Even with professional help, it takes years to overcome."

"Years?"

"That's what the TV psychiatrist said."

He groaned. "We don't have years, Moriah."

"I know, but at least, you don't have to go back yet. We still have time to try to figure something out."

"No we don't." He glanced up at her, misery written on his face. "I have to go back tomorrow."

CHAPTER 36

"Why?" She couldn't keep a note of hysteria from creeping into her voice. "Why are you leaving tomorrow?"

It was a bad joke. It had to be

Ben's eyes were serious. It was no joke.

"Abraham called this morning. Violet is sick. He's terrified of losing her, but she's worried about leaving the Yahnowa without someone there who can stabilize things. I speak several tribal dialects. I need to go and try to help."

"Can't the Yahnowa be left alone for a while?"

"Of course, they can. They aren't children. They've been taking care of themselves for centuries, but you don't know Violet. That tribe is her family. She fusses over them like a mother hen. I promised I'd come immediately because I was afraid they would delay their departure until I did."

"But what about the work here?"

"I finished laying the final run of stone on the tower this morning. You can take it from here, Moriah."

She could finish the tower, but she could not lose Ben. Not

now. Not ever. She needed his presence in her life like she needed oxygen.

"What if I said you had to make a choice, the Yahnowa or me?"

Ben looked at her a long time before answering. "You'd never do that."

"I would, too."

"You're only saying that because you're hurting."

"You already know the language." She knew she sounded desperate, but she couldn't help it. "You could finish it here and find someone else to relieve Abraham and Violet."

"You are right. I could finish the translation here. What you don't understand is that, until I created an alphabet for the Yahnowa, theirs was a language that was a spoken language only. I still have to teach them how to read and write that language. I can't just drop a Bible translation on them and walk away. It would just be a bunch of pages with marks on it. Plus, there is the problem of teaching some of the leaders the other languages they need to know to protect themselves in the future, like Portuguese, which is the language of the Brazilian government. I've already made a lot of progress with some of the young adults, who are eager to learn. My friend, Fusiwe, is already proficient in spoken English and learns fast. Soon, he will become a real leader for the Yahnowa, and as the miners and timber companies encroach, the Yahnowa are going to need men and women who can communicate enough to stand up for themselves. I can't drop the work, Moriah. I just can't."

It was all so much more complicated than she'd imagined. He really was going to have to go back.

"What if I never get any better? What if I can't ever go with you?"

"That won't happen. Someday, you'll leave this island, and

you will come to be with me. You are too strong of a person not to overcome this."

"How can you be so sure?"

"Because I know you. I know how determined you are. How strong you are. And I'll pray for you. My prayer will be that we can be together, without you having to remain imprisoned on this island."

"And if God chooses not to answer those prayers? If I can never leave?"

Ben stood and drew her to him. He held her tightly and kissed her. It was not a tentative kiss. It was not a gentle kiss. It was the kiss of a man laying claim to the woman he had chosen.

When they broke apart, she gasped.

"If you can't come to me, I'll come to you," Ben said. "but only after I've fulfilled my promise."

"How long will that take?"

"Too long, Moriah. For my sake, promise me you'll fight."

"I'm already fighting." Her chin trembled. "It's not working."

He glanced at his watch. "It's past midnight. There will be very little traffic. You've been going to the bridge alone. Go now —with me."

Moriah gave him a long, measuring look. "I don't think it will help, but I'll go one more time. With you."

CHAPTER 37

It took them a half-hour to reach the bridge. Moriah clutched the door handle of the truck and stared straight ahead.

The bridge had one lane. A light at both ends managed the traffic. There were no cars around at the moment. Everyone seemed to be tucked away for the evening. The town had shut down. A pedestrian could walk across the bridge on the walkway and pretty much have the bridge to themselves.

Ben pulled up and let the engine idle.

"What's the best way to do this, Moriah? Do you want me to try driving you across again?"

"No. Making a rush at it intensifies the fear. The farthest I've ever gotten is on foot, slowly, where I know I have some control."

"And I'll go with you?"

"You'd better." Moriah gave him a crooked smile. "You're the one who's making me do this."

Ben parked, turned off the truck, and then helped Moriah down from the cab. She usually hopped out by herself, but tonight was different. She still wore her fancy bridesmaid's clothes. He slammed the door shut and put his hand on her waist as they walked toward her iron nemesis.

"Looks pretty solid to me," he encouraged.

She stopped in front of it. "Funny thing, Ben. That solid-looking bridge has a trick of turning into a fragile, swinging rope bridge the minute I step onto it. I don't think I'll attempt it in heels."

"Want me to carry them for you?"

"Please." She removed her shoes and handed them to him.

"Your bare feet are lovely," he said, gallantly.

She laughed. "My feet are the last things I'm worried about, Ben, but thanks, anyway."

He was pleased to hear her laughter, but he had meant what he said. She had beautiful feet. Right now, in the unaccustomed sheer stockings, they looked especially enhancing. He glanced closer—was that polish?

"You got a pedicure!" he exclaimed as she placed her stocking-clad foot onto the metal.

"It seemed like a good idea at the time." Her breathing had already become ragged, but she slowly stepped out onto the walkway, grasping the iron banister with both hands. "It might help if you held onto me."

He stuffed her shoes into his jacket pockets and grabbed the hand she held back toward him

"You can do this, sweetheart." He squeezed her fingers.

Even though the bridge was solid steel, Moriah scooted her feet like a tightrope walker, holding onto him and the hand rail as though she might, at any moment, fall.

And yet, there was absolutely nothing to cause her to lose her balance. The bridge and walkway was heavy and solid.

She began to pant, as though she had been running a race, even though she had traveled only a few feet. They slowly worked their way further onto the bridge, one inch at a time, when he heard a high keening sound come from her throat.

"I'm here, Moriah honey. I won't let you fall. You're safe." He tightened his grip. She shuffled a few more feet and stopped.

"Look down, Ben." Her eyes were shut. "Look down and tell me what you see."

"Water."

"How far down?"

"You could fish off this bridge, Moriah, or easily jump in and swim to shore if you wanted to."

She nodded. "Hold me for a moment."

He wrapped his arms around her. Her heart beat so hard and fast against his chest that he could feel it through his shirt. He held her to him, willing her heart to slow, to normalize.

Ben felt Moriah's pulse slow ever so slightly. In one part of his brain, he realized that anyone observing them would think they were merely engaged in a lover's embrace. No one could possibly imagine the battle this poor girl was waging. Finally, Moriah unwrapped her arms from around his waist. She turned and stared out at the water below.

"It's only a bridge," she said angrily, "and it's only water! And I'm not five years old anymore!"

"That's right, lass," he said, encouragingly. "It's only a bridge. It's only water, and you are most definitely not a child anymore."

She pulled away from him, placed her hands on her hips and fell into the stance he had seen so often, feet planted far apart, shoulders back, ready to take on yet another project. Through some miracle, the strong, capable Moriah was back.

"Are we going the rest of the way?" he asked.

"Absolutely." She grabbed his hand. "This time, I'm going to do it! I really am, Ben. I can feel it."

Ben's heart soared.

They had almost reached the halfway point of the bridge

when a huge semi-truck approached, shifted into a lower gear, and began to cross. Ben felt the beginning vibration of the bridge escalate to a thunderous roar as every bolt and nut in the metal bridge shook in its casing.

The truck was, Ben supposed, driven by a hardworking man, who was merely delivering needed goods to the island, but as the diesel-spewing monster rattled and shook its way onto the bridge, it felt to him like the spawn of Satan.

Moriah froze.

Ben was not a cursing man, but he came close as the heavy truck chewed its way across the bridge, rumbling ominously close to them.

The wind in its wake blew Moriah's hair and dress every which way, and he felt her begin to tremble.

"I want to go back," she whispered.

"Please, sweetheart," he begged. "It was only a truck. You can finish this."

"I want to go back." Her voice was normal, reasonable, as though she were discussing the weather.

"Please try once more, lass," he coaxed.

Her fingers had a death grip on the handrail. Her knuckles had turned white.

"It's only a bridge," he reminded her. "It's only water, remember?"

"Get me off of here."

"Okay. Calm down. I'll help you off."

"NOW!"

Ben didn't hesitate. He picked her up and carried her the few yards back to the earth of Manitoulin Island, Moriah's personal haven—or prison—then propped her against her pickup.

His heart broke as she stood there, gasping for breath, in torn stockings, her pretty dress bedraggled, strands of carefully curled hair sticking to her tear-stained face. She was clenching and unclenching her hands, and her eyes were wild.

"Thank you," she gasped. "Thank you for getting me off there. I couldn't breathe."

"If it hadn't been for the truck, you'd have made it."

"There was a waterfall under the bridge. It made a roaring noise."

"What waterfall?" Ben looked around. "I didn't see a waterfall."

"The one we had to cross to get to the convent, after..."

"After your parents were killed?"

Moriah nodded.

"What happened on that bridge, Moriah?"

"We nearly fell off." Her chest heaved, and her fists spasmodically grabbed handfuls of the skirt of her dress. Her eyes were staring at something far, far away.

"How?"

"Akawe dropped both his spear and our food trying to hang on. The waterfall was so loud, and it kept the footbridge wet and slippery. Akawe had never crossed it with a little girl clutching at him, throwing him off balance. He shouted at me. He said I nearly got us killed."

"I'm so sorry." Ben grabbed her hands, turned them palms up, and kissed them. Then, he kissed her nose and cheeks and forehead, pushing away the tear-mangled hair with his hands.

She responded to his kisses by lifting her face to his warmth and comfort. Her breathing slowed and her eyes focused.

"Don't give up on me, Ben," she said. "Please don't give up on me. I'll fight this. I promise. I want so much to be with you. I'm so sorry. I'm so sorry."

"Don't." His held her and his lips grazed her hair. "It's all right. You don't have to do this ever again. I won't put you through this ever again."

"What do you mean?"

"I have to go back, and I have to finish my work, but I'll be back. If you'll wait for me, I'll come back as soon as I can. I'll get as much work done as possible. I'll ask Nicolas to hunt hard for someone who can replace me, then I'll return."

"To stay?"

"Eventually, to stay."

"How can you do that? You made a promise."

"We'll have to be apart for a while, then I'll come back and never leave you again."

Moriah shook her head. "I can't let you imprison yourself here because of me."

"Most men would consider living on this island with you a paradise, not a prison. I happen to be one of them."

"You will resent me."

"Never."

"I'm not...normal."

"I don't know anyone who is, Moriah."

"You are."

Ben laughed then, a deep, rich laugh that rose from the irony of a childhood spent pulling a father out of bars, scrounging for scraps of food, and stuffing his childhood fears so deep he was amazed he hadn't more phobias than Moriah.

"I'm not even certain what "normal" is, lass. There are only two things I know for certain: I love the Lord, and I love you. You aren't getting rid of me just because you're, let's say—a little bit bridge challenged."

"Okay." Moriah drew a deep breath. "At least, we accomplished one good thing tonight."

"What's that?"

"Tonight, with you beside me, I went the farthest I've ever gone."

CHAPTER 38

The mist rising from the lake was so dense it nearly hid the sunrise as Ben loaded his few possessions into the back of Moriah's truck.

"I guess that about does it." He swung into the passenger side.

"I guess."

He rolled down the window and hung his elbow out. "Do we have time to drive out to the lighthouse before we go? I'd like to see it one more time. With you."

Moriah swallowed past the lump in her throat. "Sure."

As they drove out the road that Jack had built, the limestone tower rose ghost-like before them, silvery in the mist.

"We did a good job together," she said.

"You'll do a good job without me." He turned toward her and laid his arm along the seat behind her. "Don't let the crew slack off just because I'm not here."

"Slack off?" she scoffed. "I'll make them work harder."

Ben tweaked her ponytail. "Right. You're such a slave driver. Keep Jack on the straight and narrow, too. Okay?"

"He had *better* stay on the straight and narrow. Alicia is pregnant again."

"Lucky man."

"You think so?"

"Yes, I think so. I can't think of anything I'd like more than you and a houseful of kids."

Moriah's throat constricted at the thought of being apart from this man for so long. "Will you be able to write to me?"

"Communication in the jungle is difficult. I can't promise much."

Moriah wiped away a renegade tear. She would not cry and make leaving more difficult for him.

"Have you heard from the guy we took the desk to, yet?" Ben said. "It won't be long before you'll be completely finished and can install that."

"No. He's really good and stays pretty backed up. When I took it to him, he said it might take a couple of months to get around to it."

The old desk held little interest to her, right now. It probably held little interest to Ben, as well. He was just trying to make conversation, trying to make this easier for her. Nothing could make this easier for her.

"We have to go if you're going to make it to the Chi-Cheemaun on time," she said. "You'll enjoy riding in it. Most people do."

"It doesn't matter." He caressed the back of her neck. It was a small gesture, but she cherished it.

As they drove to the dock, Ben, for once, wasn't talkative. He seemed preoccupied and distracted, as though he were already winging his way to the Amazon. She wanted to hear his voice, so she nervously asked questions she already knew the answer to.

"Did you get everything?"

"Yes. I didn't have that much to pack."

"Do you have enough money? There's an ATM at the ferry, and I have extra in my account."

"Nicolas paid me before he left."

"Do you need to grab anything at the store? Snacks? Magazines?"

"No."

She gave up and drove.

When they arrived, there was a long line of cars waiting to board. Moriah could see the ones in front driving over the huge gangplank and being swallowed up by the giant boat. She gave a slight shiver.

"Don't get stuck in that line, Moriah; pull over and I'll walk the rest of the way."

Moriah obediently pulled into the parking lot and climbed out of the truck as Ben lifted out his bags. She reached to help, but he shook his head.

"I've got to carry them on board, anyway."

She watched him shouldering his bags. He seemed so distracted and preoccupied, she wondered if he would even remember to kiss her good-bye.

"Ben?" she said in a small voice. "You will come back, won't you? Someday?"

He didn't answer; he just gazed at the huge ferry. Then, he removed a canvas bag from his shoulder and handed it to her.

"What's this?" she asked.

"Two dozen notebooks with the first twenty-three books of the New Testament translated into Yahnowa. Five years of my life. I planned to find a copier machine before I left, but everything snowballed, and I never did. Will you find one and mail the copies to me? Nicolas can tell you how to send them."

"You're going to trust me with them?"

"You're the only person in the world that I would trust with such a task. They'll probably be safer with you than with me."

"I'll take good care of them. You're right. There needs to be copies." Her voice was solemn, but her heart was a little lighter. She now knew absolutely that he would come back. He had entrusted his life's work to her, and she would protect it with her own.

There were people milling about them now, and she knew there would be no last, passionate embrace.

"I love you." He briefly brushed her lips with his. "Promise me you'll wait for me."

"I'll wait for you the rest of my life."

Ben smiled. "Let's pray it doesn't take that long."

One more kiss and he strode away. His broad shoulders easily carried the heavy bags.

She clutched the bag of notebooks to her chest for comfort.

He turned and called back, "If anything happens to me, give those to Nicolas. He'll know what to do." Then he waved and disappeared into the maw of the ferry.

If something happened to him? What a terrible thought! Nothing could happen to him. He had to come back here to her.

She ran then, to the edge of the island, watching the giant ferry, hungry for one last glimpse of him.

It seemed to take forever, but as the ferry pulled away from the dock, Ben reappeared on deck. Their eyes locked. She waved with one hand, clutching the canvas bag with the other. Ben waved back, then fisted his right hand and brought it to his heart.

Moriah did the same in reply. She knew what the gesture meant. Ben would come back to her, even if it took years. He had promised. And she would wait for him, even if it took years. She had promised. She had faith that, someday, a preacher would hear their vows. Someday, they would sign a marriage certificate and become man and wife. But a lasting covenant was being made, an oath taken, in that silent gesture they held until she could no longer see him because of the distance and the tears.

She grasped the rusted metal of the guardrail and strained to see. Rain began to fall, creating a gauzy curtain between her and the ferry, which now dipped beneath the horizon. The only thing separating her and Ben was wind and rain.

The panic began to set in as he disappeared. What if this was the last time she saw him? What if something bad *did* happen to him?

She could hire a speedboat to take her out to the ferry. She could hire a small plane to take her to the airport in Toronto where he was first headed. She could...she could...

She didn't even own a passport.

The only thing separating her from Ben was her own weakness and fear.

As the people around her ran for shelter, Moriah was in so much emotional pain, she fell to her knees and curled herself over the bag that held Ben's notebooks, shielding them from the rain.

As the rain beat against her body, she pounded the earth with her fist. "I can fix anything, Lord," she sobbed. "You *know* I can fix anything—but I can't fix me. I'm broken, and I can't fix me. I've tried and tried, but I can't fix me!"

MORIAH'S STRONGHOLD

The Lord is a stronghold for the oppressed,
a stronghold in times of trouble.

— PSALM 9:9 ESV

CHAPTER 1

MANITOULIN ISLAND, ONTARIO

August, 1998

Moriah's drive home from the ferry in the rain was mercifully short. As the windshield wipers kept time with her thudding heart, she managed to pull herself together long enough to get home without wrecking her truck. She was grateful that Katherine and Nicolas were still on their honeymoon. They would not see her go straight to Ben's cabin to try to comfort her. It would have been unbearable to talk to anyone right now.

She told herself she was merely doing her job, being a good caretaker, cleaning up after a departing guest, but she knew in her heart it was more than that. She wanted to breathe the same air he had breathed, run her hand over the desk where he had worked, touch the bed where he had lain.

The rain was supposed to stop soon. The crew was probably at the worksite right now waiting it out in the cottage and in their vehicles. It was her job to be there with them, but she didn't care enough to put forth the effort. She didn't care about anything right now. In fact, she looked back with wonder at the significance the lighthouse once had in her life. Nothing mattered to her now except the fact that Ben was gone.

She opened the door to his cabin and stepped into a heart-breaking silence and too much neatness. Ben had washed his few dishes and placed them in the drainer to dry. It would have been nice had he not done so. She would gladly have taken care of them for him. It would have given her something to do for him. She removed the few dry goods he had left behind; cereal and crackers, a few cans of fruit, and placed them in a box to carry back to the lodge.

She opened the refrigerator and stood for a long time, staring at a half empty jug of milk, some cheese, an apple, a couple of eggs, and then she closed the door, unable to make herself remove them.

Everything in the cabin he had touched or purchased suddenly seemed holy. It felt exactly like the days after her grandfather died, when she and Katherine had folded his clothes and packed away his life. Grief. Pure unadulterated grief coursed through her now exactly as it had back then.

But he isn't dead. He'll come back. He promised he would! If Ben makes a promise, he keeps it. Whether it's to me or to the Yahnowa, Ben always keeps his promise.

Annoyed with herself for grieving over a man who was very much alive and well, she wrenched open the refrigerator door, jerked the milk out and poured it down the sink. The apple got tossed in the trash along with the cheese and eggs before she could change her mind. She would have to harden her heart and fight this sadness if she were to continue to function.

The towels in the bathroom were still damp from Ben's shower. He had once told her that the thing he loved most about staying here was being able to take a shower whenever he wanted; a luxury he didn't have in the jungle. Again, trying to tough it out, she gathered up the towels and threw them into a laundry basket.

Then she went into his bedroom and lost every shred of resolve.

She had planned to strip the sheets and carry them to the lodge for laundering, but one look at his bed, unmade, as though he'd climbed straight out of it, and she came undone. Her fingers caressed the hollow in the pillow where his head had lain and smoothed the coverlet that had kept him warm only a short time earlier.

Giving in to a primal urge for comfort, she removed her wet shoes and carefully slipped beneath the sheets, breathing in the scent of his body left on them and nestling the side of her face into the indentation his head had made in the pillow.

It seemed like today had already lasted forever, but the clock on the wall told her it was barely noon. Ben would be in Toronto now. He was still on Canadian soil. Self-hatred coursed through her. She should be with *him* right now instead of lying in this bed alone, trying to draw comfort from his scent on a pillow.

Moriah curled into a fetal position to try to shield her heart from any more pain. Her attention was momentarily caught by a spot on the far corner of the ceiling. It looked like it might be from a roof leak, but she didn't care.

It felt so strange not to care about the spot or the leak that might have caused it, and she wondered if she could possibly ever go about her daily life again carrying this much sadness.

She must have dozed, or perhaps she was simply sunk in such despair that the knock on the cabin door did not register, but the next thing she knew, Jack was standing over her, looking down at her with a puzzled expression on his face.

"Are you sick?" he asked.

"Go away, Jack."

He ignored her request. "What's wrong with you?"

"How did you find me?" She sat up. Being caught in Ben's bed in the middle of the morning was embarrassing.

"I needed to ask you about some supplies. Your truck was at the lodge, but you weren't in there. One of your guests said they thought they saw you go into Cabin 10." He glanced around. "Where's Ben?"

"I took him to the Chi-Cheemaun a little while ago."

"Why?"

"He's going back to Brazil; to the Yahnowa tribe."

"But we aren't finished with the lighthouse yet."

"I don't think that mattered," she said. "He told me that he knew you and I would make sure it got finished."

"Is he coming back?"

"He said he would... someday." Moriah felt a lump form in her throat.

The lump grew bigger and she couldn't control it. Before she knew it, she was sobbing out the whole sad story.

"Let me see if I've got this straight," Jack said. "You love him, and he loves you. The only thing you have to do in order to be together is get over this I-can't-leave-the-island thing?"

Moriah sniffed. "I guess that's about it."

"Then," Jack said. "You need to get over it."

"Seriously? That's the best you got? You don't think I don't *know* that?" Minutes ago she'd been sobbing into his shirt. Now she felt like smacking him. In some ways Jack could be so dense. "Overcoming a phobia is not easy!"

"Neither is beating alcoholism," Jack said.

"I'm sure it isn't, but what does that have to do with me and Ben?"

"I've found that going to Alcoholics Anonymous helps a lot."

"It isn't the same. They don't have AA for what I'm dealing with."

"Probably not," Jack said. "Maybe there's something else that would help."

"Like what?" She wiped her eyes and nose on Ben's sheet, figuring she'd be stuffing it into the lodge washing machine pretty soon anyway.

"I don't know." Jack shrugged. "I'm not any good with stuff like this. I'm thinking maybe a shrink or something?"

Moriah felt a little hurt. "You think I need a shrink?"

"Having to live on a small chunk of land for the rest of your life for no particular reason might be an indication."

"There's one problem with that solution."

"What?"

"There aren't any shrinks on Manitoulin Island. At least not yet."

"Maybe you could import one."

"Shrinks don't do house calls. I think you have to go to their office and lay on a couch or something."

"Too bad." Jack rose and headed for the door. "I liked Ben. So did Alicia."

After Jack left, Moriah flopped back down against the pillows and stared at the spot on the ceiling again. She didn't usually stop in the middle of the day for more than a moment or two, but today she needed to think and to think hard. Ben's abrupt departure had blindsided her.

Over the next hour, she deliberately and carefully came up with a plan. When she was finished, she threw back the covers, stripped the bed, dumped the linens in the laundry basket, slung Ben's rucksack of notebooks over her shoulder and marched up to the lodge.

The first thing she did was place Ben's translation notebooks high on a shelf in her closet. She would deal with those later. Then she stuffed the linens into the washing machine and watched the hot water rush in.

She had created this upstairs laundry room out of an unused closet, hanging the drywall, installing the clothes dryer and washer, making shelves the right width and length to store all the bedsheets and towels they needed for the resort. . It looked nice, and everything worked.

She had fixed nearly everything that was broken around the resort for years as well as making new out of old. But she had done all of it while walking around wounded. Moriah was tired of being broken, of limping through life. Tired of having faulty circuits running through her brain. She had no idea how to rewire herself, but on the rare times something broke around the resort that she didn't know how to fix, she had called in an expert.

She left the washing machine filling up and headed out the door.

Jack was right. It was high time she called for expert help.

CHAPTER 2

"I need a shrink." She burst into the doctor's private office.

"I told her she needed an appointment..." The nurse said, behind her.

The doctor looked confused. "But, I'm a pediatrician."

"I know," Moriah said. "You were my doctor when I was little. Do you remember when I was five and came back from South America after my parents were killed?"

He peered at her more closely. "Aren't you Katherine Robertson's niece?"

"The child who didn't talk for two years?" Moriah said. "Yep. That's me."

"But you did start to speak again. It just took some time. I heard that you were doing fine." He fiddled with a paperweight contrived of miniature golf clubs. Moriah noticed that his hands shook. "Why do you think you need a shr... a psychologist?"

"Because I'm *not* doing fine." Moriah put both of her hands flat on his desk and leaned toward him, keeping her voice low and steady. "I can't cross a bridge. I can't fly in a plane. I can't cross the gangplank onto the ferry. I have nightmares. I need help and I don't know who to contact."

"Check with my office staff. They might have a list of numbers you can try." He unclipped his stethoscope and stuffed it into his top drawer. "You'll have to excuse me. Morning office hours are over and I need to go home."

Moriah, stunned, stood back and let him pass. There were other doctors on the island she could have approached, but she had been so physically healthy as an adult that she had never needed to see one. This was the only doctor she knew. Her memories of him were ones of kindness. His abrupt departure stung.

"He really is a good doctor," the nurse whispered behind her, "but he has the beginning stages of Parkinson's and tires easily. He wants to retire and there isn't anyone to take his place."

"I'm truly sorry about that, but I need some answers."

"Come to the front office," the nurse held the door open for her. "I might have some information I can give you."

"A list of shrinks?" Moriah cocked an eyebrow.

"No. More than that. My cousin suffered from severe panic attacks too," the nurse said. "She tried a lot of different therapies and therapists, but eventually found one who really helped. She said the therapist was a little different in her methods, but they worked."

The nurse found the number in the office Rolodex, scribbled it on a card and handed it to her.

"Where is he located?" Moriah asked.

"He's a she."

"Where is she located?"

"Cleveland, Ohio," the nurse said. "But I doubt she'll be willing to work with a patient over the phone."

"Actually," Moriah pocketed the number. "I was wondering if she liked to fish."

CHAPTER 3

The voice that greeted Moriah on the phone was low, warm and cultured. Unfortunately, she had gotten the psychologist's answering machine. The voice explained that the doctor was out of the office, but gave a number to call if it was an emergency.

Moriah considered for a moment. Yes. This was an emergency. Twenty years of nightmares and panic attacks and watching the man she loved sail away from her was definitely an emergency.

She dialed the number.

The same calm voice answered, but this time it was not a recording, and there were children's voices in the background.

"Dr. Crystal Barrett here, may I help you?"

Crystal? Moriah wondered how skilled of a psychologist she could be with a name like Crystal. It sounded like a better name for a head cheerleader.

"Excuse me," Dr. Barrett said, when Moriah didn't immediately respond. "Is anyone there?"

"Umm, yes. It's me." Moriah found her voice." I mean, my

name is Moriah Robertson and I'm calling from Manitoulin Island, Canada."

"Robertson. I don't remember a Moriah Robertson. Are you a patient of mine?"

"No. But I want to be."

"I'm so sorry. You'll need to call my office tomorrow. I don't have my appointment calendar with me."

The voice was kind, even though it sounded as though Moriah had interrupted the family's dinner. She could hear cutlery and the scrapping of plates. Childish voices drifted over the phone, mixed with a man's.

"I can't make an appointment to come see you, Dr. Barrett. I can't leave this island." She clung to the receiver. This wasn't going to work. But it *had* to work. It simply had to.

Her heart was pounding hard and she broke out in a cold sweat as she tried to think of what to say next.

"I have money." Then she banged her forehead with her palm. What a nutcase she must sound. Dr. Crystal was probably used to getting weird phone calls from people during supper, but Moriah really hated being one of them.

Dr. Crystal shushed the children before she spoke again. "You can't leave the island?"

"Not since I was five."

"But, I live in Cleveland."

"Here's the deal." Moriah leaned her forehead against the wall. "I own a resort, Dr. Barrett. It's a lovely place. People even travel from foreign countries to stay with us. I was hoping you and your family would like to come and have a nice vacation? A week. A month. No charge. There's a playground for the children and I can show your husband all the best fishing spots. I'll pay you for your time too."

She hated the note of begging that had crept into her voice.

There was total silence on the other end of the phone and

Moriah wondered if the doctor had hung up. She wouldn't blame her.

"It's called Robertson's Resort." Moriah tried to lend a little more legitimacy to her offer. "It's a real place. There's a light-house nearby that we're in the process of restoring this summer."

More silence while Moriah waited and watched the second hand tick away on the clock in front of her. Then finally...

"Moriah, I don't know you or what your issues are, but I'm going to take a leap of faith here and tell you that something remarkable may have happened. My husband and I had a two-week vacation planned with our children. It's rare that he and I can coordinate our schedules to have time off together and the children were so excited about our vacation. But the owners of the condominium we had rented at Myrtle Beach called and cancelled today. Something about plumbing issues."

Moriah gasped, threw her hand over her mouth, and clung to the receiver as the room spun around her.

"My husband does love to fish." There was a smile in the doctor's voice. "He rarely gets a chance. Where did you say this place is again?"

"Manitoulin Island. It's the largest freshwater island in the world and our resort is on the far south side of the island, right on Lake Huron."

"Give me a minute to ask my husband what he thinks."

Moriah heard muffled voices.

"We have three children." Dr. Barrett came back on the phone. "Is there room?"

"Yes!" Her voice was ragged with hope and excitement. "I'll have my best cabin ready for you. It has two bedrooms, a kitchen, and a couch in the front room that pulls out into a good bed. It's right on the beach and it has the most gorgeous view."

"Can it be ready a week from now?"

"It was ready yesterday."

"Please don't take offense, but Mike wants to do a little research into your resort first."

"I totally understand," Moriah said. "Tell him to call the Chamber of Commerce here on Manitoulin. They'll vouch for me."

"We'll do that," Crystal said. "But I have a strong feeling we might be meeting one another soon."

Moriah gave her the phone number of the resort and started to hang up when the doctor's voice stopped her.

"I'm very good at what I do, Moriah. There's a real chance that I can help you, but two weeks doesn't give us much time. You will need to work hard."

"Trust me, doctor," Moriah said. "If there is one thing I know how to do, it is how to work hard."

Based on the encouragement that Moriah heard in the doctor's voice, she decided to do something she wouldn't have dreamed of doing even a month earlier. She got in her truck and headed over to the post office on Mira Street. It was time to begin the process of getting a passport. Owning one had suddenly become as important to her as her purchase of the giant globe she kept in her bedroom.

CHAPTER 4

"Hi." One week later Dr. Crystal Barrett jumped out of the white SUV and extended her hand. "I'm Crystal. You must be Moriah?"

The woman was so tiny, Moriah could hardly believe she had given birth to the three children she and her husband had brought with them.

Crystal had chestnut brown hair curling down her back, khaki Capri's, a cropped red shirt and matching red flip-flops. She also had the kindest brown eyes Moriah had ever seen. How could this elfin woman help her?

"Your cabin is down there," she pointed. "Number 10."

"John, would you mind?"

"Got it covered, babe." A tall, good-looking man was standing beside the van. "Take your time."

He climbed in and started the motor. Three elementary school-age children were busy chattering together in the back.

Crystal touched Moriah's arm.

"John and the children will be fine. It was nice of you to invite us. It's been a long ride and I'm tired of sitting. Would you like to show me around your island while he and the children get everything unpacked?"

"It's a really big island."

"Then let's start with the lighthouse, I've always wanted to see one up close."

It was the exact right thing to say. Moriah had been feeling awkward about opening up to a stranger, so she was happy to have the task of showing Crystal the work they were doing on the lighthouse.

Soon, they were finished with the tour and Moriah found herself sitting on the cottage steps watching the sunset with her newest guest. The awkwardness was gone. The lovely, young doctor had somehow become a friend.

"I can certainly see why you love this place so much," Crystal said. "I can feel its power. Manitoulin Island is a healing place."

"It's always seemed that way to me," Moriah said.

"This is an especially lovely spot. It might be a good place to start telling me what's in your heart," Crystal said. "If you want."

"Like what should I say?" Moriah asked. "I don't know how to do this."

"Start at the beginning," Crystal said. "And tell me everything that's bothering you. I can listen for a really long time."

No one, not even Ben, had known the right questions to ask, the right moment to stay silent, the right verbal prompt to get her started again. This fairy-like woman *did* know. Moriah didn't just tell the doctor what was in her heart, she poured out her guts. Even *she* was surprised at how many words she had bottled up inside of her. Crystal quietly listened to every last one.

Finally, as the last rays of the sun disappeared, Moriah simply ran out of words. All her worries, fears and bad memories had been deposited at Dr. Barrett's flip-flop clad feet. Crystal now sat, chin on fist, one foot tapping, lost in thought.

"I think that's about it." Moriah awkwardly came to the end of her life story.

"Probably not, but it's a good start. Do you feel any better?"

Moriah mentally examined herself. "Yeah. I guess I do. Sort of."

"Takes some of the pressure off when one gets to truly talk. It's like lancing a boil."

"I've never had a boil."

"Me either." Crystal laughed. "I've never even lanced one. It's mainly just something people say. A boil is quite painful though, and lancing it helps drain all the poison out so the body can heal itself. Talking honestly to someone often does the same thing; helps drain some of the toxins from the mind so it can begin to heal."

The doctor stood and brushed off the seat of her Capri's.

"I'm going to think about everything you've said tonight. You'll need to go to work tomorrow and I'll have fun fishing with Mike and playing with the kids. Let's plan to get together tomorrow evening and see what insights God provides. I'll meet you back here."

CHAPTER 5

With renewed enthusiasm fueled entirely by hope, Moriah threw herself back into the work at the lighthouse the next day.

"You doing okay?" Jack buckled on his tool belt.

"Yes." Moriah tied a handkerchief around her forehead to keep the sweat from getting in her eyes. "And if Ben comes back—excuse me—*when* Ben comes back, I want to have everything about this lighthouse finished and ready to show him."

"Have you heard anything from him?"

"He called from the Toronto airport to tell me he had gotten there safely. That's the last I talked with him."

"What about Katherine and Nicolas?"

"Got one phone call from the Cayman Islands." Moriah grinned. "Katherine sounded all giggly."

"It's hard to imagine Katherine giggly," Jack said. "I suppose we can assume the honeymoon is going well?"

"Sounded like it to me."

"If anyone deserves a nice honeymoon, it's Katherine."

"I agree. Nicolas is not my cup of tea, but he seems to be exactly what Katherine has waited for all these years."

"No accounting for taste." Jack drew on his work gloves. "Alicia picking me, for instance."

"Or Ben picking me."

"He's a smart man, Moriah. He knows a good thing when he sees it."

"You suppose?"

"Suppose nothing. Nobody miters corners like you do. Now help me get this lumber off the truck. The foghorn room is not going to remodel itself, you know."

It was a two-day trek into the rainforest to reach the boundaries of the Yahnowa. Ben's clothes were either soaked or damp for the entire two days. This was nothing new to him. He was used to living wet in the jungle and had learned long ago to ignore the discomfort. That was something easily endured, but the ache of being separated from Moriah was nearly intolerable.

His mind was so occupied with the image of Moriah crying and falling to her knees, as the ferry took him away from her, and the waves pounded against the rocky Canadian shore, that his first glimpse of the Yahnowa village felt dreamlike. The scene before him of fragile huts, smoking cook fires and naked children seemed unreal, like something lifted out of the pages of a magazine.

Then he saw Abraham and Violet sweltering beneath the shade of their loosely thatched porch.

"Hello, Ben." Violet remained where she was, seated on a bench.

Normally, she would jump up and greet him with a hug. This time she could only manage a weak smile.

"What are you two still doing here?" he asked. "I thought you were going home."

"Violet was not strong enough to leave on foot," Abraham explained, with a quick, worried glance at his wife.

It was obvious to Ben that Violet had kept her secret far too long. He was shocked at how feeble she had grown over the summer. He understood now why Abraham sounded so desperate on the phone.

"She didn't tell me." Abraham said later, after drawing Ben aside. "She kept hoping the problem would go away. She didn't want to keep me from my work."

"How long has she suspected?"

"Since the week before you left."

"I could have taken her with me!" Ben groaned. "I could have gotten her to a good hospital."

"I know," Abraham said. "Trust me, that thought has been keeping me up at night."

"So, what's the plan?"

"When I trekked out to make that phone call to you, I looked up Ron Meacham. His helicopter has been out of commission for a while. It takes a lot of time and effort to track down parts for that old Huey of his, but he says he thinks he'll have it ready within the next couple of days. Some of the villagers have been clearing a space big enough to set it down."

"Thank God for the Christian Pilot's Association," Ben said.

"Truly," Abraham said. "They are such a lifeline."

"You and Violet will be sipping sweet iced tea with your son in Alabama in no time."

"Ben." Abraham's face was grim. "I don't think Violet and I will be coming back."

The two men had been close for far too long for Ben to fall back on platitudes.

"I know, brother." Ben placed a comforting hand on the older man's shoulder.

"I don't think I could bear it if you weren't here to continue our work." Abraham searched Ben's face. "You will stay, won't you, son? You'll see this work through?"

Ben's heart was heavy as he made the promise he knew Abraham desperately needed to hear.

"Yes, Abraham. I'll stay."

CHAPTER 6

The evening sessions with Crystal were often painful. The woman used questions as skillfully as a surgeon wielded a scalpel.

Moriah was shocked to discover that she had clearly seen Chief Moawa's face. That painted mask of murderous intent was permanently etched in her mind. In fact, she came to realize that all the boogeymen of her childhood had worn Moawa's face. Her childhood monsters weren't nebulous or imagined. Hers had been real. Too real.

As they sat at the lodge's dining room table, Crystal handed her a blank piece of paper.

"Moriah, can you draw?"

"Not well, but I took a couple art classes in high school."

"Good." She handed her a pencil. "I want you to draw a picture of Chief Moawa."

"I don't think I can."

"Try," Crystal said. "What color hair did he have?"

"Black, of course," Moriah said. "Everyone had black hair except some of the very old."

"So, start with that." Crystal pushed a small box of crayons toward her. "Use color if it will help."

When Moriah finished, even though the sketch was rough, she stared at a frightening, painted face, full of evil. She had no idea if it was the least bit correct, but it was a fairly accurate representation of her childhood memory.

Crystal looked over her shoulder. "Scares the dickens out of me. I'd wet the bed if that guy showed up in my nightmares. You think he still looks like this? Twenty years can take the juice out of a man. Even a bad man."

"Doesn't matter. His face will always be the same to me."

"You ever wonder if he's still alive?"

"I never thought much about it. Why?"

"Maybe you could go see him sometime and tell him what he did to you."

"Go meet him?" Moriah shuddered. "Not in this lifetime. Not ever."

"Seriously," Crystal tapped the picture with her finger. "It would be nice if you could find out if this particular boogeyman still exists."

"I don't have a clue how to find that out," Moriah said.

"Does Ben know?"

"I never asked him."

"Ask him sometime." Crystal held the picture at arm's length, then laid it back on the table. "In the meantime, let's see what we can do with this."

Crystal chose a black crayon from the box and started sketching on Chief Moawa's picture, her tongue clamped between her teeth in concentration. As the picture began to change, Moriah burst into astonished laughter. Moawa now bore a strong resemblance to Mad Magazine's "What Me Worry?" picture of Alfred E. Newman. A tooth was missing, his ears stuck straight out, and a shock of hair fell over one eye.

Crystal had taken evil and made it look goofy.

"Tape this picture to your bedroom wall and every time you feel a boogeyman attack coming on look at this and laugh."

"This will work?"

"Maybe. At least a little bit," Crystal said. "I have one on my wall at home, too."

Moriah stared at her friend in surprise. "You have a boogeyman?"

"Actually, I think of him as a giant. Did you ever hear the story of the giants who were so terrifying to the people of Israel they were afraid to cross the Jordan River into the Promised Land?"

"I know the story."

"For me, the giant was a man in our neighborhood who liked little girls way too much and very inappropriately."

"Oh no. I'm so sorry, Crystal."

"Me too. Over the years, I've discovered nearly everyone has a giant of some sort in their life. It's not always a person. Sometimes, it's a habit they want to break, or a handicap they have to overcome. Sometimes nothing more than negative words they heard in childhood that they continue to replay over and over without even realizing they're doing it."

"But you're so strong."

Crystal laughed at that with such abandon that Moriah feared she would fall out of her chair. Finally, she sobered up enough to speak.

"You have no idea how much stronger you are than I used to be, Moriah. You managed to have a whole, large island as your personal boundary. I did fine for a while, stuffed my memories down deep, attended college and made good grades." She smiled. "I even got an advanced degree in psychology. Then, shortly after the birth of my second child, I became reluctant to go outside my house. It was my haven. Then I began to spend more time in my bedroom. It was upstairs and it felt safer than, say, the kitchen or living room."

Crystal absently stirred her cup of cooling tea with one finger.

"It wasn't until my husband found me sitting in my closet with the door closed, our two older children watching cartoons on our bed, and our third baby on my lap, that he forced me to seek help. It was hard, but I fought my way out of that dark place and have been helping others ever since."

"You fix broken people." Moriah understood completely. "I fix broken things."

"You also build new with good materials, and the things you build are strong and not easily broken. I'm raising children who will, hopefully, never feel the need to sit in a closet as an adult with the door shut. I'm teaching others how to do the same. You will build a good life, Moriah. Whether here, or in the rainforest. As motivated as you are, and with some of the tools I'll give you, you'll build a life as strong and filled with purpose as... as that lighthouse you've put so much care into."

Moriah gazed out of the window at the lake and the gleaming tower. "I like the sound of that, Crystal, and I love the silly picture of Moawa. But what about the bridge? Drawing a funny picture of the bridge won't help me. How do I get across it without feeling like I'm having a heart attack?"

"One step at a time, like everything else. A major tool I'm going to teach you to use is desensitization."

"Desensitization?"

"Let me explain it by telling you a story. Did you ever hear of an author by the name of Marjorie Kinnan Rawlings?"

"I'm not much of a reader."

"Doesn't matter. Rawlings wrote a famous book called *The Yearling*."

Moriah shook her head. She had never heard of it.

"It was made into a movie many years ago."

"I don't have a lot of time to watch movies."

Crystal sighed. "It doesn't matter. What matters is that Marjorie bought an orange grove in Florida and moved there from New York City."

Although Moriah didn't spend a lot of time reading, she did like a good story, especially if it ended with something she could use to cross the bridge. She settled back against her chair, ready to listen.

"Did she like Florida?"

"She loved it. Absolutely loved it. Felt like it was the one place on earth where she truly belonged. Except for one thing."

"What was that?"

"Marjorie was terrified of snakes."

Moriah shuddered. "I can understand that. I've heard there are some bad snakes in Florida."

"Yes, there are, and while Marjorie waited and worked and tried to get published, she supported herself by growing oranges. But there was a problem. Florida farmers can't afford to be too afraid of snakes. She had to get over her fear if she was going to run an orange grove."

"What did she do?"

"She desensitized herself. There were professional rattlesnake hunters in the area, men who made their living hunting, selling and collecting venom. She asked permission to go out with them on a hunt."

"I'd die."

"Marjorie thought she would too, but she was a determined woman. She loved her farm and needed to be able to take care of it without running into the house and cowering in her bed every time she saw a snake. She loved the farm so much she was willing to fight against her fear."

Moriah was pretty sure she knew where Crystal was going with this story.

"She spent several days on that hunt. During which, she saw the men capture and handle dozens of snakes. Marjorie got to see more snakes than she had ever seen in her life. By the end of the hunt, she had stopped jumping out of her skin each time one crossed her path. Eventually, she was able to catch and handle them herself. After that she was never afraid again."

"A bridge isn't a snake."

"Same principle though. You'll need to become so familiar with the bridge that all its power over you will drain away."

"I'll do anything if it means getting to be with Ben."

"Good, because great love can conquer great fear. Fighting this because of your love for Ben is a good thing, but it might not be enough," Crystal said. "How do you feel about yourself? Do you love yourself enough to do this?"

Moriah squirmed a little, uncomfortable with the question. "I don't know. That sounds a little self-centered."

"Then let me phrase it differently. Do you ever dislike or hate yourself?"

Moriah thought about that.

"Sometimes."

"So many people feel that way. Women especially. Maybe it's a societal thing, I don't know. What I do know is that self-hatred can severely use up a person's strength and weaken their courage."

"So, what am I supposed to do?"

"Let's try an exercise that I have found helpful. Do you know any five-year-old girls?"

"Yes. Alicia's little sister, Emma. She's adorable."

"Innocent? Loving? Trusting?"

"Oh yes."

"Do you love her?"

"It would be hard not to love Emma."

"Okay then," Crystal said. "I want you to close your eyes. Imagine Emma having to see the same things you saw that terrible night. What does it make you want to do?"

"I want to shield her and run away with her to safety."

"You can do that now. For yourself."

Moriah opened her eyes. "I don't understand."

"Let me try to explain. There is a little girl who wants to be safe and loved hidden inside of every woman. Sometimes that child has gone through more than any child should have to endure. Instead of protecting that precious little girl, many of us spend our lives beating up on her. Because we were abused, we continue to abuse the child within us without even realizing we are doing it."

Crystal handed Moriah a small pillow from the couch. "Hold this in your arms for now. Close your eyes again. This time, I want you to go down deep. I want you to imagine wiping the tears from that little five-year-old face that used to be yours. Pretend that you are cradling her in your arms."

Moriah tried to envision her own face as a child. There was a photo that Katherine had taken soon after her parents died. She had been a pretty little girl with delicate features, dressed in a flowered blue dress. Her long hair was tied up with two matching bows. There was a Christmas tree in the background, and a pile of presents in front of her, but she wasn't smiling. Instead her eyes were fearful as she looked at the camera and her face was troubled.

As she thought about that frightened little girl, Moriah held the pillow closer to her chest and began to rock slightly.

"Tell her it's going to be okay," Crystal said. "Tell her that you are all grown-up now. You're big and strong and, from this point on, you will take really good care of her. Say it aloud."

Moriah opened her eyes and looked at Crystal. "Are you sure about this?"

"Trust me," Crystal said. "This is important."

Moriah tried to do as Crystal said. She went deep. In her mind, she looked down into that small, frightened face. That innocent child had gone through such a terrible experience. No one deserved to go through that.

"It wasn't your fault," Moriah began. "You didn't do anything wrong."

She stopped. Looked at Crystal, who nodded encouragement. Moriah closed her eyes again. Held the pillow a little closer.

"It wasn't your fault that those bad men hurt your parents. You were a brave little girl. You tried to run to them. You fought to get out of the hut and tried to scream at the bad men to stop, but Akawe held you back. He knew you couldn't do anything to save them. It wasn't your fault that you survived. Akawe saved your life. You were exactly where your mommy and daddy wanted you to be—where you *needed* to be. Safe in Akawe's house."

"Go on," Crystal whispered.

"You'll go through some scary things, but you will be okay."

Scene after horrific scene ran through her mind as a feeling of protectiveness washed over her toward the little girl she had once been. Yes, it was easy to love the damaged child who had grown up to become her own flawed self.

"I'm big and strong now," Moriah continued. "I'm all grown up and I can protect you now. You didn't deserve to go through what happened. You deserve to grow up and have a good life. You deserve to be loved."

"People can do amazingly courageous things for someone they love," Crystal said. "Your love for Ben is strong and it might be enough, but I'm thinking you'll also need love for yourself— for that hurt little girl within you—to break through the barrier of crossing that bridge so you can give her a normal life. Promise her that you will love her and fight for her."

"I love you." Hot tears began to course down her cheeks. "And I promise to fight hard for you as long as I live."

Crystal gave her the space she needed to cry for her lost childhood.

CHAPTER 7

As Moriah dressed for work the next morning, she felt like there had been a subtle shift deep within her. Everything felt a little brighter, a little lighter, and she could hardly wait to start her day.

Early morning sunlight glinted off the new windows of the foghorn room across the lake. She had made a dramatic change in her original plan for the large room that had once connected the lighthouse cottage with the tower and she was enormously proud of the result.

The foghorn room had sustained the greatest part of the steam explosion that created the crack in the light tower. One whole wall had been destroyed with that explosion. Originally, she had planned to rebuild the outer wall as it had once been. Then, the idea came to her that filling that space with a wall of windows would be an even better idea. By the time she finished drawing up plans, the walls on both sides were filled with the most durable windows money could buy.

It was going to be a lovely, large room that would not only

give people a magnificent view, but would capture the limited sunlight that Manitoulin Island received in the winter. Plants would thrive in that room. Whoever got to live in the lighthouse was going to love spending time there.

The lantern room at the top of the tower was coming along nicely. It was all so beautiful—a feast for her eyes and a balm to her heart.

She tore her gaze away from the window and finished getting dressed. As usual, the last thing she did before leaving her room was give the giant globe a spin. Then she closed her eyes and rested her finger lightly on the surface as it spun.

When the globe stopped spinning, the country of Brazil lay beneath her finger.

She had not expected that. Often, she ended up somewhere out in the ocean, but today her finger had stopped in the middle of the Amazon rainforest.

Superstition was not one of her weaknesses. She knew there was nothing magical about the huge globe upon which she had spent a month's income. Spinning it and thinking about visiting one of those countries was just a game. She was only pretending that she would one day be able to visit those places.

Today, however, it did seem to be an omen. What was it that Crystal had said last night? Great love could overcome great fear?

If that was true, and she had faith that it was, there was no doubt in her mind that she would someday be able to go to Ben.

Of course, there was still that blasted bridge to cross, but for the first time ever she knew she would conquer it. It wouldn't be easy, and it might not happen all at once, but it *would* happen. For Ben, for her, and for that little girl still within her she would cross it.

In the meantime, she still had a resort to run.

Alicia was already at the lodge and perched on a high stool behind the reception desk when Moriah went downstairs. Little Betsy was napping, snuggled into a stretchy blue wrap that Alicia used when she was working. It freed both of her hands, one of which held a phone to her ear, while the other one patted Betsy's tiny bottom.

"Thanks, yes, I'll tell her." Alicia hung up.

"Tell me what?" Moriah said.

"That was Tom Hawkins; the guy who has been working on the old desk that was in the lighthouse."

"Is he finished?" Moriah asked, eagerly.

"Yes. He said to have a couple men from your crew to come pick it up tomorrow, but he said for you to make sure and come with them."

"Why?"

"He said there's something he wants to show you."

"That's intriguing," Moriah said. "Anything else I need to know before I head out to the worksite?"

"The guests in cabins eight and six are leaving this morning. We don't have those two cabins reserved for anyone else at present. My guess is that we can start shutting them down for winter. I'm not sure we have enough toilet paper to get us through to the end of the season. Do you want me to order another box?"

"Yes," Moriah said. "And that reminds me. We need to have the septic tank checked soon. I don't want to risk any overflows. Can you call Amos Bradshaw for me?"

"Got it." Alicia jotted something on a notepad.

"I'm starting to wonder what we did around here without you," Moriah said.

"Me too!" Alicia grinned. "I really appreciate the job. It's great to be able to bring my baby to work with me."

At that moment Betsy awoke, poked her little head out of the wrap and gave Moriah a rosy, sleepy smile. She had her father's blonde hair and it was tousled from being inside the wrap.

"That baby is such a hit with the guests," Moriah said. "I think we might have to put her on the payroll too."

Thanks to Alicia, she felt like she could leave the resort, even with Katherine and Nicolas gone, with a clear mind. Hiring Jack's wife was one of the best things she'd done this summer. The young woman looked after the resort as though it were her own.

As Moriah drove out to the worksite, she thought about the desk that Liam Robertson had built. She looked forward to seeing what Tom had done with it. She couldn't remember a time when it wasn't scarred and blackened with the slow accumulation of grime. It was so heavy, it would take two strong men to help her lift it into the truck. Jack said the thing weighed well over three-hundred pounds and it was an awkward shape.

She had not heard from Ben in over a week. He had called once after landing in South America—then silence. She imagined him trekking through the jungle now, or maybe arriving at the Yahnowa village. It was maddening not to know what was happening.

She recalled the conversation they had the evening before he left.

"When I finish my work for the Yahnowa," he had told her. "I intend to leave nothing behind except a good translation of the Scripture, and what language skills I can give them. Other than that, the Smiths and I are determined to leave their culture intact."

"In what way?" Moriah asked.

"We've never encouraged them to wear modern clothing. In the circumstances and weather they live in, their near nudity makes sense. It's always wet in the rainforest. While the Smiths and I are walking around in wet, steaming clothes, the Yahnowa are quite comfortable. In the past, some missionaries did a lot of damage in trying to change everything about the people to whom they were trying to minister. We've learned the hard way over the years to respect the wisdom of the elders, and to pay attention to their medicine men. Sometimes they know things we do not. Of course, sometimes we know things they don't. It is good to listen to one another."

"So, you don't try to change anything?"

"The killing of people in other tribes. We've tried hard to stop that. There are unique tribes in the Amazon with as few as thirty people. It doesn't take much for a larger and stronger group like the Yahnowa to destroy a group that small. Teaching them about a loving God who expects them to also be loving, helps."

"What about the clinic Nicolas' mother established?" she asked. "Will you ever try to bring it back?"

"That's what Nicolas intends to do if he can find the right medical personnel to staff it. I know the Yahnowa would be grateful for a doctor and nurse to be available. There are so many mishaps and diseases in the jungle."

That had worried her. "You will be careful, won't you?"

"Me?" Ben had laughed. "Of course I will. 'Careful' is my middle name."

"Seriously," Moriah had said. "I've seen some of the terrible things that live there. I had a flashback of watching an Anaconda slithering across the path. I was sitting on Petras' shoulders at the time. Even he was frightened."

"Oh, Moriah." He had given her a hug. "If an Anaconda swallowed me, I'd taste so bad he'd spit me back out. Pray for me, but please promise you'll stop worrying."

So, she had promised, but she knew it would be a lot easier to keep that promise if she could be there to watch out for him.

That afternoon, with all sort of hope and courage and resolve flooding her heart, hoping to be able to tell Crystal that she had succeeded, she went to visit the bridge again. This time she knew absolutely that she could cross it. Two hours later she drove home, drained and shaking.

She had been wrong.

CHAPTER 8

"I've been thinking," Crystal said, as they sat across from each other at the kitchen table that night, each with a cup of tea in front of them. Crystal also had an extra notebook and pen with her.

"Your reaction the day you found out the truth about how your parents died doesn't seem healthy to me," Crystal said.

"Healthy?" Moriah said.

"'Authentic' might be a better word."

"Are you trying to avoid using the word 'normal,' Crystal?"

"Doesn't matter." Crystal waved the question away. "From what I understand, you absorbed the fact of your parents' murder, and of Katherine lying about it, and then simply went on with your work."

"What else was I supposed to do?" Moriah asked. "Katherine was only trying to protect me, and I can't change the fact of my parent's deaths."

Crystal didn't say anything.

"I had work to do," Moriah continued. "I needed to move on."

Crystal still didn't say anything.

"What?" Moriah asked, defensively.

"You stuffed your anger and grief down as deep as possible so you could go on," Crystal said. "It's quite admirable. People do it all the time. So, in that case, yes, I suppose you could say that it's 'normal.' But that doesn't mean it's healthy."

"What should I have done? Thrown a temper tantrum? I can't change anything that happened now. Katherine just did the best she could."

Crystal scooted the notebook and pen across the table toward her.

"I want you to write a letter?"

"To Katherine?"

"No, dear. I want you to write a letter to your mother."

"My *mother*? How will that help?"

"Tell her all that you remember about her. If you feel like it, tell her how much you miss her."

Moriah did not like to write letters.

"I hate to say this, Crystal, but that sounds like a waste of time."

Crystal's eyes snapped. "Do you consider anything else I've asked you to do a waste of time?"

"No."

"Then go find a comfortable spot and write the letter."

Moriah reluctantly took the notebook and pen into the living room to an old leather chair by the window. She expected the psychologist to leave but Crystal had brought a paperback with her and settled down onto the couch.

"What are you reading?" Moriah asked.

"A book on sociopaths," Crystal said.

"Doesn't sound like vacation reading."

"It is to me."

"Have you ever worked with a sociopath?"

"Moriah! You are avoiding the assignment I gave you. Stop

distracting yourself from your task. You know you don't give a flip about what I'm reading."

With a huge sigh, Moriah opened the notebook and clicked the pen.

Dear Mom,

I'm sorry that you died. I wish you were here.

Love,

Moriah

She tore the page out and handed it to Crystal who glanced at it.

"Seriously, Moriah?"

"I was five. I barely knew the woman."

"Try again." Crystal crumpled the letter and tossed it into a nearby trashcan. "Think back. What can you remember about your mom? Was she pretty? Was she strict? Did she cuddle you when you fell? What colors do you remember her wearing? Did she sing lullabies to you? Think, Moriah. Five-year-olds have memories. What do you remember about living here on Manitoulin with your parents before they took you to Brazil?"

Moriah leaned her head back against her armchair and tried to focus. It was hard. Had there been anything about her mother…

"Strawberries." Moriah said. "I remember my mom used a perfume that smelled like strawberries."

"Interesting," Crystal said.

"Why?"

"Because I've noticed that you often smell of strawberries too."

"I don't wear perfume."

"Is it your shampoo, perhaps?"

Moriah felt a little dizzy when she realized that the shampoo she preferred was always strawberry scented if she could find it.

"You're right," Moriah admitted. "As usual."

"I believe there might be more childhood memories there than you realized. What kind of hair did she have?"

"Long," Moriah said. "Curly. I remember playing with it. I liked to twist the curls around my finger."

"Was she kind to you?"

"I think so. I have a vague memory of baking cookies together. I remember sleeping in bed between her and dad one time when I was ill."

"How did you feel lying there between them?"

"Safe," Moriah said, without hesitation.

"Good. Do you remember any jewelry? Earrings, jangly bracelets? Things like that?"

"I remember she always wore a tiny cross on a necklace," Moriah said. "It was gold and delicate-looking. She didn't let me play with it, although I wanted to."

"I noticed a photo of an old woman in an oval frame on the wall of the kitchen. Who was that?"

"My great, great, grandmother, Eliza."

"The lighthouse keeper?"

"Yes."

"You don't resemble her much. Do you have any photos of your mother?"

"I don't think so. We have some old family photos of various grandparents and my dad and Katherine when they were small. But Katherine said my parents took the photo albums with them that had photos of themselves and me the second time they went to help at the clinic. They wanted to show their Yahnowa friends about their life on Manitoulin Island. She said she never saw the albums again."

"So, you have no pictures of your mom and dad as adults?"

"I guess not."

"Interesting." Crystal closed her book. "It's time for me to get back to help put the kids to bed. I'll see you tomorrow evening."

"I apologize for not being excited about writing the letter."

"Some techniques work and some don't," Crystal said.

"I do appreciate your help," Moriah said.

"You're welcome, but I have a feeling you won't like me much after what I'm about to say."

"Really? Why?"

"I've never met your aunt, but I can't help wondering if Katherine was telling you the truth about those photo albums."

Moriah tried to go to sleep after Crystal left. She got ready for bed and climbed beneath the covers, but she couldn't help thinking about what Crystal had said.

She knew every inch of the lodge, except what was in Katherine's room. That was off-limits unless Katherine called her in to look or help her with something specific. After Moriah had grown up, Katherine afforded her the same courtesy. Their rooms were their own private spaces. It was important to have a private space when everything else at the resort was at the disposal of their guests. Now she kept tossing and turning, wondering if her beloved aunt had lied to her about something else. Was there any possibility that there were photos of her parents? If there were, the only place they could be hidden was in her room.

Katherine was in Cancun.

She did not feel good about it, but she knew she wouldn't get a moment's rest until she'd convinced herself that Katherine wasn't lying about the photos.

Reluctantly, she went to investigate her aunt's bedroom. Inviting someone like Crystal into your life surely did stir things up.

There weren't many places to hide a photo album in a room as sparse and clean as Katherine kept hers. The closet only held a few clothes and—surprise!—a box of old letters from Nicolas she'd saved all these years. Moriah had no trouble ignoring them.

The only space remaining in which something could be hidden was a large bureau. Moriah started at the top and worked her way down. There was not much there except for nightclothes and underwear. Nothing remarkable or out of the ordinary came to light. She was starting to feel relieved she had not found anything, until she opened the bottom drawer. There, hidden beneath a handmade quilt, were two thick photo albums.

With trembling hands, Moriah lifted them out and took them to the bed, where she sat and began to turn pages. She felt the blood drain from her face as she saw picture after picture of a happy family.

She realized that she was feeling quite cold. Unnaturally cold.

Throwing on her old, blue bathrobe, she took the albums downstairs and lit a fire in the fireplace. Then, still shivering from a coldness that seemed to be coming more from inside herself than the actual room temperature, she settled down to examine every picture.

There was a picture of her mother hugely pregnant and smiling. Sweet photos of her parents in the hospital cradling their new baby. Her on her first birthday with a demolished cake in front of her and vanilla icing all over her face. Page after page of family photos. They told the unmistakable story that she had been cherished.

The photos flooded her mind with wonderful, untapped, childhood memories. She always had a vague idea that her mother was pretty; now she saw that her mother was beautiful. Yet there was no preening or posing. Her mother seemed only to have eyes for her little girl and for Moriah's father.

The albums also contained the photos from their first trip to Dr. Janet's clinic. Moriah could see herself at four, playing in the dirt with the tribal children. A small, dark-haired girl was in the photo beside her. It was Karyona, her special friend with whom she had been staying with the night of the massacre.

About one o'clock in the morning, she closed the albums, carefully sat them on the side-table beside her chair, picked up Crystal's notebook and pen and began to write the letter she had requested.

"Dear Mom and Dad,
You were wonderful parents. I miss you both terribly..."

As dawn broke over the horizon she had managed to pour her heart onto approximately eleven notebook pages in a letter to her mother and father.

It had not been easy. Tears had fallen on those pages as she allowed herself to fully realize and absorb the impact of all she had lost. She was fairly certain she had cried more in the past couple of months than she had her whole life. By the time she finished her letter, her eyelids were hot and swollen, and she was nearly cross-eyed from fatigue.

It struck her that perhaps tonight she had begun to mourn her parents as a fully functioning adult should mourn, instead of a bewildered child.

With all her heart, she wished she had Ben here to discuss all this with, but she didn't, and she wouldn't for a long time unless she was able to overcome and process all these new things she was discovering.

Why had Katherine hidden these photos away from her for so long?

She had always loved and trusted her aunt. She still loved her aunt and always would but, after the silence about her and Nicolas' relationship, the lies about her parents' death, and then hiding the photo albums—her trust was running out.

CHAPTER 9

R on got his helicopter repaired in the nick of time. Violet was so sick, Ben was afraid that her death and burial might have to take place right there in the rainforest. He prayed for her and Abraham daily, but it was with a heavy heart. Everyone's life eventually came to an end, no matter how useful or faithful. That was just a fact of life. Still, it was hard to see those two old missionaries leave with Ron.

Alone in his hut, Ben assessed the situation. It would take him at least another year to finish the translation. Much longer than that if he took over the regimen of teaching and preaching that Abraham had kept up.

The village would miss Violet. She had been such a valiant soldier, working alongside the Yahnowa women, teaching them Bible lessons as they roasted plantain together or patted out the day's manioc cakes. He had even seen her hunt for the palm heart worms to which the Yahnowa were addicted, roasting them on a stick and feeding bits to whichever child happened to be on her lap.

Deep down, he realized that the greatest struggle for him

wouldn't be the extra teaching he had to do, or the sleep he would need to miss if he were to finish the translation sooner. It was the loss of two people who had managed to be upbeat and happy as they'd worked together in a difficult mission field. Their encouragement had meant more to him than even he had realized.

He loved the Yahnowa, enjoyed working with them, and could possibly spend the rest of his life serving them. But not alone. He needed Moriah.

"Fight hard, my love," he whispered into the night. "Fight hard."

CHAPTER 10

That evening after work, Moriah and Crystal drove to Little Current. The heavy, iron bridge loomed in the twilight, monstrous and menacing.

As always, bile rose in her throat but, while Crystal watched, Moriah grasped the handrail and began to inch along the bridge walkway, drawing on every bit of willpower she possessed. This time she was going to conquer it!

She made it several yards before she hit some sort of emotional wall. The next thing she knew, she was hanging her head over the bridge railing, throwing up.

Crystal was at her side in an instant, pressing a tissue into her shaking hand.

Moriah wiped her mouth with the tissue and crumpled it into her fist.

"That's enough." Crystal hugged her. "Let's go home."

They made their way back to Moriah's truck and sat for a long time, staring at the bridge.

"You tried too much, too fast." Crystal drummed her fingers on the seat. "Don't push yourself so far. Stop before you get to that point of panic. Go a few baby steps each time. Do only as much as you can comfortably bear. Are you listening?"

Moriah nodded. She was drained from the effort and wanted only to go home.

"You can overcome this, Moriah, I promise," Crystal said. "One step at a time, you can overcome this. Literally, one step at a time. It doesn't have to be a marathon. Take a few steps on it every day. If you let too much time pass between your attempts, the fear will have time to build up again. Desensitization. That's what we're going for. Familiarity. You *are* going to beat this."

CHAPTER 11

"You look like something the cat dragged in," Jack said, after she had climbed all the way to the top of the tower.

"That's something a girl wants to hear first thing in the morning," Moriah said. "I tried to cross the bridge again last night."

"I'm thinking it didn't go well?"

"Your thinking would be correct," Moriah said. "I need for you to come with me to Mindemoya to pick up Liam's desk. He called Alicia and left word that it was ready."

"Are you trying to give me a hernia?" Jack said. "I helped drag that monster over to Tom's last month. Maybe we could talk him into keeping it permanently."

"Tom also told Alicia that he has something to show me," Moriah said. "But he wouldn't tell her what."

"Hey, Luke," Jack called to one of the workmen sanding the wooden floor of the lantern room. "You want to come with us? We've got to go bring that desk back Tom's been working on."

Luke, a twenty-five year old First Nation workman, was a man of few words. "Sure."

The drive to Tom's in Mindemoya felt a bit crowded with two large, sweaty men sharing the seat with her. Without the possible cost of purchasing the lighthouse weighing on her anymore, she began to think seriously about the possibility of purchasing a newer, larger truck.

Tom's shop was built onto the side of a small barn which was badly in need of paint. He seemed nervous when they walked in.

"I hope you're happy with it," he said. "It was a challenge."

He pulled a tarp off the desk and Moriah caught her breath at the sight of the richly glowing walnut wood grain beneath. This was what had been hiding under the dust and dirt all these years? Her great-great-grandfather had certainly known his way around a good piece of lumber.

"It's lovely," she said. "You did a fantastic job."

"You gave me a key to the larger hidden compartment," he said. "But you didn't tell me that there was a hidden drawer. Did you know?"

"I had no idea."

"Let me show you." Tom got down on his knees and opened the large cedar-lined compartment. "You have to look close to see it."

Moriah knelt beside Tom as he grasped a knob so tiny she had never noticed it before. He tugged, and a small drawer slid out.

"There's something in there," Moriah said.

"Yes," he said. "That is what I wanted to show you."

He reached inside the drawer and handed her a small, cracked, red-leather book. "It's Eliza Robertson's diary."

"Seriously?" Moriah was awestruck as she opened it. On the flyleaf, written in old-fashioned, fancy penmanship were the words "Eliza Robertson. Her diary. May 10, 1874."

"It's been there all these years and no one knew?" Moriah's voice was reverent as she gently turned to the first page, feasting her eyes on line after line of cramped, old-fashioned handwriting. "Did you have a chance to read any of it?"

"No. I looked at the first page, but that sort of curlicued, spidery handwriting gives me a headache."

She stared at the first page for a moment, then turned it sideways. "It is oddly written. Is it in some sort of code do you think?"

"No. What you are seeing is the need for frugality. I have some family letters that look like that," he said. "Paper was scarce back then. To save paper, sometimes they would fill the page horizontally, then they would turn it sideways and write vertically over the original writing. Eliza had a lot to say and wanted to save paper. Good luck on deciphering it."

She studied the diary closer. Words flowed from side-to-side, then up-and-down and finally circled the narrow margin. Eliza had written with either a quill or steel-tipped pen. Adding to the difficulty of deciphering it was the faded ink and occasional blotches. Reading Eliza's diary was not going to be an easy task.

"Thanks, Tom," she said. "I really appreciate the good work you've done on this. Now, let's get this beautiful piece of furniture back where it belongs."

They wrestled the desk into the truck without mishap and installed it in the original corner of the keeper's office. All three stood back to admire their handiwork after it was finished.

"I wonder where old Liam learned to make something like this?" Jack said.

"Katherine told me he worked as a ship's carpenter before he married Eliza." Moriah glanced down at the diary she held. "I can't wait to read this. I have a feeling it is going to answer a lot of questions."

Jack plucked it out of her hands. "You need to wait until we get the tower finished."

"Please give that back," she said.

"I'm serious." Jack held it out of her reach. "I know how obsessed you've always been about Eliza and this place. If you start trying to read this now, we won't see you again for days. Or if you do come out to the worksite, you'll be all bleary-eyed from being up all night trying to read this handwriting. You need to leave it alone until winter."

Moriah made another attempt to get it back. Jack tossed the diary to Luke. "Here," he said. "Go hide this in a safe place."

"Don't you dare!"

Luke glanced between her and Jack. Then he made his decision and trotted outside with Eliza's diary in his hand.

"It's for your own good," Jack said. "You only have a few more evenings with Crystal before she has to leave. Now is the time for you to concentrate. I'll give the diary back to you after Crystal is gone and after our lighthouse project is finished."

Jack was right. She did need to focus and the diary would be a major distraction.

"You know me well, my friend," she said.

CHAPTER 12

F or the next few days, she haunted the Little Current bridge.
The people who lived nearby grew used to the sight of her
taking a few steps, backing off, taking a few more, and backing off.

Crossing the bridge was complicated in that it swung out
over the river every hour on the hour to give tall boats a chance
to continue on their way through the North Channel. She did
not want to even think about getting trapped on the bridge while
it swung out.

Hourly she crept farther, inch-by-inch, marking her progress
with chalk, never allowing herself to force her way too far past
the line that would send her into a panic attack. It was
exhausting work—the hardest she had ever done.

"I'm not sure you can undo twenty years in a week," Crystal
said, during one of her trips to check on Moriah.

"Are you and your family enjoying your vacation?" Moriah
asked.

"Yes."

"Do you need anything?"

"No."

"Then, I have work to do here, Crystal."

"Yes, you do," Crystal said. "I'll let you get back to it."

But no matter how hard Moriah tried, she could not go past the halfway point. It was as though an invisible, impenetrable wall separated her from the remaining half of the bridge.

She was trying to figure out what else to do, when Sam Black Hawk trotted up, his long, gray braids bouncing behind him as he ran. He wore black running shorts, new running shoes, a red bandana tied around his head and a green t-shirt emblazoned with the words: "KISS ME! I'm A Herpetologist."

"You manage to cross it yet?" He jogged in place.

"No, not yet. How did you know what I'm trying to do?"

"Half the island knows what you're trying to do, child." He stopped jogging, checked his pulse and sat down on the bench beside her. "What we don't know is if you're going to do it."

"Half the island knows?"

"Probably. We got a bet going on over at the reservation. Some think you'll win. Some figure the bridge will beat you."

"What are the odds?"

"About two-to-one last I heard."

"In my favor?"

"No."

The sack lunch Moriah had packed sat unopened on the bench between them. Black Hawk noticed, investigated, and helped himself to a bag of chips and a water bottle.

"I hear you talked a therapist into coming to the resort."

"How do you *know* all these things?"

"Smoke signals." He reached into her lunch bag again and discovered the peanut butter and jelly sandwich she'd packed. "Do you want half of this?"

She didn't know whether to be miffed or amused by the old

man. Since he'd rid Cabin One of snakes, she chose to be amused. "You don't mind sharing?"

"No, I don't mind." He handed her half and took a bite out of the remaining half. "Needs more jelly."

"I'll try to remember that."

Black Hawk munched a bite of his sandwich with a faraway look in his eyes.

"Do you ever get angry, Moriah?"

"I try not to. Why?"

He took a swig out of her only water bottle. "Ahh! Nothing like a water after a five-mile run."

"Five miles?"

"Yeah. I got five still to go before I can call it a day."

"How *old* are you, anyway, Sam?"

"Old enough to know the power of anger."

"I don't understand."

"Anger can be a powerful tool when used correctly," Black Hawk said. "It can give you the strength to do what you need to do. Truth be told, I've been ashamed of you this summer."

"You barely know me," she said. "Why would you be ashamed of me?"

"All that sitting around whining and complaining you've been doing."

"I haven't been whining and complaining."

"You're doing it right now." He made his voice into a falsetto. "Poor little Moriah Robertson. Too weak and scared to walk across the bridge. Afraid she might get a bellyache or feel a little dizzy."

Anger flickered within her. "That's not fair."

"Then fight *harder!*" His voice grew strong, and he hit the bench between them with his fist. "You've got Ojibwe blood running through your veins, child. It's time you started acting like it! Our people have endured many things, but we have never been cowards."

"You don't understand." The flicker caught and her anger flared up. "I might have some issues, but I'm *not* a coward."

"Sure you are. You're sitting here thinking you don't have to overcome this. You're thinking Ben will come back and marry you anyway. Maybe you're right. The man did strike me as a bit foolish."

"What makes you think you're such an expert on my life?" Moriah said, hurt. "And don't tell me smoke signals."

"I'm a long distance runner. I hear things. I see things. I talk to people," Black Hawk said. "Ben's a linguist. He needs to be able to travel. How long do you think a marriage will last that's built on defeat? How long do you think it will take him to start resenting you?"

"Ben would never resent me."

"Possibly. But you can bet your bottom dollar Ben doesn't want to be married to a coward. What if one of your kids or Ben gets sick or bad hurt? What do you plan to do? Curl up and have a panic attack while you wait for someone else to show up and take over? You think Ben could forgive you if you lost a child because you were too scared to drive across the bridge to the hospital?

The old man was right and, for reasons she didn't entirely understand, the truth of what he was saying made her furious. Her anger had been building as he spoke. Anger at him for lecturing her. Anger at being forced into this situation. Anger at herself for not being able to overcome it.

The bridge swung back to allow the line of traffic to cross.

Black Hawk closed his eyes and began to sing in a soft, wailing, rhythmic chant as he ignored her and everything else around him. The words were not understandable, but the sound filled her heart with courage. She was a Robertson, but she was more than a Robertson. She did have First Nation blood running in her veins. Her people had never been cowards.

She picked up the chalk she had been using to mark her steps, rose from the bench and approached the bridge. As she drew nearer, the anger increased. This time, she did not try to shut it down but allowed it to grow and fill her body. Her brain swelled with it until she felt like her mind was on fire.

Behind her, Black Hawk's chant grew louder, then blended in with all the other background noise of the traffic and wind. Her fury grew until the only thing she heard was her own pulse pounding too loudly in her ears.

She had heard people use the term "seeing red" when they were angry and she had thought it was just an expression. Now, she discovered that it was not. The anger she felt was so extreme, her eyes literally saw red.

As she stepped onto the bridge, she tossed the chalk aside. It was unnecessary and bothersome.

A tour bus drove through, rattling the bridge, and Moriah didn't stop. A carload of teenagers drove by with music thundering out of their car, and she didn't stop. A heavy garbage truck lumbered through, rattling the bridge with its ponderous weight. She barely noticed.

It was at the halfway point when her stomach rebelled. She paused, breathed deeply, got the nausea under control, then with a loud cry she pushed her way past the halfway barrier—head down, butting her way through like an enraged bull. Twenty years of pain and anger flared hot and bright, fueling every step.

Through the bridge's groans and snaps, through the sound of rushing water beneath her, the caw of seagulls circling above her, Moriah crossed the length of the bridge, stepped down onto non-Manitoulin soil, scooped up a handful of dirt, and carried it triumphantly back across the bridge before the anger could wane.

"Here." She dumped the soil into Black Hawk's hand. "I did it."

Sam pulled the bandana he'd wrapped around his head, and reverently wrapped the dirt in it.

"It's just dirt, Sam." Moriah stood over him, still panting from the effort she'd expended.

"Just dirt? I disagree," Black Hawk said. "It was bought at too steep of a price."

Hands on hips, chin up, chest heaving, Moriah gazed at the bridge she had finally conquered.

"You'll need to do that again tomorrow, and the day after that, and the day after that," Black Hawk said. "Until it becomes commonplace. It's like the conditioning involved in running. You can't just walk away and forget it for a while or your legs start to get all rubbery."

Moriah nodded. "Got it."

Sam stood and gripped Moriah's shoulder. "I'm proud of you, daughter."

"Thank you." Moriah laid her hand over Black Hawk's as he grasped her shoulder. She had done it. She had left Manitoulin soil and the sky hadn't fallen.

"Thank you, Sam."

"You need to keep this." He chuckled a bit as he handed her the dirt-filled bandana tied with a knot.

"What are you laughing at?" She carefully tucked the bandana into her pants pocket.

"I'm not laughing at anything, child. That's sheer happiness you're hearing. I just won two-hundred dollars."

"How?"

"Two-to-one odds."

"You placed a hundred dollar bet on me?" She didn't know whether to be hurt or grateful. At least he hadn't bet against her.

"What are you talking about?" He acted shocked. "I don't gamble."

"Then what...?"

"I don't gamble. It was a sure thing."

"How could you have been so sure?"

"Easy. A woman with the nerve to keep herself under control while trapped beneath a cabin with a mess of rattlesnakes... well, I knew it was just a matter of time before you crossed the bridge. Did my song help?"

"It did. What was it? Another achy breaky heart song you made up?"

"Ben told you about that, did he?"

"He did."

"No. That was the real thing—an Ojibwe war song—because as far as I could see, it was high time you went to war."

He held out the half-full bottle of water. "You want the rest of this?"

"You can have it."

"Great." He drained it. Threw the empty bottle into a nearby trashcan, and jogged away.

"Where are you going?" she called.

"Got two hundred dollars to collect!"

The bridge swung out into the water, boats slipped through the narrow channel and then the bridge swung back. Moriah approached the bridge again. This time she would succeed because now she knew she could. Besides that, she was still angry, and she suspected she had been angry for a long time. She just hadn't realized it until today.

CHAPTER 13

By the time Moriah drove all the way back from Little Current, the lights were out in Crystal's cabin. That was a disappointment because she badly wanted to tell her friend what she had accomplished that day. Instead of risking waking the children, she placed Black Hawk's bandana on the porch and left a note beneath it saying, "This contains *four* handfuls of dirt from Goat Island. Now, I am free!"

When she got back to the lodge, her desire to tell Ben what she had accomplished was so great that she pulled out an old spiral-bound notebook, curled up on the couch and wrote her heart out to him. She told him about how well Alicia was doing in helping her run the place, how great Jack was getting along, how beautiful the completed foghorn room was. She told him about the desk, and the surprise of Tom finding the contents of the hidden drawer, as well as the fact that baby Betsy had gotten two new baby teeth.

She saved the best news for last. Toward the end, she told him about how she had been able to thrust herself past the halfway point on the bridge. She told him about the dirt she had brought back from the other side. She described Sam Black Hawk's part in it all. Then she told him how much she loved and missed him.

That night she slept more soundly than she could ever remember sleeping in her life. No dreams. No nightmares. No waking in the middle of the night to check the clock to see if it was time to get up yet.

Normally, she did not set an alarm clock because it was her habit to awaken as soon as the sun rose. Today, it was nearly eight o'clock. Crystal and her family had planned to leave around noon today, so she intended to head over there as soon as she got dressed.

But when she went down to the kitchen, she found a note sitting beneath a small, clear, jar with a gold, metallic lid. The note was from Crystal, thanking her for her hospitality and saying that they'd had to leave early. Something about a children's birthday party back in Cleveland. The note included Crystal's office phone number, home phone number and cell phone.

Moriah felt a stab of disappointment. She had hoped to celebrate in some small way with the woman who had become such a friend to her.

The clear jar looked like it had once housed a decorative candle. The candle was gone and, in the bottom of the jar, lay the four handfuls of earth she'd left on the porch. Beside it was Black Hawk's red bandana, neatly folded.

Taped on the side of the jar were words written in Crystal's precise handwriting.

"Don't stop. Fill this jar to the top. Don't let the giants win!"

"I won't, my friend," Moriah whispered.

She grabbed the jar and strode out to the truck. There was a great deal to do today. Jack and the men would be working on the wooden flooring in the light tower and there was a need for more lumber. She wanted to clean Number Ten cabin now that Crystal and her family had left. Guests from Toronto were scheduled to arrive this evening. The day was absolutely packed.

But first, she had a bridge to cross again. She needed to fill the candle jar with more dirt from Goat Island.

CHAPTER 14

B en stood at the top of a high gorge looking at a rope bridge with short, wooden planks laid across it. The spray from a nearby waterfall kept the planks wet and slippery. His good friend, Rashawe, stood beside him.

"So this is where it happened?" Ben asked, in Yahnowa.

"Yes," Rashawe replied, in his native tongue. "This is where my father almost fell while carrying the child."

"What saved him?"

"I heard his cry, turned, and held out my spear. It was just enough to steady him."

"Was he angry at Moriah?"

"He was more frightened than angry, but he shouted at her. I'm sure he sounded angry to her. Do you want to cross it now?"

"No," Ben said. "I can't imagine *anyone* actually *wanting* to cross it."

"It is probably sturdier now than the day we walked it with Little Green Eyes."

Ben eyed it suspiciously. "When is the last time anyone used it?"

In answer, Rashawe stepped onto the bridge and easily walked across it. When he arrived at the other side, he called back. "This is the last time anyone used it."

Rashawe and Ben had become good friends these past five years. They were about the same age and Rashawe was quick to learn. Ben was fairly certain he would someday take his father's place as leader of the Yahnowa tribe. He would make an excellent leader. Rashawe was also making headway in learning English. He loved his people and had a calm, strong spirit. He also had a sense of humor—like right now—grinning at Ben from the other side of the gorge. It was a dare, if Ben had ever seen one.

Actually, Ben had intended to walk this bridge anyway, as long as it looked sturdy enough. He had not intended for Rashawe to test the bridge for him—but it did convince him that the bridge would hold his weight. Ben grabbed hold of the two ropes that acted as handrails, and took his first careful step onto the bridge that had terrified Moriah as a child.

He did not have to do this, of course. It wouldn't have anything to do with whether or not Moriah overcame her fears, but he missed her so badly. Walking this bridge that, according to Rashawe, had not changed much since she'd been carried across it, was a way to feel closer to her. When he saw her again, he would be able to tell her that he'd crossed it and could understand why it had been so scary.

Well, actually, he didn't have to cross it to see why it had been so scary. It was a *long* way to the bottom of the gorge, and the gorge was wide. It took a lot of trust in one's fellow man's ability to construct something sturdy out of wood and homemade rope to venture onto it.

Rashawe was squatting at the end of it now, making encouraging motions for him to cross.

The wooden slat beneath his feet creaked, and the rope made

a slight groaning noise as he stepped on and allowed his full weight to be supported entirely by the bridge. He waited a moment to get his bearings and balance, then took another step. Even though there were ropes attached at waist level on both sides to use as handrails, it still took a good bit of balance to walk across the narrow bridge. It felt as though it wouldn't take much for it to twist in midair and leave him hanging from it upside down.

There was a fine spray that wafted in on the currents of wind stirred from the waterfall and it made the wooden slats slick with moisture. He felt his right foot slip, but caught himself. The waterfall was lovely, but the beauty of nature was not particularly important to him right now. Getting safely across the bridge was.

Ben took four more steps, feeling the bridge sway with each one. He glanced down again. It was incredibly far to the bottom. The thought that it might be wise to carry a parachute with him if he ever did this again, skittered across his mind.

Then it happened. He was focusing on the depth of the gorge and forgot to step carefully. His right foot slipped again, this time sideways out from under him, and his leg went over the edge. The foot bridge tipped precariously, causing his entire body to shift and then slide off.

Suddenly he was dangling in mid-air, his feet pedaling desperately. The only thing keeping him from falling to the bottom of the gorge was his death grip on the rope handrail.

As he tried to kick and maneuver his way into a better position, he was grateful for the muscle he had built these past weeks of hefting stone. He was as strong as he had ever been.

"Hold on!" Rashawe called. "I'm coming."

Ben continued to hang in midair as Rashawe worked his way over to him. He felt the bridge shift as Rashawe righted it with his own weight, and then laid down on his stomach and reached a strong arm down to grasp Ben's. He held on to Ben and counterbalanced the bridge with his own body while Ben clawed his way back up. Their faces were inches apart as Ben flopped flat onto his belly, trying to catch his breath and stop shaking after such a close call.

Moriah's horrific memory was accurate. It was very possible for someone to fall off the bridge.

"I don't understand," Ben said. "Why were you able to go across so easily?"

Rashawe carefully sat back on his haunches and lifted one calloused bare foot for Ben to inspect. "Much better for crossing a wet bridge than your white man's shoes."

"Obviously," Ben said.

"I'm guessing you want to go back?" Rashawe said.

"Oh, yeah." Ben struggled to a half-crouch, found his balance, stood up and very carefully faced the way he'd come. "I don't need to go the rest of the way to understand why Moriah has a problem with crossing bridges."

CHAPTER 15

Moriah was surprised when Katherine and Nicolas walked through the front door of the lodge a day sooner than she expected. Alicia had not yet come in for the day and Moriah was busy doing laundry before heading out to the worksite.

"You're back." Moriah was carrying a basket of freshly laundered towels. She sat the towels on the couch as Katherine rushed to hug her.

"It is so good to see you, Moriah!"

Moriah hugged her back, but she had mixed feelings about Katherine right now. For one thing, there was the issue of the hidden photos to be dealt with. She had carefully replaced them in Katherine's bottom drawer. After she and Nicolas settled in, she intended to approach her about it.

"Did you have a good time?"

"We had a *wonderful* time," Katherine whirled around with her arms outstretched while Nicolas looked on, adoringly. "But it feels good to be home."

Moriah picked up the basket of towels and settled them

against her hip while she took a good look at Katherine. Her aunt had changed. She looked ten years younger than at the beginning of the summer, and she was glowing with happiness. The dress she wore, a pastel, floral dress, was made from some sort of floaty material. It was something she would never have worn before Nicolas showed up.

She had also cut off her braids for the first time in Moriah's memory, and her hair had magically lost its threads of gray. It had been styled into a shoulder length cut that perfectly framed her face.

The change was unsettling.

"You colored and cut your hair."

"I know it's a tremendous change," Katherine glanced back at her new husband and smiled. "But Nicolas likes it."

"It looks nice."

Katherine had been gray even in her late twenties. Moriah had never seen her aunt without long, salt-and-pepper braids.

Katherine self-consciously reached up a hand to pat her hair and Moriah got her second surprise.

"You have palm trees painted on your fingernails!"

Katherine looked at her fingernails as though just discovering them. "It seemed like fun at the time." There was a hint of apology in her voice. "I think I'll go change now. It's been a long trip."

Moriah stared as her aunt climbed the stairs, her pretty skirt swirling around her knees, sandals decorated with fake gemstones glittering on her feet. The transformation was immense. Who *was* this woman with whom she had shared the past twenty years of her life?

She shook her head and turned away, stepping right into the glare of Nicolas who, unless she was mistaken, was furious.

"How dare you!" Nicolas said.

"What?" Moriah was defensive.

"Do you realize how hard I had to work to talk Katherine into making those changes?"

"If you love her, why change her?"

Nicolas wiped a hand over his face, as though trying to wipe away the anger. When he replied, his voice was measured.

"I would love Katherine in buckskin and beads, in sackcloth and ashes, with hair down to her ankles, or in a buzz cut. But what I *remember* is a beautiful, happy girl who curled her hair and wore ribbons in it. I remember what she was like before she became a slave to this resort and to you."

"That's not fair."

"You didn't ask for her to sacrifice for you." Nicolas's voice was weary. "That was Katherine's choice. But you are no longer a child, Moriah. It's time for your aunt to have her own life; to feel young. She's only in her forties and *look* at her, she's gorgeous and she's happy."

Moriah heard steps on the stairwell, glanced up, and her heart dropped. Katherine had changed into an old, drab, house-dress. She had pulled her hair back off her face and washed off her bit of makeup.

"Either of you want coffee?" Katherine said. "I'll make some."

"Nothing for me," Moriah said. "I need to drop these towels off at cabin three, then meet the electrician who is coming to install outlets in the lantern room."

"Looks like you've made a lot of progress since we've been gone," Nicolas said. "I'll be out later to see what you and Ben accomplished before he had to leave."

Her emotions were in a jumble as she left. She was still upset with Katherine over the photos, but she'd missed her terribly. Now her aunt was back—but was no longer the same person. The Katherine she had known would have been aghast if someone had tried to decorate her fingernails with palm trees. But Nicolas was right. Katherine was gorgeous and very happy.

She dropped off the towels and finished making up the beds in cabin three, then she drove toward the worksite.

Nicolas' comment about her fear of change was unfair and had hurt. The thing that hurt most was that Nicolas was right. She liked the safety of routine. She hated change. Hated the idea of Katherine being different. Change, in her life, had always meant loss. It was probably the real reason behind her dislike for Nicolas. He had managed to initiate three cataclysmic changes in her life. The appearance of Ben, the loss of the lighthouse and Katherine getting married.

Even though she was upset with her aunt for keeping the knowledge of her parent's death a secret and hiding the photos of them, she still loved her. Everyone was flawed. Everyone had secrets. Katherine probably less than most.

Her aunt had been so happy and young-looking when she entered the lodge, so filled with life. And Moriah had ruined it all with a few comments.

She swung the truck around and headed to Little Current. Jack would be fine without her for another hour or so. She wanted to go across the bridge one more time. This time she intended to *drive* over it.

She felt fairly secure in trying this. By now she had crossed it so many times on foot that she had an intimate knowledge of it. Knew exactly how many steel plates were welded together to make the pedestrian sidewalk. Had counted the rivets in those steel plates. Knew every sound, every clank, every shimmer. It was still a black, metal giant, but a benevolent giant. Her giant. She had conquered it and she owned it now.

Once she knew for certain she could drive over it, she intended to give Katherine a big surprise—a surprise that might cancel out the disapproval she had heard today in her own voice.

CHAPTER 16

When she arrived at the bridge, she entered it without feeling the least bit nervous. Ben would be so proud of her calm.

She could already visualize herself on the other side, grabbing another fistful of dirt to add to the jar Crystal had given her.

She drove with her right hand on the steering wheel, and her left elbow nonchalantly hanging out of the open window. She could feel the wind in her hair. No qualms. No lurching stomach. No heart palpitations.

Nearly halfway across, she heard a crash. The car in front of her came to an abrupt stop and Moriah stomped on her brakes so suddenly, her truck engine died. The car behind her missed ramming her bumper by inches.

The driver of the car behind her laid on his horn. She turned to look at him. Probably an impatient tourist. An islander wouldn't act that way. Couldn't he see something was wrong up ahead?

She pushed herself out her window and sat on the edge,

straining to look over the cars in front. As she had suspected, there was a wreck up ahead. People were already piling out of their cars to investigate.

She glanced back, again, at the man in the car behind her. He was gesturing oddly and continuing to honk his horn—as though *she* could do anything about the wreck!

Then it struck her where she was. She couldn't go forward. She couldn't go backward. She was pinned in on all sides, here on this bridge.

Trapped.

Her mouth grew dry and she felt dizzy. She slipped back down into the driver's seat before she could fall out. Not a panic attack! Not now when she had been doing so well...

Honk! Honk!

Why did this idiot keep honking his horn at her?

Her panic attack was suddenly replaced with annoyance. She grabbed the truck handle, opened the door, slid out and walked back to the car. Her legs were a bit wobbly but, otherwise, she was pretty steady.

"So, what's your problem?" She approached the man's window. "There's been an accident up ahead. I can't move my truck, no matter how much you honk."

"Chest pains." The man was elderly and he was pale and shaking.

"I'll get help!" Moriah was off like a shot. She flew to the front of the bridge where a large knot of people had gathered around two damaged cars.

"There's a man having a heart attack back there," she shouted. "I need an ambulance."

"One's already coming." A young man said. He was holding one of those bulky car phones. "We called as soon as we saw the crash, but it's not as bad as we thought."

Two people had been helped out of the wrecked cars. Neither

seemed to be badly hurt, although the back of one of their cars was crushed and the front of the one behind was crumpled. A siren sounded nearby.

"Send the EMTs to the blue Lincoln," she instructed. "Tell them to hurry!"

She raced back to the old man and found him breathing raggedly and clutching his chest.

"Hang on, the ambulance is on its way. They'll be here any second now."

"Bless you," the man gasped.

Two EMTs hurried toward them, pushing a gurney. They checked him over quickly. Then they helped him out of the car, buckled him onto the collapsible gurney and wheeled him to the ambulance.

As the siren ebbed away, the car in front of her began to move. The young man with the car phone who had called for the ambulance made his way toward her.

"We've pushed the wreck out of the way," he said. "People can drive around it. Cops are talking to the ones involved. If you think it's okay, I'll drive the old man's car off the bridge and park it."

"Someone needs to," Moriah said. "Thanks."

She drove off the bridge and pulled into the small parking lot on the other side. The police were indeed questioning some people and were inspecting the two wrecked vehicles. She watched as the old man's car was parked, and the young man handed the keys over to the police. She waited there until everyone, including the cops, cleared out. As she watched, the bridge slowly began its rotation out over the water again as several boats went through.

She had been trapped on it. Trapped and starting to panic. Then she had responded to the old man's suffering and forgotten that she was afraid. Funny how thinking about someone besides herself had made the panic go away.

Getting back out of the truck, she squatted in the gravel and brushed it aside until she could scoop up another small handful of dirt. The jar that Crystal had given her sat on the ground beside her. She let the handful sift through her fingers into it. She had pretended to herself that, when she'd managed to fill the jar with hard-earned dirt from the other side of the bridge, she would be well. The handful didn't completely fill it. There was still an inch of space left.

It didn't matter.

She already knew she was going to be okay.

CHAPTER 17

Moriah didn't expect to see Katherine fixing supper when she got home from meeting the electrician who was going to be installing outlets.

"I'm sorry," Moriah lifted the lid on a pot and investigated. "I would have had something ready for you and Nicolas if I'd known you were coming home today."

"It wasn't any trouble. I missed my kitchen," Katherine said. "Besides, Alicia peeled potatoes and fried the chicken while I held little Betsy. That sweet baby grew so much while we were away."

Moriah snagged a piece of celery off a vegetable tray. "It's good to have you..."

Suddenly, she noticed that the two photo albums belonging to her parents were lying on the counter—the ones she had found in Katherine's bottom drawer.

Her aunt was busy tearing up lettuce for a salad.

"What's that?" Moriah said.

"What's what?" Katherine asked, preoccupied.

"The two photo albums on the counter."

"Oh," Katherine glanced over her shoulder. "Those are for you. I put those albums away when you were little because I was afraid, if you saw those pictures, it would trigger yet something else that your grandfather and I would not know how to deal with. I'm afraid I spent most of your young years walking on egg shells, trying to protect you from any more pain."

"Why are you bringing them out now?" Moriah asked.

Katherine looked perplexed at her question. "Because you should have them, of course. I'd almost forgotten about them. Then, on our trip, Nicolas was taking a picture of me and suddenly I remembered. Maybe we can look through them together sometime. There's probably questions you might have that I can answer."

Her aunt's explanation was so reasonable that Moriah's suspicion and worry about Katherine's motives simply drained away. Wordlessly, she walked over, put her arms around Katherine's waist and hugged her.

"My hands are still wet from rinsing the salad." Katherine held her hands out away from Moriah. "I'll get water on you."

"I don't care," Moriah said.

Katherine returned her hug in spite of damp hands. "Supper will be ready in fifteen minutes."

Moriah's heart was light as she went up the stairs to her room to change out of her work clothes. Her feelings about Katherine were back to normal. Questions answered. Reasonable explanations given. She could feel her trust returning.

As she walked past Katherine's room, she noticed the door was open and Nicolas was sound asleep on Katherine's bed. That felt a little weird, but she shrugged it off. If being married to Nicolas made her aunt happy it was fine with her.

CHAPTER 18

"Anything interesting happen while we were gone?" Nicolas asked, as they sat down to the fried chicken supper Katherine had helped prepare. He seemed determined to be civil, but his annoyance about her less-than-positive reaction to the changes in Katherine that morning tinged his voice. "Any hiccoughs with the restoration?"

"No problems, but we did have one big surprise."

"And what was that, dear." Katherine sat a basket of paper napkins on the table.

"Do you remember how we removed the big desk that was in the keeper's office?"

"Yes," Nicolas said. "If I remember right, you took it to a man on the island who refinishes furniture."

"Tom Hawkins," Moriah said. "He does really good work. Something like seven layers of varnish and he sands in-between each layer. It takes him forever to finish a piece, but he's worth waiting for."

"So you're pleased?" Katherine said.

"More than pleased. Tom discovered a small, secret drawer."

"Really?" Katherine said. "I grew up with that desk and no one ever said anything about a secret drawer."

"Maybe they didn't know."

"So... don't keep us in suspense." Nicolas smiled. "Did you find the treasure map to the famed Robertson fortune?"

"You mean the nonexistent Robertson fortune?" Moriah said. "No, it was Eliza Robertson's diary."

"You can't be serious!" Katherine said. "Have you read it?"

"No," Moriah said. "Jack took it away from me."

"Why would Jack do something like that?" Nicolas asked.

"He said I would get too involved, stay up all night, and come to the worksite groggy from lack of sleep. He said I can only get it back after the lighthouse is finished and we've had our open house."

"One wonders," Nicolas said. "Who's the boss out at the job site? You or Jack?"

"Moriah is the boss, but Jack knows her well," Katherine said. "He's right. She wouldn't have been able to put it down."

"I suppose I could go to Jack and insist he turn it over to me," Nicolas said. "I'm curious too."

"That wouldn't be fair, dear," Katherine said. "Moriah should get to be the first one who reads it. She is the one who cares the most."

"Oh, okay," Nicolas grumbled. "But I lived in that lighthouse too, remember?"

"Oh, I remember." Katherine briefly covered his hand with her own. "I remember well."

A look passed between them that Moriah envied.

"So," Nicolas said, when they stopped gazing at each other and Katherine passed him the mashed potatoes. "Did you and Jack make any progress today?"

"Some. You should go see it."

"Kathy and I'll go over tomorrow morning." He lifted a crisp chicken leg onto his plate. "It's getting late."

"Actually, I had plans for Katherine tomorrow if you don't mind." Moriah savored the moment.

"Oh?" Katherine glanced up at her.

"It's a Saturday. I thought we might go shopping." Moriah nonchalantly ladled potatoes onto her plate.

"Shopping? For what?" Katherine passed a bowl of peas.

"I need some nicer clothes." Moriah dipped peas onto her plate. "Something pretty—like what you were wearing this afternoon."

Nicolas stopped chewing, swallowed, put down his fork and watched her closely. Moriah could almost feel him daring her to say something that would embarrass Katherine.

"Where did you want to go? There isn't a very big selection here on the island," Katherine said. "You know that."

"Oh! I forgot to show you something. Would you excuse me a moment?" Moriah rose.

Katherine and Nicolas glanced at each other as she left the table as though wondering what was going on. She couldn't wait to see the expression in their eyes when she told them.

After returning to the kitchen with Crystal's jar in her hand, she placed it in the center of the table, resumed her seat and began eating again without uttering a word.

"And that is?" Nicolas lifted the jar and shook it.

"Dirt."

"Dirt?"

"Yes." She spread butter on a piece of bread. "Dirt."

"Is there something particularly special about it?" Katherine asked.

"Nope. Nothing special at all. It's just common old Canadian dirt."

"As lovely as it is," Nicolas said, "why are you using it as a centerpiece for our table?"

"It's dirt I picked up from Goat Island after I crossed the bridge." Moriah lifted her chin and met Katherine's eyes, allowing her pride and happiness to shine through. "I thought maybe Katherine would like to go to the mall in Espanola with me tomorrow. I'll drive."

"Goat Island?" Katherine said. "You didn't!"

"Oh yes, ma'am, I did!"

"If you're joking about this..." Nicolas' voice was filled with warning.

"It's not a joke. I *did* it!" Both of Moriah's fists hit the table. She felt so proud. "Over and over and over again. I *crossed* it!"

"How?" Katherine's voice was filled with wonder.

"I found out about a really good therapist while the two of you were away. I gave her and her family a free, two-week vacation here at the resort while she worked with me."

"I considered importing a specialist," Nicolas mused. "But I didn't think you would accept it."

"I wouldn't have." Moriah said. "It was something I had to do for myself."

"All these years," Katherine said. "I kept hoping..."

"So," Moriah held her truck keys out and jingled them, "want to go shopping tomorrow?"

411

CHAPTER 19

M oriah lay awake long into the night after their Saturday excursion. It had felt so good to finally go shopping at the mall like normal people. She was exhausted, but too excited to settle down. The day had felt extraordinary.

First, they went to the hospital to check on the old man who had survived having a heart attack on the bridge. He was doing well. His daughter expressed her thanks to Moriah for helping him.

Then she and Katherine explored the mall together for the first time in her life. Nicolas insisted on being their chauffeur and seemed pleased by their excitement. The man had his moments.

Best of all, she had taken a quick peek at wedding dresses! Not serious shopping. She didn't try anything on. She was just daydreaming, but that was why she couldn't get calmed down enough to sleep. The world had begun to open up to her. So many possibilities once one was no longer bound by fear.

Giving up on sleep, she climbed out of bed and threw on her old bathrobe. Maybe a glass of milk would help.

Before she went out the door, she happily gave the globe another spin. This time her finger ended up on Greenland. She'd heard good things about its rugged beauty. Maybe she would go there someday. Only this time it wasn't a pipedream. There was a good possibility that soon, if she wanted to go to Greenland, she really could! The thought was exhilarating.

She trotted down the stairs after that glass of milk. Some crackers to go with it sounded good. Loading up on carbs always made her sleepy. They had church to go to in the morning and she needed to get some rest if she was going to keep from dozing during the preacher's sermon.

Nicolas was in the living room when she reached the main floor. In the past that would have annoyed her, but tonight it felt right having him here. She had definitely not enjoyed living in the lodge by herself these past weeks. Knowing that he and Katherine were here made her feel a lot better.

He was sitting at an old desk, working on his laptop computer.

He turned when he heard her.

"I'm glad you're awake, Moriah. I have something to show you."

She went and peered over his shoulder.

"While Kathy and I were in the Caymans, Ben contacted me. He told me that he'd had to leave Manitoulin, and why. When I heard that he was going back into the jungle, I planned for a solar-powered, satellite laptop computer to be taken in to him. I couldn't be entirely sure if it would be delivered, but it looks like he's received it and has figured out how to use it."

"Ben is smart."

"Yes, he is." Nicolas removed his glasses and got to his feet, offering her his chair. "I think you might be interested in this."

Moriah sat down, transfixed by her first introduction to a computer. Nicolas had already suggested that she and Katherine could run a smoother establishment with the help of one but, as always, Moriah disliked the idea of change and had balked.

She read the script eagerly.

Dear Nicolas,

Ron Meacham brought this computer last week. Fortunately, the clearing that the Yahnowa made so that Violet could be flown out, was still viable enough for him to set the old Huey down again. It is a testament to their love for her that Abraham could convince them to create that clearing at all. The Yahnowa are not fond of making access to their village convenient, and I can't blame them. Ron has gotten word that Violet is not doing well, even though she is back in the states. I pray for a recovery but I'm afraid it might be too late unless God grants a miracle.

Speaking of miracles. This laptop is only a little short of one. Thank you for sending it. I'd considered getting one at the end of the summer, but, as you now know, there wasn't time. It took me awhile to figure out how everything works on it, but what a blessing!

With the Smiths gone, my life here seems especially strange. They always softened the culture shock when I came back before.

I miss Manitoulin, I miss working on the lighthouse but, most of all, I miss Moriah. If you get this, please give her my love and tell her I'm okay.

Ben

Moriah whirled around and found Nicolas standing behind her, waiting for her reaction.

"You are a kind man," she said, with wonder. "Thank you!"

"You've decided to like me now?" He smiled. "If only I'd known all it would take was a satellite laptop..."

Moriah propelled herself off the chair and hugged his neck. "You did this so Ben and I could talk to each other!"

"Yes, I did." Nicolas hugged her back, awkwardly. "If you're happy, Kathy is happy. If Kathy is happy..."

Moriah dropped back into the seat before he could finish. "Show me how to work this thing!"

After a quick session, Nicolas went to bed, giving her the privacy to communicate with Ben alone. Laboriously, she hunted for keys and pecked out her news. Typing had never become part of her skillset.

dear ben,

> *i crossed the bridge today. it wasn't my first time, either.*
>
> *me and katherine went shopping in espanola. we even kind of looked at wedding dresses. when i can fly without freaking out we can get married if you still want to.*
>
> *i love you*
>
> *moriah*

Dear Moriah,

> *YOU CROSSED THE BRIDGE??? I know men aren't supposed to cry, but I'm bawling right now from gratitude and relief. Of course, I still want us to get married. Your strength amazes me. Yesterday Rashawe took me to the rope bridge that his father carried you across on that terrible night our parents died. It's the one you nearly fell off. It was a long hike to go see it, but I'm glad I went there. I now can understand why bridges have been difficult for you. That gorge by the waterfall is terrifying even in daytime. I can hardly imagine what it was like for you as a child and in the dark.*
>
> *Love,*
>
> *Ben*

CHAPTER 20

Schools began to open as late August settled onto Manitoulin, and the guests at Robertson's Resort dwindled even more until the cabins were completely deserted. Moriah drained pipes and prepared the resort for winter. Katherine line-dried all the linens, and stored them in the laundry room on shelves that Moriah had built for that purpose. The linens were laced, for the first time, with sachets of dried lavender—something Katherine had learned from the resort in the Cayman's where she and Nicolas had honeymooned.

Together, along with Nicolas, they turned mattresses, made certain there wasn't a crumb of food in any of the cabins to interest mice, brought in the boats and turned them belly up to repel rain and snow.

Moriah checked each boat motor then tucked it snugly into a special bin inside the storage shed. In the past, these tasks had signaled the beginning of her least favorite season, when she and Katherine would sometimes be housebound for weeks while the snow piled up around their home. Neither Moriah nor

Katherine were the kind of women who enjoyed sitting. They both went nearly stir-crazy by February every year.

This winter would probably be the same, except for one thing.

If Moriah had her way, she wouldn't be here.

It's warm here all the time, Moriah, and fragrant with the smell of flowers and rain. How I wish you could lie in my arms at night and listen to the sounds of the jungle moving about us.

Love,

Ben

Dear Ben

Wish I took typing in school! Nicolas showed me how to make capital letters last night. I'm slow as molasses on this thing, and there is so much to say! Jack and me and the crew only have a few more days to be finished. The lighthouse looks real good. Bob Wilson Jr. says he'll take me up in his piper cub when I'm ready. Now that I've walked the bridge, I'm going out to the airport to look the plane over and take pictures of it so I can start getting used to it, too. When I can face flying without going into a meltdown, I'll come. I want to hear those jungle sounds with you.

Love,

Moriah

Dear Moriah,

I am so proud of you, my sweet warrior. You are the bravest woman I have ever known. I love you beyond words, beyond life, beyond anything or anyone on this earth.

Your husband-to-be,

Ben

Dear Ben,

I stayed in the piper cub for an hour yesterday. Bob Jr. drove it up and down the runway and I didn't puke but I wanted to.

Love,

Moriah

Dear Moriah McCain

(You need to get used to the sound of your new name, sweetheart. I can't wait to hear people call you that.)

It was touch-and-go here for a while. Abraham was right. There were problems brewing. I've done what I could and I think things have stabilized. There is peace again between the tribes. At least for now. I feel I could leave the Yahnowa long enough to come to Manitoulin and bring back my bride. Do you have any idea when you'll be ready to face the flight?

I've been thinking, if Nicolas doesn't mind, Robertson's Lighthouse would be my first choice for a wedding. After all, it was what brought us together. Perhaps we could have the wedding after dark? Maybe rig a beacon in the tower and put lights in all the windows?

I dream about our wedding and about being able to hold you in my arms again. I miss you so much, I have to struggle to concentrate and do my work. Hurry and conquer flying so I can have you beside me.

Your loving Ben

P.S. Keep driving up and down the runway in that plane!

Dear Ben,

I think I can rig a beacon in the tower alright. Easier than rigging myself up. ha ha. It feels funny trying on wedding dresses but they sure are pretty. I bought one today. I hope you like it.

Moriah McCain

Dear Mrs. McCain,

I can't wait for the moment I see you in that wedding dress! You will make such a beautiful bride.

Are you also getting clothes and supplies together for the jungle? Abraham sent me a list of things Violet says you'll need. By the way, she's doing better. The surgeon thinks he got all the cancer. They're doing chemo now. She and Abraham are already talking about returning, although I think it might be too soon for them to even consider it. Maybe it's nothing more than their way of keeping hope alive. Tell Nicolas not to stop looking for someone with medical training who is willing to come. Lord knows, these people could use some help.

I can bandage a cut and hand out some antibiotics or aspirin, but that's about it.

Love,

Ben

CHAPTER 21

Dear Ben,

Alicia let me watch her teach her Sunday school class this morning. First and second grade. If I keep going into class with her I think I might be able to teach the Yahnowa children some Bible stories after I learn their language. I'll try real hard to be a good missionary wife.

Love,

Moriah

P.S. I was able to go up in Bob Jr.'s plane today for five whole minutes before I made him land. I took a bucket in case I got sick, but I didn't have to use it.

Ben's throat tightened, reading her e-mail. He hated the fact that she had to fight so hard to come live with him and wished he could make it easier for her.

"I'm finished," Fusiwe said.

Fusiwe was in his mid-twenties and had been apprenticed to the local native healer since his late teens. Violet, with her nurse training had also taught him what she could. Fusiwe was quick to absorb knowledge and had developed an aspiration to add Western medicine to his repertoire. He and his wife were already fairly fluent in spoken English, but Fusiwe also wanted to learn to read and write it.

For the past few nights, he had started coming to Ben's hut every evening to spend a bit of time working on whatever written English assignment Ben gave him. The young healer was barely at first-grade level yet in written English, but that would change. Ben had seldom seen anyone as determined to learn as this man.

Ben clicked off the satellite computer and shut the lid. It was time to look over his friend's work. Tonight they had progressed to the words 'cat' and 'dog', which Fusiwe had painstakingly copied over and over.

"Good job," Ben said. "You are gaining more English words every day."

"How is your woman?" Fusiwe asked. "Those words you read are from her?"

"Yes," Ben said. "She's doing well. Today she went up in a plane for a few minutes."

Fusiwe, who had seldom seen an airplane, let alone ridden in one, nodded sagely. "That is a good thing."

"I hope so. I would like to have her here with me. I miss her."

"My wife sometimes speaks of the days when Little Green Eyes was here. She has grown into a beautiful woman?"

"You have no idea," Ben said. "Beautiful, kind and capable."

"How soon will she come?"

"It might take a few months," Ben said. "She was only in the air today for five minutes before she panicked and the pilot had to set her down again. The trip here takes many hours. I'm certain she won't be ready to get on a commercial flight until she knows for certain she can withstand it without falling apart. At that point, I will go marry her and bring her back here to live with me."

"I will leave now," Fusiwe said. "When you talk with her, tell her that we look forward to seeing her."

"I will do that," Ben said.

"But I think it might be wise not to tell her about Moawa."

A look passed between them.

"You're right," Ben said. "I won't tell her about Moawa until after she arrives. I will explain things to her then."

"Good." Fusiwe left to go back to his own family's hut.

A mosquito landed on Ben's arm and he swatted it. It seemed that no matter how much bug spray he used, the dratted things wouldn't leave him alone. He had heard that insects were particularly drawn to redheads. He could certainly attest to the fact that, at least in his case, it was most definitely true.

Ben opened the computer again and began to type.

Dear Moriah,

    You stayed in the air five whole minutes! I'm so happy and proud of you!

    How are the newlyweds? Still blissfully happy?

    Love,

    Ben

Dear Ben,

    Blissful? The love birds I live with are ridiculous. They are so happy even the air feels all sweet and sticky around them. ha. ha. Jack is working on the wood flooring of the cottage. I wish we had the Fresnel lens back, then all would be perfect. I don't know what Nicolas will do with the place now that he has moved into the lodge, but it is beautiful. We did a good job.

The heavy humidity outside made his hut feel like a steam bath. He closed the laptop, pushed it aside and scooted his Bible and spiral notebook over in front of him on the makeshift desk. In spite of the computer's capabilities, he felt more secure working with paper and pencil when it came to his translation. Hard copy was a good thing. Besides, he seemed to think better with a pencil and paper in hand. He was grateful he'd left the rest of his work with Moriah. It would be safe with her.

He worked long into the night until the pages began to swim in front of his eyes and the Yahnowa words lost their meaning. He was used to exhaustion, having been pushing himself ever since his arrival. But this time felt a little different. He felt feverish and achy and was rapidly getting worse.

With the walls of the hut swirling around him, he stumbled to his pallet and fell face down.

CHAPTER 22

Moriah put her tools away and locked the storage shed after finishing a plumbing job on Cabin Seven. Then she drove to the lighthouse. Everything was finished there except varnishing the newly-sanded wooden floors in the keeper's house. Jack was working on them today. She had picked out a honey-colored stain for the oak flooring and couldn't wait to see how it looked.

"Don't come in!" Jack shouted as she approached. "The stain isn't dry. I don't want your feet messing up the job I've done."

She stood at the open door and looked in. The room gleamed. The woodwork had been stripped, sanded, and stained the same honey-color maple as the floor. A buttery yellow covered the walls. Early autumn sunlight flooded through the new windows.

"It's beautiful," she said.

"Nice place for a wedding, eh?"

"A small one. I figure this room can only hold about twenty people. How long before we can put furniture in?"

"I'd give it a day or two. What furniture?"

"My grandmother and grandfather's things are stored in the

attic of the lodge. Some of it is original from the beginning of the lighthouse."

"You planning on charging admission on the place, or what?"

"I'm not sure what Nicolas has planned for it. Now that he and Katherine are married and living at the lodge, he seems to have completely lost interest in it."

"Are they still acting like lovebirds?"

"Pretty much. Katherine seems very happy."

"And Nicolas?"

"Nicolas is... well, Nicolas. He's tightly wrapped, but he seems to have focused his life on being good to Katherine, so I'm not complaining."

"Seems a shame for him to stop practicing medicine."

"He hasn't," Moriah said. "He and Katherine are working together these days over at Wikwemikong. She talked him into it but he doesn't seem to mind as long as she's with him."

"We can use another doctor on the island."

"I agree."

"Have you decided on the date for your wedding yet?"

"It depends. I want to be absolutely certain I can fly for a long period of time without falling apart before we set a date."

"How's the flying going?"

"I was able stay in the air a little longer yesterday than the day before. I do pretty good as long as we're above Manitoulin, but whenever Bob Jr. tries to head out over the lake I start having a rough time."

"You'll beat it."

"I will eventually, but I'm grateful that Bob Jr. is a patient man."

"You sure you can stay away from us once you do leave?" Jack asked. "The Amazon is very far away. You're going to miss us."

"Of course I'll miss everyone but, if I can be with Ben, I'll be okay." Moriah smiled. "Besides, we've decided we'll come back each summer so I can help Katherine run the resort when the tourists come. Ben says for you to keep an ear open for stonemason jobs he could do next summer while I'm working at the resort."

"I'll do that. Shouldn't be hard. People around here are impressed with the way he put that tower back together."

Moriah watched as Jack gathered his tools together. "Alicia has been wonderful help this summer. You two still doing okay?"

"Absolutely. Having steady work has helped. It isn't good for a man to be cooped up in the house for too long without a job."

"Do you have anything lined up when this job is over?"

"Not yet. I've put some feelers out."

"I hope something comes up."

"I do too." Jack pounded the lid down on the remaining bucket of stain and opened his toolkit. "It's going to be hard to walk away from this place. I've enjoyed the company and the work. Felt like we accomplished something important."

"We did."

"In fact," Jack pulled a zip-locked bag out of the bottom of his toolkit and tossed it to her. "I think I can safely give this to you, now. You've earned it."

Inside the zip-lock bag was Eliza Robertson's leather diary.

"Thanks," Moriah said. "Did you read any of it? Do you know what it says?"

"Nah," Jack said. "Alicia and me tried to read some of it together one night. With all that spidery handwriting and the faded ink, we couldn't make out much. Better get a good magnifying glass before you attempt it."

CHAPTER 23

"Where's Katherine?" Moriah laid the zip-locked diary on the counter and washed her hands in the sink.

Nicolas sat at the kitchen table, his laptop in front of him. "Upstairs in our room. She has a headache."

"Is she okay?"

"She's fine."

Moriah noticed that he was frowning as he stared at the laptop.

"We finished the cottage today." Moriah was proud of what they'd accomplished. "The floor is completely finished and it is gorgeous. Jack and the others did such a good job on it. The only thing left now is installing the big windows in the lantern room and rigging some sort of light. Oh, and if you don't mind, I'd like to purchase an excellent telescope. The lantern room needs one. When the weather is good, you'll be able to see for miles up there."

Nicolas ignored her.

"What are you looking at?" She searched for a towel, but the one Katherine usually kept near the sink was missing. "You seem concerned."

"I am. Ben sent me an e-mail."

Her heart nearly stopped. "Is something wrong?"

"He doesn't sound coherent."

She dried her hands on her jeans and bent over Nicolas' shoulder to take a look.

"It's as though he's hallucinating or something. The message is garbled and misspelled," Nicolas said.

"Ben doesn't misspell words."

"I know. That's why I'm worried. Here, read it for yourself."

The message was short and disturbing.

kum fast ben bad hot

"What in the world?" Moriah said.

"I don't know. I sent a reply and I'm waiting for an answer." Nicolas forked his fingers through his hair. "When did you last hear from him? Yesterday?"

"Actually, no. There was no message from him yesterday or last night. He had mentioned he might be visiting another tribe in a neighboring village. I thought perhaps he needed to stay over." Fear wrapped icy tentacles around her stomach. "What do you think is going on?"

"I don't know. But something's wrong."

He typed a sentence. "Ben. Do you have a fever?"

no ben fusiwe

"Fusiwe?" Moriah said. "Who is Fusiwe?"

"A good friend of Ben's who lives in the village. He speaks decent English, but I didn't know he could read or write yet. Apparently Ben has started teaching him."

"Is Ben sick?" Nicolas typed.

yas

Are you sick?" Nicolas asked.

no

"Ben is hot?"

bern lik fir

"Burn like fire." Moriah gripped Nicolas' shoulder. "What's happening to Ben?"
"Wrap Ben in a wet sheet," Nicolas typed. "Fan him. Do not stop."

i do

"Is there a rash?"

yas

"On his face?"

no pleze kum

"High fever. A rash that hasn't spread to his face." Nicolas shook his head in dismay.
"Is it Breakbone?" he typed.

mabe

"Maybe," Moriah said. "What's Breakbone?"

"Another word for Dengue Fever."

"What's Dengue Fever?"

"The Brazilians call it 'Breakbone Fever' because a person who has it aches so badly he feels like his bones are breaking."

"How could Ben have gotten it?"

"It's mosquito borne."

"Like malaria?"

"Different mosquito. A day-biting one."

"But Ben said he was taking malaria medicine," she argued. "Wouldn't that help?"

"Not with Dengue. There's no vaccine to prevent it or medicine to cure it. The only line of defense is Deet and mosquito netting. Problem is, a man can't live his life beneath mosquito netting and it's easy enough to sweat Deet off and forget to reapply it."

"But he'll be okay?" she pleaded.

"He might." Nicolas' voice became cold and clinical, as though he were detaching himself. "As long as it doesn't turn into Hemorrhagic Fever."

"What's that?"

Nicolas didn't answer. "Fusiwe," he typed. "Is Ben bleeding?"

sum

"Where?

skn

"Under his skin?"

yas

"He's bleeding beneath his skin?" Moriah ranted. "Ben is bleeding beneath his skin! Nicolas, how bad is that?"

"It's not good."

"Do not give him aspirin," Nicolas wrote. "Keep him cool. Give him as much water as he will drink. I'm coming."

"Me too," Moriah said. "I'm coming too."

"Impossible," Nicolas said. "You don't have a passport."

"You're wrong."

"When did you get a passport?"

"While you were gone."

"You aren't ready yet."

"It doesn't matter. I'm coming."

"Think about it, Moriah. What other phobias might this trip stir up within you?"

"I'm going."

"Ben's life is at stake," Nicolas argued. "Having to stop to deal with your emotional problems isn't worth the risk. Besides, you have no medical training and I can travel more easily and quickly alone."

"I love him."

"If he is as sick as I think he is, he won't even know you're there."

"I can *fix* things!" she said. "If something breaks I can fix it."

Nicolas gave her an appraising glance. "Okay then. Sometimes there is a great need in the jungle for someone who can fix things. Go pack." He reached into the top drawer of the desk and pulled out a prescription bottle. "I got these for you last week... just in case. They are sedatives. Pack quickly and then take one. I don't intend to deal with hysterics while we're in the air."

It was a reasonable request, although it galled her to accept Nicolas' directive. "You want to knock me out until we get there?"

"You spent exactly five whole minutes in the air before

431

begging Bob Jr. to land the plane. Just take the pill and don't argue."

He closed the computer. "I have phone calls to make. If they go well, we can leave within the hour."

"I'll go tell Katherine," Moriah said. "She'll want to come too."

"No."

"But Katherine has medical training."

Nicolas picked up the telephone and dialed a number.

"No."

"Why?"

"Kathy's pregnant." He turned his attention to his phone conversation.

It took Moriah a moment to absorb the shock of his abrupt announcement. She heard the words "private jet" before she backed away from him and stumbled up the stairs.

The bedroom was dark, and Katherine lay on the bed with a washcloth over her eyes. Moriah stood at the doorway, calming herself before she sat down on the bed beside her aunt.

"Why didn't you tell me?" Moriah gently stroked her aunt's hair.

"Why didn't I tell you what?" Katherine pulled the washcloth away from her eyes.

"That you're pregnant."

"Oh that." Katherine waved a hand as though dismissing her concern.

"Yes, that."

"I knew you'd make a fuss."

"Well, of *course* I'll make a fuss." Moriah gazed into her aunt's eyes. "I'm worried about you. I'm so sorry this has happened to you."

"Excuse me?"

"You know, accidentally getting pregnant. At your age. I know having babies after forty is dangerous."

"You think this was an accident?" Katherine sat up and scooted against the headboard. "You are so wrong. Nicolas and I *desperately* want this child."

"You got pregnant deliberately?"

"Yes. I'm healthy as a horse, and I'm perfectly capable of carrying a child full-term. The only reason I'm lying down *now* is because I have a slight headache and I don't want to take any medicine for it because of the baby."

"So, you're happy about this?"

"You'd better believe I'm happy." Katherine laid her hand over Moriah's. "Just think. I'm going to have a *baby*! I'm so happy I can't even talk about it without crying."

"Is Nicolas pleased?"

"Ecstatic."

"Nicolas? Ecstatic?"

"Yes, Moriah. Ecstatic. He just doesn't jump up and down to show it."

"When are you due?"

"June."

"You guys didn't waste much time."

"We knew we wanted a child." Katherine shrugged. "As you keep pointing out, I *am* past forty."

"Okay, if you're happy, I'm happy. But I can't talk anymore about this right now. Ben is sick and Nicolas and I are leaving for the Amazon within the hour."

Katherine grasped her by the arm. "What's wrong?"

"Nicolas thinks Ben may have Dengue Fever."

"That can be fatal!"

"I know. Will you help me pack?"

"Of course!" Katherine was suddenly all business; headache and pregnancy temporarily forgotten. "You already have some jungle gear selected, don't you?"

"I've been getting things ready. They're in my closet."

They hurried to her room and began filling a nylon backpack with cotton underclothes, quick-drying shorts, pants, socks, hiking boots and t-shirts. Katherine went to her own room and came back with a handful of energy bars that she shoved into a side pocket.

"Where did you get those?" Moriah asked.

"I seem to be hungry all the time since I became pregnant. You'll need these. I can get more."

"Moriah!" Nicolas called from the bottom of the stairs. "You ready?"

"Doesn't he need to pack too?" Moriah asked.

"Nicolas keeps a packed bag in his car and another one in his plane at all times," Katherine said. "He's like a boy scout, always prepared."

Katherine's "boy scout" appeared in the door, his expression grim and determined. "The weather is good. I'll fly my plane to the Toronto island airport. There will be an Extended Range Leer jet fueled and readied by the time we get there."

Moriah slid the passport she had recently obtained into a side pocket of her bag and zipped everything up.

"Don't forget this." Nicolas tossed the bottle of medication to Moriah.

Moriah stuck it in her pocket.

"Take one now, Moriah," Nicolas said. "This trip is too important to risk you falling apart in the air. I won't order the pilot to land if you have a meltdown."

Moriah opened the vial, tossed one capsule in her mouth and swallowed. The capsule stuck in her throat. She pushed past Nicolas to go into the bathroom, filled a glass, threw her head back and drank until the pill reached her stomach.

She sat the glass down, gripped the sides of the sink, looked at the mirror and stared into her own eyes. Even if she had to stay sedated the whole way, no matter what it took, she *would* go to Ben.

Moriah ran down to where Nicolas' pontoon sat in the water, fully aware that she would be traveling across Lake Huron, the continental United States, a portion of the ocean and deep into a South American jungle.

Nicolas stowed her bag as she buckled herself into the seat, grasped the armrests with an iron grip, and whispered. "Stay alive, my love."

Then she squeezed her eyes closed, clamped her jaw, and fought her desire to scream as the seaplane lifted into the air.

CHAPTER 24

The capsule she had swallowed back at the lodge had begun to work its magic by the time Nicolas landed at the Toronto island airport. At least Moriah thought that was what was happening. She definitely didn't feel like herself. She also thought it was a sad state of affairs when not feeling like yourself was a *good* thing.

The private jet they boarded looked powerful enough to carry them non-stop to Honduras, where Nicolas said they'd refuel before flying to the airport nearest to the Yahnowa. The smell of expensive leather laced with jet fuel permeated the cabin.

"The weather looks clear most of the way," the pilot said. "With a bit of tail wind, we could make it into Sao Paulo in nine or ten hours."

"Radio ahead, please, and see if you can make arrangements for a helicopter to take us the rest of the way," Nicolas instructed. "A pilot by the name of Ron Meacham picked up a missionary and his wife awhile ago. The temporary clearing the tribe created might still be open."

"I'll check, but the jungle closes up fast," the pilot warned.

"I know," Nicolas said.

Moriah ran a hand over the glove-soft leather of her seat after she'd buckled herself in. "What does renting a jet like this cost?"

"A lot." Nicolas said.

"What's 'a lot?'"

"I've delivered hundreds of babies, Moriah. Some of those pregnancies were extremely high risk. Fathers can be quite grateful when you save the life of their wife and child. Tonight I called in a favor."

"Thank you for doing this, Nicolas."

"You're welcome, but I'm not doing this for you."

The plane was so luxurious that she felt slightly apologetic for even sitting in the lovely leather seats. With Katherine's help, she had stuffed a bag full of clothes and necessities, but she had not taken the time to change out of the clothes she had worked in all day. Every minute was too valuable.

"Is the medication still working?" Nicolas asked, as she felt the jet start down the runway."

"I think so. I'm more sleepy than scared."

"Good." Nicolas pulled a blanket out of a storage cabinet. "Then sleep as long as you can." He handed her the blanket. "If Ron isn't available, or if his old helicopter is out of commission again, or if the landing area they cleared for Violet has closed up, we might have to hike in. It's best to be well-rested before you do that."

"What about you? Don't you need to rest?" She spread the blanket over her legs and leaned her seat back. She heard the jet engine start up. The medication had definitely taken the edge off. That and the fact that the jet was so elegant and well-appointed that it felt like being seated in a small living room. She thought that, if she pretended really hard, she could almost convince herself that it wasn't a plane at all.

"I don't require much sleep," he said. "I learned to go without when I was delivering babies."

The jet began to roll down the runway. As she gripped the armrests and closed her eyes, another repressed memory bubbled up.

The priest was kind, but he was a stranger. She wished Mommy or Daddy were there to hold her as the big airplane roared off into the sky. She did not want the priest to hold her and he did not offer. She felt small and very alone as she sat in the seat beside him and stared out the window. After a while she needed to go to the bathroom, but she was afraid to go there by herself. Being on the plane with this man who dressed funny was so alien to her that she couldn't make herself ask him to take her. So she simply waited. And waited. Until it was too late.

The priest was surprised when they stood up to leave the plane and discovered that her clothing and seat were wet. He waited until everyone else had left the airplane, then he called the stewardess over and quietly told her what had happened. The stewardess was unhappy about the wet seat and frowned at her. The priest held Moriah's hand as he led her off the plane.

It felt awful walking out of the plane with wet clothes. She glanced back over her shoulder and saw there were now two stewardesses shaking their heads over the wet seat. She knew from the expressions on their faces that she had done something very bad.

Moriah felt her stomach lurch as the jet lifted from the ground, but that was all she remembered. A prescription drug-induced sleep took over, deep and dreamless.

CHAPTER 25

M oriah awoke with a start, disoriented. She was surprised
to discover it was dark. It had been daylight when she
fell asleep. Where was she?

The only light was a dim one directly above Nicolas' head. He
looked neat and professional as he worked at a small desk.
Vaguely she remembered getting on the jet with him.

A jet! She was in the air?

She scrambled to sit up and glanced out the window beside
her seat. The inky space outside the jet's window was relieved
only by stars. She didn't like this feeling of flying at night. In Bob
Jr.'s piper cub, she had at least been able to look out the window
and anchor herself with familiar landmarks.

Being inside a Leer Jet, at night, was nothing like flying with
Bob Jr. Nor was it anything like the large commercial jet she'd
ridden in as a child—which had felt cavernous to her. This
tightly built, encapsulated craft was beginning to make her feel
as though she was inside a tomb. As full realization came of
where they were, she broke out in a cold sweat, and her stomach

heaved. She pressed her forehead against the cool glass of the window and tried to force the nausea down.

Nicolas glanced over at her with concern. "Get up, Moriah. You're turning green."

She couldn't make herself move. He jumped up and half-carried her to the miniscule bathroom.

She lost the contents of her stomach into the toilet while Nicolas held her long hair out of her face.

When there was nothing left to bring up, she flopped back against the doorframe, her stomach still spasming. Her whole body trembled from the violence of the past few minutes.

"I was afraid something like this would happen." Nicolas squatted down beside her. "Here. Rinse your mouth out." He shoved a cup of water into her hand.

She rinsed and spit into the toilet without getting up.

Nicolas was annoyed. "I have half a mind to leave you off in Honduras when we land for gas."

"No!" She still felt sick, but her will to go to Ben remained unchanged. "I'm going with you. I don't care how many times I get sick. I'll just keep going."

"Where's your medication? Obviously, it's worn off. Take another pill."

She searched her pockets. "I don't have it."

"You've got to be kidding."

"I—I think I left it on the bathroom sink back home."

Nicolas' face was a study of resignation. "Of course you did. Nothing is ever easy with you."

"I'm okay. I can do this." Moriah stretched out on the carpeted floor, her head a few inches from the bathroom door. Lying there, she felt slightly less nauseous than sitting in a seat, staring out at the dark sky. With her head against the carpeted floor, she could also hear the comforting thrum of a well-kept engine.

"I'm okay," she repeated, closing her eyes.

She heard a snap, then a fizz and, when she opened her eyes again, she saw Nicolas bringing her a can of ginger ale. He grabbed a pillow from an overhead compartment and handed both items to her.

Gratefully, she sat up and sipped the soda. "Thanks."

"You're welcome."

When she'd finished her drink, Moriah lay back down on the floor with her pillow and felt marginally better. She tried to distract herself by concentrating on plans for her wedding. It was easier to visualize getting married in the beautiful lighthouse cottage, than to think about Ben fighting for his life right now with no one but a young tribesman caring for him. Emotionally exhausted, she finally dozed once again, waking only briefly when Nicolas tucked a blanket around her.

CHAPTER 26

Hours later, Moriah watched as Nicolas perused a faded map along with Ron Meacham and Ron's co-pilot son, Matt. The map was tacked onto the wall of a rickety plywood airport hanger. Ron's gray hair was cut military short and he wore a spotless white shirt with pressed khaki pants. His face was tanned and creased with years of squinting into the sun. Matt was simply a younger carbon copy of his dad.

The tropical sun blazed down on the corrugated tin roof, which made the hanger feel like a sauna. She felt slow and dumb, as though her mind was starting to shut down from having too much to process.

In less than a day, she had come from a Canadian late summer with the crisp snap of autumn in the air, to this oppressive South American heat. She couldn't remember ever being so unbearably warm. The weight of the moisture-laden air was suffocating. She tried to tune back into the conversation, but it was difficult to concentrate.

"You're sure?" Nicolas folded up the map.

"The jungle grows back so fast," Ron said. "Unless the tribe has kept it clear, it will be next to impossible to land."

"How close can you take us in then?" Nicolas asked.

Moriah swayed slightly. The combination of weariness and heat was making her dizzy.

Nicolas glanced at her. "We'd better get her out of this hothouse. Ron, let's get there and circle the village. If the landing place isn't clear, I know there's a tribe a few miles directly to the south that Ben has visited. There's a large landing field not too far from there that a lumber company uses. It wouldn't be too hard to walk the rest of the way."

"Normally that would be a good idea," Matt said. "But not right now. There's been some unrest again there the past couple weeks. The lumber company left until things settled down. That tribe is not up to welcoming company right now."

"Our 'copter carries enough fuel to circle Mrs. Smith's clearing and get back here," Ron said. "If it's clear, we'll land. If it isn't we'll come back and figure something else out."

"Sounds like a plan." Nicolas shouldered his bag of medical supplies. "I'm ready."

Moriah felt better outside the hanger. She followed the three men to where an army-green helicopter was tethered. Unfortunately, the aircraft looked quite a bit worse for wear. In fact, in her opinion, it looked like it should be sold for scrap.

"How old is this craft?" she asked.

"Our Huey?" Ron said. "It flew in Vietnam. We picked it up from war surplus."

"Then that would explain the bullet holes?"

"It was a mess when we got it. Matt and I had our work cut out for us, but it purrs like a kitten now."

"A kitten that has to cough up a hairball every now and then." Matt laughed. "There's still a few small mechanical kinks we need to work out—nothing for you to worry about—but we're making progress."

Moriah stared at it with dismay. With Nicolas' seaplane and with the Leer jet she had confidence in the crafts, even if she didn't have any confidence in herself. However, with this Huey, she had grave misgivings. She wished she could take a long, hard look at that Huey engine, but there wasn't time.

Matt slid the side door open, pulled out a vest, helmet, headset and goggles then handed them to her.

"I'm supposed to wear all this?" she asked.

"Standard procedure." He helped her slip the vest over her arms. "We'll be following the Amazon river for part of the trip. If we go down in the water, pull this nozzle on the container of pressurized oxygen you have here on this pocket, and the vest will inflate."

"And that will save me?"

"Sure, unless a croc or piranhas get to you. Try to swim fast and get onto land as quickly as possible."

"Okay." Moriah tried to keep her voice from shaking.

He placed the helmet on her head and helped her adjust the goggles. "This will keep the bugs out of your eyes."

"Bugs?"

"We keep the doors open for ventilation when we fly."

Moriah repeated his words like a parrot. "Doors open. Ventilation. Life vest. Oxygen. Crocodiles. Piranhas."

The panic was rising and she wasn't even off the ground yet.

Nicolas read the desperation on her face.

"You'll be fine," he said. "Ron is famous in this area for getting into and out of tough places. He knows what he's doing."

Matt climbed into the Huey and folded a canvas and aluminum seat down from the wall.

"Get in and sit down," he said.

Moriah got in and sat down.

Together, he and Nicolas strapped Moriah into her seat.

"This is an intercom." Matt said, as he plugged a long wire from her helmet into the electrical system of the helicopter. "Push the button here on the wire if you want to talk to any of us while we're in flight."

"Push button," she repeated, her head spinning.

In the other two aircraft, it had been possible to close her eyes and at least *try* to pretend that she was inside a safe little room. In this too-open helicopter there was no possibility of pretending. There was no carpeting, no soft music, no luxurious leather seats. There weren't even any *doors*, for crying out loud.

Nicolas, clad in the same type of life vest and helmet as the others, calmly buckled himself in while Matt climbed into the co-pilot's seat.

She saw them flipping switches, and then the high-pitched whine of the engines slowly started up and the blades began to turn. She could smell the fumes. She didn't know if that was the exhaust of burnt fuel or hydraulic fluid. Neither pilot reacted or seemed concerned, so she assumed it was normal.

Soon the popping sound of the blades on the Huey began and then escalated. The sound became deafening where she was sitting. She felt every pop like an impact against her chest as the old bird began to vibrate. Her body tensed as the blades became a blur and then the ancient beast lifted into the air.

The aircraft bounced once as it rose and hovered above the trees, then Ron slanted the blades to bite into the air and they moved forward at an alarming angle, pitching Moriah sharply against her seat straps. The single pill she had taken to placate Nicolas had definitely worn off. Now, she was protected by nothing, not even by the blanket of night. She could see quite well, unfortunately.

As Ron headed toward the Yahnowa village, wind rushed at her through the open door as the valiant motor of the old military craft roared in her ears. Although the helicopter wasn't moving anywhere close to the same speed that the jet had flown, it somehow felt like it was flying faster as she absorbed every vibration, every bounce and every shimmy.

The sensory overload, after staying on the island for over twenty years, was overwhelming. She had had enough. Everything was moving too fast, rushing toward her, like the wind that kept whipping against her from the open doors. The fear was unbearable, filling her mind with so much pain that she didn't know if she could bear it. She could hear Matt, Ron and Nicolas talking to one another through the speaker inside her helmet, but she didn't comprehend what they were saying. She was too absorbed in fighting her own, intense battle.

The helicopter felt like a fragile eggshell as it chopped its way over a coffee-colored river snaking its way through an ocean of green vegetation. Sometimes Ron flew the helicopter so low, she feared that the treetops would scrape its belly.

Her fear escalated into sheer terror.

She fought against the desire to rip off the helmet and tear off the seat harness. Although there was no lack of fresh air, she found herself having difficulty catching her breath. In an attempt to regain emotional control, she bit the inside of her cheek until it bled, clenched her fists until her fingernails made cuts into her palm, grabbed her hair with both hands and pulled as hard as she could—focusing on the pain she was inflicting on herself—trying to concentrate on anything except the most dizzying, heart-palpitating, paralyzing terror she had ever experienced.

After what felt like two eternities, she saw Nicolas tense and lean forward.

"There's the village!" Nicolas shouted, pointing.

They were here? They'd made it? Moriah glanced down. There was a tiny village of huts below them. The village looked like a small sore that had opened up inside the rolling green carpet of healthy vegetation that stretched as far as her eyes could see. People, who from her vantage point looked like dark ants, were pointing up and running toward a spot directly beneath where the helicopter was now hovering.

"Son of a… biscuit eater!"

She had a strong feeling that Ron had intended to say something besides 'biscuit eater' but changed his mind at the last minute.

Nicolas hung his head outside the door and looked down.

"What?" She leaned forward. "What's wrong?"

"Bamboo can grow more than a foot a day in the jungle. I gambled that the villagers would keep the clearing open. They did not."

"Looks like they are making an attempt now," Matt said.

It was true. In an area that looked slightly less dense than the rainforest canopy all around them, several villagers were hacking away at the new growth. It looked like difficult work because the bamboo towered far above their heads. Their efforts were too little, too late.

"Fusiwe must have told them we were coming," Nicolas' voice was frustrated. "But they haven't had time to make enough progress. We can't land in this."

"But they are trying to clear it." Being so close to Ben and unable to land was maddening. "Can't we give them a little more time?"

"How much fuel do we have left?" Nicolas asked Ron.

"Just over half a tank. It was full when we left. If we don't have any problems we can make it back to Sao Paulo, but just barely. This old bird is thirstier than usual today. We'll need to do something to fix that when we get back."

"We can't turn back," Moriah said. "Ben is in that village. Don't helicopters have ropes or something they use to rescue people?"

"Sorry, sweetheart," Ron said. "We aren't equipped for that. Nick—do you think Ben can survive waiting a day or two for the villagers to finish working on the clearing?"

"Probably not." Nicolas glanced at her.

"Well then," Ron said. "If that's the case, it's time for an old trick I learned from a buddy back in Nam. Best pilot I ever knew. Scared the bejeebers out of me the only time I ever saw it."

"Dad?" Matt sounded worried. "What are you doing?"

"I'm turning this old bird into a weed-whacker!" Ron roared. "It might be a one-way trip, but if it's Ben's only chance I gotta try. I like that boy. Always have."

Ron hovered over the landing area for a few seconds to make it clear to the people below that he was coming in while Matt and Nicolas gestured frantically for the villagers to get out of the way.

Moriah felt the Huey being lowered further and further until suddenly the blades began biting into the bamboo and debris flew everywhere.

Bits and pieces of vegetation started pelting her and she instinctively covered her eyes with her hands. The sound of flying bamboo striking the metal of the helicopter was thunderous.

Finally, with a hard thump, the Huey touched earth and Ron slowed the rotation of the blades.

Someone pried Moriah's hands away from her face. She opened her eyes and saw Nicolas staring at her with concern. She glanced around, dazed and uncertain.

"I'm okay," she said. "I think. Are you?"

"I'm fine." Nicolas brushed pieces of leaves off his shirt. "We're here now. Let's go."

Nicolas climbed out of the helicopter while the blades continued to turn. She hurriedly pulled her helmet, goggles and headset off, unbuckled her seat belt and slid out of the helicopter. While they waited for Matt to join them, she silently blessed the fact that she was once again standing on firm ground.

"So," Nicolas said, dryly. "Did you enjoy your first helicopter ride?"

CHAPTER 27

M oriah felt as drained as if she had run a marathon...
twice. The earth around her was littered with pieces of
leaves and bamboo.

"Matt, would you grab the stretcher?" Nicolas asked.

"Got it," Matt said.

"I'm staying with the Huey," Ron said. "I'm afraid we might
have sustained a bit of damage. If I turn it off it might not start
up again."

"Will it take us out of here?" Nicolas asked.

"Hope so," Ron said. "But it wasn't made for what I just did
to it."

Villagers began to cautiously emerge from the forest where
they had hidden to escape the rainfall of bamboo.

"Might be a good idea to hurry," Ron shouted, his voice
strained as he stared up at the rotating blades.

Instead of just the solid sound of rotors beating the air,
Moriah heard an eerie sort of whistling. It sounded like it was
coming from the Huey's blades but she couldn't be sure.

In what sounded like halting Yahnowa, Nicolas quickly

greeted and thanked the villagers, then shouldered his medical bag and strode forward.

"Follow directly behind me, Moriah," he instructed. "Don't touch anything. If you fall, make sure you fall straight down onto the path. Whatever you do, don't try to grab onto anything to break your fall."

"Why?" Moriah was still coveting the feel of firm ground beneath her feet and fighting the urge to hug the nearest tree.

"Because it might be alive and deadly, sharp as a razor, or filled with poison. Ignorance can get you killed very quickly in the jungle."

"Oh." Suddenly, the lush beauty of the place felt threatening. "I'll be careful."

"Don't let him scare you." Matt brought up the rear as they walked beneath the rainforest canopy. "You'll learn what to touch and what to avoid. It's not really that hard. It's just that you don't know anything yet. Nicolas is right. Ignorance can be deadly in the jungle."

She stuck her hands firmly in her pockets to remind herself not to use them if she tripped and fell. It would be tough.

After a short hike, they arrived at the small village. Nicolas headed straight toward a hut that looked like it had been made from dried grass. It sat slightly outside the others. As they entered, she saw Ben. He lay as still as death, his body on a raised platform of bamboo, his body swathed in a wet sheet.

On the flight to Sao Paulo, she had prayed for a miraculous recovery. She had hoped that Ben would somehow be able to welcome her with open arms, laughing about her great fear for him. One glance, and she knew that would not be happening. Not this time. Ben was completely unconscious. His face was flushed, his breathing ragged. A rash covered the upper part of his chest. He did not show any sign of knowing that she and Nicolas were there.

An exhausted-looking young tribesman stood over Ben, fanning him with a palm leaf.

"Fusiwe." Nicolas' voice was respectful. "How is our friend?"

"Not good. I kept wet sheets on him all night," the young tribesman said. "Rashawe helped. He spent much time putting drops of water into Ben's mouth."

Moriah was surprised that the young man spoke English so well. From the misspelled email, she had expected Fusiwe's English to be practically incoherent. Evidently, he had only recently begun his spelling lessons.

"Are others in the village affected?"

"Three. They all went with Ben to another village. Bad mosquitos there. Two died. Many villagers stay in their huts now; afraid."

"Talk to them," Nicolas said. "Explain that Dengue isn't contagious. Is Ben better or worse than he was yesterday?"

"Worse."

Nicolas quickly examined Ben, then turned to her. "We have to get him to the hospital as fast as possible. I'll start an IV as soon as we get back to the helicopter. Let's move!"

CHAPTER 28

Matt and Fusiwe held the canvas stretcher steady while Nicolas and Moriah muscled Ben off his pallet and onto it. Ben was so solid, it took all her strength to help lift him. Once they got him secured, Matt and Fusiwe took off on a fast walk through the jungle with Ben's limp, fever-ridden body between them.

Moriah's mind was leaping ahead, making calculations as she and Nicolas followed. At best, it would take maybe five minutes to load him, strap him in and get into the air. Nicolas would start the IV that had been among the medical supplies a doctor friend had placed on the private jet before they left. Thanks to Nicolas, they had gotten here in time. Soon they would be at the hospital where Ben would have a fighting chance.

Fusiwe helped load Ben into the helicopter, got out from under the still rotating blades and then stood in the shade of the forest while Matt and Nicolas secured the stretcher and Ben as well. Then she crawled into the helicopter and knelt beside him.

Ben's face was so unnaturally pale. She smoothed back his unruly red hair and kissed his forehead. Her lips registered the heat. He was burning up. How long could his body sustain a fever like this? His eyelids did not so much as flicker at her touch.

Nor did he flinch when the IV needle went in. Nicolas hung the bag of life-saving liquid on a hook that appeared to have been attached to the Huey for that very purpose. Moriah held Ben's hand and wondered how many other lives this old helicopter had saved.

"We're getting you help, my love," she said. "You're going to be okay."

Nicolas buckled himself in and donned his helmet, goggles and headset.

Once again Ron and Matt started flipping switches and the whine of the engine escalated. As the blades began to rotate faster, that troubling whistling sound she had noted earlier increased.

Ron looked back at them. His face was deadly serious. He said something into his mic and Nicolas' head snapped back as though he had just received a blow. He glanced worriedly at her, still kneeling beside Ben.

While the men communicated with one another she made her way to her seat, donned her helmet and plugged in her headset. Something was wrong and she wanted to know what it was.

She interrupted their conversation. "What's going on?"

"Ron and I have decided that you need to get off the helicopter, Moriah," Nicolas said.

"Why?"

"For your own safety."

Ron's voice interrupted Nicolas. "The hydraulic pressure is low. It will be running hot soon. The fuel needle is barely past a half of a tank. You need to get off."

"But…"

She tried to argue, but Ron wasn't interested. He jerked a thumb at the open door.

"Out!"

"I don't understand. I want to be with Ben."

"We don't need your weight adding stress to the 'copter," Ron said. "Out!"

She glanced around at the inside the helicopter and keyed her mic. "That's ridiculous. This thing was built to hold at least a dozen soldiers. My weight isn't going to make any difference."

"Please leave, Moriah," Nicolas said. "Fusiwe will take you back to the village."

"No," she said. "I'm staying with Ben."

The whistling sound continued.

Ron threw his headset down, climbed out of the helicopter and came around to the open door beside her. He was a man of few words. Without asking, he unbuckled her restraints and tried to pull her out of the open door as the blades picked up speed.

Even as she clawed at the seat to keep from being dragged off, it struck her that only yesterday she would have fought anyone who tried to make her get on one of these things. Now, she was fighting to stay on.

All because of Ben.

Love did, indeed, overcome fear.

Vaguely, through the headset, she heard Matt's voice talking fast. "The bird is damaged, Moriah. The blades are compromised. Some of the steel is missing. The honeycomb structure beneath has been exposed, which is why the blades are whistling. The hydraulics *are* low and will be running hot soon. That means we'll burn even more fuel going back than coming. There is a chance we might not make it. There's no reason for you to be at risk too."

"But…"

"If anything happens to us," Nicolas said. "I need you to go home and take care of Kathy and the baby. I'm begging you. Get off the helicopter. Now!"

Her heart plummeted. Nicolas was right. Katherine would need her. She had to get off.

With tears streaming down her face, she let go of the door-frame. Ron staggered backward two steps at her quick release. Then, realizing she had given up, he went back to the cockpit and climbed in. She tore off her headset, goggles and helmet as Nicolas threw her bag out after her.

The wounded metal bird immediately flew into the air.

Once again, Ben was leaving her behind.

CHAPTER 29

Moriah watched in silence as the helicopter turned into a speck in the sky and the sound of rotors evaporated.

She heard someone cough, and realized it was Fusiwe trying to get her attention. She turned and looked at him—this man who had saved Ben's life. Fusiwe wore nothing but a breechcloth. His hair was long and plaited down his back. Moriah glanced down at her blue jeans, sweat-soaked t-shirt and tennis shoes. In spite of her intense worry about Ben, if she was going to be under Fusiwe's care, she thought it best to start things off on an honest footing.

"I'm dumb as dirt. I don't even know how to feed myself here."

"I know," Fusiwe said. "Follow me. And do not *touch* anything!"

She wiped the tears from her cheeks with the tail of her t-shirt, picked up her bag, then obediently followed him, arms stiffly down at her side. Things had taken a turn she could never have anticipated. How would she know if they had made it safely to the hospital? What would she do if they didn't?

In the meantime, her life pretty much depended on the man walking the path in front of her.

"Thank you for taking care of him," she said. "If it weren't for you, we wouldn't even know he was sick."

"Ben is my friend," Fusiwe said.

"How did you learn to speak English?"

"Violet and Abraham teach me. Ben teach me Portuguese, too. It is the language of Brazil and valuable to know."

"So you speak three languages?"

"Four. Ben teach me Spanish, too."

"Four languages?" Moriah said. "Why?"

Fusiwe stopped in the middle of the path, turned around and looked at her as though she might be a little stupid. "To protect my people, of course."

"How will learning all these languages help protect the Yahnowa?"

"Ben says knowing the language of the people around us gives us power. Especially if they think we are ignorant. My wife and my wife's brother, Rashawe, learn too. We are not ignorant."

"I thought you were still pretty isolated here."

"Yes, for now. I fear we cannot be isolated much longer. The farmers eat away at our land. They clear it with fire and grow crops, but the soil is thin. It only supports a few plantings. Then it gets tired and the crops do not thrive. The farmers move on. Ben prepares us to survive in the future as well as give us a Bible translation."

"Nicolas says you're some sort of apprentice to the local witch doctor?"

The young man winced, then he turned and continued down the path. "The correct word is Shaman. Yes, I'm learning to be a healer. In our ignorance and need, my people turned to what you might call witchcraft. I am not interested in chants and magical spells, but I *am* interested in what there is to be learned from the old people who have much knowledge about herbs and plants."

"Did I offend you?" Moriah reached out to touch an exotic-looking flower, but remembered at the last moment to jerk her hand back. "I didn't mean to."

"I am not offended, but I am tired. I care for Ben for two days. Before that my people need my help."

He stopped outside a neatly built hut and called softly. A lovely young woman peeked out at Moriah with brown eyes as soft and lovely as a young doe.

"This is my wife." Fusiwe wearily entered his one-room hut. "She take care of you." He climbed into a hammock, closed his eyes and fell asleep immediately.

It was obvious that caring for Ben had taken quite a toll on the man.

"Hello." Moriah wondered how much his wife understood. She had long, shiny black hair much the same as Moriah's, but she wore little in the way of clothing except swirls of paint.

"You have green eyes!" The woman stepped closer, touching Moriah's face. It felt strange having another woman caress her face, but Moriah thought perhaps it was one of those strange tribal customs she might have to get used to.

"A friend of my childhood had eyes this green. Ben says you are my childhood friend."

Moriah's eyes opened wide. "Karyona?"

The young woman nodded and smiled.

Moved beyond words, Moriah embraced her, paint and all.

"We always wondered about you," Karyona said. "We worry about you many years."

Fusiwe stirred restlessly in his sleep. Karyona looked at him with concern.

"Our voices disturb him. Should we go to Ben's hut to talk?"

"Good idea," Moriah said.

After they arrived at Ben's place, they climbed onto his sleeping platform and continued their conversation.

"I would have gotten word to you if I had known." Moriah stared at her friend in wonder. "But I had no memory of anything that happened here until a few months ago. Is your father and mother still living?"

"Oh yes. He is on a long hunting trip. My mother visits relatives in a different tribe. They will come back in a few days. Until then, we have much to talk about."

CHAPTER 30

The two women stayed late in Ben's hut, facing each other, sitting cross-legged on his sleeping platform, whispering as the years fell away. Moriah felt the same gentleness emanating from Karyona that she had felt as a child.

"Why didn't Ben tell me about you?" Moriah said. "After he got the satellite computer, we were in contact nearly every day."

"He was afraid you might not want to see me again for fear it would bring back more bad memories, and he wants so much for you to come here."

"You are a happy memory, Karyona. Not a bad one."

"Do you remember Little Man?" Her friend smiled. "I think he is a happy memory."

"My monkey? Of course! I loved him. I was so proud that I had a monkey for a pet. Whatever happened to him?"

"We cared for him until he die of old age. He have a good life."

"Thank you for doing that. How's your brother?"

"Rashawe?" Karyona's face lit up. "He does well. His wife is with child. We are happy to welcome another little one into our village."

"He put his life at risk to save me. So did your father."

"They are warriors. It was what they are born to do. Moawa's attack was a surprise to them. If they knew, he and his followers would never make it to your parents.'"

Moriah shivered involuntarily at even hearing the name Moawa.

Karyona touched Moriah's arm with concern. "You are still frightened of him?"

"Yes."

"I was too," Karyona said. "Until he came out of the hills begging food."

Moriah stared. "What?"

"Moawa is blind and very helpless now."

"You mean he's *here*?" Moriah jumped off the sleeping platform and whirled around as though expecting Moawa to pounce at her from some dark corner.

"He can no longer hurt anyone, Moriah. You do not need to fear him."

"Where is he?"

"Our villagers never forgave him for what he did. Because of him, we lost the good doctor as well as your family. But he was once a headman, and he is blind. A village meeting was held and it was decided to build him a hut far outside the village. We isolated him to punish him for what he had done, but we still provide water and food. He does not have a happy life, Moriah."

"I can't believe Ben never told me!"

"Perhaps, again, he was afraid you would never come to him if you knew."

"It would have made it harder for me to do so," Moriah admitted.

"Would you like to go see him?"

"Moawa? No! Absolutely not."

"I think it would be wise. He is no monster now."

"I can't, Karyona. I just can't."

"I understand." Karyona slid off the bamboo platform. "I will leave you to rest now. You have had a long day. We will see each other in the morning." She smiled as she left. "I am so glad you are here, my sister."

After Karyona's departure, Moriah ran her hand over a primitive desk Ben had made from wooden crates and boards. The satellite laptop was in the middle. It was here that Ben had sat, writing to her about his world and his life. It was attached to what looked like a car battery. She wondered who had carried the heavy object here.

The kerosene lamp she had lit cast shadows all about her. The jungle rose in a cacophony of sounds as nocturnal carnivores went about their grisly business. Next door to her there was a cough, then a child called out in its sleep. She heard the sounds of a mother soothing it.

This had been Ben's world for five years while he patiently worked at bringing the written word to these people, along with the languages that would help equip the young adults of the village to communicate with the outside world if necessary.

His Bible lay in front of her. The one he'd used back on the island. It was well worn, its spine held together with silver duct tape. She traced a finger across the cover. She had wanted to buy him a new one, but he had said he liked this one best because he knew where everything was in it.

Beside his Bible lay a fresh spiral notebook filling up with the language she knew to be Yahnowa. She riffled through the last pages. His handwriting had grown sloppy toward the end, as though he had tried to continue in spite of the fever.

Apparently, her lionhearted Ben had been trying to finish the translation so he could come back to her if, after all, she wasn't able to make herself come to him.

Beside the translation notebook was another, smaller one.

She opened it, wanting any small piece of him with which to comfort herself. As she read the first page, she realized that this was his prayer diary. She had not known Ben wrote down his prayers, but it did not surprise her.

What did surprise her were the words.

"Father, she is more beautiful than any woman I've ever known. I dream about her at night and think about her all day. I've memorized the scent of her hair and the perfection of her eyelashes. I don't know what the future holds for us, if anything, but I know this much—she hurts, Lord. Please take the pain, whatever it is, from her heart."

Tears crowded her vision as she checked the date. May 10th. Two days after Ben had arrived on Manitoulin. Long before he could have had the faintest inkling about her past. But he had seen into her heart, anyway.

Brushing away the tears, she read on.

Father, would you mind blinding her to my faults and teach her to see me with loving eyes? I don't think I'm going to want to live without her.

Moriah smiled. Ben had been coercing God behind her back. No wonder she had fallen in love with him so quickly. Ben didn't play fair.

Fascinated, she read on—the details of their journey together chronicled on these pages. Sometimes she laughed, sometimes she cried, but the final pages made her sit up.

Lord God, I'm afraid Moriah will never forgive me for bringing Moawa to this village, but I didn't know what else to do. When I found him, he was wandering alone, sightless, half-starved. His own tribe decimated by disease. What could I do? Watch another human being

suffer? I cannot tell her. And yet I must. If only she could see him;
could see that her monster no longer exists.

Moriah frowned. No way was she going to set eyes on
Moawa. He could stay in his hut out there in the jungle until he
rotted, as far as she was concerned.

She was so exhausted; even the thin mat on Ben's bamboo
bed looked good to her. It was probably still drenched in his
sweat, but she was too tired to care. Everything felt damp
anyway, including her own clothes. There was mosquito netting
above, but apparently it had not been enough to save Ben from
the toxic mosquito that had bit him.

Mosquito repellent sat on a shelf. She splashed it on liberally.
Then she blew out the kerosene lamp, lowered the mosquito
netting around her and lay in the dark. Eventually she fell into a
fitful sleep, rousing at every sound. A child's cough, a puma's
growl, the snapping of a twig, all wove themselves into a pattern
that melded and blended and swirled with dreams in which her
father, Ben, and Petras fought barehanded with a giant chieftain
wielding a gleaming machete.

She awakened in the early morning hours, drenched in sweat.
Her bladder was crying out to be emptied and she didn't know
where to go. There were no windows; the only opening was the
door, but from the soft light that was starting to show through
the small cracks in the hut's wall, she could tell that it would be
dawn soon. Ben's hut didn't exactly have indoor plumbing, so if
she was going to go outside to relieve herself without the entire
village watching, it had to be now.

She would have been grateful to have even an outhouse to go
to—but that apparently wasn't part of the culture. Presumably,
the people of this tribe went in the forest, which was a place
she'd repeatedly been instructed not to touch.

Carefully, she eased the door open and peeked out. No one

465

was stirring that she could see. Quickly, she scurried around to the back of the hut and squatted in the dirt. There were times when pain overrode modesty. This was one of those times.

Quickly zipping her pants, she looked around. No one was there. No one had seen. She felt much better as she went back into Ben's hut and closed the door.

The light through the cracks in the wall gave her enough light that she didn't have to light either of the lamps. There were two gallon-sized containers marked "DRINKING WATER" sitting on the ground. She lifted one, screwed off the lid, tipped it up and sipped carefully, wishing she could turn the container of water upside down and pour it over her head to cool off. Of course that was out of the question. She needed to save it. She did not know where Ben had gotten it or how to get more. The people in the village must have a water source but, until she could find out where Ben got this, she would have to be careful.

Even though she had to be careful not to waste water, had there been any soap lying around, she would have loved to wash her face, but she couldn't find a bar anywhere. Didn't Ben bathe when he was here? Or perhaps there was a place somewhere in a river or lake where the people took their baths. Maybe they used some sort of primitive soap made from roots or berries or something. Or perhaps no one used soap in the rainforest.

Her ignorance annoyed her. She should have pestered Ben with questions about everyday things—like how to use the bathroom in the jungle without getting killed, and how to get a safe drink of water when these two gallons run out.

One thing was for certain, Ben's possessions were minimal in the extreme. There wasn't a lot to work with here, and she had packed in such a fever to get to him that dragging along something as mundane as a bar of soap simply had not occurred to her.

She felt sweaty, sticky and sleep deprived. She also felt scared and abandoned and worried about whether or not the men had made it to Sao Paulo. If they did make it, she was still worried about Ben's health. He was strong. He was young. He would fight through this, she tried to reassure herself. But what had Fusiwe said? Two had died. One had gotten better.

Those were not great statistics.

The lack of soap was the final straw.

She felt a panic attack coming on. What was she doing here? What if Ben died? What if Nicolas didn't come back? Then in the corner, on a makeshift shelf, she spied Ben's razor, a small mirror and a ceramic soap cup with a shaving brush in it.

Pulling the cup off the shelf, she tipped a few drops of water into it and used the soft-bristled brush to make a lather. The familiar scent of Ben's favorite shaving soap wafted up and calmed her.

Completely alone, she removed her clothes and, careful not to waste a drop, poured another small amount of water on a portion of the t-shirt that she had worn all day yesterday. Using some of the lather of Ben's shaving soap, she washed her face and body the best that she could with nothing more than the dampened t-shirt.

When she was finished, she folded her t-shirt over Ben's desk chair to dry—at least as much as it would dry in the rainforest. Then she unzipped a pouch in her duffle bag and pulled out one of Katherine's energy bars. Her legs dangled from Ben's waist-high sleeping platform as she chewed and watched the light grow brighter through the cracks of the hut. The morning air felt good on her body; the menthol of Ben's soap cooled her skin.

As she surveyed the interior of Ben's home, she was impressed with the ingenuity of whoever had built this small hut with nothing more than what could be gathered in the forest. Some sort of woven grass made up the walls and roof, all of which was held up by large, bamboo poles tied together.

Her guess was that these were not structures that lasted more than a few years. Insects alone would make it unlivable eventually. Still, it impressed her.

She built with electric circular saws, battery-operated drills and lots of trips to the hardware store in Mindemoya. Her cabins, although not large, had cost quite a lot as she'd purchased the materials. Apparently, these people had built this structure with not much more than their bare hands.

With dawn approaching, she pulled fresh clothes out of her bag. The familiar smell of Katherine's fabric softener rose from the bag and brought on a wave of homesickness.

"What was I thinking?" Moriah whispered as she pulled on fresh underwear, khaki shorts and a sleeveless blue shirt. "What good did coming here do? Nicolas was right. I'm useless here."

She was sitting on Ben's bed, brushing her hair, wondering fruitlessly about Ron's helicopter. Wondering if, as hot as it was, it might be a good idea to cut her long hair short, when Karyona quietly opened the door. It was a relief to see a friendly face.

"You sleep?" Karyona said.

"A little. You?"

"Fusiwe went out again in the night. One of the village children had a bad cough."

"I heard the coughing. Was he able to help?"

"Yes. Both Fusiwe and the little one is asleep now."

"You have a good man, Karyona."

"Yes." Karyona smiled, pleased. "Are you ready to go now?"

"Go where?"

"I need to go check on Moawa and take him food. Ben and Fusiwe usually take care of his needs, and sometimes Rashawe will take a turn, but he is on a long hunt today and tomorrow, so it is up to me today. The other villagers will not go near him. I am not afraid of him, but I do not enjoy going alone. It would be nice to have a companion."

"I can't do that." Moriah shuddered. "I'm sorry."

"I know how hard it is." Karyona eyes held deep understanding. "It was difficult for me, too, the first time I went." She walked over to the bed and took one of Moriah's hands in hers. "After my father and brother took you away, my mother and I were alone for days. We were frightened. We were afraid Moawa would come to kill us for having hidden you from him. I had nightmares too."

"I'm sorry," Moriah said, and she was. The world felt a little less lonely knowing that there was at least one other person on earth who truly understood her fear, but still, she wished Karyona hadn't experienced it.

"When Ben and Fusiwe found him and brought him to our hut, I refused to stay. I shouted at them and ran away to my mother and father's hut."

"What did they do?"

"They let me cry for a while. When all my tears were gone, Ben came to me and told me the story about how Jesus had washed his friends' feet—including the friend that he knew would lead murderers to him. He asked me to try to overcome my fear so I could help him and Fusiwe do what was right. And so I did."

"Oh, Karyona," Moriah said. "Then what happened?"

"I went back to my own hut with Ben and I helped Fusiwe bathe Moawa and we put healing salve on all his cuts and scrapes. There were many. It was the hardest thing I've ever done, but I was no longer afraid of Moawa when we finished. He was so starved and shrunken. It was heartbreaking to care for his poor body. I realized that he was just a man. A scary man, maybe, at one time. But just a man."

"You are a braver woman than I am, Karyona."

"I am not. I think you can do this thing too."

"I'm not going to bathe Moawa."

"No, but you will help me go see him?"

"I can't," Moriah said. "I admire you for what you are doing, but I can't."

"I understand," Karyona said, after a short hesitation. "And it is different for me. My parents lived."

Karyona's simple words and extraordinary faith shamed Moriah.

"When I come back," Karyona said. "You may help me harvest some of my manioc crop. I think you will enjoy that."

"I would love to help you with anything," Moriah said. "As long as it does not involve seeing or dealing with Moawa."

"I will be back soon."

"Karyona?" Moriah said, before her friend could leave. "Where am I supposed to um... go to the bathroom?"

Karyona's head tilted. "Bathroom?"

"Where do I go to... relieve myself?"

"Oh," Karyona's voice was matter-of-fact. "In the forest, of course. But do not touch anything."

CHAPTER 31

Nicolas was not happy. The x-ray of Ben's chest showed that there was a buildup of fluid in his lungs. So far, Ben had been rehydrated with IV fluids along with an IV solution of electrolytes to correct the electrolyte imbalances. A transfusion of platelets had been given to try to stop the bleeding problems, but now Ben's oxygen level was abnormally low and the epidemiologist here at one of Brazil's finest hospitals was not hopeful.

"I have ordered oxygen therapy," Dr. Rodriguez said, making a quick sign of the cross. "Now, it will be in God's hands."

The doctor's statement and gesture did not surprise Nicolas. Brazil had the largest number of Catholics in the world.

Studying Ben, watching his coloring, his low oxygen levels, his continued fever—he agreed with the epidemiologist. It was, indeed, completely in God's hands now.

"You need to fight harder, my friend," Nicolas whispered to an unconscious Ben. "We've done all that we can do."

Moriah would have given anything to know if the men had made it to the hospital, but she couldn't figure out how to use Ben's satellite laptop. Fusiwe must know how to work the thing, but she had not seen him up and about yet. Even if she had been adept at using it she had no idea how to contact Nicolas. The only computer she had seen Nicolas use was the one back at the lodge. It would have been comforting to communicate with Katherine, but her aunt was not interested in such technology. After all, until now, she had Nicolas with her. They spent practically every second together. Her aunt had not possessed the need to use such things to talk to the man she loved.

Therefore, Moriah sat on Ben's chair in the middle of the morning, not knowing if Ben was alive or dead. She had initially tried to leave the door partly open for light, but so many children and adults had come to peek in at her that she had closed it because she didn't know what to do with them. No doubt, they were curious about her but, unlike Fusiwe and Karyona, they knew no English, so she couldn't talk to them.

Once she closed the door, she sat there in the semi-darkness, listening to the sounds of village voices, of which she could understand nothing. She felt useless, scared and miserable as she waited for Karyona to come back.

Karyona, the friend who had asked for her help to go see the old, blind headman. The friend who had confessed that she did not like going there alone. The friend who had asked if she would go with her.

It went against Moriah's nature not to help someone when asked. In fact, she couldn't remember ever having done so, but going to see Moawa was expecting too much. Even if it *was* Karyona who asked.

Besides that, there were practicalities involved. Katherine's stash of energy bars were not going to last forever. Moriah had been serious when she told Fusiwe that she didn't even know how to feed herself here. From a survival standpoint, alienating the only real friend she had in this place was not wise.

The possibility of having to survive here alone was starting to make the struggle she'd had crossing the bridge in Little Current look like child's play. As she hid in Ben's hut, sunk in worry about him and self-pity for herself, Karyona opened the door.

"Why do you stay in here in the dark?" Karyona said. "It is much nicer on the outside."

"I don't know anyone out there except you and Fusiwe."

"Fusiwe is in a neighboring village trying to help a man who has a sore tooth. And of course you do not know anyone else yet," Karyona smiled. "That is why you must come outside and meet my people. Will you come help me with our garden?"

"Gladly!" Moriah hopped off Ben's bed and followed Karyona. As they walked through the village, they collected a band of curious children.

Karyona stopped in front of a group of tree-like bushes, as high as her head and thick with green leaves.

"This is your garden?" Moriah asked.

"Part of it. This is my manioc grove."

"I've never seen anything like this in the gardens back on Manitoulin. How long have these plants been growing?"

"A year," Karyona said. "That is about the right amount of time for a manioc plant to grow. Here, let me show you."

Moriah watched Karyona, helped by several of the children, dig away the dirt from the roots of the first manioc plant with their hands, sticks and anything else they could use.

"Now help me pull," Karyona said.

Moriah helped her friend pull at the small tree-like plant. A clump of manioc roots, the size and shape of large, sweet potatoes was pulled away from the earth. Karyona brushed the loose dirt off with her fingers. The children, used to the spectacle of harvesting manioc roots, ran off to play.

"I will teach you how to make flour from the root," Karyona said. "This is our most important food. You will need to know how to prepare it for Ben when he comes back. That is a wife's job."

"Okay," Moriah said. "What is the man's job?"

"The men hunt for meat."

"What kind?"

"Many things like wild pigs, monkeys, deer, jaguars and snakes."

"Snakes?"

"Yes." Karyona did not seem to find anything peculiar about eating snakes. "The men also help with fishing, although we women like to fish too. And if we are attacked, it is their job to protect us," Karyona said. "Sometimes there are raids from other tribes when they want more women. Then our men have to go fight to get us back. Our men do not want to lose their wives and daughters, so they learn to be vigilant warriors."

"How often does such a thing happen?" Moriah had a mental image of being carried through the jungle flung over some neighboring tribesman's back. Living in the rainforest was even more complicated than she'd realized.

"Not nearly as often as it did when my grandmother was young. She was kidnapped twice. My grandfather had to go fight to get her back both times."

"That was nice of him," Moriah said.

"My grandmother thought so," Karyona said. "Now, I think it would be good to fix a meal together. If you are going to be Ben's wife, you will need to know how to feed him. The forest can provide everything you need as long as you know what to use and what to avoid. Our children learn these things from the time they are small. I will teach you like a little child."

Moriah wasn't sure she liked the analogy, but she had to admit that it certainly fit.

CHAPTER 32

The combination of fever medications, electrolytes, IV hydration and platelet transfusions—not to mention Ben's body's ability to heal—slowly began to take effect. For the first time since Nicolas had gotten to him, Ben opened his eyes and there was recognition in them.

"Nicolas?" he said. "What are you doing here?"

"Saving your butt." Relief flooded Nicolas' body. "Or at least the doctors and staff here at the hospital have been trying to."

"I'm in the hospital?" Ben craned his neck and tried to see out over the window sill next to his bed.

"We're in Sao Paulo," Nicolas said. "You've been deathly ill. We thought we'd lost you."

"What happened?" Ben said. "All I remember is feeling a little achy and tired and falling asleep."

"That was several days ago," Nicolas raised the head of Ben's bed so he could see outside. He knew that being able to see out of a window could help a patient who was disoriented to ground themselves. "You had a bad case of Dengue hemorrhagic fever."

"And it didn't kill me? I can't say I'm surprised I got it. With all the mosquitos that have taken a bite out of me this season, I suppose it had to happen eventually."

"I suppose."

Ben glanced outside, now that his bed had been raised. "So I'm in La Paz."

"You are," Nicolas said. "Ron and Matt helped fly you out."

"How did you get here?"

"I hired a private jet."

"Because I was sick?"

"Yes." Nicolas handed Ben a bottle of water. "Here, you still need to drink as much of this as possible."

Ben was too weak. The bottle slipped from his hand. He looked at the bottle lying on his bed, and then held up his hand and examined it. "It used to work."

Nicolas found a straw, opened the bottle, and inserted the straw into it. Then he held it while Ben swallowed several times.

"Be patient," Nicolas said. "You'll get stronger. It will take some time."

Ben laid his head back against the pillow and closed his eyes. Then he opened them as another realization hit.

"How did you know I was sick?"

"Now that's an interesting story." Nicolas gave him another sip, then sat the water bottle on the bedside table. "Fusiwe has been paying a lot more attention to your computer than you probably realized. He was able to contact me and tell me you were bad sick."

"Fusiwe did that?" Ben said. "He saved my life by contacting you?"

"He did," Nicolas said. "He also kept your fever down by keeping wet sheets on you and fanning you constantly until I could get there."

"Fusiwe is an amazing young man," Ben said. "I won't be surprised if he ends up being an emissary between the Brazilian government and the Yahnowa someday. His people are going to need someone like him."

"I can see that happening. Fusiwe would do a good job."

"How was Moriah doing when you left?" Ben took another sip.

"The last I saw her, she was with Fusiwe watching our helicopter take off. She looked okay to me, but she was not happy she couldn't come with us."

Ben sprayed water. Choked. Wiped his mouth. And looked at Nicolas wild-eyed. "Are you saying that Moriah is *here?*"

"Well not *here*, exactly," Nicolas said. "Ron's helicopter was a little iffy and I didn't want to risk the possibility of Kathy losing both of us. I made Moriah stay there in the village."

"Moriah is in the village? Alone?" Ben tried to throw back the covers so he could get out of bed. "I have to go to her!"

"You can't even lift a water bottle, Ben." Nicolas restrained him as easily as if he were a kitten. "Even if you manage to get out of this bed, you'll collapse on the floor. You haven't used those muscles for a while. Plus, you have an IV in you *and* a catheter."

Ben fell back against the pillow again. Nicolas could understand his frustration, but even that small amount of effort had caused a sheen of sweat to gather on Ben's forehead.

"She'll be fine," Nicolas said. "I'm sure Fusiwe and Karyona will take good care of her."

"You don't understand," Ben said. "Moawa is with us now. Fusiwe and I found him wandering around, blind and hungry. His villagers didn't want him anymore—they had problems of their own—and he became a burden. Our village has a long memory about what he did, and they didn't want him either. So, Rashawe, Fusiwe, Karyona and I tried to do the best we could. We fixed him a hut outside of the village and we take turns bringing him food and water. When Moriah finds out he's living nearby, she is going to freak out."

"You mean, you haven't already told her?" Nicolas said.

"I was afraid she'd *never* come if she knew. If she ever did make it here, I was going to let her get acclimated to all the strangeness of the village first and introduce her to the people, and then after a few days break it to her really gently."

"You think Karyona and Fusiwe won't break it to her gently?"

"Fusiwe is too distracted by all his responsibilities, and Karyona might look sweet and gentle, but she's a bulldog once she gets an idea in her head. Without me there, I'm afraid she'll try to get Moriah to go with her. That would be a disaster."

"I tried to keep her from coming," Nicolas said.

"I don't blame you. I can hardly believe she did!"

"She thought you were dying," Nicolas said. "And she loves you. I have to admit, the girl has grit. The helicopter ride was especially terrifying, but she endured it."

"Just like that?" Ben said. "She just sat there and endured everything?"

"No," Nicolas smiled. "I'm pretty sure I'll be getting a cleaning bill from the company that owns the Leer jet. She almost made it to the bathroom in time, but her stomach didn't quite cooperate. Then, in the helicopter, she was more terrified than I have ever seen anyone in my life."

"But she made it."

"Yes, she made it."

"I need to get back there, Nicolas."

"As soon as you're strong enough. Kathy would never forgive me if I came all this way and didn't do my job."

"Is she pregnant?" Ben asked.

Nicolas was surprised. "Why do you ask?"

"Katherine would be here with you unless she was either sick or pregnant."

478

"You have a good understanding of people. We're expecting a little one in seven months. God is good."

"All the time." Ben closed his eyes and was sound asleep before Nicolas could say another word.

"Amen, my friend," Nicolas said, as he smoothed the red curls back from Ben's freckled face. "All the time."

CHAPTER 33

The meal Karyona taught her how to fix was made up of a mixture containing manioc flour patted out and baked on hot stones into a flat bread. This was eaten with a sort of stew of chopped tapir meat along with fresh pineapple, which Karyona had also cut from her garden.

"We will wait until another time to prepare snake for you," Karyona teased. "That was hard for Violet to eat at first too, but she grew to like it."

None of this cooking was done alone. From the moment Karyona and Moriah harvested the manioc roots, they were accompanied by chattering, curious women and several children. They were a healthy people. The children had strong teeth and sturdy little bodies. Two of the little boys ran around with tiny homemade bows and arrows, competing with each other without much expertise. Several of the women wore vestiges of paint—perhaps left over from some small celebration for which they wanted to look nice.

The tight-knit relationships struck her as admirable. These

women apparently spent nearly all day every day in one another's company and seemed to want to do so.

One elderly woman took a special interest in her. With no children to keep an eye on, she seemed to delight in teaching her how to do small tasks. She would demonstrate and then pantomime for Moriah to copy her actions. When Moriah did something well, the old woman would smile and nod in an exaggerated manner, as though encouraging a small child. She also pointed at objects and had Moriah repeat certain Yahnowa words as she pointed. It didn't take an expert in linguistics to know that the old woman was trying to teach her the names of the items.

She had seen not one store-bought article among them. What bits of clothing they wore were made out of plant fiber. The decorations they wore around their necks and in their hair were made up of shells, feathers, bone and more plant fibers—all brightly colored. She thought she understood why Ben's hut was so bare now. He must have decided to live with as few Western possessions as possible so as not to disturb this culture that had used only the things they could gather or make from the natural world for thousands of years.

Fusiwe came back from his dental work at the other village and found her working with the women.

"I have news," he said. "I stopped at Ben's hut and found a message on his computer."

"What does it say?" Moriah jumped up from where she had been sitting.

"I do not know." The weary tribesman shrugged. "I cannot yet read well."

She ran to the hut with Fusiwe and Karyona following close behind.

The message was from Nicolas; it had been there since

yesterday and it was maddeningly short but held the most important information.

"If you get this—the Huey held together. We are at Sao Paulo hospital. Ben is alive. At this point, that is all we know."

That evening, as she climbed back into Ben's bed and pulled the mosquito netting around her, she wondered what the future held. Would she soon be living here permanently? Would she learn to live with the heat, the dangers and the lack of privacy?

Or would the unthinkable happen. Would she end up accompanying Ben's body back home? Even though she now knew he was safely in the hospital, she could not erase the fact from her mind that two villagers had recently died from the same disease.

She did not sleep well that night. It was the heat and worry over Ben. There was also the sound of hungry mosquitos buzzing around outside the netting.

Worst of all, she kept replaying the sympathy that was in Karyona's voice as she described Moawa. She felt guilty for not accompanying her friend when she went to care for the old man. Then she felt angry over feeling guilty. She kept telling herself that he was not her responsibility. Moawa could starve to death out there for all she cared.

In the morning, another quick bath using yesterday's under-wear as a wash cloth—less clumsy than the t-shirt. Maybe her underwear would be clean enough after it dried to use again. She was trying to be sparing with her clean clothes because she had no idea how long she would be here. Another protein bar was washed down by tepid water.

This time she did not wait for Karyona to come to her, but

walked into the circle of Yahnowa huts looking for her friend. She found her cooking pieces of fish over a small fire using only green twigs as a sort of grill.

"I didn't know you could do that," Moriah said, fascinated.

"Sometimes the sticks catch fire and we lose some meat," Karyona said. "But fish cook so fast there is little danger."

"Do you need any help today?" Moriah asked.

"I am making this fish as part of Moawa's morning meal," Karyona said. "It would be nice if I had some company when I take it to him. Last night it was difficult."

"What made it so difficult?"

"It is always hard for me to go to see him. He sits in the hut Ben and Rashawe built and waits for someone to bring him food and water. Having someone to talk to for a few minutes seems even more important to him than the food we bring. One of the saddest things is that he is so hungry to talk each time we come. He asks about the men; what they have brought home from the hunt. He asks if there have been any new children born. Anything to make me stay a bit longer."

"But he is alive," Moriah said. "Which is more than I can say for my parents."

"He knows what he did, and is grateful to be cared for at all," Karyona said. "But we are a people used to living together. We are seldom alone. We don't want to be alone. It is not in our culture to live apart like he is being made to do."

"Why did his village reject him?"

"They think he brought illness and bad luck into their village."

"Did he?"

"I don't know. Last night I ran out of things to tell him and so I told him about you being in the village."

"I wish you hadn't." Moriah suddenly had a sick feeling in the pit of her stomach. "What did he say?"

"He asked to see you."

Oh goodness. Would her friend *never* stop pestering her with this?

"I can't, Karyona," she said. "Please don't keep asking. I just can't."

In her own, sweet, gentle way, Karyona was relentless. "But you need to do this."

"No," Moriah said. "I don't. It is not within me to do what you want me to."

"You are not telling the truth," Karyona said, in a matter-of-fact voice. "You can do this. You can go talk to an old man."

Moriah was silent. What was it that Crystal had said? Something about asking if she thought Moawa would look the same after all these years, if seeing him might help?

"It would be a kindness for you to go talk to him," Karyona said. "And it would make Ben so happy and proud of you."

"How do you know it would make Ben happy and proud of me?"

"Because we talked about it. Ben said you were strong and kind. He said he thought you would be able to do this... eventually."

"You aren't going to let up until I go, are you?"

"Probably not." Karyona gently lifted the fish onto a clean banana leaf and expertly wrapped it into a neat package.

CHAPTER 34

"How is Ben?" Matt asked, as he entered the hospital room. "He's getting crankier," Nicolas said.

"I'm not cranky," Ben said, irritably. "I just want to get out of here."

"He wants to get back to the village," Nicolas said. "I'm afraid he'll try to escape if I turn my back on him."

"He'll have to walk then," Matt said. "Dad's still trying to get the Huey patched up."

"Is that even possible?" Nicolas asked.

"I'm not sure. The other mechanics at the airfield are still scratching their heads over how we even made it back. What with the damaged blades, the damaged hydraulic line and only a few drops of fuel left in the fuel line—some of them are calling it a miracle flight. Dad's eating it up."

"Your dad has both faith and courage," Nicolas said. "That's a great combination for a missions pilot."

"Yes," Matt said, fondly. "My dad is also a little bit crazy."

Another day passed, and Nicolas had sent a message that the doctors said Ben was passed the worst and was slowly gaining strength. That eased her mind greatly.

Now that worry over Ben had eased, the thought of Moawa being only a short walk through the forest began to crowd out everything else in her head.

Cowering inside Ben's hut until she could escape back to Canada wasn't much of an option. Especially since Karyona and her own conscience was apparently not going to give her any peace until she went to see the old man.

Deep down, choosing to face him had little to do with Karyona and everything to do with the fact that she was being given an opportunity to neutralize her last great fear. She had a strong feeling that she would never be completely healed of the trauma of the past until she could face the man who had been the root cause of all of it.

She had conquered the bridge. She'd conquered her fear of flying... sort of. She could conquer this final challenge. Chief Moawa was old and blind, she reassured herself. He could no longer hurt her.

It's like ripping off a band aid, she told herself. Go to his hut. Say whatever it is that Karyona wants you to say. Get it over with and get out. Five minutes max, she told herself. She could bear anything for five minutes.

Put like that, it didn't sound so hard. Except that it was. It was very hard.

"Time to get a backbone, Moriah," she said out loud.

Stiffening her spine and squaring her shoulders, she left Ben's hut and walked to Karyona and Fusiwe's hut where Karyona was grilling another piece of fish over a small fire.

"Okay. I'm ready," she told Karyona.

"Ready for what?" Karyona said.

"Isn't this the time you usually take Moawa's breakfast to him?

"Yes. I am preparing it now."

"I'll go with you."

Karyona glanced up and a slow smile spread across her face. "I am pleased." She quickly gathered Moawa's food together and stood.

"The path is narrow. Stay directly behind me... and please don't touch anything."

In spite of what lay ahead, Moriah smiled inwardly at Karyona's admonition. She vowed that if she lived here, she would make it her business to learn every tree, plant, insect and animal so she would know which ones were dangerous and those that were not.

People had survived in this rainforest for years. They'd given birth, hunted, grown gardens, laughed and told stories. It *must* be possible to live here safely once one learned how to deal with the environment.

Carefully, she followed her friend through the jungle upon a narrow path that had seen but little foot traffic. Karyona carried a wooden bowl filled with what appeared to be a sort of porridge made of manioc in addition to the package of fish. In a small clearing, a tiny, ragged, hut sat utterly alone.

Her first thought was that it would be dangerous to live out so far from everyone. He wouldn't be able to protect himself from any sort of predator, or know if a poisonous snake had slithered into the hut. He wouldn't be able to call for help if he fell and hurt himself or got sick.

She hardened herself. The punishment was harsh, but he deserved it.

Moriah could feel her heart pounding harder the closer she got to the hut. Her feet began to drag as she forced herself forward. Every step felt as though she were pushing through quicksand. This was a familiar feeling—something she'd experienced repeatedly while crossing the bridge at Little Current.

Karyona stopped several feet from the hut and called out.

A frail voice answered in Yahnowa from within.

It became difficult to breathe.

Her friend politely motioned for Moriah to enter before her. Moriah shook her head, refusing. A memory of gruesome images flashed through her mind.

Karyona entered.

Moriah stared at the opening of the hut. If there was one thing she had learned during her work with Crystal, it was the value of pushing her way past the fear.

Almost in a trance, forcing herself to take each individual step, she made herself move toward the door of the hut. She stood there taking deep breaths as she reminded the little girl within that this old man could no longer hurt her. Then she ducked her head and entered. Once inside, it took a moment for her eyes to adjust to the dim interior of the hut. What she saw was disturbing.

An old man huddled on the ground with his back against the circular wall. The interior of the hut was nearly bare except for a hammock attached to the poles at the top.

Karyona spoke softly to Moawa as she offered him the bowl of porridge and then opened the package of fish which she spread out upon the ground. He reached eager hands out to her and grasped the wooden bowl. His clouded eyes stared straight ahead as he hungrily fed himself by scooping the porridge into his mouth with his fingers. The bowl was quickly emptied. Karyona took it from him, sat it aside, then grasped his hand and gently led it to the pieces of fish lying beside him. He smiled widely after tasting the fish, and murmured something to Karyona that Moriah assumed was the Yahnowa equivalent of thank-you.

Moriah stood rooted to the spot, directly in front of the door, struggling to equate this frail, blind man with her parents' killer. How could this be the man she remembered? This shrunken old man could not possibly be Moawa. There were no similarities at all.

After he had finished the fish, Karyona removed a hollow gourd from a peg, dipped it into a container of water in a corner, and handed it to him. After he had drunk deeply and noisily, Karyona spoke to him again at some length, glancing from time to time at Moriah.

His face lost the look of pleasure he had worn while eating his simple meal. He grew sober, his head lifted and it seemed as though he was looking straight at her even though he was obviously blind. Then he spoke and Karyona translated.

"He asks if I am completely certain that you are the little girl who got away."

"Tell him that I am. Say that I still hold the memories of him killing my mother and father," Moriah said. "Tell him I survived only because of the courage of your father and brother."

Karyona translated, then listened carefully to his reply. She questioned him again, as though clarifying his answer.

"He says you did not get away. He says he let you go."

"Really?" A laugh of disbelief burst from her lips. "I seriously doubt that."

Moawa spoke a few more words as though he understood what Moriah had said.

"No," Karyona said. "He did let you go. He says he and his men tracked my father and brother planning to kill all of you. They caught up with you when you were crossing the long rope bridge at the big waterfall. He says my father was at the midway point when Moawa called his men off."

Moriah was shocked. "Why didn't he kill us?"

Karyona spoke with the old man a few more moments and then translated.

"He says it was because you cried out so pitifully. Moawa says it reminded him of his son's cries the first time Moawa carried him across. His son had been about your age."

"His son?"

"The one Nicolas' mother could not save."

"What are you talking about?"

"Oh? I thought you knew. Moawa's son developed gangrene after breaking both his legs in a bad fall. Moawa carried him to the missionary clinic, hoping the good doctor could save his life."

"And she couldn't." Moriah voice was dull.

"It was too late. He died here. Moawa didn't understand. He believed the people at the clinic had deliberately killed him. He blamed himself for not trusting the Shaman, for trusting his son's life to Western medicine."

The old man spoke again. Moriah didn't understand the words, but she heard the sound of regret in his voice.

Yet again, Karyona translated.

"Moawa says he was crazy with grief and anger at the death of his only son. He knew only revenge killing and so he killed."

Moriah rubbed her hand across her face. The knowledge that Moawa had killed out of misdirected grief was a revelation. She had experienced enough of grief herself to have some idea of the control it could have over someone's emotions.

"Tell him it was an evil thing he did."

Karyona spoke softly, listened and then turned back to Moriah. "He says he knows that. He says that he and his people suffered much because of his actions."

Moriah had come here out of duty to Ben and friendship to Karyona. She had come to overcome her fear, to prove to herself that she was brave enough to face anything, even her parents' killer.

Now, to her surprise, she felt her heart softening toward the old man. This was not something she wanted to happen. She had not come with the intention of forgiving him. It had never even occurred to her that she could.

Deliberately, she tried to harden her heart against him. "Tell him I hate him."

Karyona glanced up at her friend, shocked. "I won't!"

"Then tell him I've been a prisoner on an island for twenty years because of the damage he did. Tell him he nearly destroyed three families."

Karyona sat back on her heels, gave it some thought and then began to translate.

The old man interrupted her, his voice cracking with emotion.

Karyona's gentle eyes filled with sadness. "He says he knows. He wants you to forgive him."

Moriah looked at the sad old man sitting in the dirt, heard the pain in his voice and felt her heart shatter.

The old man waited in silence.

Moriah stumbled back out the door, her body shaking, her chest heaving, her thoughts tumbling wildly.

She had overcome so much. Wasn't it enough? Did she *have* to forgive him?

That was not possible.

A child's two-year silence.

A family torn apart.

Nightmares. Wet beds. Terror…

She paced back and forth in front of the hut, fighting with herself. Fighting the desire to start running and not stop. Away from this hut, this man, Karyona, the village, the heat, the danger. When Ron came back she was going to climb on that helicopter and get out of this place. She'd been a fool to come, regardless of Ben's illness. She suddenly craved the crisp, pure, lake air flowing over her beloved island instead of the smothering humidity of this place. Homesickness flooded her.

The suddenly, instead of Manitoulin Island, a different image flooded into her mind. That of a man forgiving his murderers even while he hung dying on a cross.

Who was she to do less?

This pitiful old man was no monster. He never had been. He was nothing more than a father who had lost a son, and who had lashed out against the foreigners whom he believed to be responsible.

Once again, she entered Moawa's dimly-lit hut.

Three steps in, she felt her legs give way and she fell to her knees onto the dirt floor of the poor hut, her bitterness draining away from her broken heart, her head bowed in submission.

"Tell him that I understand, and I forgive him."

Karyona spoke to Moawa. His face creased into a smile. He stretched his arm out into the space reaching out for something.

Moriah knew he was reaching out to touch her.

On her hands and knees, as though propelled by a force outside herself, she crawled the four remaining feet across the dirt floor between them and allowed him to lay his hand upon her head. He held it there, speaking with dignity and purpose. The years that he had led his village was in his voice.

"Moawa says for you not to grieve anymore," Karyona voice was choked with tears. "He says that he will be a father to you."

CHAPTER 35

Ben strained to catch a glimpse of his village, but all he saw was an unbroken sea of treetops until the helicopter landed. He was disappointed that Moriah wasn't there to meet him in the tiny clearing.

Several of the village children ran to greet him, ducking under the blades of the borrowed helicopter despite Ron's shouts to stay away. As the blades ceased to rotate, Ben and Nicolas climbed out.

"Whoa." Nicolas reached out a hand to steady him when Ben swayed. "You aren't a hundred percent yet, friend, take it easy."

He did not want to take it easy. He wanted to see Moriah. He wanted to see with his own eyes that she had truly come to him.

Lying in the hospital bed with little to do except think, he had driven himself nearly mad with worry about what she would do when she learned of Moawa's presence near the village.

He had meant to tell her, of course. Eventually. When he got back to Manitoulin Island and when they were face to face so he could personally deal with the emotional fallout.

He had been so desperate to get back to her that Nicolas had become convinced he would heal more quickly in the village.

"I know you are anxious to see her," Nicolas shouldered his bag with one arm and assisted Ben with the other, "but Fusiwe saved your life. Don't neglect to thank him."

Ben was so weak, the children nearly pulled him down as they clung to him in their happiness at having him back. While Nicolas shooed them away, Fusiwe walked toward him, hand extended.

Ben ignored Fusiwe's Western gesture and pulled him into a close embrace. "Thank you, my friend. Thank you for saving me."

"It was nothing," Fusiwe said, modestly.

"If you hadn't figured out how to work the computer and send a message, I would be dead by now—not to mention keeping my fever down until Nicolas could get here."

"Karyona and Rashawe helped with the fever, but I worked the computer," Fusiwe said, with some pride.

"How did you know what to do?"

"I watched you."

"I should have thought to teach you. I'm sorry, Fusiwe. I didn't know you were interested."

"I am very interested."

"Then as soon as I get settled, I'll teach you more." Ben glanced around, "Is Moriah alright? Why isn't she here?"

"Little Green Eyes is too busy to come." Fusiwe grinned, as though holding back a secret.

"Doing what?"

"Fixing things."

"I know she likes to fix things… but *here*?"

"Come see."

Fusiwe placed Ben's arm around his shoulder, taking over the job of supporting him from Nicolas as the four men made their way through the jungle.

Ben's first glimpse of Moriah astonished him. It was definitely Moriah, and she was most definitely busy. Busy building a new hut. She stood, holding a crossbeam of lashed bamboo above her head, while two of the village men secured it to supports they'd dug into the ground. From what he could tell, she had somehow managed to improve slightly on the design.

"Hello, Ben." She grinned at him mischievously when she saw him "Good to see you again. Nice day, isn't it."

Her hair was in a ponytail and she had a blue handkerchief tied around her forehead. Her white t-shirt was stained with sweat, her khaki pants were smudged with dirt. Her arms were stretched above her head grasping the bamboo and her face was flushed with the effort.

She was the most gorgeous creature he had ever seen.

"I see you found a way to keep yourself busy while I was gone."

"Oh you know me," Moriah said. "Always looking for a project."

They both burst out laughing at their absurd commonplace tone, as well as the sheer delight of being able to once again be together.

He wanted to run, grab her, twirl her around and kiss her senseless. Unfortunately, he could barely stand alone. It also appeared that, even if he were strong enough to do so, the structure she was supporting would collapse if she let go.

"Want to explain what you're doing?" he asked.

"Well, I seem to have gotten myself adopted while you were away."

"Adopted?"

"Yep. I'm building a home for the newest member of our family."

As happy as he was to see Moriah, and as badly as he wanted to hear this, his legs felt like they were quickly turning to rubber.

Rashawe came running out of Ben's hut with his chair and Ben gratefully collapsed onto it.

"Thank you," Ben gasped. "I'm weaker than I knew. Now, tell me, Moriah. For whom are you building this new home?"

"I had nothing to do with this." Fusiwe held his hands up and stepped away. "It was all Karyona and Moriah's idea."

Ben turned to Nicolas. "Do you know what they are talking about?"

"I've been at the hospital with *you*, remember?" Nicolas said. "Moriah, what are you up to? Wasn't Ben's hut big enough?"

A familiar voice quavered in Yahnowa from behind Moriah.

Ben was startled at the sound.

Moawa shuffled into view, supported by a rough stick, led by one of the children.

"Uh, Moriah, honey?" Ben said. "Do you know who that is?"

"Yes." Moriah was finally free to release the crossbeam. She scooted out from beneath it, brushed her hands on her pants, then ran over and gave Ben a kiss. "I know exactly who he is and I know who he was. I also know why he did what he did. I'm building this new hut for him."

"Why?"

Moriah glanced meaningfully at the villagers crowding in around them, eavesdropping as Karyona translated every word.

"He asked my forgiveness and I gave it. Then he offered himself in place of my father whom he killed. I accepted that offer."

Who *was* this woman! Apparently she was not the same person he had carried sobbing off the Little Current bridge. "I'm impressed. But why the hut?"

"Oh that. He shouldn't be out there in the bush by himself, Ben.

He's old and blind. He needs to be close where we can take care of him." Moriah walked over to where Moawa stood, placed one hand on his shoulder and glanced around at the people as though daring them to argue with her. "Family should take care of family."

Ben felt tears sting his eyes. In all she had done, in all she had overcome, he had never been prouder.

Moawa stood up straight as Karyona translated Moriah's last sentence. He lifted his chin as though challenging anyone to question his right to live within the village. No one did.

Moriah untied the handkerchief and wiped the sweat from her face.

"You need to excuse me now, Ben. I can't talk any longer. I was hoping to get this finished and Moawa moved in by nightfall."

Nicolas had quietly watched the entire scene from behind Ben's chair.

"So." Nicolas' voice was emotionless as they watched Moriah go back to work. "The man who murdered my mother is now to be considered some sort of an in-law?"

"Apparently so," Ben said.

"Interesting." Nicolas was quiet for a while as they watched Moriah work. "Hatred is a heavy thing to carry."

"I've found it to be so."

Nicolas sighed. "I suppose if Moriah can forgive this man, I shall try to as well. She's the one who has suffered the most."

"We all suffered from his actions, Nicolas. But no longer, by the grace of God, no longer."

Nicolas cleared his throat. "We need to get you to bed now. You've done enough for one day."

"Nicolas?"

"Yes?"

"Thank-you buying the lighthouse. Thank-you for saving my

life. Thank-you for bringing the four of us together so we can help heal one another."

"I am a selfish man, Ben. I bought the lighthouse solely as an excuse to be close to Katherine. I hired you because you were a skilled stonemason and available. I saved your life because that's what doctors do. I never expected any of the rest of this to happen. It never once crossed my mind."

"A selfish man wouldn't have put his own life in danger to save a missionary's life," Ben said. "A selfish man couldn't possibly love Katherine as whole-heartedly as you do. But I believe you when you say you never expected any of this to happen. God used you, my friend."

"I would be pleased to believe that." Nicolas steered Ben toward his hut. "Come. You need to rest."

Reluctantly, Ben allowed Nicolas to tuck him into his sleeping platform. Exhaustion soon overtook him and he fell asleep listening to the unbelievable sound of Moriah building a hut for Chief Moawa.

"Ben?" Moriah whispered.

He awoke with a start.

"Everything is alright," she reassured him. "It's me."

"Did you finish the hut?" Ben said.

She sat on the platform and he wrapped one arm around her waist, loving the feel of her. So many times he had dreamed of this. It was hard to believe she was here and real. Living, breathing—and smelling like she had done a hard day's work in the tropics. Yep, she was real, alright.

"I have a little more to do in the morning, but it's mostly finished."

"Never, in my wildest dreams did I ever think you would react this way to Moawa."

"Neither did I."

"Why did you?"

Moriah hesitated. "One minute I was so filled with hatred I could barely breathe. The next minute, my heart was in pieces and all I could feel was compassion for him. It's hard to explain."

"I know. I went through a similar experience when I found him."

"It felt as though God, himself, touched my heart."

"Maybe that's because He did."

"You felt it too?"

"I couldn't have forgiven Moawa on my own. I loved my father too, Moriah." He gently tweaked her nose. "But you didn't have to adopt the man, babe."

"He adopted *me*. At least that's the way I remember it. He's no monster, Ben. He's just a sad old man. Karyona said that, since I've chosen to adopt him, the rest of the village will accept him too. Building the hut for him is sort of a visible symbol to them."

"And besides that, you're enjoying it."

"I am. Is there any rule that says a missionary wife can't build?"

"Honey, you can swing from the vines and sing *Zippity Doo Dah* for all I care. Just as long as you'll stay with me. I'm afraid you'll leave now that I'm better."

"Why would I leave?"

"I don't know. To prepare for that wedding in the lighthouse? Wasn't I supposed to fly up there?"

"Well, about that wedding..." She pulled her feet onto the platform and hugged her knees to her chest. "...is having that lighthouse wedding really important to you?"

"No. I just want be married to you. It doesn't matter to me how we get there."

"I talked to Ron. He said he can fly a preacher in when he comes to pick up Nicolas. I hope I'm not being too pushy."

"Moriah. Please. Be my guest. Be pushy."

She smiled and gave him a quick kiss. "Good. You rest. I'll take care of everything."

CHAPTER 36

"Are you finished yet?" Moriah winced as Karyona sectioned off yet another hank of hair.

"Almost." Karyona braided it tightly. "Now, you're all done. Stand up and let me see you."

Moriah stood. She was wearing a white tank top, khaki shorts... and a skirt made of some sort of dried grass she couldn't identify. Her hair was braided and bedecked with flowers, *and* she was wearing paint.

Karyona had carefully explained that, although traditionally, the Yahnowa didn't have any sort of formal wedding ceremonies, they considered it rude to attend special occasions without painting themselves. Even paying a friendly visit to a neighboring tribe involved an elaborate ritual of body painting. Moriah supposed that, for a people with few clothes, it was their answer to formal dress. Karyona and Fusiwe were no exception. Not only had they painted themselves with festive colors, Karyona had insisted on beautifying Moriah as well.

Moriah knew that to Western eyes she looked a sight, but Karyona was so excited about preparing her for her wedding, she couldn't hurt her childhood friend by refusing. Still, she was a little relieved there was no mirror in which to see her reflection.

With longing, she remembered the lovely, long white wedding gown hanging in her closet. It was four thousand miles away and completely inappropriate for this jungle village. Moriah tried to find humor in her predicament, in spite of cringing inwardly a little at the thought of going to Ben as a bride in such a garb.

Chopper blades sounded in the distance, hopefully indicating Ron bringing in the preacher. Karyona glanced outside. "It's nearly time," she said. Then she looked again. "Oh! My mother and father are home. I'm so glad. I sent one of the young men to find them and to tell them you were here."

Moriah peeked around Karyona and saw a familiar-looking middle-aged Yahnowa couple walking toward her. Akawe proudly carried a wooden chest.

"I think my mother and father are bringing you a gift," Karyona said.

Akawe's expression was serious as he approached Moriah and ceremoniously laid the wooden chest at her feet.

Napognuma then knelt, opened the lid and lifted out a bundle wrapped in cloth and handed it to her. She carefully unfolded the fabric. In her hands lay a cracked, cheap, white leather Bible. She handed it to Moriah. On the front, printed in fading gold letters, was the name "Mary Ann Robertson."

"It's my mother's!"

Napognuma spoke and Karyona translated.

"Your mother left her Bible in our hut the night she brought you to stay. It was the only thing of hers not consumed by the fire. My mother has cared for it all this time. Now, she wants you to have it on your wedding day."

Moriah opened the onionskin pages. They still smelled

faintly of strawberries, her mother's favorite scent. A thin sachet lay pressed between the pages.

For twenty years a woman had guarded another woman's Bible—which she could not read. Moriah felt like weeping at the lack of thought and importance she had once given to Ben's work.

"I don't know if I should accept this, Karyona. How great of a sacrifice is it to your parents?"

"Probably even greater than you know. It has been a treasure in our home. If you are uncomfortable receiving it, perhaps you could carry it with you for your wedding and then give it to my mother for safekeeping? For so many years, when she was sick or frightened, she would hold it and pray."

"Then, of course I'll give it back. Please tell your mother my intentions along with my heartfelt thanks."

Karyona did, and Moriah saw a look of relief come over Napognuma's face. Although older, it was the same sweet face that had cradled and protected her on the worst night of her life.

Akawe smiled now and held out his arms. Moriah was shocked to find herself flying into them. He had put his life at great risk to save a little white girl. Akawe patted her on the shoulder. "Safe," he said. "Safe."

The village buzzed with excitement when Moriah emerged from the doorway of Karyona's hut. Ben glanced at her, raised his eyebrows and a grin slowly spread across his face.

Moawa waited nearby. She had told him that, in her country, fathers walked their daughters to their husbands-to-be and then gave them away. Moawa said that he thought this was a barbarous practice and carefully explained that there should be some sort of goods exchanged for her. She agreed wholeheartedly.

Ben, in deference to his new father-in-law, respectfully gave

Moawa a small pouch of Canadian coins that Moawa carefully counted, then tied the pouch around his neck.

Now, she took the old headman's arm and they slowly proceeded toward Ben. Moawa supported himself on a new cane she had made for him.

Moriah could tell the minister was struggling not to gape. Nicolas had given up the struggle and merely stared with his mouth open. Neither of the men mattered. The only person that mattered was Ben, who looked at her, in spite of her odd dress and paint, as though he couldn't wait to spend the rest of his life with her.

"Gentlemen," Moriah said when she and Moawa arrived in front of Ben and the minister. "I believe we're ready."

Later that night, Moriah and Ben lay beside each other in his hut, nearly paralyzed with giggles.

"I wish I'd had a camera," Ben said.

"To take a picture of your lovely bride?"

"No, to take a picture of Nicolas. I was afraid a bird would fly into his mouth and make a nest."

"I thought the old headman was a nice touch."

"He lent our marriage dignity," Ben agreed.

"Do you suppose we're truly married?"

"*That*, I can assure you, is one thing I'm absolutely certain of. Rick Carver is a bonafide Baptist minister and the marriage certificate he brought is as official as it comes. Rick said he would register it for us as soon as he got back to Sao Paulo."

She turned on her side and stroked Ben's face. "I'm so glad you're back here with me, but I wouldn't have missed the past few days here for the world."

"Life does get interesting along the Amazon."

"I have a feeling that life with you is going to be interesting no matter where we are."

"I'm proud of you, you know." Ben drew her close.

"In what way?"

"Pretty much everything. The way you fought to come here. The gift of forgiveness you gave to Moawa. How you managed to look regal in a grass skirt and with your hair sticking out all over your head."

"We're going to have a good life, Ben."

"That we are."

She snuggled her head against his neck. "I saw Nicolas give you an envelope before he left with Ron. Did you open it?"

"Forgot all about it. He said it was a wedding gift. It's over there beneath the lantern if you want to look."

Moriah went to the table and pulled the envelope out from under the lantern.

She didn't think Nicolas would have given them money. Currency was pretty much unusable this far in the jungle.

What she saw when she opened the envelope nearly made her heart stop.

"You aren't going to believe this, Ben. "

"What am I not going to believe?"

"It's a letter. Here, you read it out loud. I'm not entirely certain I saw what I think I did."

Ben sat up and took the letter out of her hand.

Dear Moriah,

I know you've never liked me and I don't blame you. I don't deserve Katherine or you and I probably never will. But I am aware that the real reason you and I got off on the wrong foot was my purchase of the lighthouse. You are right. The lighthouse belongs to you, in spirit if not in deed. You are the one who's loved it, cared for it, tried to protect it, and finally restored it. It should belong to you.

Fortunately, I have no need for it anymore. I have, instead, a life with Katherine, which is all I ever wanted in the first place.

When I get back to Canada, I will have my attorney draw up a deed, which will put the lighthouse in your name. You and Ben will need a home whenever you are between mission trips and although you will always be welcome in the lodge with us, as your family grows, you might want a place like the lighthouse to which you can come.

I know I am sometimes stiff and awkward with words, and that is why I am writing this instead of saying it. Moawa has already claimed you for a daughter here in the Southern Hemisphere, but if you're willing, even though I'm twenty years late, I would like to claim you as a daughter in the North.

Sincerely,

Nicolas Bennett, MD.

Both Moriah and Ben sat in stunned silence as several seconds ticked by.

"Should we allow him to do that?" he asked.

"I don't know," Moriah answered, slowly. "But a big part of me is wanting to yell 'Yippie!' right now."

"It's your decision."

Moriah tapped her chin with the letter, considering. "Then it's my lighthouse. I'll make him the best northern daughter he ever dreamed of. That is, if he treats Katherine right. She's pregnant, you know."

"Nicolas told me. That's such good news. She's always wanted a baby of her own."

"Did she tell you that?"

"No. I saw it in her face when she held Camelia's newborn."

Moriah folded Nicolas' letter, placed it carefully in the envelope and put it back beneath the lamp. Then she blew out the lamp and padded across the floor to Ben, who lifted a sheet for her to crawl beneath. She adjusted the mosquito netting so it covered them both.

"How far along is Katherine?" Ben asked.

"Barely six weeks, why?"

"If something were to happen tonight…"

"Don't even say it." Moriah shut him up with a kiss. "I refuse to be pregnant the same time as Katherine. That's just way too weird."

CHAPTER 37

MANITOULIN ISLAND, ROBERTSON LIGHTHOUSE

From far away, Moriah heard the cry of a child. She opened her eyes and saw Ben holding a naked newborn with a fuzzy head of red hair.

Their son.

Ben was sobbing so hard with happiness and relief, she was almost afraid he might drop the tiny, purplish infant. Fortunately, his hands were so large, the baby was securely cradled in them.

"Push again, dear," Katherine said, calmly.

Moriah summoned the strength to push once more, felt the release of afterbirth and collapsed back onto the pillows Ben had stacked behind her.

"Is he alright?" She felt herself slowly coming back from the private, primitive place she had gone while she had fought her way through the birth.

"Perfect," Katherine said. "And you didn't tear. You'll have an easy recovery."

"I had a good doctor and midwife," Moriah said, as Katherine kneaded her now empty abdomen.

"Don't cry, Petey, Daddy's here," Ben crooned to the furious newborn.

"Petey?" Katherine asked. "Where did that come from?"

"It's a McCain tradition, we alternate between three first names." Ben shrugged. "Petras, Ebenezer and Peter. It's a stone-mason thing."

"How so?"

"Both Peter and Petras means rock."

"And Ebenezer?

"Ebenezer means 'stone of help'."

Moriah gazed at her stalwart husband with loving eyes. "Ebenezer means 'stone of help'? You never told me that."

"It's not important."

"It fits you."

Katherine laid a blue receiving blanket on the bed. Ben placed the baby in the middle of it and stood back while Katherine turned his son into a sort of blue flannel burrito and placed him back in Ben's arms. Then she deftly bound Moriah with soft cloth, and helped her prop herself up to nurse her son. He was a hearty little guy and latched on as he had been programmed to do from time before time. Moriah smiled contentedly at his greed.

"Not too long this first time," Katherine said, after a few minutes. "I don't want you to get sore. Those little newborn tongues can be rougher than you realize."

"Can I hold him again?" Ben said, reaching out his arms. "I can hardly believe he's really ours."

"Sorry if I hurt you," Moriah noticed red marks on his arm and was fairly certain she'd put them there. "I didn't mean to."

"Hurt me?" Ben laughed. "You mean digging your fingernails into my bicep with one hand and nearly pulling a hank of hair out of my head with the other?" Ben said. "That was nothing. Piece of cake, lass. Totally worth it."

Katherine set a tall glass of water on the bedside table. "You'll need to drink a lot of this if you are going to nurse that baby."

"I'm thirsty already," Moriah said. "Thanks."

"I want to go tell Nicolas the good news, and I want to introduce Petey to his new little cousin," Ben said. "I'll be right back."

"It's over?" In the adjoining room, Nicolas sat holding a small bundle of his own in the crook of his arm. He had remained close by so that he could take over if Katherine needed him, but had chosen to give Moriah her privacy as long as everything was going well.

Ben carefully pulled the receiving blanket away from his sleeping son's face. "We have a healthy little boy. His name is Peter Jacob."

"I'm happy for you," Nicolas said. "Another boy. Isn't that something? We are rich men, McCain, with these sons to raise."

"Your Lucas David and our Peter Jacob are going to have a lot of fun together in a few years."

"You planning on sticking around for a while?"

"For a while. At least until Moriah recuperates and the baby stabilizes. Plus, she wants me to carve out a special stone before we leave,"

"What for?"

"To put in front of the lighthouse. It's to say, 'Robertson Lighthouse—In memory of Dr. Janet Bennett, Petras McCain, Mary Ann and Jacob Robertson."

"They would like that, I think, especially now that you're using this place as a respite for missionaries."

"How many have come now for sabbaticals?"

"Check it out." Nicolas nodded toward a table. "The guestbook is right over there."

Ben opened a massive leather-bound book Katherine had found that resembled the old logbooks kept by the original light keepers. He turned to the first page. Five different ministers' families from around the world had enjoyed a no-cost, much-needed vacation here in the past nine months.

"It is a good use of this place," Nicolas said. "I'm glad you thought of it. They were all so grateful."

The sound of a pickup truck coming up the lighthouse road filtered in through the open window

"Who do you suppose that is?" Nicolas said. "Moriah certainly isn't up to company."

"Looks like Sam Black Hawk's truck." Ben opened the door as Sam scrambled out of his truck.

"Did Moriah have that baby yet?" Sam asked.

"About a half-hour ago."

"I figured. Heard she was in labor."

"How did you know?" Ben asked.

"Smoke signals." Sam caught sight of the infant in Ben's arms. "Well, would you look at that! Boy or girl?"

"Boy."

"Poor little fellow," Sam stroked the silky red fuzz on the baby's head. "Ugly little thing. Too bad he took after his daddy."

"I wouldn't let Moriah hear that if I were you." Ben laughed. "She thinks me and the baby are gorgeous."

"There's a baby present out in my truck for her, but I need help lifting it out."

"What kind of baby present is that heavy?"

"One she's going to love. You'll see. Better hand off your son to someone else and give me a hand."

Ben took the baby back to the bedroom. Moriah was sitting up in bed and eagerly held out her arms.

Ben laid the sleeping Petey in her arms and watched as she cradled him.

"Oh, Ben!" she said. "Isn't he the prettiest little thing? Can you even believe how beautiful he is?"

"Absolutely," Ben said. "I'll be right back."

He joined Sam and Nicolas out at the truck, curious as to what sort of baby present would require two men to carry it.

Then he saw it. Gleaming in the sun. Cushioned in layer after layer of pillows and blankets. Sparkling like a diamond.

"I drove five miles an hour all the way," Black Hawk said. "Took forever. Didn't think I'd ever get here, but I had to be careful."

"Your timing is perfect," Ben said. He was awestruck at his first look at a Fresnel lens. "You're right. Moriah is going to love this. You couldn't have possibly brought her anything she would appreciate more."

"I know," Black Hawk said. "That's why I brought it back."

Together, they carried the giant prism into the cottage while Nicolas held the outer door open for them.

While Ben and Black Hawk waited, Nicolas knocked at the door leading into the bedroom where Moriah lay.

"Katherine? Moriah has a visitor. Is it okay to come in?"

Katherine opened the door. "A visitor? Of course not..." The look of annoyance on her face turned into a look of wonder.

"Oh, Moriah. You aren't going to believe this." Katherine backed into the room as Ben and Black Hawk carried the gift to the foot of Moriah's bed.

Moriah glanced up from adoring her baby, her expression changing from maternal softness to astonished delight.

"It can't be! It was stolen!"

"You're right about that. I'm the one who stole it," Black Hawk said. "It was the only way I knew to make certain it was safe."

The Fresnel lens, over four-feet tall, every prism of glass polished to a diamond-like gleam, caught a beam of sunlight.

Color spread across the bed, covering Moriah and her child in a rainbow.

Moriah caught her breath at the beauty. The baby turned his head toward it and blinked.

"This was the light your great-great-great-grandmother kept, little Petey," Moriah said. "We'll put it in the tower and someday you can help me light it for the ships out on the lake."

She looked at Sam Black Hawk who stood beaming at her from the foot of the bed. "How can I ever thank you, Sam?"

"I've already got that figured out. Can I be the one who strikes the first match to light the lamp the first time we fire this thing up?"

"Absolutely." Moriah turned to Ben. "Do you think it will be terribly difficult to install it, Ben?"

"Probably," Ben said. "But difficult things are what we do, isn't it?"

A look of understanding passed between them.

"Yes, my love," Moriah said, kissing the downy head of her newborn son. "That is exactly what we do."

CHAPTER 38

Wearing nothing but pajama bottoms, Ben paced the floor of the lighthouse cottage with their tiny, squalling bundle of joy. Moriah had tried to comfort the child until she was exhausted. Petey did not want to nurse, did not need new diapers, did not seem to be ill, but he was definitely not happy. Nor was he interested in going to sleep.

The baby honeymoon they had experience filled with awe and excitement had waned somewhat. It was amazing how a tiny scrap of humanity could show up and completely take over two people's lives. Unless he missed his guess, Petey was not going to go down tonight without a fight.

With a sigh, Ben gave up pacing, laid the baby on the couch while he squalled and began wrapping the stretchy material around himself that Moriah often used to carry the baby. It was only a long length of stretchy fabric, but it involved an intricate wrapping procedure that he was only now getting the hang of.

With Petey pitching a red-faced fit on the couch, tiny feet kicking and little fists waving, Ben finally got the wrap securely tied, picked up the furious infant and tucked him down inside the wrap. Then he began to walk in circles, singing in a low voice.

"A mighty fortress is our God.

A bulwark never failing..."

He didn't know any lullabies. His own bedtime songs, once his dad had gotten sober, had been hymns, so he figured that was about as good as any.

For variety, he sang the same verse in Yahnowa. Then Spanish and Portuguese. It was good practice for him, plus he thought maybe it would make learning languages a little easier for Petey when he got older. He thought the fact that Moriah had been exposed to Yahnowa at the age of five had made it a lot easier for her to pick up the language these past months. She had astonished the village as well as herself with her quick mastery. It was amazing how powerful things were that got imprinted early on a child's mind—both good and bad.

He caught sight of himself in a mirror and nearly laughed out loud. He was grateful for the privacy of the lighthouse cottage tonight. There was no one to see him marching around with his hair on end, looking about nine months pregnant with the baby tucked inside the wrap. It was attractive on Moriah, but it just looked silly on him.

Whether it was the feel of being against his daddy's bare chest, the womb-like security of the tight wrap, the comforting rumble of Ben's voice against his ear, or perhaps having already worn himself out crying, Petey finally fell asleep.

Ben stood still and took stock. With any luck, his son would sleep maybe as much as two hours before needing to nurse again. Moriah desperately needed sleep. And an excellent way to make certain Petey started crying again was to disturb his slumber by removing him from this wrap.

Therefore, the smartest thing to do was to stay awake, watch over the little fellow until he awoke hungry, and give Moriah a bit of time to recuperate.

He knew exactly what he wanted to do with the next two hours. Their lives had been quite topsy-turvy ever since they'd gotten home, but tonight might be a good time to begin translating the diary that the furniture refinisher had found in the old lighthouse desk.

Ben had already taken a look at it. Eliza's handwriting was as hard to read as everyone said. Especially since the ink had faded. So he had recently purchased an excellent magnifying glass.

With plenty of time to kill, he pulled a chair close to a table, sat out a fresh notebook and positioned a good lamp just so. Then, with Petey snug and content against his chest, he started to really examine the diary. Carefully, he thumbed his way through it all the way to the end. In the very back, inside of the back cover, he discovered a final and slightly more legible message written separately from the rest of the diary.

I am Eliza Robertson, a God-fearing woman. I am the third light keeper of the Tempest Bay lighthouse. Hard things happened within these walls. Let whoever finds this know that I did the best I could.

AUTHOR'S NOTE

I was surprised to discover that during the 1800's and early 1900's, an era when it was taken for granted that a woman should be paid less than a man, over a hundred women kept the lights burning in lighthouses all over the United States and Canada. Most were women who were already familiar with the job, and who were granted the right to continue the work of their deceased husbands and fathers. They were given pay equal to their male counterparts long before women won the right to vote.

Many took on this hazardous job while also raising large families. Most impressive of all were the women who rowed out alone in storms to rescue those who would otherwise have perished.

Sometimes they faced starvation in the north when the ships that tended the lights could not break through the spring ice to bring provisions. They made hundreds of weary trips up staircases to carry fuel and supplies to keep the light burning. They went without sleep night after night to ensure the lights did not go out. They struggled with loneliness, danger, sickness, sleeplessness, and isolation while keeping those beacons of hope and guidance shining out upon the turbulent waters.

It is impossible to calculate the vast numbers of lives and ships they saved.

Modern day people love the romantic notions of lighthouses.

The endurance and dedication of the old light keepers grabs the heart and excites the imagination. Many history buffs devote much of their lives to researching and preserving the lore and history of our remaining lighthouses.

As I researched this series of books, that fact created a problem for me as an author. I try to record the settings of my books as accurately as possible. In this case, it was my beloved Manitoulin Island that I wanted to describe. I did not think choosing an existing lighthouse as a backdrop for a fictional family was going to be well-received by those who have meticulously researched the struggles of the actual families who lived in specific lighthouses.

So, I made one up.

I chose the general location of Providence Bay (which I rename Tempest Bay) where a lighthouse once stood before it burned down. I took great license with the immediate area, creating a peninsula and nearby fishing resort that does not exist. The characters I put in the lighthouse were not based on anyone I know. Michael's Bay (which I rename Gabriel's Bay) is Manitoulin's only ghost town.

Lighthouses similar to the one I describe do exist, however. I chose to pattern Moriah's lighthouse after the Imperial Towers built around the Great Lakes in the early 1800's. They had the stonework that I needed for the story. I read extensively and visited Great Lakes lighthouses to be as accurate as possible in my descriptions. I apologize to lighthouse historians for any mistakes I might have made.

The Yahnowa tribe where Ben lives and works does not exist. However, I tried to make the customs, habits, and habitats as believable and accurate as possible based on my research into some of the larger Amazonian rainforest tribes. A warning, though. Studying the treatment of the indigenous tribes of the Amazon is heartbreaking.

The phobia with which Moriah struggles, does exist. My hope is that as we watch her battle against fear unfold, it might help us face our own demons with a bit more courage.

-Serena

MY HEARTFELT THANKS TO:

Charlie Robertson, owner of the once-famous rock shop on Manitoulin Island. I appreciate the example you have been of choosing joy in spite of great loss.

Mamie (Coriell) Robertson, my transplanted cousin, who followed her heart to Manitoulin Island to be with Charlie. Thank you for telling us about the island so many years ago.

Wanda Whittington, Charlie's granddaughter. Thank you for patiently sharing your knowledge of your beloved Manitoulin Island with me and for your amazing hospitality.

My family, for taking the time to help me explore and research the island. The depth of your continued support and encouragement continues to astonish and humble me.

My church, who so lovingly took care of me and my family during my husband's final illness.

Launie Gibson, the master stonemason who's work inspired this series.

ALSO BY SERENA B. MILLER

Love's Journey on Manitoulin Island Series

- Moriah's Lighthouse (Book 1)
- Moriah's Fortress (Book 2)
- Moriah's Stronghold (Book 3)
- Moriah's Lighthouse, The Collection
- Eliza's Lighthouse (Book 4)

Love's Journey in Sugarcreek Series

- The Sugar Haus Inn (Book 1)
- Rachel's Rescue (Book 2)
- Love Rekindled (Book 3)
- Bertha's Resolve (Book 4)

Michigan Northwoods Historical Romance

- The Measure of Katie Calloway (Book 1)
- Under a Blackberry Moon (Book 2)
- A Promise to Love (Book 3)

Uncommon Grace Series

- An Uncommon Grace (Book 1)
- Hidden Mercies (Book 2)
- Fearless Hope (Book 3)

ALSO BY SERENA B. MILLER

THE DOREEN SIZEMORE ADVENTURES

- Murder On The Texas Eagle (Book 1)
- Murder At The Buckstaff Bathhouse (Book 2)
- Murder At Slippery Slop Youth Camp (Book 3)
- Murder On The Mississippi Queen (Book 4)
- Murder On The Mystery Mansion (Book 5)
- Murder In Las Vegas (Book 6)
- Mystery At Little Faith Community Church (Book 7)
- Mystery At Alcatraz (Book 8)
- The Accidental Adventures of Doreen Sizemore (1-5 Book Collection)

UNCATEGORIZED

- A Way of Escape
- More Than Happy: The Wisdom of Amish Parenting

ABOUT THE AUTHOR

USA Today Best-Selling Author Serena B. Miller has won numerous awards, including the RITA, the CAROL, and was a finalist for the CHRISTY Award. A movie, Love Finds You in Sugarcreek, was based on the first of her Love's Journey in Sugarcreek series, The Sugar Haus Inn, and won the coveted Templeton Epiphany Award. Her novel, An Uncommon Grace, was adapted into a movie of the same name which airs on The Hallmark Movies & Mysteries Channel regularly. Her latest contribution to The Hallmark Channel is her novel, Moriah's Lighthouse, premiering summer 2022 by the same name. She resides in the beautiful southern Ohio countryside surrounded by three hardworking sons, three talented daughters-in-law, six utterly brilliant grandchildren, and four lazy porch dogs. When she isn't writing, researching, or traveling, she spends her time playing with grandchildren, failing at yet another decluttering mission, or sitting on the front porch counting her blessings.

For More Information, Please visit
serenabmiller.com

 facebook.com/AuthorSerenaMiller
 twitter.com/Serenabmiller
 instagram.com/serenabmiller

CPSIA information can be obtained
at www.ICGtesting.com
Printed in the USA
LVHW100724190622
721602LV00018B/94